WATCHING THE KNIFE AS IT CUTS

Georgia went crazy somewhere between the Hall and the cliff tops. She ran barefoot across the tarmac and onto the grass. It was the one thing she knew, that she was running, in the cold and anger and the dark inside her head. She could feel her feet and she held on to that. They were the only part of her she had any control over, but she didn't know for how long. They were pushing her out again, the voices that filled her up, that had pushed her out in her bedroom, and even though she couldn't understand their words, she could understand their frustration, their eagerness. *There just wasn't enough space, not for all of them, not yet, they couldn't all fit in here...*She screamed loudly into the darkness.

The hands that were hers and not hers held a knife, and as her body came to a panting stop on the headland, from somewhere behind her eyes she saw it rise. Her own silent scream of panic joined the multitude inside her. Coldness overwhelmed her and as they took control Georgia was sure that her organs exploded. With a last inhale of breath she was pushed out again. This was wrong. This was very badly wrong.

She looked down at her arms and feet. They flickered jerkily in and out of vision like a bad TV transmission. Her solid body stood three feet away carving at its face with the knife and screaming and twitching as it cut....

Sarah Pinborough

TOWER HILL

LEISURE BOOKS NEW YORK CITY

For Lucy, Jimmy and Kylie,
my partners in crime at lunchtime.

A LEISURE BOOK®

July 2008

Published by

Dorchester Publishing Co., Inc.
200 Madison Avenue
New York, NY 10016

ISBN 10: 0-8439-6052-3
ISBN 13: 978-0-8439-6052-5

The name "Leisure Books" and the stylized "L" with design are
trademarks of Dorchester Publishing Co., Inc.

Printed in the United States of America.

10 9 8 7 6 5 4 3 2 1

Visit us on the web at www.dorchesterpub.com.

TOWER HILL

PART ONE

CHAPTER ONE

TOWER HILL 40 MILES.

Admitting defeat, Father O'Brien pulled off the road and into the service area. He'd left Route 95 at Bangor and followed the coast road upward through the thinning towns for the best part of two hours without seeing a rest stop. A younger man may just have squeezed his legs a little tighter and pushed the car a little harder, but at fifty-eight the priest knew when his bladder was ready to scream that enough was enough. The speed with which you could go from first twinge to fit to burst crept right up once a man reached the age of fifty, and O'Brien didn't think that even out here in northern Maine the sight of an ordained priest taking a pee by the side of the road would go down well with any passing traffic. Forty miles may not be that great a distance but it was far enough to get yourself caught in an embarrassing fix.

He pulled into the parking lot next to the small Burger King and stepped out into the chill, clean air that cut straight across from the ocean. Tucking his head down against the wind as he moved, he didn't pay any attention to the SUV that slid into the parking space next to his, the engine purring silently, no one stepping out. He was preoccupied. The cold chased its way toward the hot liquid in the base of his belly, and he hurried through the doors and into the smell of cooked fries.

Ahead of him hung the sign pointing to the restrooms, and he offered an apologetic smile to the acne-ridden boy behind the counter. The boy wasn't looking at him—he probably hadn't even seen him come in—but O'Brien would still buy a coffee on the way out. It was good manners, after all. And given that there were only two or three other people eating at the plastic tables, the place could probably use his patronage.

Pushing through the heavy door and into the cool of the bathroom, he felt for the discreet zipper concealed among the blackness of his cassock and, tilting his head back, he smiled slightly as he peed. There were joys to be had in the simplest pleasures; the good Lord had been right about that. The water hit the back of the urinal in a strong steady stream, the sound echoing around the tiled room for nearly a minute before his privacy was broken. Behind the priest the door opened, bringing with it a draft. The chill forced a few more seconds flow out of his depleted bladder, but no one came to stand in the empty stall alongside him.

"It's all right, son," he said, shaking himself dry. "Underneath the robes I'm a man like any other." He paused before laughing gently. "Although maybe slightly bigger." Even after thirty years away from the home country, his Irish lilt was still audible in every word. He'd worked to keep it. The congregations he'd served had found it comforting, although why they'd prefer his to their own was beyond him. Maybe it gave them a link to a heritage in a faraway land that would never be visited and could therefore be imagined as perfect. Perhaps a little like the kingdom of heaven.

The man behind him remained still, and, re-doing his fly, O'Brien turned. His face fell, slightly surprised, before it beamed. "Well, fancy that. Two fathers in the restroom together out here in the middle of nowhere. Surely there's got to be a joke in that."

The priest that faced him smiled thinly. "Are you Father Peter O'Brien?"

"Yes, yes I am." He was confused. "Do I know you?"

"Father Peter O'Brien on your way up to Tower Hill? Going to replace Father James at St Joseph's?"

"Sure, that's me." He held out his hand, despite not having washed it. It felt like the right thing to do in the situation. How did another priest know that he'd be here? "I don't understand—are you from the bishop? Is there a problem?"

The priest that faced him left O'Brien's hand hanging, but grinned widely.

"Yes, I'm afraid there is a problem."

They stood in awkward silence. It was O'Brien that broke it.

"And that is . . . ?"

"You're not. Not anymore."

He stepped forward and O'Brien found himself stepping back. He couldn't reason why. Sweat broke out on his forehead and he couldn't reason that either. The other man wasn't making any sense.

"I'm not what?" His feet stumbled slightly and he felt the cool ceramic of the urinal brushing against his cassock. Somehow the germs of strangers no longer seemed important.

"You're not Father O'Brien. Not anymore."

Father O'Brien was becoming claustrophobic, as if there was no longer enough air in the bathroom for the two of them to breathe. O'Brien took it as a sign. Maybe this was a priest of the cloth in front of him, or maybe it wasn't. One thing was for sure though: the man's mind was gone. He'd warn the kid at the counter on the way back to the car. Standing tall, he stepped toward the door.

"You must be mistaken, Father. Now, if you'll excuse me . . ."

His journey was stopped short as the stranger blocked his way.

"Consider yourself excused."

The arm came around too fast for the priest to duck, and for a brief moment he thought that the man was embracing him as if they were truly two fathers meeting as strangers in a public restroom. The hand was firm and cold on his shoulder and there was an absence of emotion in the way that it pulled him inward that gave O'Brien his first real shiver of dread in this surreal moment.

The coldness spread suddenly to his stomach and he sucked in a shocked breath, his wide eyes staring into the empty blue of his antagonist's. He didn't feel the pain. Not at first. Not until the man stepped backward, pulling the knife roughly out. Not until he looked down and saw his blood spilling out thick and fluid between his fingers. His legs slipped, the strength gone from them, and he hit the ground hard. A part of him thought he should scream, but there was no air for it. Darkness crept into the edges of his vision as the stranger crouched and rummaged in his pockets, removing his keys and wallet.

The pool of red spread across the tiled floor and his hand slipped away from the wound, limp and useless. The man had hit a home run with the knife, that was for sure, and O'Brien knew somewhere in the dimness that enveloped him that the precision had been no accident. The confident determination in the man's eyes had told him that there was a story here in which he was involved, and the knife had been swift and controlled as it cut into his organs. He idly wondered how the story would unfold. There were no answers coming to him. He hoped there would be answers afterward. He hoped the Lord would forgive him the lack of a prayer, and the lack of rites. He figured he would. He was a forgiving God, after all. He was glad that it had all happened so fast that there was really no time for fear. He had always worried about being afraid at the end, and at least he'd been spared that. Maybe the Lord did work in mysterious ways. There was a final chill as the opening restroom door let in a breeze, and as it slowly closed, the world faded to black.

Letting the door swing shut behind him, the man casually wiped the knife on his cassock before tucking it away. The smell of grease had been replaced by the stronger odor of gas. He smiled and peered over the counter. The spotty youth lay staring upward, the hole in his forehead almost indistinguishable from the rest of the boils that ruptured there. The back of the boy's skull, the man reflected, would no doubt be a very different proposition.

The gas can rattled as the man's partner emptied the dregs of its contents over the fat woman who was facedown in her burger.

"You done in there, Jack?" The second man pushed his hair out of his eyes. "Or should I say Father O'Brien?"

"Yes, I am, my son." He smiled and paused to watch his friend at work. "Don't get any of that shit on yourself, Gray. You won't be so handsome with third degree burns."

Gray tossed the can and nodded at the dead fat couple and their supersized meals. "They say those things'll kill ya. Guess they're right."

"Always the joker, Gray. Now help me get the body into the van before any more customers turn up."

"And you've always been so fucking bossy." Gray beamed his Hollywood smile and Jack felt his excitement rising. All the girls at Tower Hill would want to screw him and all the jocks would want to *be* him. Gray's classes and clubs were going to be full; he had no doubt about that. The rest of the town he would take care of himself.

Jack watched the wind tease an empty Whopper carton across the parking lot while he waited for Gray to bring the body. The road ahead was quiet. He'd seen only one car passing but he'd still be happier when the priest was stowed and they were on their way. It wasn't so much the prospect of more lives being lost, but rather the potential damage to their plans. Or themselves. They were good with both guns and knives but you could never be sure you might not come up against someone better. On a couple of occasions in their travels through the Middle East he and Gray nearly had, and underneath the clerical garb he had the scars to prove it. Still, maybe not for much longer. There was movement behind him.

"Open the door, then." Gray held the priest over his shoulder as if he didn't weigh any more than a shadow, but then physical strength had always been one of his talents. Jack pushed open the door.

"I'm glad you understand our need for speed. You must be growing up at last."

"Whatever, man. I was thinking of my clothes. I'm going to have to change but if possible, I don't want to ruin this shirt, and this guy is still definitely leaking."

The wind was cold as they trotted over to the two cars. Jack pulled open the back door of the SUV and Gray dropped the body in before looking down at himself. Red bloomed over the linen. "Shit, it's wrecked." Unbuttoning despite the chill, he started to walk back to the restaurant. "Start my engine and then head off. I'm going to be coming out of here fast and I don't want that heap slowing me down." He smiled over his shoulder. "See you in Tower Hill."

Jack nodded. "See you in Tower Hill."

It was about five minutes later that somewhere in Jack's rearview mirror the flames and black smoke from the burning Burger King rose up angrily toward the sky. He smiled.

Gray would be somewhere behind him heading toward the reservoir to get rid of the priest's earthly remains before getting back on course. A sign loomed large by the side of the road and he allowed himself to relax slightly as it came into view.

TOWER HILL 38 MILES.

CHAPTER TWO

Tower Hill isn't a town that has a lot to recommend it. Even with the coast lining its borders it doesn't draw the tourists. The cliffs are gray and ragged and the beach is all sharp shingle. Occasionally one or two more adventurous wanderers who find themselves off the beaten track traveling up toward Canada will rest there and take in its quiet sights before moving on. Just enough people to keep May's Bed-and-Breakfast on Main Street in business, and that's only because May doesn't really need the income other than as pin money now that her Ted's insurance has come through nearly a full year after he passed, God rest his soul.

If it weren't for the small university nestled within its heart, Tower Hill might have become the haven of the elderly alone, forgotten by the bigger towns just out of its reach. The university itself is tiny by any city standards, confined to only one campus of old gray brick buildings, the exterior of which have been unchanged, apart from the odd touch-up here and there, for over two centuries. This is something that makes the residents of the town proud. It gives them a heritage, and that's more than the people who live in some of the bigger towns can claim. The folks that choose to stay in Tower Hill love their town. They unthinkingly protect it from an outside world that might try to change it, keeping its borders safe.

Perhaps that's why the university has never expanded into the fields and empty land around the town and offers only a limited number of courses. They are top quality, of course, delivered by solemn professionals who feel drawn to the peace of its beautiful corridors.

The students who come are those who in the main aren't seeking the fast pace of the big cities for whatever reason, bucking the trend of each generation trying to prove itself wilder and crazier than the one before. They may want to party occasionally, but it will all be wrapped up by two and the next day they'll get up and clean the mess, which keeps the janitor happy.

A few wild ones may slip in each freshman year, coming either because the fees are a little cheaper than elsewhere, or because their folks want them to cool off for a while, or just because they didn't research their application well enough, but their wildness either fades as they settle in to the steady rhythm or they drop out and head to LA or New York, or even just Bangor. The town isn't sad to see them go.

CHAPTER THREE

Steve Wharton unloaded the last two boxes from the trunk of the battered station wagon and slammed it shut. He could have sworn the back passenger door wobbled a little with the impact. However far Liz had driven it to get here, she was lucky to have made it in one piece. He smiled at the rear windshield sticker that read MAINE BORN AND BRED. He guessed maybe she hadn't wandered too far from home, and even though he barely knew her, it didn't surprise him much.

It was a warm day and sweat prickled under his T-shirt as he mustered his strength and picked up the two boxes, balanced precariously on top of each other, from the sidewalk. He couldn't see past them, but he'd made enough trips today to know his way blindfolded, and his feet were sure as he started up the stairs to his new home.

The quaint wooden house on the edge of the campus had been divided into two separate apartments, each with three bedrooms, and music filled the hallway coming from the rooms downstairs, a clash of Gwen Stefani and Nickelback playing at pretty much equal volume. The mix was never going to hit the *Billboard* chart, of that he was certain, but at least the rock hinted at another guy in the building, maybe also a couple girls. A different man might have wished the

housing officer had housed him with another guy, but Steve
was pretty cool with how things had turned out. The girls
seemed fine, even if Liz was perhaps a little quiet and
tense. Angela, on the other hand, seemed to be able to talk
enough for both of them. A pretty even balance, all things
considered.

Still, he thought, nudging their front door open with his
foot and leaving the neighbors' music behind, it would be
good to have another guy downstairs, especially while the
weather was warm. The house had been divided on the inside, but outside there was still the huge porch and yard
with a barbecue area. And turning a burger on a barbecue
while cracking open a beer or two was definitely the man's
domain.

"Hey, I've got the last boxes," he called out. "Where do
you want them?"

"In here, please!" Liz poked her head around the kitchen
door. "Thanks, Steve." She shrugged slightly, almost apologetic. "I'm not sure I'd have got them up the stairs in one
piece."

"No problem at all, ma'am." he said, all country and Western, and her smile relaxed a little as she turned back to taking out carefully wrapped dishes from the box she was
working on. Steve watched her as she tucked some flyaway
blond hair behind her ear. Neither he nor Angela had
thought to bring any cutlery or dishes, but it seemed that
Liz had come with at least four of everything, and if he
wasn't mistaken, she seemed a little embarrassed by it. But
then he figured she seemed embarrassed about pretty much
everything. She was a strange girl. Nice enough, but definitely strange.

"Are you all unpacked in your room?"

She nodded. "Yeah, I didn't bring too much. Just a couple of suitcases."

That was probably all there would be space for in the
small bedroom she'd chosen next to the bathroom. The

tiniest of the three bedrooms, it was about a third the size of Angela's and half the size of his own. But Liz had scurried into it pretty much as soon as she'd seen it. Steve figured she was probably the kind of girl who never wanted to be any trouble. Never wanted to get in anyone's way and never wanted to be noticed too much. He could see why she'd chosen Tower Hill. Both seemed quietly pleasant and understated.

Unaware of him studying her, Liz pulled two tumblers from the box and rinsed them clean before putting them in the cupboard. There was something homely about the action that made him feel a sudden pang of warmth for her.

"And you brought all this. I feel like a total dumbass for not even thinking about plates and stuff. You've saved us."

Her face flushed slightly, but some of her shy embarrassment had faded. "Well, my mom has loads of kitchen stuff so I figured I may as well bring some." She giggled—a small noise that barely escaped her chest. "There's even a food processor in one of those boxes. Not that I know how to use it."

"Well, don't look at me. It's going to be a whole new way of life just doing my laundry. Blenders are alien technology."

"Maybe Angela will know how to use it."

Steve laughed. "I doubt it. On my last trip from the car I poked my head in her door and she was swearing her head off while trying to get her stereo plugged in. And judging from the way her stuff was emptied out all over the floor I wouldn't bet on her being too domesticated."

"Yeah, I figured the same." She grinned back. "Girls that paint their toenails black don't tend to be the best homemakers."

Crouching down, he pulled the food processor from the cardboard box. "I'll just stick this on top of the refrigerator for now." As he tugged at it, yanking it free, a large wooden crucifix tumbled to the tiles. Abandoning the crockery, Liz scooped it up and hugged it to her chest, covering its shape with her nervous hands.

"Oh, I didn't know that was in there. My folks packed the kitchen boxes." The embarrassment was back, clinging to her pale cheeks and making the skin on her neck blotch. "It's not for in here. I'll put it in my bedroom." She scurried past him, shoulders hunched over the cross as if he'd discovered her with a dirty magazine. He stared after her for a second. Sighing, he followed her. He knew better than most that the world was made up from a whole heap of different kinds of people, and he figured that Liz with her cross wasn't going to be the worst of them.

She hadn't shut the door of her room; that would be too much of a statement for Liz to make, but she had pulled it almost closed. Steve rapped on the wood. "Hey, can I come in?"

Rather than answering, she opened the door as if he were a visitor calling, and for the first time he noticed the flash of gold jewelry around her neck and the symbol that hung discreetly from it.

"There's nothing wrong with having religion, you know. You don't have to feel awkward about it."

"I know." She smiled but the expression wavered a little, some of her confidence gone. "But some people can be funny. You know how it is. I guess I'm just private about it." She stepped backward and he took it as in invitation inside. The room was neat as a pin, no sign of her suitcases or any scattered teenage junk. On top of the small chest of drawers were a hair brush, a small black book and a photo frame. He was too far away to make out the picture in detail, but he was pretty sure it would be a smiling image of her family. Liz was definitely a family kind of girl. The bed was made, the sheets neatly tucked in, and a blanket was spread tightly across the duvet. A pair of pink slippers sat on the carpet beside it.

He reined in his curiosity. She was awkward enough without him gawking at her things. "Well, I'm not religious myself, but plenty of my relatives go to church on a pretty regular basis. Once a month at the very least. And that doesn't include Christmas and Easter." He smiled.

Her shoulders dropped a little, tension going out of them, and she raised an eyebrow. "Well, it has to be said, my parents are a little stricter in their observances than that." A dark cloud flitted across her face for the briefest of moments before she smiled it away. "But don't worry—I've got no intention of trying to convert anyone."

Steve glanced over at the book on her dresser and the fine silk thread that divided the closed gilt pages, and then back at the wooden crucifix that Liz still held. A Bible and a cross. Religion was looking to be a serious part of Liz's world.

"Hey, are you okay with sharing your home with a man?" Her surprised awkwardness when they'd first met that morning suddenly made sense. "Will your folks be fine with it? You know, if they're totally religious?"

She laughed, and there was something clean about the sound of it, like looking through washed glass. "Yeah, I'm fine. I was a little surprised at first but that was just silly." She drew herself up tall and lifted her chin almost defiantly. Steve found it endearing.

"This is college, after all." She said. "We're supposed to live at least slightly dangerously. I figure I just won't tell my parents that you live here too." She paused. "Well, not straightaway. It'll take them some time to get used to me being all grown-up and away from home." She put the cross down on the bed. "Anyway, this is better than living in the dorms. We have more privacy here. It'll be less intense."

Catching a glimpse of how uncomfortable the whole idea of sharing was to Liz, Steve was about to ask if she had any siblings when Angela bounded into the room, a big grin on her face.

"Speaking of dorms"—she waved a piece of purple paper at them both—"this was downstairs tucked under the door knocker. There's a kind of welcome party going on tonight in the sophomore hall. Look—first floor chillin', second floor disco beats, third floor hard house!" She bounced up and down for a second. "It'll be a blast!"

"Well, I'm a bit tired, and I'm not sure I'm—" Liz didn't get to finish the sentence. She was never going to get to finish a sentence. Angela was on a high velocity roll.

"It says here that it starts at eight. Seems a little early, but hey, let's get that party started! Now, what the hell are we going to wear?" Her dark eyes flitted over Liz and then Steve. "I guess jeans will be good. You know, first night, check out the lay of the land. Don't want to wow the guys too much!" Energy buzzed out of her. "I'll grab the shower first!"

She was gone before either Liz or Steve could get another word out. Although he was fine about the idea of heading out and mixing a bit, looking forward to it in fact, Steve raised an eyebrow in support of Liz's obvious nerves. "Well, it seems we're going to the party."

Liz smiled. "Yes, I guess we are."

Tower Hill may be a quiet college compared to some, but its students were still essentially the same as young people were most places, and as the three freshmen entered the sticky warmth of the busy building a tall man a couple years older than them reached into the barrel of iced water beside him and handed them each a cold beer, a broad, friendly grin on his face. "Hey, I'm Matt Brinkley, student president. Welcome to Tower Hill! Just go on through and make yourselves at home."

They nodded and mumbled their thanks, but Matt had already moved on to the group of people arriving behind them, dipping into his bucket and introducing himself. For a moment, Steve idly wondered if inside the student president was just a whir of machinery under a plastic skin and perfect grin, programmed to meet and greet, and then he laughed at his own cynicism. Just because there was something wholesome about the small college community didn't mean he had to seek out its flaws. Wholesome was good. Wholesome was what he'd wanted. It would just take a little getting used to. It all seemed like a long, long way from home and the life he'd left behind.

Still, he figured, watching Angela half dancing, half walking into the crowd and already laughing with a stranger ahead of them, his *home* was not exactly most people's idea of heaven. Yes, this was different, but maybe different would turn out to be good. He took a long swig of the cold beer and followed the disco beats further into the party.

By eleven, they'd all danced and chatted to various wide-eyed freshmen and a few idly superior sophomores and then found themselves some floor space in a room off the hall, away from the main thrust of the party. Angela flopped down beside Steve, her dark, sweaty hair sticking to her face.

"Damn, that was great!" Reaching into her pocket she pulled out a pack of Salems and lit one, inhaling hard, as if making a point of it. Steve wondered if there was anything that this girl did at half pace. After watching her dance, he doubted it. Where Liz had carefully moved from foot to foot in time with the music, Angela had jumped and twisted and turned and sashayed, spinning and jiving with anyone at hand, immediately befriending them with her easy smile. It wasn't even that there was anything particularly sexual in the way she danced, but she was a surge of energy.

Over her jeans she wore a black tank top and Steve could see the definition in her slim arms. Her bare midriff was toned too, and it didn't surprise him. Angela may have liked to party, but he'd bet she worked out pretty hard too. She blew a smoke ring into the air and grinned in the gloom. He couldn't help but smile back and saw that beside him, Liz did too. Her blond hair was pulled back into a ponytail and she too had gone for a black shirt over jeans, although hers had proper short sleeves. He figured he'd lucked out with his roommates. They were three very different people, but so far, so good. As far as he was concerned anyway. He hoped the girls didn't think too differently.

"What made you pick Tower Hill, Angela?" Steve leaned back against the wall, his legs crossed. "You seem like you should be, I don't know, maybe at one of the state universities. Somewhere with a bit more action."

"Yeah, well, I'm not always a party girl." She raised an eyebrow, mocking her own words. She took another long inhale of her cigarette and flicked the ash into an empty beer bottle. "If you must know, I got a scholarship to study divinity."

"Divinity?" Liz almost spat out a mouthful of beer. It was the same bottle she'd had since they'd arrived, and she'd taken only occasional sips from it. She raised a hand apologetically before wiping her mouth. "God, I'm sorry. I didn't mean to sound so shocked. You just don't seem the divinity type." She looked over at Steve. "I mean, she really doesn't, does she?"

He smiled and shook his head. "No, I definitely wouldn't put you down as a churchgoing type, Ange."

"Well, you shouldn't judge a book by its cover, should you?" Angela drained the rest of her beer before laughing, pushing her hair away from her face. "Although in this case you'd be right. I'm not religious. Not at all. My interest is in studying religion to disprove it." She paused, her face suddenly serious. "Not entirely disprove it. I mean, I do believe in something. I believe in the weird and wonderful and ghosts and all that stuff. I just don't believe in the moral code man applies to it." Her dark eyes were thoughtful, and in that contemplative moment, Steve caught a glimpse of why Angela had her scholarship. They were clever eyes. Her brain was as much of a whir of energy as her body seemed to be.

"This place may well be nearly off the radar as well as the coast, but its divinity program is second to none, and there's no point in setting out to disprove something if you don't understand it." She snorted. "Obviously I had to tell the odd lie about my religious affiliations to get the scholarship, but hey, I'm here now. And I'll save the radical stuff for my PhD."

She shrugged, then pointed at Liz's discreet crucifix. "But don't worry, I won't try and change your mind about the church. If you're happy with it, then that's fine by me."

Liz laughed, and Steve was surprised by the warm earthy quality of it. "And I won't try and change your mind either."

Angela spat in her hand and held it out. "Deal, sister." Liz didn't spit, but she did shake.

"Well, to me Tower Hill virtually is the big city. I'm from the islands. North Haven?"

Angela stared at her. "I didn't think people really lived out on the islands anymore. I figured they were only open for summer."

"Not North Haven. We're all year-round up there. Sure, it gets busier in the summer, but there's about four hundred year-rounders." Liz's shoulders hunched up slightly. "It's a real community. I didn't even have to go to the mainland for school."

"Shit, girl, how many kids were in your class?"

"Well, the school had seventy." She raised an eyebrow. "My class was pretty full with eleven."

"Wow. That is something else."

Liz sipped her beer. "To me, that is normal. *This* is something else."

"Hey, within a week or so, you'll feel like you've been

here forever." Steve nudged her gently in the ribs. "And anyway, the three of us will stick together until we're all settled."

"Certainly will." Angela added. "We're homies now. This is our hood." She grinned at Liz. "We'll be ruling this school before long, trust me."

Both girls laughed, and then Liz turned to Steve. "Your turn."

He paused for a moment and almost made up some bullshit excuse for coming here before just blurting out the truth. "I'm here because it's cheap." He shrugged. "And I can still barely afford it. I'll be out job hunting first thing tomorrow. I doubt this place is heaving with student employment." He didn't add that he'd have to send some money home to his mom, at home in the trailer collecting her disability check and slowly growing fatter from unhappiness. There was only so much honesty you could share with people.

"I was going to go job hunting too," Liz said, and smiled.

"Not me, guys. I probably do need a job, but tomorrow my ass is going to be sleeping off tonight!" She looked around. "It's emptying out down here. I might head up and see what's happening on the other floors. Find myself some more dancing and a couple more beers. You guys coming?" She stood up in one fluid move, and with her hair hanging wildly down the back of her lithe body, Steve figured she wouldn't have any problem finding a dancing partner or three.

Liz shook her head, but did get to her feet. "I'm going to head to bed, I think. I'm beat. It's been a long day."

Angela gave her a hug. "I'll walk you out and get some fresh air. What about you?" She looked down at Steve.

He checked his watch. The hands were just touching midnight. Theirs must be the only college in America where the freshmen party was starting to slow down. Even back at home the kids he hung out with at school would just be warming up for the night. "I'm going to hang here for a while. Have another beer and maybe talk to some of the guys. I'll see you all back at the house."

He waved good-bye and then settled back against the wall and drank his beer, enjoying a moment on his own before finding some company. A couple girls were in the middle of a serious conversation on the other side of the room and to his left a group of three or four guys were laughing. They all had beers in their hands but none of them seemed even half drunk. Not by the normal standard of kids suddenly released out into the wild by their families.

In some ways it felt more like a house party at high school than a college first night. He let the warm beer run down the back of his throat as the bottle emptied. So much for the crazy nights and half-naked chicks too out of it to know what they hell they were doing with themselves or anyone else. Still, that didn't really bother him. He'd seen enough of what too much booze could do. Getting shit-faced for shit-faced's sake wasn't something that overly impressed him.

Although he had to admit, it was a weird feeling to be in a college full of kids that seemed to feel that way too. Shit, as far as he could fathom, there weren't even any frats here. And that didn't overly bother him either. Dragging himself to his feet, he laughed a little at himself. Part of him felt too damned old for his age. He needed to find himself another beer.

It didn't take long to find either a beer or some company in a small sea of names and faces, and it was about half past one when he finally slipped out and wandered across campus back to the house. The air was still warm but a sea breeze added some crispness, and by the time he quietly shut the front door behind him, he'd pretty much lost his beer buzz. Which, he figured, pulling his T-shirt and jeans off and lying on the bed, was probably a good thing. He wanted to be up early and scouting the town for a job. Stinking of beer probably wasn't the best way to get himself an interview. Outside, the town and campus were silent, the noise of the first night party not carrying to its borders. Listening in the dark, he thought for a moment that he could hear the to and fro of the ocean as it danced under the influence of the moon, but decided after a while that it was perhaps just his own breath. He yawned. Maybe he still had a little beer in his system after all. His eyes were heavy. Liz was right: it had been a long day.

He woke only once in the night, to the sound of Angela cursing as she tripped up the hallway, the door slamming behind her. His eyes scanned the luminous dial of his watch. Three thirty. Rolling onto his side, and almost asleep again already, he smiled. At least one of them was acting their goddamned age.

CHAPTER FOUR

Jack peered through the window of the small wooden house next to the church and took in the night. Out on the deck he could see the swing chair rock slightly back and forth as if the sea breeze had taken a seat in it. He smiled. Tower Hill was entirely and quietly all-American, and all the best parts of that. There had even been an apple pie cooling in the kitchen when he'd arrived. It had tasted perfect, and he'd eaten half of it in one sitting. But he'd been starving and it had been a long day. He should've probably helped himself to a burger or two at Burger King before Gray torched the place, but a man can't think of everything. He thought of the way the place had gone up in his rearview mirror. Those burgers were certainly flame-broiled now.

The town was silent as was to be expected but he was sure he could hear a low hum coming from the old stone church, the oldest house of prayer in the state, and certainly one of the oldest in whole country. Maybe it was just his imagination but he didn't think so. He'd never been a man with much in the way of imagination. If he thought the bricks were humming, striking a chord with the un-locked knowledge inside him, then they probably were.

He paused from his night watching to pour a whiskey from the full decanter on the small drink trolley next to the

TV. It was good quality, thick and brown, and he'd bet it was Irish. Whoever had left that apple pie would no doubt have made sure there would be good Irish whiskey for their new priest. *Father Peter O'Brien.* He raised the glass slightly, making a silent toast, before sipping from it. *May you rest in peace.* He hoped Gray had secured the body before ditching it, but the thought slipped away. Gray was not careless. Not with things like that. Like the fire, the body disposal would have been executed with slick efficiency. And amen to that. He smiled again and thought of himself and Gray and how far they had come. It was surprising that they were here at all. He'd never been much for superstitious bullshit. He supposed it came with his lack of imagination. He sighed and listened to the hum. But still, *it stops being bullshit when you have hard proof.*

On the wall the old grandmother clock softly released three chimes before settling back into a gentle tick. The world slept around him and he wondered at them. He wondered at how much they didn't know and how oblivious they were to so much of heaven and hell and the universe around them. Still, not so long ago, he had perhaps been similar. Similar, but not the same. He and Gray had always known that something great would come their way.

Somewhere on the other side of the small town Gray would be fast asleep in his apartment on campus. Jack smiled wider. Unlike Jack, Gray could sleep through anything. He's slept through plenty in the twenty years they'd known each other. In fact, it was his own lack of sleep that had brought them together. When he'd snuck out of his parents house to take a walk in the park—anything to relieve the boredom of insomnia—and found Gray in that unfortunate situation with the girl. They'd bonded that night, sorting the mess out. Gray had come back to the house with him, clambering back up the trellis and in the window with ease. Even at sixteen they knew they needed a cover story, and a sleepover was as good as any. And Gray had slept. Slept

like a baby even with the trace of the girl's blood still staining his hands.

The cassock itched in the muggy night air. He hadn't
taken it off yet even though he could have without arousing
suspicion. This was a sleepy town. He was banking on doing a lot before arousing any suspicion. He hadn't taken
the gown off yet because he just hadn't thought about it. It
was becoming part of him. Or he was becoming part of it.
He was a method actor getting into character. He was becoming Father Peter O'Brien. He walked slightly taller in
the cassock, he'd noticed, and his stride was slightly shorter.
Strange how his body was adapting to the part.

He'd enjoyed wearing the religious garb while walking
through the old stone church earlier that night, looking up
at the breathtaking biblical depictions in the stained glass,
and the symbols of idolatry that struck the eye with each
turn of the head. The things these small people with small
minds would believe. Still, it was good to have a population of sheep. They would be weak and stupid and easy to
lead. His flock.

He sighed and looked at the moonlight reflecting on the
ocean beyond the cliffs. He sipped his whiskey. It burned
inside. The water was calm and the town was calm. It was
an empty, blank canvas. He glanced at the locked trunk behind him and felt the key against the skin of his chest.

He was ready to start painting.

CHAPTER FIVE

By ten A.M. on Saturday morning, Liz and Steve were out of the apartment and on the short walk from the campus to the center of the small town. They'd left Angela to sleep, Liz making sure she'd pulled the door shut real quietly, even though they could probably have left stereos blaring and the other girl wouldn't have woken. Liz had peered into her bedroom before leaving and Angela had been flat on her back, dead to the world, and gently snoring. Liz doubted she'd be much more than just getting up by the time they got back.

She had decided early on that she liked Angela. She made her smile. Angela's apparent wildness took her breath away, and watching her dancing the previous night she'd wondered how it would feel to be so unrestrained and joyful. There had been a lot of talk of Joyousness at home, but very little plain old joy with a small *j* felt. Hopefully it wasn't too late for her, even though she felt totally at odds with the young people around her at the college. At the party she'd felt almost middle-aged. Still, she thought, lengthening her stride, it was only the first day of her great adventure, and so far, so good. The good Lord had not felt fit to smite her yet.

The sea wind lifted her blond hair right out behind her,

and she relished the feel of it on her face. She looked over at Steve and saw that he too had lifted his head slightly.

"It's good, isn't it? Wakes you right up." Although the sun was shining and the land air was warm, the air being carried in from the sea had a sharp chill that made her skin tingle. She watched Steve smile beside her. "You wouldn't get that in the city. I love the sea air. I loved it at home too. You just can't beat it."

"It sure makes you feel alive." Steve grinned. "I haven't walked by the sea in ages. I feel like a kid again."

"I don't think I could ever live too far away from the ocean." She looked out to where a few boats seemed to hover on the skyline. "I can't imagine not hearing the water at least once a day. I guess it must be in my blood. Being an islander and all."

"Well, I can see how it would get under your skin. I feel great."

"It's your skin it ruins. Back home, by the time you're forty, most people look fifty, just from being beaten by the wind every day. Still, I figure it's a fair trade."

"You should quit college and go home," Steve said. "Set up a store selling those expensive face creams that you see on TV. You'd be rich!"

Liz laughed. She decided she liked Steve too. He was easy to feel relaxed around even though she figured that he too was trying to leave more behind than just his childhood. It took one to know one, as the old saying went. And his eyes had deep, dark patches under the humor.

Despite what he'd said the previous evening, she'd thought the party might have gotten the better of him and had been pleasantly surprised to see him tumbling out of his room just after she'd got up. He'd made them both coffee while she was in the shower, and had seemed more awake than she was. But then, she may have been the first back from the halls, but she hadn't slept well. It was strange lying in an unfamiliar room. Strange, a little frightening, and at the same time, liberating. She'd woken at five, just like she would have done at home, her body clock too set in its routines to change by will, but this time, for the first time in forever, she'd stayed wrapped up beneath the covers and listened to the birds instead of joining her parents and sister for an hour of prayer. She'd promised them that she would continue the routine on her own, of course, but the minute she'd spoken the words, she'd known them a lie. The lie had stopped her mother's crying, though, at least for a while, and she figured a little white lie was no great sin.

Lying there under the covers, hearing that first hour of religious observance ticking by, she'd felt like a pagan, but it had been a good feeling. It would take small steps to get totally rid of the grip overzealous religion had on her, but she was at least starting. From now on she'd keep her relationship with God low-key and personal. She figured he'd be okay with that.

It didn't take them long to find Main Street. The small town didn't exactly seem to have that many bustling hubs, and with the cliffs and ocean spread out along one side the two students could hardly get lost. The rows of picturesque clapboard houses thickened, various colored picket fences protecting perfectly trimmed front yards. There were already a few people out taking advantage of the late summer sun to pluck tiny weeds out from between bright flowers and feed the topsoil. Liz waved hello as she passed, and most nodded back.

Aside from the student population, she figured that most of the residents of Tower Hill were going to be older. At least married and settled, and she'd bet there were a lot of old people filling the perfect houses. She didn't mind that. She didn't mind it at all. If she was honest she'd probably feel more at home among them than with her own peers, however much she wished it different. Somewhere off to her left a bell rang signaling a small boat leaving the harbor, and she promised herself that if she had time today, she'd go down and take a look. Maybe there were even boats that could be hired for a day to take out on the water. She couldn't afford it right now, but if she managed to find a job then she probably could. She could take Steve and Angela out one day before the summer died completely.

A wooden street sign declared MAIN STREET to their right, and as they turned Liz realized she was grinning. It was a good feeling.

"Shit, this place looks like something out of a postcard. Or that town in *Murder She Wrote*. What's it called?"

"I don't remember," Liz answered. What else could she say? TV was not something that was watched much in the Clapton household. Sometimes they'd watch the newscast and of course they rarely missed *Father Macklin's Daily Hour of Worship*, but other than that the machine was kept switched firmly off. Sometimes, if her mother had heard something she considered particularly sinful on the news, she would unplug it completely, as if the devil could creep into their sacred home through the wire.

Still, she thought, whatever town Steve was referring to couldn't be quite as pretty as Main Street in Tower Hill.

"God, it's beautiful. Candy-box perfect." He said.

The old-fashioned streets on the island had been pretty, but this was something else. Ahead of them, the street opened out like a boulevard, awnings of storefronts tidily lining each side, and under their feet the sidewalks were cleanly swept. Color still flooded from the tree branches even though the summer was nearly done. Purples and pinks shone from within the full green leaves, adding to the quaint deliciousness of the street. It seemed almost unreal. Liz looked up at Steve and they both giggled.

"Like I said," she smiled. "You wouldn't get this in the city."

They strolled past a florist and a hardware store and several other small boutiques selling a variety of knickknacks and gifts designed to satisfy the needs of the residents and with a few more obvious choices to please the few tourists that the town must get. Small wooden toy sailing ships of differing sizes filled one bay window, and both Liz and Steve paused to admire the tiny detail of the decks and cabins. Although they were painted in different shades of green, red and blue, they all had the town name painted carefully on the side.

"Yep." Steve looked almost like a small boy beside her, his eyes wide at the simplicity of the toy. "You wouldn't get this back home."

Liz looked up at him. "And how different is this from home?"

He laughed out loud. "Oh man, you wouldn't believe it. This is as far from Detroit as you can possibly get."

She felt herself blush with ignorance. He probably thought she was a real inbred island hick. "I guess you'll have to tell me what it's like someday."

He looked at her, and then back at the window. He seemed almost wistful. "Yeah, maybe. Maybe I'll just leave it behind and concentrate on this place instead."

Liz watched him almost visibly shake the dark moment away and pull himself up tall. "Well, this sure is grand, but it ain't getting us no darned job." Leaving the window behind, he strode forward, eyes scanning the shopfronts for job postings, and she trotted to keep up.

He faked a deep Southern drawl, and although it made her smile, she couldn't help wonder what he used his humor to hide. She may come from a backwater island, but she could read people pretty well. And she figured there could be a whole lot of reasons for someone to choose a small college like Tower Hill. For her it was a small breakaway. Not enough to ruin her relationship with her family but enough to allow her to breathe, so who knew what the move was for Steve? Maybe she'd find out and maybe she wouldn't. She guessed it didn't really matter that

much. They were here now, and embarking on a new stage
of their lives, with so much more lying uncharted ahead of
them.

"Hey, look!" Steve was staring down a side street. "There's
a Hannaford's. It's tiny, but it's an all-American store.
Thank God, for a while there I was thinking we'd moved to
Stepford, everything's so frigging perfect." He turned back
to her and laughed. "I guess maybe they didn't put this
store out front in case it spoiled the view."

Following his gaze, Liz could see the store. She smiled.
Even the secondary streets looked pretty in this town. Sure,
Tower Hill was bigger than she was used to, but it wasn't as
if she'd never been to the mainland and seen other towns.
None of the ones she'd seen compared to this quaint calm
tranquillity, though.

"I'm going to go and see if they've got any work going.
I bet I've got a better chance in there than anywhere else."
He raised an eyebrow, wiggling it playfully. "I think I'm
definitely side street in Tower Hill."

"Cool. I think I'll keep looking around and exploring.
I'll catch up with you back at the house."

"Sure. If we don't bump into each other before then in
this bustling metropolis."

"Oh, you're such a wit, Mr. Wharton." She smiled and
waved good-bye, heading back to the busier central boulevard.

Away from the open edge of the cliffs the wind had
dropped, and the morning sun was warm on her skin as she
followed the gentle curve of the street as it turned slightly
left. Up ahead the road widened and split into two, one
bend in the fork heading farther inland while the other
smaller street bent back on itself and headed to the cliffs.
Pausing, she weighed her options.

On the wider road, the stores appeared to thin out and be
replaced by more formal offices on one side and a small car
lot up ahead on her right, and so still seeking out more of

the town's cozy charm, Liz took the narrower road that twisted back toward the water. She walked until the charming street wound around and she could see the ocean stretching to the horizon, the sea breeze once again sending a shiver of goose bumps pleasantly across her skin.

She'd passed several little outlets, pausing in a sleepy bookstore to see how many of the texts on her reading list they stocked. She was pleased to be told by the elderly man behind the counter that they worked hand in hand with the university, and if she needed to purchase several volumes they could arrange for them to be delivered to her during the first week. It was a long way to walk for a young girl with an armful of books, he said, winking at her in way that might have been sleazy if done by another man, but in his case was purely kindly. He'd wait till all the orders were in and then drop them up there in his small truck. There was even a little bell that tinkled merrily to signal her exit back onto the street. She almost couldn't wait to see the town at Christmas, imagining how strands of lights would no doubt adorn the streets and shopfronts, twinkling down on dressed trees and hanging Santas. It would almost be too cute.

Turning so that the ocean was on her right, she strolled along the front, happy to have some time to herself after the madness of yesterday's arriving and unpacking and the party. A large shadow crossed the road and sidewalk, and looking up from her daydream, she saw the huge stone church rising imposingly from the ground next to the sidewalk. She paused for a second to stare at the weather-beaten dark stone walls.

"It's the oldest in the state. Maybe even the oldest in the Union. Impressive, isn't she?"

Liz hadn't noticed the priest sticking a large, bright poster to the noticeboard until he spoke, and she jumped slightly before flushing and smiling. He raised an eyebrow.

"But then, I guess I'm probably a little biased." The poster in place, he held out his hand. "Father Peter O'Brien. Just arrived last night."

Unlike Father Macklin on the TV, and her own father, who delivered most of the sermons at home, both of whom were gray, stern and unsmiling, this priest was only perhaps in his midthirties, and his hair was sandy brown above his blue eyes. Liz wouldn't call him handsome, but he at least looked friendly. Her grin relaxed and she reached for his hand. His grip was firm as she shook it. "Elizabeth Clapton. I just arrived last night too."

"Ah, of course. The college."

She nodded. His eyes flicked down to the chain around her neck, where the small crucifix carried a tiny gilt forever-suffering Christ, and he smiled some more.

"Ah, Miss Clapton, I see you're one of the fold. I hope I can count on your support for my debut Mass tomorrow morning." He nodded in the direction of the newly placed poster, declaring THERE'S A NEW PRIEST IN TOWN! FIRST MASS SUNDAY 10 A.M.! COME AND HELP WAGE THE WAR ON SIN! Alongside the words was a cartoon image of an old-style sheriff like something from a fifties Western movie.

She stared at it for a second and her face must have looked a little perplexed, because the priest shrugged.

"I know. Cheesy, isn't it? But, to be fair, it wasn't my idea to put it up. The orders came from on high."

"*God* told you to use that sign?"

He laughed out loud. "No, Miss Clapton, He did not. I think the good Lord may be a little preoccupied with more important matters, and I don't have that kind of direct line quite yet. The poster came from the bishop's office."

"Oh, I see. Of course." Her skin felt hot where she was blushing. Sometimes she wished she would think a little before opening her mouth and releasing the first words that came into it.

"So," he said, picking up his bucket of glue, "I'll be seeing you tomorrow, then?" His eyes seemed to stare right into her, and despite all her prior resolutions, she found herself nodding. "Yes, I'll come."

"Good." He grinned. "And spread the word. Let's keep at least a little corner of Maine Catholic."

Leaving her on the sidewalk, he headed back to the house beside the church, and even carrying the bucket, took the stairs to the front porch two at a time. Liz watched him disappear inside and suddenly felt angry at herself. So much for keeping her relationship with God personal. So much for trying to assert some independence and see what it was she wanted out of her life, and, more importantly, so much for taking some time to find out what beliefs were really hers and what were those of others. She'd been here twenty-four hours and already had agreed to go to church. She was a blind sheep; that's all she was. Air escaped her in a big sigh as her earlier good mood deflated.

She looked again at the tacky poster. Despite her irritation, she almost laughed. The cowboy looked ridiculous, and she felt slightly sorry for Father O'Brien. The sun was warm in the bright sky and it was hard to stay in a bad mood. She supposed one Mass wouldn't really hurt. She said she'd go, so she'd keep her word, but after that she'd just not come back. No doubt the father wouldn't really notice.

Allowing herself a smile she crossed to the other side of the road. It was nearly midday and the town was filling up with more students wandering in awe around the parades of shops and heading down to the cliff-top walks on the far side of the church. The fresh air had made Liz slightly hungry and she headed toward a café with a few tables and chairs outside like she imagined they had in France and the other exotic cities of Europe. Checked tablecloths covered their surfaces, held down with clips and bottles of ketchup, mustard and mayonnaise. Maybe not too European after all. She didn't imagine that they went too much for ketchup and hotdog mustard in Paris.

Inside the café a few customers were sipping coffee but in the main it was pretty quiet. A busty middle-aged woman behind the counter turned from where she'd been looking out from the window and smiled.

"Well, I see you've met the new father." Her face was overweight but pretty and her dark hair curled to her shoulders although it remained frozen when she bobbed and moved her animated face. Liz imagined she slept in rollers to get it to stay like that all day. If she leaned in farther she was sure she'd be able to smell the thick scent of hairspray. She smiled back, immediately liking this woman and her honesty. She wasn't trying to hide the fact she'd been watching from the window, and Liz figured that maybe she didn't have to. There was nothing to be ashamed about in having a healthy interest in your community.

"Yes. He seems quite . . ."—the right word seemed to elude her—"friendly." She looked down at all the cakes behind the counter. "Can I get a coffee and a raspberry muffin, please?"

"Sure, honey. Take yourself a seat." She reached behind her for a mug and filled it with steaming liquid from the jug on the hot plate. "I guess he couldn't be any duller than old Father James, the Lord rest his soul." She crossed herself with her free hand. "And it's always nice to have new blood in town. Adds a little spice to the population."

"I'd have thought you'd get fed up of new people every year."

The woman brought her drink and muffin over, setting it down on the table. She looked perplexed, and then her face cleared. "Oh, you mean you young people." She smiled, folding her full arms across her equally full bosom. "To be honest, honey, we don't really *see* you students, if you get what I mean. To us lifelong residents of Tower Hill you kids come and go, and don't get me wrong, we love your energy and the life you bring, but I guess you're more like ghosts than real people to us." She winked. "And I wouldn't

SARAH PINBOROUGH

36

be surprised if it's the same the other way around. We all rub along, but we live in two different Tower Hills."

Liz nodded. She understood where the woman was coming from. Back on the island they had an annual influx of summer visitors and the residents felt the same about them. "This muffin is delicious. Do you make them yourself?"

"Sure do. I don't make everything, but my muffins are famous all the way to Bangor." She laughed. "Well, maybe I'm exaggerating a little, but there are a few people around here who would say I'm not too far off."

Liz smiled, and her eyes drifted back across the road at the church. The woman followed her eyes. "I may even take a plate of my next batch over to the new father while they're still hot. Not that I'm overly religious, but it'll sure set May over at the bed-and-breakfast twitching if I'm the first to get to know him." The comment was mischievous rather than malicious and it made Liz laugh out loud.

"What's your name, honey?"

"Elizabeth Clapton. Liz." She held out her hand and the woman shook it. Her grip was warm and soft like bread dough.

"Nice to meet you." She pronounced it *meetya*, the accent hinting that maybe Maine hadn't been her home forever. "I'm Mabel George. Well, I was christened May Belle with two words but as soon as my folks moved up here from South Carolina I changed it to plain old Mabel. I don't think my daddy really minded once he'd settled into Maine's ways."

Liz got the feeling that Mabel could talk for hours, but she didn't mind. There was something warm and comforting about her. She ate the moist, berry-rich muffin, only half listening to the woman's story, one eye still on the church outside. The poster was bright and garish under the gilt letters proclaiming it to be ST. JOSEPH'S CATHOLIC CHURCH SERVING TOWER HILL SINCE 1783. It was such an imposing building, the charcoal-colored stone not suited to an American shoreline. It looked more like it belonged in medieval Britain making up part of a castle. She wondered at its heritage. The eighteenth century was pretty much the dawn of United States history. It was amazing that the church had stayed standing through all that time. But then, like the college, it was more solidly built than the rest of the town, Gothic and strong. The middle ages had always been an area of interest for her, and she was taking a class on it this semester. Maybe if they were assigned a research project then she could use that as an excuse to dig into the history of St. Joseph's. Something about the design of the building and the stones used made her feel that there was some link to the medieval period.

"So, Liz, are you going to be taking mass with the new priest tomorrow?" Mabel was watching her. "You seem a little drawn to that church."

Liz shrugged. "Yes, I guess I'll be going. I said I would." She looked up at the older woman. "Not really the kind of thing a student should be doing, though. Sleeping off a hangover is probably more the norm."

"Hey, there's nothing wrong with having a little faith. We all need faith in our lives." She looked right into Liz, and although her hair wasn't soft, her eyes were. "You just got here, right? Is this your first time away from home?"

Liz nodded. "Yes. It's okay though." She didn't want Mabel feeling sorry for her. "The town looks lovely. I've taken a good walk around it looking for somewhere with some part-time work going, but so far I haven't found anything. I don't suppose that you know of anywhere, do you?"

Mabel rested one hand on her rounded hip. "How many hours you looking for?"

Liz shrugged. "Well, my schedule's light on Tuesdays and Thursdays, so I was hoping to get an afternoon job for each of them and a few hours on Saturdays. But it looks like my luck isn't in just yet."

"How well can you handle a cake slice?" Mabel asked, grinning.

"I beg your pardon?"

"If you're lucky I may even teach you how to make my raspberry muffins."

"Oh my gosh, thank you!" Sheer excitement overwhelmed Liz's natural reserve and she leapt out of her chair to hug Mabel. "Thank you, thank you, thank you!"

Mabel had no choice but to hug the girl back. "Whoa, that's okay, honey. I need a part-time waitress anyways, so you were just in the right place at the right time. And I think we're going to get along just fine."

Liz hopped from one foot to the other. "Oh, thank you. Thank you so much!"

Mabel laughed out loud. "It's only serving coffee, sweetheart. Now, you'd better run along back to that college of yours. I'll see you at mass tomorrow."

"I'll be there. Ten o'clock sharp."

"Hey, you can be as late as you like for that, honey. That's just church!"

CHAPTER SIX

Looking out over the headland, the sea wind lifting his blond hair, Gray dug his hands into his jean pockets. "Jesus, we must be in the right place. I'm itching like shit."

Jack fingered the ground where he was hunkered down, his eyes narrowly focused on a formation of moss-covered rocks. "You've got to watch that mouth of yours." He muttered. "No swearing in class." He carefully worked some of the dense green carpet away.

"Yeah, tell that to the kids. Little fuckers."

Jack looked up suddenly. "What's itching like shit?"

Gray continued to stare out over the water. Over to the far left of the horizon the buildings of the school stood proud against the skyline, and in the dip below where the two men stood, where the level of the cliffs dropped down a little creating a naturally protected enclave, the white buildings of the small town flashed in the afternoon sunshine. The church that stood guard over it was like a gray rain cloud casting its shadow in the light.

"The freaky little scar tattoo thing that I've got on my chest. That's what's itching." He said. His blue eyes turned to face his partner. "I'm guessing you've got one too."

Jack stood up, his movement fluid. "Show me."

Gray laughed. "What is this, you show me yours, I'll show you mine? Whatever floats your boat, man."

"Just show me, Gray."

The blond man undid his shirt, revealing tanned, taut skin. A thick leather thong hung around his neck. From it hung a coiled snake worked in dull gold, covered in detailed carvings, each scale worked into the soft metal, interspersed with strange small letters covering the reptile's back. The ancient jewels set in the sharp fangs flashed a silent hiss. One impossibly red eye glared back at Jack.

Gray pulled the pendant to one side. Where it had lain a burnt brown shape, that of the snake, was etched into the man's sternum. "Now, my guess is that about the time I got this, you got one in the shape of the key around your neck. Am I right?"

Jack nodded. "Came up a couple of weeks ago."

Gray laughed. "I knew it."

They said nothing for a moment or two and Gray's eyes roamed the view, resting on the church. "This shit is real, isn't it?"

There was awe in his voice, and Jack looked up, surprised. Gray had never been in awe of anything. There had been times when Jack had found himself in awe of Gray and his capabilities, but Gray was normally totally unaffected by the world, however much he might affect it.

"I knew we'd stumbled on something big back in that cave in Afghanistan, but I never for shit thought it would be this big." He looked at Jack. He was still smiling but there was wildness in it. "My scars are fading too."

He undid the rest of the buttons on his shirt. Against the curve of one muscled shoulder a thin stretch of sickly white skin stood pale where a bullet had once cut through him. "That one's at least an inch smaller than it was. And one on my leg has disappeared totally." He raised an eyebrow. "It's fucking awesome."

Jack met his eyes. "Yes, it is." They grinned at each other.

Gray nodded in the direction of the church. "I've got this buzzing in my head most of the time. Drives me fucking crazy when it's quiet. Do you think it's coming from there? Do you hear it?"

"Yeah, I hear it." Jack crouched again, rubbing away moss from the rocks and clearing the excess pebbles. Strange symbols were carved into a small square stone embedded in the earth. "You're right. This is one of them."

"Good, then let's hope this fucking itching stops when we walk away from it."

"I'll come back tonight and dig it up."

Gray pulled him to his feet. "You want me to come?"

"No. We should avoid being seen together. And definitely not in the middle of the night."

Gray smiled as he started to stroll away. "Suits me, dude. I might rustle myself up some entertainment then. I've got a different kind of itch."

"Hey." Jack's voice was sharp, and Gray paused. "Nothing stupid, Gray. And nothing in town. No mess."

"I'm not dumb, Jack." The smile had fallen a little.

"Oh, I know you're not dumb, Gray. You've never been stupid, but we need to be focused. We've both got a busy morning tomorrow."

Gray saluted, his humor returning. "Enjoy the Mass, Father. I'll be thinking of you."

"Likewise, Dr. Kenyon. Likewise."

The two men nodded at each other before heading back down the cliffs, taking different routes back to the town below.

CHAPTER SEVEN

Despite the late night had by most, by the time Liz got back through the college gates, the campus was fully alert and awake, both freshmen and sophomores alike strolling in and out of the imposing halls, laughing and chatting in twos and threes. Looking around her, Liz was glad that she'd stood her ground and come to Tower Hill. And she was doubly glad that her grandmother had left her a college fund. She sent a silent prayer of thanks to the woman she'd never known. She had an idea her mother's mother was smiling down on her from heaven's equivalent of the Miami condo she'd lived in for the final part of her life. Not that Liz had ever seen it, much as she'd secretly have loved to. There was no visiting Grandma for Liz and Sally. Uh-uh, not while she refused the good Lord's word. And then, of course, it was too late for anybody's words. Grandma was gone.

Liz looked at the casually dressed teenagers around her and refused to let her mood drop. There was nothing outrageous about their T-shirts or even the minidresses a couple of the girls were wearing. They were just young people behaving normally. Exactly as it was supposed to be. Exactly as she wanted to be. She loved her folks, she really did, but she was sure going to learn from their mistakes. She'd heard her mom crying quietly late at night and it didn't take much to figure that her guilt was going to be with her forever; God's love couldn't soothe that. Grandma had died of a heart attack and there had been no time for good-byes and I-love-yous. It weighed heavy enough on her; how her mother felt, she could only imagine.

Still, her grandmother had understood how the Clapton family was wrapping itself in a dangerous cocoon of isolation, so she left Liz the fund, and one for Sally if she decided to use it. Without that money, no matter how much she'd wanted to study away from home, her parents would have got their wish and she'd be starting a long and painfully slow degree by correspondence courses. On reflection, she had quite a lot to be thankful for. At least she'd got to go to high school. Sally hadn't even got that. It was homeschooling for her, as their parents got more and more involved with the word of their God. Still, it was pretty much all Sally knew, and that made Liz's heart contract. If Sally was happy that was fine, but Liz hoped her little sister would want to see some of the world for herself.

Liz picked up her step, automatically avoiding the cracks in the sidewalk as if she were a kid again. Maybe if she made a success of things her parents would realize that there was nothing too terrible out there as long as you lived clean, and then things would be easier for Sally. Yep, that's what she'd do. She'd use her time here to show them just how good a place the world could be.

The air was fresh and sweet, with the kind of crisp cleanness that only comes on the cusp of summer and autumn, and she took the stairs up to the house two at a time. Pulling the porch door open, she almost collided with Angela and Steve coming the other way.

"Hey, watch out, chick!" Angela held her hands up. Her face was scrubbed clean and her hair was pulled back into a tight ponytail. Liz thought she suddenly looked almost fragile, her tight dark T-shirt and skinny jeans making her slight frame seem smaller. Her grin was all mischief though, and it made Liz smile back.

"You're up, then?"

"Oh, you're funny. I'm a college girl. Eleven is supposed to be early on the weekend, isn't it?" She raised her eyebrow. "You look fit to burst. What are you so happy about?"

"I got a job! In a really great little coffee shop. They sell muffins to die for and—"

"You're excited because you got a job?" Angela shook her head. "You two are as bad as each other."

Liz looked up at Steve. "You got a job too?"

He shrugged, smiling. "You're looking at Hannaford's next employee of the month."

"And you should see the uniform." Angela rolled her eyes dramatically. "Jesus, I can't wait to see him in it. He'll have to change at work if he's going to keep any vague sense of cool."

Steve nudged her. "So you're saying I'm cool?"

"Only when I'm drunk."

Liz laughed, loving their banter. There was something about the way Angela so flippantly took the Lord's name in vain, which along with her exaggerated responses made her even more endearing. There was something exciting about Angela. Liz was going to become more like Angela, she decided.

"Where are you guys going?"

"To the cafeteria to grab a sub." Steve said. "Then someone said last night that all the lists of clubs and stuff have gone up in Medway Hall, so we were going to go and see if there was anything worth signing up for."

"Sounds good." Liz turned around and the three of them headed back into the sunshine. Angela stood between the other two and linked arms.

"Then we thought maybe we'd see if the neighbors wanted

to have a barbecue with us. May as well use the yard while the weather's still good."

Medway Hall was light and airy, the high vaulted ceilings making it cooler than outside, and Liz felt pleasant goose bumps tickle the skin of her arms. The arched windows created the impression of a church or cathedral, but the walls were painted a neutral magnolia, making it welcoming but somewhat modern. The dark wood under their feet was polished till it shone like amber, and the heels on Angela's boots clicked with each step, sending the whisper of an echo around the hall that probably never seemed busy no matter how many people wandered through it.

"This place is beautiful," Liz said, swallowing the last of her ham salad sub.

"Yeah, and it's where history and divinity are both taught, so we'll be coming here for lectures. How great is that?" Angela looked over at Steve. "What's your major?"

"I'm doing accounting. I think I'm mainly in Gallileo, the smaller one, with the tower."

A long table had been set up under the notice board and various leaflets and flyers were spread across it. Angela's eyes lit on a flyer. "Hey, Steve. There's one for you. Soccer!" She waved it at him dramatically, and then nudged her way past a girl to get to the main board. Liz rummaged through the various bits of paper inviting her to join various societies. There was the debating club, chess club, book club, the young Christians—she pushed that one aside. Guilt rose up like acid in her chest and she hurriedly moved over to where Angela was staring at a bright poster pinned up on the board.

"What's got your attention?"

"Look at this! The paranormal society. That sounds like fun!"

Liz looked. It didn't sound like fun to her. Trying to relax her religion was one thing, but dabbling in the weird and wonderful was taking things a step too far. And aside from that, she was too easily spooked.

"Not really my cup of tea."

"Yeah, but look. It says 'scientific and hands-on exploration of the unknown.' That's just too curious to ignore." She grinned at Liz. "I love all that stuff. And anyway, I can probably use some of it in my debunk-religion crusade." Her eyes flicked back to the poster. " 'First meeting, ten A.M. tomorrow with Dr. Kenyon, MH3.' Cool. I'm so going." She looked around. "What about you, Stevie?"

He shook his head. "Not really my thing either, and anyway, I've got some staff training at Hannaford's tomorrow. Got to be there at nine."

Angela shook her head. "Well, you guys will be missing out." She glanced down at a couple of the smaller notices. "It'll sure as hell be more fun than Scrabble club."

CHAPTER EIGHT

The night wind came in fast from the ocean as the man dug into the hard cliff-top earth. It seemed as if the small town had sucked in to blow him from its surface. If that were the case, then it wasn't successful. Focused on the job at hand, he ignored the wind's strength and let it beat at his back. On his hands and knees, working at the ground with a trowel, Jack Devaine or Father O'Brien or Sergeant McClellan, the name dependant on the time and place of meeting him, concentrated in the small triangle of yellow light. The flashlight was hidden under a tented jacket held down with pebbles, so the light shone only where it was directed and not out into the silent darkness for anyone who was awake to see. Jack Devaine did not want to draw attention to himself. Not yet, at any rate.

The stone embedded so many years ago did not want to budge. It remained firmly settled in the thick mud, resisting the invasion of the gloved hands that clawed at it with a trowel. The man continued with cold determination, his eyes narrow and focused, pushing his fingers into the gaps he was slowly making around the gray stone that had no place in the chalky limestone of the cliff. He showed no sign of frustration, nor did he seem to feel the damp chill from the air that whipped angrily around him.

Eventually the ground spat out the stone, and Devaine tossed it to his left. He reached into the hollow that had been sealed and protected, and he pulled out the small box. He grinned, the first outward sign of emotion, and held it to his chest, resting back on his heels. Somewhere mixed in with the wind, his low chuckle danced. The moment over, he pulled himself quickly to his feet, extinguishing the flashlight and putting on the jacket. He slipped the small box into an inside pocket. The ocean glittered, matching the shine in his eyes. He could feel the power of centuries running through his veins, and he wondered about the men who had buried the box and wondered where their moldering, useless dust lay now. They had buried three, but now that he and Gray had the first, the others would come. They hadn't been hidden well enough to keep men like them away. But then, he was coming to believe that there was more than a touch of destiny at work. If there were a mirror he would see something of the fanatic in the shine of his eyes, and he would recognize it. He could feel it in himself. Self-awareness had always been one of his strongest character traits.

Still, these were lost times, and perhaps the madmen of the world recognized the edge of the apocalypse and felt the calling. The same bright, determined eyes could be seen on countless grainy video broadcasts, the taped words simply ghost echoes of angry men already blown up in the name of some angry god or another.

Standing tall, he gazed out over the black ocean. Jack Devaine learned a lot about angry gods in the past year. What he'd learned had made him smile, and his eyes shine. The humming was louder and with his free hand he scratched at his chest as the wind threatened to tumble him backward. Below, the town lay still and quiet and momentarily he felt like its god. It was a town that had forgotten its purpose. It believed its own lies and had commended its heritage to the book of legend.

The institution of the Church no longer believed in gods and devils and life after death. If it had kept its faith at the core, he reflected, then it would have sent better, stronger men than Peter O'Brien to be the sentinels. It would have kept an army of faithful here, all through the years. Fanatics. Dangerous men were needed to do dangerous jobs.

He grinned and turned away, his legs slipping from stillness to a fast jog with fluid ease. People were generally slack. The church and the town had proved to be no exception. They were slack and happy for someone else to do all the hard work, and if there was no one available, well, then hell, they'd just let it slide. And that was why special people like he and Gray could do what they did. They weren't sheep. Never had been. And what they would be in the future? Well . . . time would tell.

His breath still steady and even, he emerged from the darkness of the cliff tops and into the sporadically lit town. Increasing his pace slightly, he moved silently through the quiet streets. A few lights glowed from within houses, but not even dogs banished to the front yard for the night whimpered as he passed. He was used to moving with stealth and invisibility. Sprinting the last few yards, he slipped into the house by ducking down the dark alley beside the church, jumping the back fence and going in through the back. Most of the other side of the street was taken up by stores but it was best to be careful. He knew the fat bitch over at the café had a habit of peering out through the curtains at him whenever she could, and he hadn't figured out just yet whether she lived in the apartment above. Not that she'd be awake at this time.

The light sweat irritated his chest but he ignored it. Leaving the main house lights off, he pulled his key ring from his pocket and felt expertly for the correct grooves with which to unlock the study door. Clocks ticked through the silent house as he relocked the solid wood behind him. Moonlight shone through the slits in the blinds, making

shadows of the furniture until he clicked on the Tiffany
lamp, giving the shapes substance.

Leaving the box on the worn surface of the large desk,
he poured himself a whiskey. He'd have preferred a warm,
aged Merlot, but for now he'd take the Irish liquor. Father
O'Brien could turn into a wine man during the next couple
weeks. Sitting back in the leather chair, letting it creak with
the movement, he sipped his drink and stared at the box for
a while. It was made of a material he didn't recognize, dark
and heavy enough to have been made from stone, or wood
so old it had fossilized. The whiskey burned his mouth, and
he swallowed slowly. There was no visible seal or lock on
the surface of the box; it appeared to be one solid piece, no
hint that anything was held inside.

The itch on his chest was turning to a burn and he tugged
off his jacket and black long-sleeved T-shirt, letting the air
cool his skin. The key resting there, so much older and
more worn than the one he'd felt for earlier, quivered
slightly. Pain shot down Jack's right arm. He clenched his
teeth and ignored it, focusing instead on the key and the
box. There were things he already knew the key could do,
but nothing as dramatic as this. The tarnish that covered it
was fading, the gold beneath resurfacing and exposing its
true glory. A rising hum drowned out all sound from the
grandfather clock as the key shook and the box began to
tremble. Its surface shone and rippled, the solidity oozing
away like black mercury as it sought out a new shape,
stretching into an oval before returning to its original rec-
tangle, but this time with a more definite edge. The box
clicked and the humming stopped. For a few seconds Jack
didn't move, and then eventually he let out a long slow
breath that seemed to hang invisibly between him and the
desk before escaping into nothing.

Leaning forward, he opened the carved wooden lid, which
was now clearly visible. The contact sent an electric tingle
through his fingers and despite his normal cool, he held

his breath. On the surface sat an old piece of parchment—thick, worn and leathered. Jack rubbed his hand on his trouser leg before gently picking it up, revealing a desiccated twig underneath. He looked back at the hardened paper. Words were scratched into it in crimson ink. Genesis 3:22–25. Some of the ink had dried in a solid drop, and looking at its deep color and thinking about the bottle in the trunk, he wondered if it was ink at all. He sipped his whiskey some more before placing the paper back in the box and shutting the lid. It was likely that the open air had already damaged the delicate contents, and he didn't understand its purpose yet. The twig and the parchment needed to be preserved for as long as possible; of that he was sure.

He reached for the thick Bible on the desk and leaned back in the chair, resting his feet on the desk. Putting his glass within easy reach on the floorboards, he flicked through the thin pages until he found the one he wanted.

> *22 Then the Lord God said, "Behold, the man has become like one of us in knowing good and evil. Now, lest he reach out his hand and take also of the tree of life and eat, and live forever:*
> *23 Therefore the LORD GOD sent him out of the garden of Eden to work the ground from which he was taken.*
> *24 He drove out the man, and at the east of the garden of Eden he placed the cherubim and a flaming sword that turned every way to guard the tree of life.*

He stared thoughtfully at the extract, reading it over several times before shutting the heavy book. The whole thing was, as Gray was fond of saying, too much fucking metaphor. Nothing was ever told straight. He smiled slightly. Still, he understood a lot more than most. *Genesis. The beginnings. The origins.* Yes, he understood what that meant

well enough. He drained what was left of his whiskey and
enjoyed the burn. It matched the one on his chest. Placing
the glass next to the box, he glanced again at the Bible. It
was funny how sometimes the most important characters
in a book were on the sidelines, forgotten until the great
denouement. Not that he'd ever had that much time for fic-
tion. It bored him. He didn't have the imagination for it.

Turning, he moved over to the trunk and crouched beside it, unlocking it conventionally with the key around his
neck. There was no trembling or quivering this time, but he
could still feel the surge of power as the lock mechanics
slid to open.

He moved aside the other items until he pulled free the
large bottle encased in ornate silver fretwork. Inside, the
crimson liquid glowed. He smiled. Tomorrow the true Communion would start.

CHAPTER NINE

The sun was bright but lacked the previous day's warmth as Liz walked the last few yards to the church. Despite still being pretty pissed at herself for agreeing to go, she was in a good mood. She'd got a job and was making friends. The barbecue had been fun too. Dan, Eric and Mona, who had the apartment below theirs, seemed pretty cool, although they were sophomores, so they would probably mix in different circles. Their insights into life at the school had been interesting, and the description of the relative calm of student life at Tower Hill had made Liz even happier that she'd made the move away from the island.

The playful wind teased the hem of her long summer dress, and she clutched at one side just in case a sudden gust decided to show her panties to the world. Her hair was pulled neatly back from her face, and a salmon pink jacket covered her bare arms, making her look every inch the respectable churchgoing girl she always had been. Mom and Dad would be so proud. Still, she figured, it was always respectful to be conservative in a church, and it seemed the rest of Tower Hill thought so too, judging by the smartly dressed men and women who were eagerly scurrying up the stairs of the old gray building.

From beneath a wide-brimmed cream hat, the large

woman standing by the notice board waved at her. Mabel. Liz smiled and raised her hand, picking up her pace to join her new boss.

"Morning, Liz. And don't you look pretty!" Mabel's fuscia lipstick matched the color of her dress and the strong aura of perfume that surrounded her, and suddenly Liz felt almost scruffy. Her smile stretched though. There was something almost motherly about Mabel that made her heart feel warm.

"Hi. You look so great!"

Mabel winked. "Well, you've got to make a good first impression, you know." She looked up at the man beside her, who smiled indulgently. "Oh, where are my manners? Liz, this is Sheriff Russell. James, this is Elizabeth, who I was telling you about. The college girl coming to work in the coffee shop."

Shaking the man's hand, Liz smiled. Even though he was wearing a dark suit and a tie, and his hair had been wetted down to sit politely in a part, he had the look of law enforcement. His eyes twinkled with a calm intelligence, and although he was perhaps carrying a little extra weight in the stomach and was on the wrong side of forty, Liz felt strength in his firm grip. She watched him stand a little straighter as Mabel held his arm, and following them in, she smiled. She figured she may be seeing quite a lot of the sheriff at the café. The pair were obviously sweet on each other.

Out of the sunshine, the temperature dropped a couple degrees and Liz shivered slightly as they found themselves some space in one of the long pews. The wood was dark and old and scarred with scratches in the varnish from years of services. Above the general chatter music played, and taking her seat, Liz listened. It wasn't coming from the organ as she would have expected from a church this old, but from the speakers. It was trancey and beautiful, but she didn't recognize the tune. Mabel nudged her in the ribs.

"I'll tell you this for nothing, the church is never this full. I think the last time most of these folks came to a service was when the last father first arrived." She laughed slightly.

"Mabel"—the sheriff's voice was low—"you ain't exactly a regular churchgoer yourself."

This made Mabel laugh a little louder. "You may have a point there, James. That you may."

She was right though, the church was filling up and Liz followed Mabel's finger as the older woman quietly pointed out various members of the Tower Hill community, attaching to them little snippets of gossip. There was May from the bed-and-breakfast out on the cliffs, whose husband died just over a year ago, and the insurance company had only just paid out after giving her merry hell, which was such a shame, because May was one of the best. And then there was Dr. McGeechan sitting with his wife, who probably had a right to look so miserable because rumor had it that the good doctor was working late with the pretty receptionist at his practice a little too often for a happily married man. The list went on until Liz's head was swimming with names and faces and random bits of information. Only half listening, she let her eyes wander. It seemed that there were very few people under forty, let alone under thirty, and she wondered if that had to do with the town or just the state of Christianity in the modern world. Maybe it just didn't have enough appeal to people her age anymore. She felt a twinge of sadness.

"Oh, and that is the young Christian society from the campus." Mabel pointed out a small clutch of kids about Liz's age sitting silently and somberly waiting for the sermon to begin. Mabel pulled a slight face. "They take themselves very seriously. Don't join up with them, honey. Life is too short for all that misery."

Still staring at them, Liz shook her head. "No, I won't. You don't have to worry about that." She hadn't left one claustrophobic religious environment behind just to join another one.

The music faded a little but not completely and as the door from the vestry opened, the chatter around them died. All eyes were on Father O'Brien as he walked up the stairs to the pulpit. He paused there for a second, placing his hands firmly on the wood and looking down on them before starting to speak. He smiled.

"I'd like to thank so many of you for coming to share in my first Mass here at St. Joseph's. I hope it will be the first of many that we partake in together. This is a new beginning for the church here, and we will take it forward together. Therefore my first sermon is about Communion and what that word really means. . . ."

Angela swore quietly under her breath as she looked up at the class door. MH6. Great. Why the hell couldn't the rooms be in some kind of order? The last one had said MH2. She glanced down at her watch. Nine fifty-five. Shit, she was going to be late. Her hair was loose and she'd pulled on a pair of baggy jeans, a T-shirt and sneakers before running out of the house only ten minutes before. Ten was way too early for all this. At least she'd managed to brush her teeth. She couldn't believe that Liz and Steve were already up and dressed and gone by then. They needed to learn a little more about college life. Still, she had three years to train them.

Looking both ways, she hesitated. The long corridor gave no clues which way she should go, but then she was saved by a figure rounding the corner. The girl smiled at Angela. "If you're looking for MH3, then it's up the stairs at the end of the corridor."

"Thank God for you, because I'd never have found it. You going there too?"

"Paranormal investigation? Shit, yeah. Who could resist? I'm Georgia Keenan." She was pretty, with bright, lively eyes and a small array of pale freckles across her nose.

"I'm a freshman. I guess you must be too if you don't know your way around yet."

"Yeah, I'm new. Angela Wright." She fell into step beside Georgia. "Why the hell do societies meet so early on a Sunday? I could have used another hour in bed." If she was honest, she could always use another hour in bed. She loved her bed. She and her comforter had a special relationship. Especially when she didn't have a boyfriend.

"This is Tower Hill. It's not exactly party central. Still, most of the clubs don't run till eleven on the weekends. I don't know why this one is earlier. I guess this new teacher is an early riser."

They took the stairs two at a time and true to her word, Georgia led them to MH3, tucked away in the corner on the next floor. The two girls hushed a little as they pushed open the door, the awkwardness of meeting fresh strangers suppressing their high spirits.

It was a big space, not a lecture theater as Angela was expecting—more like a regular classroom. The desks were pushed to one side and neatly stacked against the wall, and instead of rows, the seats were laid out in a wide circle. There was some music playing in the background, but Angela didn't recognize it. It was kind of mellow, kind of weird. The sort of thing the emos would go for if they were in a reflective mood, not that emo was ever her thing. Despite her tendency to wear black T-shirts, Angela had never been tempted to join the ranks of the permanently depressed and black-kohled. She liked her soft rock and pop way too much. She shared a grin with Georgia as they grabbed a couple seats next to each other. Despite having only just met, Angela liked this girl. She was sure that Steve and Liz would like her too.

The room wasn't full by any stretch of the imagination but there were a few kids already there, maybe eight or ten, most trying to be cool, sitting lazily in their chairs, looking at everything and nothing. A couple of guys sitting at the farthest side of the circle from them checked them over in the way that men do when they think it's going unnoticed. It wasn't unnoticed by the blondes sitting on either side of them, however, one of whom stretched out her perfectly manicured red nails and dug them in slightly as she casually rested her hand on his thigh, before sending a sparkling smile Angela's and Georgia's way.

Ignoring the underlying message, Angela smiled back, open and friendly. Jocks and their girlfriends weren't ever going to feature in her social circle, so the girl had nothing to worry about from her. Not that she messed with other girls' dates. She'd seen her mother's heart broken down that path and had no intention of ever causing that pain for someone else. And she'd yet to see evidence that the men who cheated were worth having in the end. Her own father was a great example. After leaving her mother, it wasn't long before he was playing the same tricks on the next one.

Georgia flashed Angela a quick, knowing glance, her clever eyes twinkling. The interplay hadn't been lost on her either, and something about it made Angela want to laugh out loud at the sheer ridiculousness of it. Why the hell were the perfect blondes always so damned insecure?

A man stepped confidently out of the office at the side of the room and smiled at the small gathering. He was tall and unexpectedly dressed in battered jeans and a casual shirt. Angela stared at his sandy hair and tanned face for a second before Georgia whispered, "Is it just me, or is he gorgeous?" Angela couldn't argue. Even the bookish girl on their right, sitting hunched forward, hugging her notebook to her chest and hoping not to be noticed, flushed a little and looked as if she'd pee herself if that dazzling smile shone her way for more than a second.

"Hey, thanks for coming. I'm Dr. Kenyon. It's great to—"

"What's the tune, dude? It ain't exactly top forty." The broad-chested wannabe football star whose girlfriend's talons had slipped away from his thigh when the older man had entered the room was now measuring Kenyon up, albeit in a very different way. Angela watched the way he leaned a little farther back in the chair and sniggered with his friend. Now who was feeling threatened?

Dr. Kenyon just smiled. "Good question. It may not be easy listening, but it's relevant to our group. It's an ancient piece of music I discovered on an adventure in the Middle East a few years back. I've funked it up a little but the tune's the same. Roughly translated, it's called 'The Dance of the Serpent.'" He paused and winked in Angela's and Georgia's direction, and Angela felt her stomach twist. Georgia was right. He was damned gorgeous for an old guy. What was he? Midthirties?

"Apparently," he continued, leaning toward the boy a little, "a long, long time ago, the tune was used to summon the dead." He grinned. "You gotta love it just for that, don't you?"

Angela felt like the wind had been knocked out of her from the toes upward. He was *so* not what she had expected from a college teacher. She was staring at him; she couldn't help herself. Beside her, Georgia looked equally wide-eyed and fascinated. Even the boys were nodding a little with a kind of warming respect.

"What do you teach?" The breathless question tumbled out of her before she'd realized she'd spoken. Inside, her cynical voice of reason totally suppressed by the massive crush she could feel developing, she desperately prayed he was going to say divinity.

"History."

The girl clutching her notebook almost gasped with delight, and Angela flashed her a dirty look. No guessing what she was majoring in, then.

"I'm an archaeologist. Well, I used to be, before I got older. A kind of Indiana Jones but without the hat." He grinned again, and Angela laughed along with the rest of the small gathering. Maybe ten o'clock wasn't too early for a club. Dr. Kenyon was worth hauling her ass out of bed.

He sat in a chair almost directly opposite her and leaned his elbows on his thighs. "Okay, let's get started. This session I'm just going to introduce you guys to the kinds of things we'll be looking into as part of the society, and then I'm going to teach you something we'll spend a lot of time coming back to over the weeks. It's something I picked up in Tibet, a method of putting yourself into a suggestive state. It'll be useful for when we try things like astral projection."

One of the blondes giggled and was hushed by her boyfriend. Kenyon waved a hand at them. "It's okay, you're allowed to giggle a little. Laughter is the way we react as animals when presented with things that make us feel awkward or nervous. Remember—some of this stuff will seem weird and downright foolish at times, and that's why this is an *investigation* society. I'm sure as hell not saying that I'll believe in everything we're going to investigate, but you have to be open to belief. This society is all about maintaining an open mind." He paused and studied them each seriously. "You got that?"

Along with the rest, Angela nodded eagerly. She was definitely open to Dr. Kenyon. Yes sirree.

The strange music continued as Father O'Brien delivered his sermon, and Liz wondered if he'd just forgotten to ask someone to turn the tape off when he started speaking. Not that he couldn't be heard over it, but it just didn't seem right to have music during the service. Hymns, yes, but this strange modern-and-yet-not-modern melody continually in the background? No. It just wasn't in keeping with St. Joseph's. Still, maybe Father O'Brien was trying to do something different to mark his arrival. All in all, she wasn't sure it was working. Stifling a yawn, her attention wandered from the pulpit. Sunshine battled its way in through the stained-glass windows, casting a rainbow of light across the stone floor and the backs of the rows of people in front of her, dust dancing in the light.

The church had gotten warmer with the volume of people, and she drifted in her own thoughts, gazing at the depictions carefully worked into the mosaic of glass high in the walls. The faces of saints gazed sternly down at her. She looked again. In one image, predominantly of a huge serpent coiled around a tree, in the background there were three figures. She stared at their gray armor with St. George's crosses emblazoned across their chests. Crusaders? Why would there be Crusaders in the stained-glass windows of a small town church in Maine? Once again, she found her curiosity about the church piqued. Maybe she'd come back and see if the priest had a history of the building somewhere.

From the pulpit, Father O'Brien's voice flowed in a smooth, confident river of sound. She only half listened to his words as he talked about sharing and community and belonging, the words hovering around her rather than sinking in. If she was honest, then she was vaguely bored. She shouldn't have come. Her skin itched to be out of here. But then, she'd heard more sermons than most, delivered with far more passion and fervor.

Looking around, it seemed the boredom was solely her own. Even those who had come along probably just for the gossip and to take a peek at the new father appeared to be listening attentively. The content of the service was slightly seductive. Everyone wanted to belong to something, after all. Glancing to her left, she caught Mabel's eye and smiled. Mabel smiled back, but it was a quick mechanical gesture, as if she didn't welcome the distraction to her listening. Liz shivered again.

By ten thirty Angela was hooked on every word that came out of Dr. Kenyon's mouth. She couldn't help herself. It

was the same for all the others too. They were like starstruck
kids in front of a gig they never expected to get tickets for.
He was just too awesome for words. The girl with the notebook was now sitting upright, the impressive chest that
she'd obviously been hiding under her hunched shoulders
definitely sticking out in Kenyon's direction, her face glowing. Georgia too couldn't wipe the grin off her face, and
Angela just knew that she was probably in the same state
herself. But what the hell, a little crush on the teacher never
did any harm. And it wasn't like he was just good-looking.
He was fascinating and intelligent and funny. *Christ, girl,*
she thought, biting down on the inside of her cheek to stop
from laughing, *you have got it bad.*

"Okay, so everyone ready to give this a go?" Dr. Kenyon
drew down the blinds, shutting out the sun and leaving the
room in cool gray darkness. A murmur of eager voices as-
sented. He turned up the volume slightly on the music before fetching a tall candle on a pole from the office. It
wasn't a candle like the ones Angela had seen in pretty gift
shops, all smooth and cream and ready to be brought out at
Thanksgiving or Christmas. This one was dark and lumpy
and poorly formed; man-made, not custom. Placing it in
the middle of the circle, Dr. Kenyon flicked open a Zippo
and lit it.

"Did you find that on a dig too?" asked one of the jocks.
Angela thought he'd said his name was Will, but she wasn't
sure. The jocks were Will and Dennis, so he was one or the
other, anyway. There was no arrogance in his question now.
Just a kind of awe.

"Something like that." Dr. Kenyon stepped back out of
the circle. "Everyone shut your eyes. No giggling now, if
you're going to get the hang of this."

Angela did as he asked and let the blackness inside her
eyes take over.

"Now take three deep breaths. In and out. Nice and slow."
The scent from the candle drifted slowly outward and

Angela could taste it in her mouth. It was thick and heady, almost like good weed: a mix of sweetness and herbs. There was something else there too, a tang that stuck cloyingly at the back of her throat for a moment or two as she dragged air in through her nose.

"Good." Dr. Kenyon had lowered his voice, making it softer, barely audible over the strange tune. "Now I'm going to come around and whisper a few words into each of your ears. Listen hard and make sure you hear me right. You won't recognize the words. They're just to help you meditate and empty your minds. As soon as I've moved on I want you to start repeating those words, keeping your eyes shut. Everyone with me?"

Angela nodded and swallowed. There was no giggling now. Between the darkness and the scent coming from the candle she felt half sedated already. A couple of seconds later someone a few chairs to her right began to softly chant. The sounds blended into one and meant nothing to her.

"Amanniparadosisparadiso . . ."

She gasped slightly as warm breath tickled her ear. Her heart pounded faster with the sheer closeness of him as he repeated the phrase and then was gone, stepping away and whispering into Georgia's ear. Lost in her inner darkness, Angela shook off the pleasant shiver, focusing on the words he'd poured into her. Quietly she joined the others in the chant. The scent of the candle seemed stronger as her breathing relaxed. After a while the words in her quiet whisper filled her head, pushing all else out. And then there was nothing.

CHAPTER TEN

Gray looked at the kids seated around him.

Their mouths hung open, lips slack but still trying to mumble out the words he'd given them. He snapped his fingers. Nothing. He grinned. They were like fucking zombies. Whistling Lynyrd Skynyrd's "Sweet Home Alabama," he took the small bottle that Jack had given him from the trunk and syringed a couple of drops into each teenage mouth.

Pulling a pack of Salems from his pocket he leaned forward and lit one from the candle. Screw the rules. He'd open the window on his way out. He checked his watch. Ten forty-three. Perfect timing. Damn, he was good.

CHAPTER ELEVEN

Liz's fingers drummed on her thigh as the minutes ticked away. Father O'Brien was delivering a good enough sermon and he did have a certain amount of charisma, but by ten forty-five she was just itching to get out and back to the weekend. It was a relief when the priest finally called the congregation up for the Eucharist. A few in the front row didn't move, and O'Brien gave them a broad smile.

"Come on up, all of you! I want everyone to share in our first Mass as a new congregation. It's a fresh beginning for all of us. Come and share in the blood of Christ with me."

Those that had remained seated got to their feet and shyly joined the rest at the altar, waiting their turn and then sipping from the cup. The people in the row in front of Liz shifted in their seats impatiently until it was their turn, and then a few minutes later Mabel was grabbing at Liz's sleeve.

"Come on, honey."

"Oh, I don't think—"

The older woman looked down at her. "You don't think what? Come on."

With both the sheriff and Mabel staring at her, Liz sighed and got to her feet. Nothing was going quite as planned. She was supposed to be trying to leave religion behind, and here she was going up to take the Eucharist on her first weekend away from home. The line moved slowly until she took her place on her knees next to Mabel, her hands cupped in front of her. The curate came past and, muttering the ritualistic words, placed a wafer in them. It felt light in her hands, but in her head it was a heavy symbol of everything she was trying to put behind her. She raised her hands to her mouth but let the wafer slip unnoticed down the sleeve of her jacket. She should have been more honest and stayed seated. She was tired of doing what others expected of her, and it wasn't as if Mabel would have minded much if she hadn't taken part in the Communion. Father O'Brien's dark robes blocked her vision. He held the gold chalice in both hands, level with her head. She was up here now, and there would be no point in causing a commotion and heading back to her seat. Raising her head, she allowed the priest to tip the cup on her mouth, but she kept her lips sealed tight around the metal edge. It was cold and the warm liquid stung her lips. A second later the cup was gone, the priest moving on to Mabel.

Her heart thudded triumphantly in her chest. She didn't feel ashamed of her cheating in the house of the Lord. It would have been more of a lie if she'd taken the wine and bread, and God, if he existed, would understand that. She shouldn't be taking Communion, not while she was having a crisis in her faith. Her lips burned slightly with the trace of wine and she licked it away. The familiar taste was edged with bitterness, and she shivered slightly, as if she'd just tasted a lemon. Maybe it was just the metal residue, or maybe the wine had been left over from a previous service. Whichever, she was doubly glad she hadn't taken a full swallow.

Following the movement beside her, she was happy to be heading back to her seat. The line seemed to shuffle more slowly back than it did going up, but maybe that was just her own eagerness to get away from the altar.

She slid into her place, and the congregation sat in silence while waiting for the final rows to be blessed and return. The sun still shone in golden rays through the glass, and Liz hoped it was going to be a glorious day when she got outside. An afternoon lazing in the yard reading a book was what she had in mind. A little downtime before the chaos of classes that would start the next day. She looked around her. Most people, Mabel and the sheriff included, were staring fixatedly at Father O'Brien as he finished up the Communion. Only one or two others were like her, glancing around, slightly bored and distracted. Even the children were focused. Liz was slightly surprised. From what Mabel had said, the town hadn't seemed overzealous in their religious observances, but this congregation seemed pretty serious about their praying.

Eventually everyone was back in their seats, and Father O'Brien stood in front of the altar and smiled. The strange music was playing in the background again; the only time it had stopped was when they'd sung a hymn. It was beginning to grate on Liz's nerves. And only one hymn in an hour? Even in the services her parents conducted at home they'd sung more than that. She bowed her head out of habit as he led them in the Lord's Prayer.

"And now I'd just like to once again thank you all for coming along to share my first prayers here in Tower Hill. I hope to see you all again next week. And remember, for those of you that like to spend a little more time with God than that, there is the midweek mass on Wednesday evenings. This is your church. Come share in it."

Murmurs of enthusiasm and approval rippled along the pews.

"And remember to spread the good word. Bring along a friend next time. Someone that maybe needs the love of the Lord in their life. Someone who needs our help." He paused. "God bless you all."

The seat was itching under Liz and she smiled at Mabel as they finally rose to leave. The older woman smiled at her. "James and I are going to go grab a coffee and a muffin. You want to come along?"

"Yeah, that would be great. I didn't get any breakfast this morning and I'm starving."

"It's the advantage of owning your own coffee shop. If every other darned place in town is closed, at least you can open up, if only to serve yourself. And you know who to complain to if the cakes are a little stale." She laughed aloud and Liz smiled. She wished her mother was like Mabel—warm and wholesome and earthy. Just like a mother should be.

Getting out of the church was slow going; everyone wanting to spend a few minutes talking to the priest, who stood in the vestry, wishing them well. He grinned when he saw her. "Well, hello there, Miss Clapton. Glad to see you here. Did you enjoy the service?"

She nodded, but felt sure that he could see her lie burning out from her cheeks. She gripped his hand for only a moment before letting it go. It was cool and clammy. Somehow she didn't find him so friendly anymore. Mabel and Sheriff Russell obviously felt differently though, and she waited for them at the bottom of the steps as they both shook his hand vigorously, Mabel literally gushing at him about how she would be back the following week. Finally they came down to join her.

"What a charming man, wouldn't you say, Liz? James?"

Liz just smiled, but the sheriff nodded. "Yes, he most certainly is. I think he's going to be good for the town. Tower Hill needs someone like him. Get some of the old community spirit back." He squeezed Mabel's arm. "Now, didn't you promise us some coffee and muffins?" He winked at Liz. "I wouldn't want to have to arrest you on a charge of deception."

Mabel nudged him hard in the ribs. "Oh, you could try, mister. If you don't watch your cheek, I may find I only have enough muffins for two."

James laughed out loud. "Now, honey, that *would* be a crime."

Listening to their banter as Mabel unlocked the small café on the other side of the road, Liz felt her spirits lift, the residue of her boredom in the church dissolving into her smile.

CHAPTER TWELVE

"That was pretty awesome." Angela said as they took their paper coffee cups out from the refectory and into the sunshine of the quad.

"Don't you mean *he* was pretty awesome?" Georgia grinned as she found a space on the grass for them. Angela sat cross-legged, putting her coffee and the small bag Dr. Kenyon had given them in the nook between her legs.

"Hmmm. Maybe I do. But the whole thing was pretty exciting. The meditation was good. I felt so sleepy." She looked down at the white bag. "How cool that he gave us each one of those candles."

"Yeah." Georgia sipped her coffee. "But I bet I can't get myself in that kind of trance without his help." She wiggled an eyebrow. "Hey, maybe he'll give me private lessons."

"Slut." Angela peered across the lawn and returned a half wave from the jocks and their girlfriends who were sitting on the other side of the square, their white bags neatly piled beside them. "I feel like I've joined a frigging secret society."

"Yeah, me too. That makes this thing even cooler. I don't think they've ever had a society like this one at Tower Hill."

"How come you know so much about this college if you're a freshman too?"

Georgia pointed a stern finger at her. "You can't call it a college. They call it a university. The founders of the place, and the town for that matter, came from England. From London, in fact. That's where they copied the name from, some part of London." She sipped her coffee. "My sister's here doing her finals. I've made her swear to stay out of my way. All the Keenans have come here. My mom and dad met here, in fact." She grimaced. "Cute, huh?"

"Didn't you feel like maybe applying somewhere else?"

"Nope." She paused. "The way I see it, as soon as we graduate and head out into the big wide world, there'll be enough excitement and strangeness to deal with. There's something safe about Tower Hill. I like it. And hell, if it wasn't for this place, I wouldn't even be here!"

Angela smiled. She had a point. And she was right. There was something peaceful about the gray stone buildings and tranquil setting. It kind of suckered you in. "So, are you going to go to the next meeting?"

"You kidding? Of course I'm going. I wouldn't miss it for the world! Are you going to do the home meditation?"

"I'll try." Angela yawned, stretching out in the sunlight. "I'm not even sure it worked, but it definitely relaxed me. I feel like I could sleep for a week."

"Yeah, me too. Kind of like after a massage. Not even this awful coffee is perking me up."

"Well, I'm not going to fight it. My bed is my favorite place, especially on a Sunday. I think I might head back to the house and catch some z's for a couple hours." She pulled herself to her feet. "What are you going to do?"

"Oh, I may just lay here for a while and doze."

"I'll catch you tomorrow sometime around lectures. Maybe lunchtime?"

"Sure." Georgia mumbled, her eyes already shut as she stretched out on her back. Angela grinned. She'd be asleep in seconds. She just hoped Georgia didn't snore. Not something you'd want to be doing out here in the middle of everyone on your first Sunday at school.

The house was cool inside, none of them having drawn back the drapes before rushing out earlier that morning, and Angela slipped the candle into her top drawer before lying down on her unmade bed. Maybe she should put some music on or something. Her ears buzzed slightly with the absence of sound. Her limbs felt too heavy to move and it took all her energy to kick off her sneakers. Just half an hour of sleep; that was all she needed. Just to make up for the early morning. God, she felt so deliciously relaxed. Her eyes shut and within three deep breaths she was asleep.

When she opened her eyes again, she stared for a moment at the digital numbers glaring from her alarm clock before wiping sleep dribble from the edges of her mouth. How could it possibly be frigging five o'clock? That would mean she'd slept for nearly four hours. Jesus. Dragging herself up so she was seated, she ran her fingers through her sleep-mussed hair, trying to straighten it up and clear her head. She pulled the drapes open a little, letting some light in. At least it was still day out there. She yawned and flicked the remote, turning the tiny, battered portable TV on, letting the voices in without really paying attention to the words. Her mouth felt dry and she was starving, which wasn't really surprising because apart from the coffee she hadn't had a thing to eat or drink all day.

Standing up, she stretched, feeling the tight muscles in her legs slowly loosen. That was better. She was awake. Or at least nearly. Her head still felt pretty drowsy. God, she must really have needed to sleep. Shuffling to the door, she thought for a second about the candle Dr. Kenyon had given her. She was supposed to use it to practice the meditation that evening, but she couldn't see it happening. She was just too tired. And too damned hungry. She'd give it a go tomorrow.

In the kitchen Liz sat at the small table while Steve kept an eye on the pans on the stove. Something smelled good. Something smelled very good.

"What you cooking?"

"Hey, sleepyhead, nice to see you." Steve grinned. "Pasta and meatballs. My first staff discount purchase at Hannafords. There's plenty here, so pull up a chair. It's just about done."

"Hey, Liz, how was your day?" Getting three tumblers from the cupboard, Angela poured them each a large glass of juice as Steve served up their dinner.

"Great, thanks. Nice and lazy. I've been reading in the yard for most of the afternoon."

"I had to sit through an hour of health and safety, and then spent the rest of the day lugging boxes from the stock-room and into the store." He passed a full plate to each girl. Angela grinned.

"This looks great. I'm starving." She shoveled a forkful into her mouth. "So, what were the people like? Okay?"

Steve rolled his eyes. "Jeez, you wouldn't believe it. They're nice, but there's not a lot happening at home, if you get me."

Liz whacked him on the arm. "Intellectual snobbery is not nice, Mr. Wharton. The world takes all sorts to tick along."

"Yeah, well you come in and take a look for yourself. I'm working late on Tuesday, and then a short shift Saturday and shelf stacking Sunday. It's not great hours, but it's a start. It's all money in the bank."

Liz nodded and spooned Parmesan on her pasta, looking up at Angela. "How was your paranormal thing?"

"Damn, it was good. Dr. Kenyon, who runs it, is pretty awesome. He's done so much stuff. He was an archaeologist and he's traveled pretty much everywhere, from what he was saying." She paused to swallow another mouthful. The food was good and her stomach was screaming out for her to fill it. "And on top of that, he is just so hot!" She laughed and then stopped. "Hey, he's teaching history. You'll be in some of his classes." She felt a wave of disappointment tinged with more than a little jealousy. She pushed it away. Shit, he was just a teacher. It wasn't as if either of them was going to date him.

Liz rolled her eyes. "I can't wait."

They talked and laughed until about nine, comparing the classes they had the next day. Angela was pleased to see her day was pretty light. It was always better to ease in gently to something new. By nine thirty, she was yawning again.

"God, I'm going to have to go back to bed. I'm beat." She shrugged. "I know you guys think I'm just lazy, but all the sleeping I've done today isn't like me." She smiled, yawning some more. "Maybe it's the ocean air or something."

"I've been feeling groggy all afternoon too." Liz said, stacking her diary and books neatly in a pile for the next day. "I don't know why, because I woke up feeling great. Maybe there's a bug going around or something."

"Yeah, maybe. Anyway, I'm going to go and sleep it off. I'll see you guys at lunch if I don't see you in the morning."

Waving good night, she washed quickly and brushed her teeth before curling back up under her comforter. She flicked the remote on, but kept the TV on silent, staring at the screen for a while as her eyelids grew heavier. The news was on, with more dead soldiers in Iraq or Afghanistan, one or the other. The images were depressing and she was glad she didn't have the sound up. She thought about maybe changing the channel, but then her eyes were shut and her breathing slower and she was gone.

When she awoke, it was with a start. The TV was showing a silent rerun of *I Love Lucy*. Blearily, she reached in the darkness for the remote to turn it off. She froze and yelped.

Jesus. Georgia was standing in the middle of the room, gazing at the screen. God, she'd scared the crap out of her. Angela stared at the girl for a moment. Her heart thudded, calming from the surge of adrenaline her body had pumped into her. Maybe she was dreaming. What the hell was Georgia doing in her room?

"Georgia?" she whispered.

The girl turned to face her, her hands stuffed into the front pouch of her yellow sweatshirt. She had bare feet under her jeans and her hair was wet, as if she'd just got out of the shower. This was way too much detail for a dream. Angela sat up on one elbow.

"Georgia?"

The other girl seemed to see her properly for the first time. *"Sethenoshkenanmahalaleljaredenoch . . ."*

Angela frowned. "What the hell are you saying? Are you awake, Georgia?"

Georgia looked down at herself and then at the TV, and then back at Angela. "What am I doing here?" Her eyes were wide. "I feel funny. What am I doing here, Angela?"

If Georgia hadn't looked so terrified, Angela thought she might have laughed. She sat up on the side of her bed. The clock read just about eleven. "I don't know, honey. Who let you in?"

Walking awkwardly, Georgia turned her back on Angela as if she'd forgotten she was there, and opened the door to go out into the hallway.

"Shit," Angela muttered, and pulled her robe from the back of the door before following her out. The hall was empty.

Steve's door opened and he peered out. "Who was that? You got friends over?" His voice was sleepy.

Angela opened the front door and scanned the gloom. There was no one there. How could she have left so fast? She turned back to Steve. "I think it was Georgia. Did you see someone out here?"

He scratched his hair and squinted. "No, but I woke up about five minutes ago and could swear there was a girl standing in my room. And then she was gone."

Angela's feet tingled on the carpet. This was weird. "She was in my room too. She spoke to me, and then she came out here, and when I came after her, she'd gone." She looked up at Steve. "Did you really see a girl in your room too?"

He shrugged. "I don't know. Maybe I just heard you talking and dreamed it?"

"What was she wearing?"

"I'm not sure. Jeans, I think. And a yellow sweat shirt."

"Yeah, that's what she was wearing in my room too. Not a dream, then. How did she get out so fast?"

Steve yawned. "Maybe she's a sleepwalker. Woke up in your room, freaked herself out and ran."

Angela nodded. "Yeah, maybe." What Steve said did make sense. It was possible that Georgia could have been sleepwalking, even if it was a long way from the student residential hall to the house. Still, what else could it be? She smiled apologetically at Steve, and he smiled back.

"You can rip her for it tomorrow."

"Yeah. G'night."

It was only when she was back in bed that she realized that she hadn't actually told Georgia where she lived. And what were the chances of someone leaving the main door to the house unlocked, as well as their apartment door? She thought about going to talk to Steve some more, and then thought better of it. He'd only think she was being stupid. And maybe she was. There was bound to be a simple explanation for it. There always was. Still, she trembled slightly and turned the volume up on the old sitcom to help her drift back to an unsettled sleep.

CHAPTER THIRTEEN

Tower Hill is a town unsettled but unaware. A tumor has started to grow in its bowels but the early symptoms are hard to spot and easy to ignore. Most of the residents still sleep soundly in their beds, as yet untouched by the events that are bubbling under the surface. The ocean stirs the waves, forcing them to hit the shingle harder, as if nudging the buildings that hold the townsfolk, hoping to wake them to the danger lurking within. They sleep on, of course, used to the ebb and flow of the water and its occasional attack on the border that divides them.

Some, though, the church congregation and those as yet few students from the paranormal society, toss and turn, unable to rest. They call out strange names in the night and lick the memory of liquid from their lips.

In the house built of the same cold stone as the church, a man, a wolf in sheep's clothing, stares at the box on the dead priest's desk. A key burns at his chest and the box opens. He pulls out the parchment as he has done before, but things in the box have changed. The parchment reads only two words now, scratched in Latin: *ME CENA*.

He peers into the box. Where last time there had been only a dry, long, dead twig, there now sits an apple, round and red. He takes it out. It's cool and waxy in his hand. He looks at the parchment again.

ME CENA. Eat me.

Smiling, he raises it to his lips and does what he's told.

CHAPTER FOURTEEN

Gray drove through the quiet streets and left the small town behind. It was nearly eleven and he had lectures to deliver early the next morning, but there were some things that just couldn't wait until later. He'd been a good boy for long enough and he needed to do what came naturally to him; what was in his makeup to do. He knew that Jack would prefer it if he could hold off until after, but he would never say it. Jack also knew that Gray focused better when he wasn't stressed; when he was allowed to let off some steam from time to time. As long as he was careful, then Jack would be A-OK with this. He always was. They were like brothers. Always had been and always would be. Jack was the only person he'd ever felt anything close to love for; even his parents had seemed only like alien necessities. Jack *got* him. And he got Jack.

The street lighting soon filtered out, leaving him with only his headlight and the moon to guide him through the darkness as the miles flashed under him, marked by white lines in the road. He drove an hour inland until he came to the outskirts of a larger town. A place big enough for people to be anonymous. A place big enough to have dark corners within which most people didn't much care what happened.

He drove carefully but not too carefully, knowing how to avoid late-night police attention. He'd had plenty of practice at it. Turning away from the Main Street, he took a side road, seeking out seedy, badly lit bars and clubs—the haunts of the abandoned and the lonely. There'd be some, he was sure. After all, the world was full of destroyed people.

He sighed as he saw the first cluster of women smoking on the corner. Normally, he'd avoid hookers. There was little appeal for him in them. They were hard and cynical with none of the sweetness he sought. They expected pain. They knew their lives were fucked, and when they found themselves with him, with his true self revealed, they often looked as if the fate they had always expected had finally found them. They were resigned. It wasn't what he liked, what made his blood surge with enthusiasm. What he liked was back at the university, but he knew that was off-limits. There were bigger things at work there and he had no intention of fucking them up. He wondered how his urges would be affected *after*. He hoped they'd still be there. He'd miss them if they weren't.

The car's engine thrummed as it prowled like a predatory shark through the dark night, moving deeper into the town. He was definitely in the right area; now all he needed was to find the right woman. Ignoring those standing in groups or huddles of twos and threes, knowing he couldn't afford witnesses, he scanned the streets for solitary women. He passed two or three. They were too old and wasted to be much fun, and not worth the risk for such a limited return. And then he saw her. *Bingo.*

She stood on the corner, alone under the streetlight, her eyes darting this way and that, as much out of fear as looking for her next job. Her thin jacket was pulled tight around her even though the night was warm, and below the hem of her minidress she had the chubby yet firm thighs of a teenager.

Gray slid the car over to the curb and rolled the window

down. She leaned in, her eyes wary, and under the makeup Gray figured she was maybe nineteen, max. She hadn't been doing this long; he'd bet money on it. Her skin was too fresh and her pupils didn't shake like a junkie's. He grinned at her. She hesitantly smiled back, her arms draped into the car in what she must have thought was a seductive pose. She wore an garish, oversized green ring on her finger. It was cheap, like something you'd get from a dime store. The color matched her eyes, though. Gray stared into those emerald irises. Behind the color there was still some hope in them. He was pleased about that as she climbed in beside him, and he drove away.

An hour and a half later and all that hope had gone. Little Lucy had grown up a lot in that time. A lifetime. Lying out on the headland, covered in her own blood, she begged to die.

And Gray obliged.

CHAPTER FIFTEEN

Liz put down her pen for a moment and stretched her fingers. It had been a long morning of classes and her hand ached from writing. She was sure that as time passed she'd take less care with her notes, but she was full of first-day enthusiasm and wanted her folder to be perfect. She swallowed a yawn and looked at Dr. Kenyon, who was just finishing up the potted history of Alfred the Great.

As much as she was enthusiastic about college, the classes so far hadn't really inspired her. Yes, Dr. Kenyon was more interesting than Dr. Blackmore, who'd spent two hours that morning defining the Middle Ages but really telling them very little of substance, but watching Kenyon smiling and joking with the class, she couldn't help but think he was somewhat in love with himself. He was good-looking, she couldn't deny that, but he didn't appeal to her. Not in *that* way. He was too old, for a start. Not that she'd had that much experience with boys to really know. Maybe if she'd ever done more than just kiss a boy she might see the professor differently, but she didn't think so.

She thought about the way Angela had flushed when talking about Dr. Kenyon. Had Angela "done it"? Probably. Most girls their age had. Her thoughts drifted to Steve. Of course he'd done it. There was something adult about

Steve, something safe and strong. A prickle of a blush crept up her neck from just thinking about him like that. Oh, great. She was getting the hots for her roommate. Gathering her books together as the class started to filter out, she wasn't sure if she felt good or embarrassed about thinking of Steve that way. She got to her feet. Probably a bit of both. And not that it mattered. It wasn't as if it were ever going to go anywhere.

"Dr. Kenyon?"

He flashed his white teeth at her and grinned. "Yep, Liz? It is Liz, isn't it?"

She nodded. *Yep.* No, he wasn't her type at all. It seemed he was trying a little too hard. Still, he was probably a perfectly decent man, and who was she to judge him?

"Hi, and yes. I was just wondering if you had any information on the history of the church in the town."

"The church?" His eyes narrowed slightly, but the grin was fixed. "I may somewhere, but I'm new to town myself, just like you freshmen. Why do you ask?"

"Oh, no reason." Liz hugged her books to her chest. She wasn't sure why. "I was there on Sunday and I just thought the architecture was medieval. Like the college, I guess. I was just curious about it."

Dr. Kenyon winked. "Well, I may go down and take a look for myself. But between you and me, I'm not much of a churchgoing man."

Liz smiled and headed to the door. The others would be waiting for her for at lunch. "So I gather. My roommate came to your paranormal society meeting on Sunday."

"That would be me." Angela was leaning against the wall outside the classroom, her hips thrown provocatively forward. She smiled and straightened up. "I got out early so I came to find you for lunch."

Liz watched the way the other girl looked up at Kenyon for approval and bit back a smile. She wondered if Angela would have come to meet her if she'd had Dr. Blackmore before lunch. Probably not. But hey, if Angela got a buzz out of it, then that was fine with her.

"Hey, Angela. Good to see you. You coming next Sunday?"

"Of course." Angela had slipped herself between Liz and Kenyon as they walked to the stairs.

"Try and bring someone along. Let's get our numbers up." He looked across at Liz. "Why don't you come along?"

She shook her head. "Not my kind of thing."

He grinned. "I guess you'll be in church, huh?"

"Maybe. Although I'm not sure that's my kind of thing either."

Kenyon laughed. It was a warm, throaty sound, and although Angela giggled along with it, it just didn't reach Liz like that. It seemed fake. A lot of things about Kenyon seemed fake.

"Well, you should do one or the other. What else is there to do on a Sunday?"

"Read a book?"

He shrugged. They'd reached the stairs, and he turned to head up while they were heading down to the refectory. "Hey, Angela. Don't forget to practice your meditation."

"Sure. Of course I will."

Angela's eyes followed the man as he took the stairs two at a time; then she turned to Liz. "Didn't I tell you he was hot?"

Liz smiled. "Not my type, I'm afraid."

Angela laughed. "Yeah, whatever. That man is every girl's type." Linking arms, she dragged Liz down into the busy corridor. They bustled thought the crowd of students tumbling out of classrooms and heading either out into the sunshine or to get some food. Angela paused for a moment as the hall opened out into the atrium. "Hey, that's Georgia. Georgia!" She waved in a dark-haired girl's direction and then yanked Liz's arm. "Come on, this'll only take a minute."

Georgia stood with a very pretty blond girl, and with

Angela giving them no time for introductions, Liz just smiled at them both.

"This might sound stupid, Georgia"—Angela lowered her voice—"but were you sleepwalking or something last night? I woke up and you were in my house."

"In your house?" Georgia looked over at the blond girl with her. "No, I fell asleep really early. I was beat." She shrugged. Liz thought she looked tired. "I guess I could have sleepwalked, but I never have before." She paused. "You say you saw me in your house?"

"You didn't sleepwalk, honey." The blond girl's accent was all Oklahoma, soft and smooth. "I went in to check on you at about eleven, just before I went to bed. Your room light was off and you were fast asleep. You were restless, though. Tossing and turning." She laughed, but there was nothing mean in it. "But you weren't walking."

Angela still stared at Georgia. Her natural humor was absent from her face. "That's so weird. Maybe I was dreaming." She paused. "But you're wearing what you were wearing when I saw you. That's too freaky."

Georgia's roommate shrugged, bored. "Honey, I'll grab a table. Come find me."

Liz looked around them. The tables were filling up. There'd be nowhere left for them if they didn't hurry. Her foot tapped, only half listening as Georgia leaned in to Angela.

"You know, you were in my dream last night. Isn't that odd? I'd completely forgotten until you just came up right now. You were there, and some old TV star. I can't remember her name. She was funny. Had her own show."

"*I Love Lucy*?" Angela's mouth fell open. "That's what was on my TV when I saw you." She looked at Liz and tugged her sleeve. "Did you hear that? Isn't that just too fucking weird?"

Liz laughed, flinching a little inside at the expletive. She was just going to have to get used to that kind of language out here in the big wide world, she guessed. Angela and Georgia were both gaping. Her books tucked under one arm, Liz nudged Angela playfully. "Yeah, of course you two have a psychic link. There couldn't possibly be a perfectly rational explanation like you both had the same channel on while you were sleeping. I mean, come on."

Georgia didn't smile. "But I didn't have the TV on."

"Yeah, but your roommate might have. You might just have heard it through the walls while you were sleeping." She looked at them both. "I mean, get real."

Georgia's attention was caught by her roommate waving her over. "Yeah, you're probably right." At last the dark-haired girl grinned. "Angela's infecting me with her over-active imagination." Heading to her friends, she called over her shoulder. "I'll catch up with you later."

Filling their trays with sandwiches and yogurt, Liz wormed her way through the busy room and found some spaces at the end of the long central tables. She'd hoped to sit somewhere quieter, maybe by the windows, but they were too late for that. It was going to take some time to get used to being with this amount of lively strangers, and her throat felt tight with self-consciousness as she bit into her sub.

They'd only been sitting a few moments when two broadly built, handsome, confident boys stopped at their table. Liz felt the food go dry in her mouth and forced herself to swallow. Angela looked up and grinned.

"Hey, Will, Dennis. How's it going?"

"You know, classes. Boring." Liz didn't know if it was Will or Dennis speaking, but she did wonder how these two football meatheads knew Angela.

"Have you tried, you know, the meditation?" The taller blond one spoke, without even looking in Liz's direction. She obviously wasn't cool enough.

"No, not yet. I was going to do it last night, but I was too tired. What about you?"

"Nah. We're going to do it Thursday after football practice. It might help us with the game on Saturday if we can get that relaxed. Dennis is going to ask some of the other guys if they want to come along on Sunday. Sandra's going to talk to the cheerleaders too." He paused. "Dr. Kenyon's so cool, isn't he? Someone said he used to play college football. Could have been a pro if he'd wanted to."

Liz looked up from her sandwich to look at the three students. What was it with Kenyon that had this effect on them?

"That girl you hang with—Georgia? We saw her this morning. She says she's doing the meditation every day. And that other girl, the one with the . . ." He paused, and Angela laughed.

"The huge rack?" she asked.

"Yeah, that's her."

Angela looked at Liz. "You've probably seen her. She's taking history too."

Liz shrugged, wishing Angela had just left her out of the conversation. She glanced away and then smiled. Steve was weaving his way toward them. Her heart thudded slightly. Thank the Lord. Someone she could talk too. She slid over in her seat a little, giving him room on the end of the bench.

"Anyway, see you Sunday." The two men smiled at Angela and nodded at Liz and Steve before regaining their cool and sauntering away.

Steve raised an eyebrow. "Admirers? They don't look like your type." He grinned. "Not mean and moody enough."

"Well, maybe you don't know my type, Mr. Wharton."

"I do," Liz said. "Dr. Kenyon."

Pulling a piece of lettuce from her sandwich, Angela chucked it at Liz. "Enough already. Actually, they were from the paranormal society." She looked at Steve. "You should come. It's great—it really is. Really interesting."

"Thanks, but no thanks. I've got work Sundays anyway. Someone's got to keep those Hannaford shelves stacked!"

"Suit yourselves. You don't know what you're missing."

Steve looked over at Liz and winked. Her heart and stomach flipped, meeting somewhere in her middle. Great. Just great.

By the time Liz had served three of four coffees, a cappuccino and a toasted sandwich, she'd got the hang of working at Mabel's. It wasn't particularly difficult once she'd figured out the milk frother, and there weren't a huge amount of tables to serve. Smoothing her apron down over her black pants, she smiled at a little old lady, who smiled back. Liz decided it was all about friendly service here, and most people just wanted to feel relaxed and at home while they chatted over cake or simply read a paper.

Behind her Mabel wiped down the already spotless counter, so Liz busied herself with polishing the cutlery. She had a feeling that Mabel had given her the job because she liked her and she could, rather than because she needed the help. It made Liz like her all the more. Her mom would be glad that she'd met someone like Mabel. Maybe she'd call home later to talk to them. Hopefully they'd relaxed a little. The short call she'd made on her first night in Tower Hill had been horribly strained. Still, they'd get used to it. They didn't have a lot of choice.

Two middle-aged women who'd been sharing a plate of sandwiches got to their feet and, still chatting, gathered up their shopping bags to leave. Mabel waved at them and smiled.

"Bye, now, Ettie. Don't forget your leaflet." She nodded toward a bright piece of paper still on the table.

"Oh, yes." The other woman picked up the small sheet and put it in her purse before once again gathering together her belongings. "I suppose I may well come along on Sunday. Been a while since I've been to church."

"Maybe you should bring young Sam along too. I've

seen some of the boys he's been going around with lately. They'll be leading him into trouble before long."

Liz watched the two women. Mabel had a way about the manner in which she said things; you just didn't take offense. The other woman, Ettie, nodded a little. "You may be right, Mabel. But what can you do? At sixteen they think they're more men than children. And our Linda just won't be told how to bring him up." She reached the door and smiled. "I'll see what I can do. I'm not sure church is going to help him, but I'll see if I can bring him along."

Liz waited until the two women had left, and then cleared their table, loading the dishes into the washer before joining Mabel behind the counter.

"What was that leaflet you gave her?"

Mabel pointed at a small pile of colored paper on the counter. "I put one or two on every table. Father O'Brien asked me to, and I was more than happy to help."

Liz picked one up. It was a miniature version of the poster that hung outside St. Joseph's but at the bottom it had times for the services that would be running every week.

"The father's forming a town church council," Mabel continued. "He wants James and me to sit on it as leading members of the community." Her face was flushed with pride. Liz looked at her and then back down at the flyer.

"I didn't think you were all that religious. Are you sure you want to be getting this involved in the church?"

Mabel rested against the counter and folded her arms across her large chest. "You know, it's a funny thing, but I wasn't, not at all. But ever since we went to the service on Sunday I've felt differently. James too." She paused. "Maybe I've had an epiphany or something." She peered out the window. "I'm definitely drawn to the church. I can't stop thinking about it." A buzzer sounded quietly from the back and she smiled. "That'll be the next batch of muffins ready. I'm sure there's enough in there for us to try one each, don't you think?"

The air smelled hot and sweet as she pulled open the oven door. "I'm going to the midweek evening service tomorrow. Are you going to come along?"

Liz felt her heart sink a little. She knew she was being selfish, but she didn't want Mabel to find religion. She'd loved that Mabel was so warm and giving without it. There was an earthy freedom at the core of the older woman. Religion would change that. Liz had seen it happen.

"No, I've got a paper to work on."

"Already? You've only been there a couple of days."

"I know, but I don't want to get behind now. If I do, then I'll never catch up."

Resting the tray on the side to cool, Mabel smiled. "You're a good girl, Liz. But you'd better come along on Sunday." She winked. "I'll be disappointed if you don't!"

Liz tried to smile back and hoped her own disappointment didn't show.

"Hey there, ladies." A man called to them from the counter. "That smell has dragged me right across the road."

The two women turned. It was Father O'Brien. Liz felt her heart thump a little, and she wasn't sure if it was guilt from her thoughts that was causing it. Mabel was gushing breathlessly at him as she hurried through to the counter. "Oh, that'll be my fresh muffins, Father. You should try one. Can I get you a coffee?"

"You certainly can." He smiled at Mabel as she scurried around after him, and then looked up and winked at Liz. Liz smiled uncertainly but stayed in the kitchen.

CHAPTER SIXTEEN

The housekeeper, Mrs. Argyle, who came in to do a little light cleaning for a couple of hours three times a week, had left for the day. When she'd been dusting and tidying she'd brought a cup of coffee to Father O'Brien as he worked quietly on his sermon, the large Bible open. She'd smiled and told him not to work too hard. Father O'Brien had smiled back serenely and continued taking his notes.

Two hours later he'd taken her advice. The Bible was firmly shut. Jack leaned against the desk and Gray sat on the leather chair, one leg casually tossed over the other, swallowing the last of a muffin and reaching for a second.

"Shit, these are good."

Jack held out the plate to him. "The fat woman across the road makes them. She sent me away with half a dozen earlier. Think I could have taken twenty and she would have loved it all the more." He didn't have a muffin himself. They were too sweet for him. "She's on my newly formed church council. Taken to it like a duck to water." He paused. "Or maybe more like a whale to water."

"She probably dreams about you spreading those huge fat-ass thighs and going down head first." Gray laughed.

"I'm a priest, Gray. I'm unattainable. That's my attraction."
He smiled, but his eyes narrowed slightly watching Gray
rip into the huge muffin.

"So, what did you do?"

"How do you mean?"

"I know you, Gray. Remember? You only ever eat like
that when you're . . ." he searched for the right word. There
wasn't one. "Exhausted."

Gray shrugged. "You got me, bro." Sighing happily, he
swallowed some more muffin. "But it was out of town. I was
careful." He smiled—all natural ease and charm. "That
chick went into the ocean in so many pieces that there's no
way anyone will be putting her back together again. She
was a hooker. No one will notice."

"Fair enough." Jack opened the box on his desk and
pulled out the fresh apple. He bit into it. Taste exploded in
his mouth.

"You sure you should eat that?"

"It's what the paper in the box told me to do." Jack said.
"There's been one in there every day. And it's got to be better for me than that kind of crap."

Gray snorted, his mouth full of raspberry muffin, while
Jack chewed thoughtfully. He looked down at his hands,
feeling every nerve working at the tips of his fingers. "I'm
changing though. I can feel it. I can feel every part of myself in a way I never have before." He looked up. "And this
is only the beginning."

"Now we just need to find the other boxes so I can have
a piece of the action." Gray looked at the plate of muffins,
but didn't take a third.

Jack stood up. "I've got the second, buddy. Why do you
think I got you over here?"

"No shit." Gray sat upright, his eyes alive. "How the hell
did you find it? I checked over the coordinates and looked
out on the headland but there was nothing there. I couldn't
find any kind of pattern."

"I'm not sure there is a pattern. You know the parchment from the first box? The writing changes on it. When I opened it last night all it said was 'the graveyard.' I went out and had a hunt around and found a gravestone. It had no birth or death dates on it, but the name was A. Stone. And then it said 'Rest Peacefully.' The carvings on the headstone were the symbols. I can't believe it sat there untouched for all these centuries."

Gray burst out laughing. "Holy fuck. Who said those old monks didn't have a sense of humor?"

"Yeah, well, I only had to dig around for a couple of minutes and it almost slid into my hands from the earth, like it was waiting for me to pick it up. I was itching like crazy until I got it back here."

"Maybe it *was* waiting for you to find it. Fucking destiny at work here, bro, and you know it. So, where is it?"

Jack crouched and reached inside his cassock for the heavy key.

"What about the third box?" Gray asked. "Do you think there actually is a third box? I mean, there's only two of us. And the old man wasn't making any sense by then."

Jack lifted the lid carefully. "Well, the third box is the joker in the pack. It either exists or it doesn't. It's either meant for us or it isn't. We'll find out soon enough, I'm sure. And I think a couple more weeks and nothing will be able to stop us."

"I just wish all the shit had been clearer to follow. Why can't people just write things down plainly?"

Jack stood up. "Because then just about anyone could do this." He held a long, smooth red stone. "And we're doing pretty okay so far, wouldn't you say, metaphor and confusion included?"

Gray stared and scratched at his chest. "Is that it? It doesn't look like much?"

"Neither did the first one until it changed. Here, you take it."

Gray wrapped his hands over the smooth surface. "Shit, it's hot."

Jack's brow furrowed. "No, it's not. It wasn't a second ago."

"Well, it is now." Gray laughed.

Eyes wide, Jack watched as the stone changed, wriggling and hissing in Gray's hands. "Don't let go of it."

"I'm not planning too, but it's slippery, the little asshole." Gray's strong arms fought to control the changing rock. "And my pendant is burning me." Keeping one hand around the rock, which was forming scales and a bulbous, malformed head, he ripped open the top buttons of his shirt. The coiled gold serpent resting against his chest blazed red. "Holy fuck, that hurts." He looked up at Jack and laughed.

Jack stared at what had been a smooth rock when he'd taken it out of the trunk just a few seconds before. There was now no doubt in his mind what it was turning into. The lumpy head pushed out glowing eyes and broke its mouth open in a hiss of fangs. Its scales shone in a myriad of colors.

For a long second it stopped its movement and stared at Gray, before lashing out with its tail, wriggling powerfully out of his hands and leaping at the glowing pendant. Jack knew his own shocked mouth hung open with fear, but Gray just watched, fascinated, as the snake from his hands and the snake around his neck became one fluid living creature twisting angrily against the leather thong that held it.

"Holy shit," he said again, as the snake pulled back and then, with a final snarl from its forked tongue, dived into Gray's chest, disappearing into his skin. Grey fell back in the chair, convulsing slightly, his breath sucked away from him. His eyes rolled in his head. An unpleasant gargling sound filled the room.

Jack sat back against the desk and waited for it to stop. He didn't look at Gray, but concentrated instead on the leather strap that had fallen to the floor, the pendant gone. After five long minutes, Gray's breathing slipped back to somewhere near normal and the chair stopped rattling. Jack looked at his friend.

Gray grinned. "Did that fucking thing just go inside me?"

Jack nodded. "You okay?"

Gray stood and flexed his fingers. "I think I'm better than okay." He took another muffin and bit into it. "No going back now, is there?" His eyes met Jack's, triumphant. "I can feel what you mean when you said that shit about changing. I can really feel it now."

Jack smiled. "Yes, but still, go easy on the muffins. No point being a God if you're going to be a fat one."

He watched as Gray ate. He wondered what Gray would say when he looked in a mirror and saw that his eyes had changed. He'd probably just laugh. That was Gray. Not that they'd changed too much. Not so that anyone else would notice, but Jack did. Gray's pupils had become more oval than round, their rims edged with white. And where they had always been a clear cornflower blue, definite flecks of green and yellow had appeared. Almost snakelike, he decided.

No. There was no going back now.

CHAPTER SEVENTEEN

The first week flew by in a mass of new names, new rooms to get lost finding, and the sheer excitement of settling into college life. Before Liz knew it, the weekend had rolled around again, but still she'd barely had time to catch her breath. Pulling the drapes open, she unlatched the window to let the room air a little.

Saturday at Mabel's had been quite busy and she'd got to meet a few of the longtime residents of the town. It seemed that most of the older people liked to drop in to the coffee shop a couple times a week to just have a chat and feel alive for a while, and it gave the place a real homely atmosphere that Liz already loved.

When Liz had been grabbing her coat to leave, Mabel had been talking to May from the bed-and-breakfast. As she'd waved her farewells they'd both asked if they'd see her at church. Biting the inside of her cheek, Liz had stuck to her guns and said no, and she'd meant it, she really had, despite their disappointed faces. And then May had surprisingly started in on her, sharply pointing out that the next time she needed the Lord to carry her through a difficult time, then she'd find herself alone and she'd be sorry. Mabel chided May for that, and that's why Liz found herself saying that of course she'd be there and that her paper could wait.

So here she was again, all dressed up for church, and all because Mabel had stuck up for her. She gave her reflection a stern glare in the mirror. The only good thing to come out of her inability to stick to her word was that when she'd spoken to her mother again the previous evening, she'd been able to answer with hand on heart that she'd been going to church regularly.

Her mother had still cried on the phone and her dad wouldn't speak, and neither of them would let her talk to Sally, but at least her answer to that question hadn't been a lie. As far as her family was concerned, she was determined to keep calm and keep trying to make them see reason. She loved them; they were good people and she knew they loved her too, but she just couldn't share their growing extremism. Someone had to be the grown-up, and it was turning out that it had to be her. They had of course begged her to come home. But as much as she may be swayed on the attending-church issue, there was nothing they could say to make her give up college. She needed to stay at Tower Hill. She could feel deep down inside her that it was important. To who she was and who she wanted to be.

Steve was in the kitchen making his lunch. It was the first time Liz had seen him in the tan uniform, and she giggled. "I can see what Angela meant. Not the most flattering look."

He waggled the butter knife at her. "Enough of that already. I have to wear it—I expect support from my roommates, and maybe even a lie or two about how good I look in it." He looked at her properly. "You, however, do look good, and I don't even have to lie about it. Where you going? Church?"

She nodded.

"You don't look happy about it."

"It's a long story." Liz sighed and watched him as he wrapped the stack of sandwiches in foil.

"Why don't you meet me during my lunch break?" He held up the packed food. "I've got enough for two. It's a nice day. We can sit out on the cliffs and you can tell me all about it." He grinned. "As long as it doesn't take more than an hour. My break's from one till two."

Liz smiled and tucked a strand of hair behind her ear. "Okay, that . . . that'll give me time to come home and change." She'd been about to say "that's a date," but stopped herself just in time. It obviously wasn't a date and she didn't want him thinking that she was thinking about it like that, even if she wasn't and it was just a turn of phrase. She could feel a blush starting in patches at her throat and was saved from it fully developing by Angela wandering in. Her eyes barely open, she shuffled past Liz to fill the kettle from the faucet. She was pale.

"You look dreadful," Liz said. And she meant it. Angela was normally a whirlwind of energy. Right now she looked like just a breath of breeze would knock her down.

Angela managed a weak smile. "Gee, thanks. I just didn't sleep very well."

"Why don't you go back to bed?" Steve said. "It's Sunday, after all."

"No, I've got the paranormal society. I can't miss that."

"What do you actually do there? You going ghost hunting?"

Angela rubbed her face and yawned, before spooning coffee into a mug. "No, nothing like that yet. We're kind of learning techniques to open our minds first. Kind of make us more receptive to things." Her eyes shone slightly. "Dr. Kenyon's just so fascinating."

Liz laughed and raised an eyebrow. "Hmmm, yes, we all know how fascinating you find Dr. Kenyon."

"You wouldn't understand," Angela snapped back. "You're too closed-minded to really get it, so you just laugh at it. And coming from Little Miss Religious, I find that quite funny."

Liz stared at her friend, feeling the flush rise up in her face, out of shock this time rather than embarrassment.

"Hey." Steve had paused in the middle of putting his jacket on. "She was only kidding." He looked Angela over. "Maybe you should go back to bed and get some sleep if you're going to be so nasty."

Angela held both hands up. "I'm sorry. I really am. I don't know why I said that. I didn't mean it. I feel awful. I just keep having these freaking dreams that I don't quite remember. It must be because everything's so new." She looked over at Liz. "I really am sorry."

Liz shrugged. "Don't worry about it. We all have our off days." She glanced down at her watch. "Anyway, I've got to go. I'll catch you later." Neither she nor Steve had mentioned that they were meeting up for lunch, and she was glad. It was a private thing between them and she didn't feel, especially after what had just been said, that she could open up in front of Angela. Not today at any rate, and not about religion.

The church was full and Liz had to squeeze herself in on the end of a pew next to two elderly strangers. She gave them a brief, embarrassed smile, which they returned before shuffling along a little to make more space. She'd thought that Mabel and the sheriff would sit with her, but although they'd met her outside, once they'd climbed the steps Mabel had told her that they had to sit in the reserved seat down by the front because they were in the council. She'd said this quite loudly and Liz wondered who she was trying to impress and how it didn't seem like Mabel to be quite so concerned with what other people thought. Maybe she'd got the older woman wrong. She hoped not. Sheriff Russell stood in the aisle herding people to the left or the right and sending those that had attended the Wednesday service to a separate section.

"What's so different about the Wednesday service?" Liz asked, and Mabel had just beamed at the sheriff.

"Don't you worry about that," she said before bustling down to her own seat.

Sitting squashed in with strangers, Liz figured she wouldn't worry about any service again, let alone the Wednesday one. She almost laughed out loud at herself for coming, especially now that she was sitting here alone. What a joke. Glancing around, she was just wondering if she had time to sneak out before the service started, when the congregation hushed and the strange background music that Father O'Brien seemed to favor rose a notch or two. Her heart sunk. That was it. She was stuck here for the hour.

Sighing a little, she glanced around, surprised at how full it was. It seemed that the crowd was divided into two types: those who had come to church the previous week and those who hadn't. The former were all expectantly looking toward the rear of the church, and those who had come for the first time today were all sitting as she imagined she was—a little awkwardly and uncomfortable in their seats, wondering how on earth their aunt or uncle or friend had persuaded them to come to church.

Finally Father O'Brien appeared from the rear of the church, and Liz could swear a small buzz of excitement rippled around her. At the front she could see Mabel's face positively radiating joy as he smiled at her. She stared at him for a moment and then at the congregation. Lots of people were looking at him with that same almost fanatical glow. As if he were something special; more special than a priest. She looked at the upturned faces of the people she thought she knew, at least a little: Mabel and the sheriff and May from the bed-and-breakfast. They were totally entranced. She couldn't think of another word that fit. She looked back at the man in the cassock, who was taking his place in the pulpit and smiling down on his flock.

A messiah, she thought. *They're looking at him like he's a messiah.*

When Angela scurried into MH3, Georgia was over on the other side of the room, already seated. Her purse was on the chair beside her, and she smiled and lifted it when she saw Angela. She looked tired. Gratefully taking the saved seat, Angela figured she wasn't one to talk. From what Liz had said and the mirror had confirmed, she wasn't looking too hot herself. Still, she'd dragged her ass out of bed and had made it on time. Just.

"You okay?" she asked.

Georgia nodded. "Yeah, I just feel beat."

"Me too. Must be the first week of school catching up with us."

"Yeah," Georgia snorted. "We're not as young as we used to be."

Angela dug her in the ribs. "Oh, you're so funny." She looked around. "Hey, there's way more people here this week."

"Yep. Dennis and Will and their Barbie girls have been on a recruiting drive. I asked a couple of people but they said no." She shrugged. "Guess we're not popular enough to pull in a flock."

"No, I guess not." Looking around, Angela gave a nod to the boys and the girl from Liz's history class. She was wearing a much tighter top this week and was sticking that chest right out, and Angela knew why. Not that she thought Dr. Kenyon would go for it. She hoped not. If she wasn't screwing him, there was no way she wanted any of the others to. Smiling a little at her own thoughts, Angela looked back at Dennis and Will. They looked tired too. The football crowd must have had a late Saturday night after the game.

Wriggling out of her jacket, she leaned forward to put it under her chair. Her eyes rested on Georgia's nervous fingers.

"Hey, what happened to your hands?"

Georgia tried to tuck them away inside the sleeves of her shirt, but Angela stopped her, carefully turning the other girl's hands over in her own. Each palm had about four large bandages stretched across them. One had gone pink where blood had oozed out from the cut underneath. Angela stared. Whatever she'd done, those had to hurt.

Georgia pulled her hands free. The nails were bitten down to the quick. Her eyes darted over Angela's as if she couldn't look her in the eye. "I don't really know," she whispered. "And that's the truth. I'm not self-harming, if that's what you think."

That had been exactly what Angela had been thinking, and she raised an eyebrow. She was surprised though. Georgia didn't strike her as an insecure girl. If anything she had a quiet self-confidence; the kind that appealed to Angela's own. "So, when did they turn up? You can't cut yourself and not know how. That's crazy."

"I just woke up with them. I remember dreaming that I was kind of exploding. Kind of. Something like that, anyway." She paused. "It felt like I was being pushed out of myself. I've never had a dream like that before. It was freaky. Then I woke up and I was sitting in bed and my hands were wrapped around my vanity scissors." She glanced up and Angela could see dark rings around her friend's eyes. "But they were open, and so as I squeezed them, they'd been cutting me. It was so weird. My candle was still burning. I'd been doing my meditation and I must've fallen asleep."

Angela looked at the bandaged cuts. "Maybe you should talk to Dr. Kenyon about it after. Maybe it's a side effect of the meditation or something." Hearing the words, Angela didn't know why she'd said them. It was obvious that Georgia needed to see a proper doctor to at least check that there was no infection, but somehow those weren't the words that came out.

"Yeah, maybe." Georgia looked up and smiled. Following her eyes, Angela found herself smiling too. A big, fat fuck-me grin. Dr. Kenyon had come out of his office. Over his jeans he wore a black T-shirt. Not too tight, like the

football squad did, but just a little loose, showing his definition underneath, but without looking attention-seeking.
His bare arms were strong and tanned. Angela felt her concern for Georgia melting along with the pit of her stomach.
Her lower belly felt on fire with nerves.

"Great to see so many new faces here! Well done, those
of you that dragged your friends along." He grinned at
Dennis, Will and the girls, and their faces almost burst with
pride.

"How many of you have been practicing your meditation?" Georgia and a few others shot their hands up. No
one was looking so tired anymore. Angela didn't even feel
so tired anymore.

"Okay," he continued. "Well, let's start this session by
giving it another go for twenty minutes or so, so that the
newbies are onboard before we talk about what paranormal
activities we might want to start our research with." He
placed the tall candle in the middle of the room where it had
sat the previous week and lit it. Angela became aware that at
some point the weird music had started up in the background. *What did he call it?* she thought as she shut her eyes.
"The Dance of the Serpent"? Something like that. The
strong smell of the burning candle came to her. Heart thud-
ding, she waited to feel the doctor's hot breath in her ear as
he whispered her chanting words into it. She only had to
wait a moment and he was there, and then gone.

"Ammaniparadosisparadiso." The sounds tumbled from
his mouth and then from hers, and she repeated the phrase
over and over as if it belonged to her. It was her language
now, her words. Her eyes were heavy. Behind her lids she
thought she saw a snake slithering, seeking purchase on
her slick eyeballs. She thought she saw a lot of things. And
then, as the fumes and the words and the room overtook
her, she saw nothing at all.

Lost somewhere deep inside herself, she didn't feel her

mouth open greedily for the dark liquid Dr. Kenyon dripped into it with a smile.

Before the previous week, it had been a while since Liz had been to an organized church service, but she was surprised at the way Father O'Brien chose to deliver his Mass. Perhaps if her parents had heard him spouting fire and brimstone and warning people of the perils of abandoning the Lord, of being cast out of Eden, then they may have been tempted to come back to the church for their worship instead of doing it for themselves. There was certainly nothing moderate about it, which she found at odds with his easy manner. Maybe Tower Hill was a more religious community than she'd first realized.

When it came to the delivery of the Sacrament, O'Brien didn't call for them to come to the altar.

"I know there are many of you amongst us who are old and infirm." He smiled. Liz wondered if it was supposed to be a benevolent gesture. If so, it didn't work on her. "And so I would ask you to remain seated. Members of our newly formed church council will bring the Sacrament to each and every one of you."

The gathering of smartly dressed people seated to his left rose proudly. Liz watched as they filed to the altar and took their own Sacrament before collecting either a cup or a plate of wafers. Mabel was just like the rest of them, her head held high as they walked up the aisles and positioned themselves facing the pews. The strange music echoed loudly in the silence. When they were all in place, Father O'Brien nodded, and the wafer tray was passed along the line. One space behind, the cup followed. The church was filled with the sound of hushed chanting.

"May the body of Christ bring me to everlasting life."

"May the blood of Christ bring me to everlasting life."

As the silver reached her, Liz did as she had the previous week, she lifted the cup without drinking and slipped the wafer through her fingers, letting it drop to the ground. It was difficult to do under what seemed like the stern glare of the middle-aged man standing above her. She wished she wasn't sat at the end. Passing the cup, she kept her head down.

Father O'Brien came down from the pulpit and wandered up and down the aisle, watching and smiling. Staring at her knees and wondering why she felt so awkward, Liz could hear audible sighs around her as people swallowed the wine. The old woman beside her gasped, and glancing over Liz was sure she took a big gulp of the liquid rather than the required sip. The woman handed her back the cup, her eyes shut and mouth still muttering the words. Confused, Liz gave the cup back to the councilman, who strode back up the altar. She was sure he was whispering the prayer too. As the others joined him, their job done, they retook their seats and immediately shut their eyes.

Father O'Brien stood silently at the front, surveying the congregation. From her point at the back, Liz did the same, her heart pounding with uncertainty. The music blended with the constant repetition of the words and she wondered if maybe she'd drifted into her own world at some point, because she couldn't remember any instruction given to either shut their eyes or continue the prayer once they'd taken their communion. She let her hand brush the old woman's skirt, as if it were accidental. The woman didn't hesitate with her words, nor did she flinch or open her eyes. It seemed that everyone in the church was in the same state. This was freaky. It felt more like a cult than a church, and she was in a good position to judge, given her ever-stranger religious upbringing.

Her head still slightly bowed, her eyes scanned the room. Her breath caught when she saw a man looking back. He was seated two rows ahead of her in the opposite bank of pews, and he was twisted around slightly in his seat. He was thin and his suit hung untidily from his shoulders.

Above the pale face, his brown hair was halfway to gray. All in all, he didn't look healthy. More than that, he looked almost afraid. Their eyes met for a second and then Father O'Brien glanced his way and his eyes shut, mouth moving with whispered words. Liz stared for a moment. He was pretending. Just like her.

"And on Thursday we'll be having our first coffee morning." Father O'Brien's words came out of nowhere, and Liz jumped. Eyes flicked open around her and listened as if he hadn't really broken into their prayer, starting midsentence.

"Over at the town council hall. The mayor has kindly given us some space there. Please bring along some cookies or cakes to share, and we look forward to seeing you there. I may even have a go at baking some myself, although I may need the good Lord's intervention to get that right." A smattering of good-humored laughter broke out. Everything was back to normal. Liz wondered if they even knew that they'd sat and chanted for the best part of five full minutes. What on earth was going on? The church felt cold and hollow and she itched to get into the sunshine.

Rising to file out, she joined the hubbub of people. Bits of conversation attacked her: "Oh, what a beautiful retelling of the Sermon on the Mount. Lovely story." "Yes, he's just what this town needs. A real community man." "A liberal. Room for everyone here, isn't there?"

Liz's ears throbbed and the world felt unsteady beneath her feet. What on earth were they talking about? The sermon she'd heard had been totally different. All hell and damnation, not turning the other cheek. Her stomach contracted slightly. Maybe it was her, not them. Maybe Daddy had been right about the wicked ways of college and someone somewhere had put drugs in her drink or food. Maybe that's what this was. All in her head. Her face burned. She had to get out. She had to get out now.

Escaping into the fresh air, she fully intended to bypass the priest, but his hand reached out from nowhere, touching her on the shoulder. Stepping away from the crowd of well-wishers who surrounded him, he shook her hand and held it. His grip was firm and cold. Liz wished he'd let go. He stared into her eyes and in that moment there was just her and him; the exiting congregation merely shadows.

"Hello there, Miss Clapton. And how are you?"

She stepped back slightly, but he still kept hold of her hand. "I'm fine. I'm just in a bit of a hurry. . . ." She wondered if that sounded rude, and found that she didn't much care.

Father O'Brien smiled and pulled her in closer. She felt the tug and gasped. She wondered if anyone else had noticed. Probably not. And she didn't dare look around. She had a terrible, irrational fear that he might bite her face if she looked away.

"If you're not going to take my Communion, then you may as well not come to church at all." His words were melodic but there was steel underneath. "There's no room for nonbelievers in the house of the Lord. Not while I'm in charge." He paused. "I think maybe it's time you were cast out."

Liz stared, her mouth dry, and suddenly her hand was free. Unable to move, she watched for a moment as a gaggle of old women flocked to him. Everything normal. Her heart thumping, she finally found herself turning away and striding on shaky legs toward the college. She wasn't waiting around to say good-bye to Mabel and hear her gush on about the priest. This was worse than at home. At home the person delivering the sermon may be slightly crazy, but he was her father and she knew he loved her. Even with leaving home, leaving them, she knew that he'd never abandon her. If she needed him, he'd come. This man, this Father O'Brien, was different and she didn't like him one bit. Whatever his beliefs were, she didn't want any part of them.

"How cool is it going to be researching reincarnation?" Angela was buzzing as the noisy group emerged from MH3. They hadn't spoken to Dr. Kenyon about Georgia's cuts. Somehow by the time the session was finished, it didn't seem important anymore. So she'd cut herself by accident. Big deal. Cuts heal themselves. Energy tingled through Angela's limbs. Any tiredness she'd had that morning had completely disappeared. "Do you think we'll do regression?" She laughed, and followed Georgia down the stairs. "I'd love that. Maybe I was Cleopatra or something in a past life."

"Yeah, right. Or maybe I was Cleopatra and you were just my slave." Georgia sighed. "God, I feel great. That meditation must really relax me."

"Me too. I feel fantastic. Like I could run for miles or something."

"Yeah, maybe I'll go for a swim later. I used to swim every other day at home. Probably about time I started here, before my butt gets too fat to float."

Looking down at her friend's slim frame, Angela raised an eyebrow. Like her, Georgia had a naturally athletic build, all long toned limbs and easy strength. It would take more than a couple of weeks of no exercise to change that.

"I just wish the meetings lasted longer. They always go so fast, don't they?" Georgia hit the bottom step and headed toward the cafeteria. "I guess that's the weird part about the meditation. It never feels like it's lasted long at all, but it must do."

"We must just be naturally receptive. The doc almost said as much. I think we're his favorites, or at least in his top ten. Are you going to get a coffee?"

"Yeah, I've got a really funny taste in my mouth. Maybe it's the candle smoke." Angela licked her lips and frowned a little. She knew what Georgia meant. Her mouth tasted like shit too.

Stepping out of the store, Steve was surprised to see that Liz had brought the car. It wasn't as if it were a long walk from the college to the store, and it hadn't seemed to bother her before. She beeped and he waved, trotting over to climb in. He held up a bag. "I got us a couple of Cokes too. And some doughnuts, just in case my sandwiches aren't enough to keep us going. How come you brought the car?"

"I thought it would be nice to go a bit farther along the coast to eat, and as you only get an hour for lunch, driving's probably the best bet." She smiled. "I just feel like getting out of this town, if only for an hour."

Steve watched her as she pulled away. "Are you getting claustrophobic here? No offense, but I'd have thought that coming from the islands you'd be more likely to suffer from the opposite."

"I guess it's not the town. The town is beautiful. I just shouldn't have gone to church today. It was a bit freaky. I'm shaking it off now, but it was weird." She followed the road until the ocean was glistening alongside them. "Or maybe it's just me. I promised myself that I was going to take some time out from religion while I was at Tower Hill, and so far I haven't managed it." She glanced toward Steve, and blushed slightly. He liked it. There was something really cute about her self-consciousness. Maybe it was just that it was so different from the girls back home. Seemed that all the girls in Detroit were very self-aware by the time they were fifteen or sixteen.

"I don't know why I'm telling you this. It's probably boring and not really your problem." She tucked a loose strand of blond hair behind her ear to stop the breeze blowing in her face. He liked the way she did that too.

"Hey, I'm interested. Sounds like there's a story there."

"Okay, well, you asked for it! But it stays between you and me, okay?"

"Sure. I'm the king of keeping my life private."

They didn't go far out of town, picking the first headland rest stop to pull into, and within ten minutes they were sat on the grass, munching sandwiches. With her free hand, Liz tugged at daisies as she spoke.

"My folks were always religious. I mean, that's how they met, I think. At a church dance. My grandmother used to take my mom to Sunday school when she was a kid and I think it grew in her from there. I don't think my grandparents were particular churchgoers, but my mom sure grew into one." She paused. "Not that that's a bad thing. I mean, I believe in God. Well, I'm pretty sure I do. I just need to get a perspective on religion, you know?"

Steve nodded, but he wasn't sure he did know. He thought of his own mother, fat and stinking and unhappy, and of the way she'd cried and cursed when he'd left. He might not get exactly what Liz meant, but he did know how well your parents could screw you over if you let them. "So, what went wrong from them meeting at the church dance to now?" he said. "I mean, I take it something did go wrong?"

"Well, they got married and bought a house on the mainland. I don't even know the town's name. They've never told me. They don't like to talk about the past." She giggled slightly, but Steve didn't hear any humor in it, only sadness. "They call it their sinful past—you know, TVs, cars, modern appliances, the outside world.

"Anyway, things were, I think, going well for them. My dad worked in finance and made big money for a young man, and my mom finished training as a legal secretary. It's weird to even think about them like that. Those people sound like strangers and I probably wouldn't even know anything about that life if my grandmother hadn't told me. Back before they banished her from our lives." She shook her head slightly. "I just can't see my mom and dad being normal. I especially can't see my mom being a paralegal or whatever. Seems to me she's spent my whole life, at least, baking bread and praying." Pausing, she took a bite of her sandwich, chewing slowly.

"She got pregnant about two years after they were married—that's what my grandmother told me. She carried on with her job, and one evening after she'd been working late, she was walking to her car and got mugged. They almost killed her. She was beaten up real bad. She still has small scars on her face, although we don't talk about them. Anyway, by the time she was found and taken to the hospital, she was losing the baby. My dad had sealed a good deal at work and had gone for a beer with some guys and no one could find him. He didn't get to the hospital until much later. The baby was gone by then."

Steve nodded. He didn't say anything. Sometimes there was nothing you could say. Liz looked up.

"They never caught the men that did it. They only got away with her purse and there wasn't much in that. Maybe they were high or something. I guess no one's ever going to find out. I don't know if it would have even made any difference if they had been arrested. Somewhere in their grief my parents started to blame themselves for what happened. They decided it was because they'd been distracted from the Lord and become obsessed with material wealth instead of spiritual wealth. From what my grandmother told me, my mom wouldn't even leave the house when she came home from the hospital. I guess she had post-traumatic stress, and I can't blame her. But they came up with the plan to sell up and move to the islands. And so that's what they did. They moved to North Haven.

"And it worked, you know? They had plenty of money and even though he didn't need to, my dad got a part-time job at the bank and they settled into island life. They joined the church and became part of the community. And then my mom got pregnant with me and somehow that triggered them to become more and more involved with their religion, as if they were worried that something would happen to take another baby from them."

Reaching into the bag, she took a doughnut and broke it in two, handing Steve one half. "It's been a gradual decline since then. My little sister came along five years after me, so things are worse for her. I mean, I was allowed high school and can remember when they had friends and a social life. For her, it's all homeschooling, chores and a lot of praying. The TV only goes on for the news and some religious shows." She blushed again, as if embarrassed by her life. Steve thought once again about his own mother. He understood that shame that you could do nothing about but you still carried with you.

"If it wasn't for my grandmother leaving me a college fund, I doubt I'd be off the island now. But she did, and we went through all the arguments but I still broke free and came here, which was a huge deal for me. I'm not wild and free like Angela. It was hard for me, hurting them like that. But I did it, only to find that the church here is equally weird. That Father O'Brien totally freaks me out."

A cloud passed over her face. "Maybe it's me, but I can't help feeling that something is wrong there."

"Hey," Steve said, "I tell you what. I'll make it my personal business to make sure you don't go to the church next Sunday, okay? It's not good for you right now. That much is obvious from what you just said. And if anyone tries to bully you into going, I'll sort them out Detroit-style." He grinned.

Liz smiled back.

"I don't think you need to beat Mabel up—she's actually quite sweet, and more important, she's my boss. But thanks for the offer."

"Okay, but remember it's there if you need it!" He bit into his doughnut and grinned. "These are good."

"Not as good as the muffins we sell!" She raised an eyebrow.

"Okay, well you're bringing those next time."

They didn't speak much for the rest of his lunch hour, instead just looking out over the water. Steve figured that was okay. Sometimes it was nice just to sit quietly with someone and feel comfortable, and after everything Liz had just said, small talk wasn't necessary. It would have felt wrong. He wondered what she'd make of his own story if he ever decided to share it. The sun was warm on his face, and glancing at his watch he saw they had at least ten minutes before they had to leave. Shutting his eyes and feeling content, he lay back on the grass. Tower Hill was going to be good for him. He could feel it.

CHAPTER EIGHTEEN

Eventually, night fell.

CHAPTER NINETEEN

And the town dreamed.

Small lights rippled across the surfaces of the hidden shapes of the buildings, glowing in the darkness through closed drapes—tiny dull fireflies in the night, hinting at conscious life within.

Angela sat cross-legged on a small zebra-striped faux fur rug on the floor beside her bed. She'd rested her hands, thumb and forefinger together, on her knees as she imagined a Yogi would do. They still rested there forty-five minutes later.

The flickering candle dripped muddy blue and red onto the plate that held it, a foot or two in front of her. Angela's mouth moved but only the echo of a whisper carried the words she chanted. Her mouth was too dry and cramps were edging into her feet, but she didn't feel either. Slowly her shoulders slumped forward as if she were asleep. Her head lolled down heavily. Briefly the candlelight flared a little stronger and the thick smoke escaping from its tip curled and twisted itself into a ghostly black rope. Constantly turning to hold its shape, it reached out toward her, oozing its way into her nostrils, finding its way to her lungs and organs.

Angela let out a long sigh. The dark smoke stayed inside, her exhaled breath clean and invisible. As if she were a puppet that's strings had been pulled hard, her body yanked upright again, her slack spine and neck suddenly stiff and straight. Her eyes remained closed though, and although the ocean air sent a warning blast through her open window, she didn't shiver. She didn't feel it. She was lost. She was there and not there.

If, in his room across campus, Dennis had been able to open his own eyes, he'd have seen Angela standing in his room. He'd have heard her calling his name when she realized where she was. He'd have heard the confusion and fear in her voice and he would have got up and helped her because that's what big, strong guys like him did when girls were in trouble. And, although he'd never tell the guys on the team or let Alicia see, there was something he found particularly hot about Angela Wright and her dark hair and wild, exciting ways. If he'd been able to open his eyes, then Dennis would have been pretty made up to find Angela in his room. But his eyes stayed shut even though his mouth moved with the murmur of words. The smoke was thick and strong, and Dennis was lost. He was there but not there.

A couple hundred yards away in the sophomore dorms, Kate Jensen, an English student, stepped into the shower block just moments before Dennis James appeared from nowhere into her empty hallway. If she'd waited till the end of the late-night rerun of *Newlyweds: Nick and Jessica*, she would have been able to watch his ghostly shape tugging at door handles and whispering, his voice dead and empty, "Let me back in. Let me back in. What am I doing here?"

But as it was, she'd seen the show the first time around and knew that it would end with Jessica and Nick arguing in a hardware store, and it wasn't the best in the series anyway.

The caretaker, Abel Roseman, did, however, see Dennis's girlfriend, Alicia Crossway, moments after she appeared in the quad in her thin T-shirt and pajama shorts. It was hard to miss her, standing on the grass on her own, her pale skin glowing in the dark. Far too much pale skin as far as Abel could tell, and he was glad he wasn't a younger man and that it was dark, because there was no way she was wearing a bra under that top and that kind of distraction a man could do without. Not that he had ever played away or ever wanted too, but a half-naked girl with a malicious mind could get a man in trouble easily enough.

Abandoning the trash can he had been emptying, he strolled across the grass toward her, stopping a few feet away, careful to leave a big enough gap between them. Her eyes met his, and they were wide and shaky. "Where am I?" she asked him, her hands tugging a little at her long blond hair. "Where am I?"

There was something about her voice that didn't seem right, as if it wasn't quite there, but Abel supposed maybe her words were just getting dragged away by the ocean breeze. "You're in the quad. You'd better get back to your dorm."

She stared at him. "Where am I? Where am I?" The question tumbled out of her like a stuck record, over and over in the same monotone.

Abel sighed. He'd been a caretaker at Tower Hill for a lot of years and he never thought he'd see the day kids started walking around the campus in their underwear. Tower Hill just wasn't like that. It never had been and he hoped it never would be. Turning, leaving her to answer her own damned question, he hawked some dark tobacco-stained phlegm into the grass with disgust.

It must be drugs, he figured. Why couldn't the kids today just stick to reefers like they did back in the sixties and seventies? Why couldn't they just have a halfway high, a mellow buzz? Why did they have to fry their brains in the name of fun? Shaking his head, he strolled back toward his abandoned trash bin and the can he'd been in the middle of emptying. It was a shame. A pretty girl like that could get herself in trouble being wasted and out here in the middle of the night. She could walk into town or maybe out over the cliffs. Anything could happen to her. He reached for the trash bag. And what if it did? How would he feel if something did happen to her? He thought of his own daughter and his fast-growing-up granddaughter and sighed. Turning around, he started to walk across the quad. He'd take her back to her hall, he decided, and then say no more of it. But when he looked up, she'd gone. Vanished like she'd never been there.

A thin man with prematurely gray hair wasn't sure if he was dreaming or not. Either he was asleep or he was having a severe case of the DTs. A genie had slipped out of the whiskey bottle and sat on the rim. The man thought it looked a little like Tinkerbell. She was pretty with bright eyes and dark hair curled up on top of her head like Brigitte Bardot. The toes of her gold shoes curled. She looked like she was built for play, but her face was solemn.

"People are going to die, you know, Al." She swung her legs. "You have to warn them. They might not listen." Leaning forward, she cupped her mouth to whisper. "Bad things are happening in the house of the Lord. You know it. *She* knows it." She nods. "She's important."

He couldn't think of anything to say to that. He wasn't even sure what the genie was talking about. He watched as she wriggled back into the neck of the Jim Beam bottle. "Oh, and one other thing," she said before disappearing into the glass. "Clean up."

Mabel dreamed she was baking. The kitchen was hot and flour itched under her nose but she smiled as she cracked eggs and beat sugar and butter in the sunlight that watched from the window. She was baking for the Good Lord and all was well. Leaning against the fridge, arms folded across his chest, he smiled at her as she worked. The Lord sometimes looked like the caricature of God her daddy had ripped out of a newspaper once, because it was an anti-Vietnam cartoon and that wasn't "damned patriotic," as Daddy had said, and sometimes the Lord looked like Father O'Brien. Mabel was pretty sure that in his natural state the good Lord looked like neither President Johnson nor the new priest, but she figured he could look like whomever he wanted. He was the good Lord Almighty, after all.

She was baking muffins, but as she reached past him, shooing him to mind himself in her kitchen while she cooked, and pulled out a tub of plump fresh raspberries from the refrigerator, God shook his head.

"Uh-uh. Don't need those. Make chocolate ones," He said. "Thick, rich chocolate ones."

Mabel wondered if maybe the heat was going to the Lord's head. Everyone from here to kingdom come knew her raspberry ones were to die for. Why the hell would God want chocolate ones? She figured He must have read her thoughts because the Good Lord smiled, and it was beautiful.

"It has to be chocolate to cover the taste, May Belle." He drawled out the second half of her name just like Daddy used to when she was a little girl. "To cover the taste of the special ingredient."

Mabel rested her hands on her ample hips. Well, now He was just confusing her. Maybe the heat was going to *her* head. Despite any rumors to the contrary—which she had to admit she may have fueled herself—there were no special ingredients in her muffins.

He smiled at her again and winked, nodding toward the shelves. She glanced over. There was a condiment bottle there, but not one she recognized. She picked it up.

"That's the one."

The Lord was happy and that made her happy. Mabel unscrewed the lid and sniffed the dark liquid. Her nose crinkled. "Phew. That's bitter. It doesn't smell like any kind of chocolate I know." She resealed it and put it back on the shelf.

"It will do by morning. Trust me," He said. "You keep that bottle safe and put four or five drops in every batch, you hear? You bring lots of those chocolate muffins to the church coffee morning." He was grinning now. "In fact, why don't you take some down to the kids' school and up to the college? I'm sure those teachers would love it."

Mabel nodded. Of course she would. If that was what He wanted, Him being God and all. The kitchen dissolved around her. She sighed. After that, she slept more peacefully.

Liz did not sleep peacefully. Her bedsheets had fallen to the floor, kicked off as she tossed and turned and struggled and fought. Her dream was a battleground in her bedroom.

The serpent slid toward her once again, its hissing mouth turning into Dr. Kenyon's easy grin as he shed the scales, abandoning the snakeskin and reforming as a man.

Liz's own flesh was slick with sweat under her pajamas from fighting him off. It felt like they'd been playing this game forever.

"Hey there, pretty lady."

She blew hair eyes out of her eyes as he launched himself at her, toppling them both backward onto the bed. Air punched out of her lungs as she hit the mattress with his full weight landing on her. He pinned her arms down and grinned, rising to look at her face. "Why don't you just relax? You know you'll like it."

Her legs wriggled in an attempt to knee him hard, but he'd learned his lesson during their last bout. They'd both learned a lot of lessons during the eternity of the dream. Liz had learned that this snake, this Dr. Kenyon, this whatever the hell it was, was a master of disguise, constantly changing. Sometimes it looked like Steve and its hands were soft on her and it felt so good, but then she looked in its eyes and saw it. They were snake's eyes, cold and deceptive.

Her arms hurt as she struggled, and laughing, Kenyon lowered his face and licked her face in a long, slow, wet movement. It was a mistake.

Screeching her assault, Liz twisted her head and bit down hard on Kenyon's cheek. His blood tasted bitter. Hissing and wailing, Kenyon pulled back, retreating to the floor and reforming as the snake.

Pulling herself to her feet, standing on the bed, Liz grinned over at her parents standing in the doorway. Her father held a large crucifix in front of him as if the snake were some kind of vampire.

"You keep that devil out, no matter how he comes to you. You hear, Elizabeth? You keep him out!" Her father's voice was firm but he didn't come any closer.

She nodded. "Amen to that, Daddy. Amen to that." Turning her attention back to the snake, she found that it had curled itself around Father O'Brien's feet. The priest was seated in her chair in the corner of the small bedroom. She noted with dismay that he was crumpling her dress. The one she'd worn for church that day. He smiled at her.

"You belong in the house of the Lord, Elizabeth. You know that." He held a silver goblet out to her. "Drink. Eat. It's me or the serpent. There really isn't any other choice." The serpent wrapped around his leg was growing again. Liz looked at the cup. And then she looked at Father O'Brien. She wondered if he knew his collar was black and his tongue darted out forked, just like the snake's.

"I'll pass," she said, and got ready to fight again.

Georgia went crazy somewhere between the hall and the cliff tops. Her feet ran barefoot across the tarmac and onto the grass. It was the one thing she knew, that she was running, in the cold and the anger and the dark inside her head. She could feel her feet and she held on to that. They were the only parts left of her she had any control over, but she didn't know for how long. They were pushing her out again, the voices that filled her up, that had pushed her out in her bedroom, and even though she couldn't understand their words, she could feel their frustration, their eagerness. *There just isn't enough space, there isn't enough space, not for all of them, not yet, they can't all fit in here. . . .* She screamed loudly into the darkness.

A hand that was hers and not hers held a knife, and as her body came to a panting stop on the headland, from somewhere behind her eyes she saw it rise. Her own silent scream of panic joined the multitude inside her. Coldness overwhelmed her and as they took total control, Georgia was sure that her organs exploded. With a last inhale of breath she was pushed out again. This was wrong. This was very badly wrong.

She looked down at her arms and feet. They flickered jerkily in and out of vision like a bad TV transmission. Her solid body stood three feet away carving at its face with the knife and screaming and twitching as it cut. For a moment it froze and stared at her. "*Not enough room. Not enough room. Make more space.* Sethenoshkenanmahalaleljarede-noch. One and not one."

She didn't recognize her own voice. Her vision was blurring. Her body started to crumple to its knees, knife in hand and still cutting, slicing long lines into her thin arms. She couldn't breathe anymore. Why she needed to breathe without a body, she didn't know. As the wind took her and broke her she stared at the church a few hundred feet away and hoped that there was a God and a heaven and a life after—

And then she was nothing.

CHAPTER TWENTY

At this time in the morning the watery sun had yet to warm the atmosphere and Sheriff James Russell shivered a little before sniffing loudly. The ocean air always affected his sinuses, and although his nose was running, he knew it wouldn't be enough to clear the thick pain that shot across one side of his face whenever he moved his head. Still, it couldn't be helped. He probably should have moved away years ago, but there was something about Tower Hill that was under his skin, always had been and always would be, and a little sinus pain was not too much to deal with as a payback.

He stifled a yawn. Damn, he was tired. Not that he had a reason to be; he'd slept like a baby all night. But then, what man wouldn't in Mabel's arms? He thought of her for a moment and wondered if she'd still be in their mussed-up bed. Probably not, he decided. She wasn't no lazybones, his Mabel. Her energy and enthusiasm for life was part of what he loved about her. Always had and always would.

He looked again at the scene in front of him. *This is a bad business,* he thought. *Bad indeed.* Behind him, the young deputy was finishing up taking a few notes from old John Hansen, who'd found the body. Not that he'd get much from him. There wouldn't be anything to get.

The sheriff sighed, disappointed with the corpse that had sullied the face of his town. There was no doubting where she came from, but he expected more from the students at Tower Hill. But then, he supposed, every town or college had a bad apple or two hiding in the tree. Maybe theirs had just fallen early this year.

Taking his hat off, he punched some shape back into it as Lou jogged over.

"I've told Mr. Hansen to go home. That's okay, isn't it? He doesn't have anything to do with this. He was just out walking his dog." Lou Eccles had been the deputy for nearly four years now, but despite being twenty-six and having a fine analytical mind, the thin frame of his body had yet to fill out. That hadn't stopped him getting wed to lovely Emma Brewster though. Eccles had the makings of a good policeman, and James figured in two or three years time when he retired, the town would be happy to have Louis Eccles fill his shoes. Watching the young man holding on to his hat in the wind, James was surprised he wasn't blown over entirely. He was still a thin streak of piss, just like he'd been when he was a boy.

"That's fine, Lou." Squinting in the breeze, the sheriff watched Mr. Hansen walk away, the equally life-beaten mutt walking beside him. Once again James gave himself a slap on the back for resisting the urge to ever invest in man's best friend. As well as the fact that the beasts always made you love them and then went and died on you just when you couldn't imagine them not being around, it was always people with dogs that came across the bad messes that life left behind. They sniffed them out in the early morning or late at night. Just like today. It was only seven A.M. and John Hansen's day was already ruined. Somehow James didn't think the old boy's bacon and eggs were going to taste too good when he got home, and maybe not for a few days to come.

Still, he thought, pulling a handkerchief out of his pocket

and blowing his nose for what felt like the hundredth time that morning, it wasn't as if life left a lot of its mess in Tower Hill. And he liked to keep it that way.

"What's Doc McGeechan doing examining the body?" Lou Eccles' brow furrowed. "When's the county man coming in?"

James opened his mouth to answer but paused. There was a place in his head that felt a little furry. He remembered being about to call the coroner, and then . . . not. Well, wasn't that the damndest?

"I called him." He heard himself say. "I don't think we need to bother the county coroner with this. Seems obvious to me what happened." And suddenly it did. Everything was clear again, the fog lifted. Crystal clear, in fact. This was town business. They'd do their cleaning up in-house.

"It does?" The young deputy didn't sound convinced. "Seems to me very *un*obvious what happened. I mean, Jesus." He looked back toward the body. "She's sliced to ribbons. Her face is damn near half cut off, and it looks to me like she may have been forced to do it herself." He shook his head. "And that is some serious shit, James."

The doctor finally covered her, zipping up the bag. James was glad. He'd done his time in the army, but there was never any getting used to a dead body—especially not one in that condition.

"Drugs." he said. "She's probably got a history of it. I'll call her family when we get back to the office."

"Do you know who she is?"

"No, that's your job. Get up to the college and see if they're missing a student that fits her description." He paused. "They will be."

"I'll get on it." Eccles' eyes narrowed. "Hey, what's that badge on your uniform? And I don't mean the sheriff's one."

James looked down to see what had caught the young man's eye. A small silver pin sat on the flap of his right-hand chest pocket. A tiny serpent hung from a tree in the decoration. He stared at it. When did he put that on his uniform shirt? This morning? Again, his mind felt a little furry. Maybe Mabel had done it last night, but that didn't seem likely. Last he remembered he'd put the pin at his top drawer at his own place after the meeting. He didn't even have it at Mabel's. Wasn't that just the strangest thing? He sniffed, his head clearing slightly even though his nasal passages downright refused to. How it got there didn't really much matter. It would come to him.

"It's my church council badge. I didn't even realize I was wearing it." He looked at the deputy. "You need to come to church, son. It'd be good for you."

Eccles shook his head. "I don't think Emma holds much with the church."

"Well, maybe it's time you changed her mind. How old is little Jacob now, two or three?"

"Yep, three next month. She takes him to that preschool now. He's loving it."

"Yeah, well, I think you could do worse than raise him as a churchgoer." He nodded in the direction of the blood-soaked ground. "Look at the kind of things that can happen to kids if you don't raise them right. And that's right here in Tower Hill." He smiled. "And anyway, it could be good for your career."

The sheriff felt his stomach turn a little with annoyance when he realized his deputy was only half listening. He was staring at the body and the doctor who was attending it.

"Look, boss, are you sure we shouldn't call the county on this one? Even if it is drugs, she's still going to need all the proper procedures. We could get ourselves in trouble from the family at the very least if we don't handle it by the book." He shrugged. "I mean, we don't know anything about what happened to her yet. And I respect Doc McGeechan as much as everyone else in this town but he's not a properly trained coroner."

James Russell stared at his deputy. "Lou, I've been doing this job since before you were even out of diapers, so don't you start telling me what's best now or I may have to teach you a lesson or two in respect."

For a moment Eccles said nothing, chewing on the inside of his mouth. "I'll go get up to college, then." He took a couple of steps away and then stopped. "I'll go with your call James, but I don't understand it. And I'm going to reflect that in the paperwork."

"I wouldn't have it any other way, Louis. But I'm the boss around here still, and don't forget it."

Doc McGeechan hovered a few feet away until the deputy had got the door to his car open and gotten in; then he stepped up alongside the sheriff. James thought the other man looked tired, and as if acknowledging his point, the doctor rubbed his stubble and yawned.

"I've taken some blood samples to check if there's any drugs in her system. I'll run some tests when I'm back at the lab." He met the sheriff's eyes. "It definitely looks like death by self-inflicted injury at the moment. I can't see any sign of a struggle, and her clothes seem okay." He paused, a wave of confusion passing across his face. "Is the county coroner coming? Should we really be moving her without them looking at the scene?"

James smiled. Unlike Eccles', McGeechan's concern seemed hollow. "Don't you worry about it, Doc. This is Tower Hill business. We'll take care of it."

The doctor nodded. "You're the sheriff, James. You know what's best."

Something glinted on McGeechan's jacket, and before Jame's eyes had even focused on it properly, he knew what it was. A little pin, just like his own. He wondered if John even knew it was there.

"I'll get her back to the lab. We'll have to keep her cool until the family comes to get her."

"Don't you worry about the family, Doc. I'll deal with

them." They strode back toward their cars. After a moment, Sheriff James Russell put his big arm around the doctor's slight shoulders. "You know, it would be really good if you do find some evidence of drugs in that blood you took. Really good." He watched the doctor to see that he understood, and when he nodded, the sheriff smiled. The fuzzy places in his head were getting clearer.

Things were under control. Always had been, always would be.

CHAPTER TWENTY-ONE

The college was in shock. Liz was in shock, and she'd barely known Georgia. Even so, it was hard to believe she was gone, and in such a terrible way. She'd seemed so straight-forward, so normal, whatever that was, and now all this talk of drugs and suicide. It was everywhere you went—the hushed excited anticipation of information and more shared gossip. The rumors had started flying in the morning, whispered from seat to seat in classes, a wave of short gasps of air rippling between the halls.

By lunchtime the whispers had risen to loud chatter and trays of food were left untouched. Liz couldn't eat her sand-wich above the noise and instead hunted among the crowds until she'd found Angela in a huddle with the football boys and the girl from her history classes who she now knew was called Jemima. Angela had fallen into her arms too quickly for Liz's own reserve to kick in, and she hugged the other girl tight.

After lunch all classes were canceled, and Liz gathered with Angela and the other students for the official an-nouncement that Georgia had been found dead. The dean had been somber and red-eyed. His hands had trembled. By half-past two, Angela had had enough of all the noise and excited gossip and they'd gone back to the house. Liz was glad. There was something horrible about the energy an unexpected death could create. Maybe it was natural; maybe it was just a *Thank you, Lord, for making it her and not me,* reflex, but it still left a bad taste in her mouth.

Sitting on the other side of the small kitchen table, Angela drew hard on a cigarette. "I can't believe they're saying it was drugs. Georgia just wasn't like that."

Liz watched her friend's hand shake. She was taking this hard. Steve set down three mugs of coffee. "Hey, you know what rumors are like. They start out of nothing. Don't listen to them. We don't know what happened yet. It might have just been a terrible accident, you know?"

Angela's eyes threatened to spill over again. "Her sister's a senior here this year. I wonder who had to tell her." She wiped her nose on her sleeve. "Her parents met here while they were here studying. How romantic is that?"

Liz didn't say anything. Sometimes there was nothing you could say. She thought about the poor Keenans, who were probably driving silently up the Maine coast, pale and tear-ridden and not quite believing it to be true. How terrible for them. It made her heart squeeze slightly for her own folks. She'd call them again tonight. She wouldn't tell them about Georgia; that would probably send them over the edge with worry, but she'd remember to say she loved them.

Steve stared into his coffee. "I didn't think shit like this happened in Tower Hill. How naive is that? I guess bad things happen everywhere."

Liz knew what he meant. On top of the strange church service yesterday, this had broken the magical spell the town had over her. It wasn't so picture-postcard perfect after all.

Angela lit a second cigarette from the butt of the first. "I know she wasn't like family or anything, and I know I only just met her, so it probably seems really lame that I'm so upset." She looked up at Liz. "But I really liked her. I thought we were going to be friends."

"You were friends, sweetheart. You don't have to know someone long for them to have an impact on you." Liz kept her eyes firmly forward to stop them from helplessly sliding toward Steve. There were more important things to deal with here than her stupid crush.

Angela nodded a little, and then sighed. "Tony Archer on the football team says that some of the guys were out running this morning. They saw the police cars on the headland." Getting up, she went to the window and stared out. Her voice was soft. "They say there was a huge red mess of blood on the grass."

"People say a lot of things." Steve didn't sound too convinced and Liz wasn't surprised. She'd seen one of the joggers recounting the story in the cafeteria, and he'd looked pretty shaken up. He didn't look like he was bragging; he just looked like he wanted to share something to make himself feel better.

"Yeah, but suppose it is true." Angela's cigarette dropped ash to the floor. "What could have happened to her for all that blood to be there?"

Liz didn't have an answer. She didn't want to have one. She didn't really want to think about it. She sipped her coffee and it was good to feel the burn in her throat. It reminded her she was still alive.

"I don't believe she killed herself." Angela looked out to the ocean. "I just don't."

A loud rap came from the direction of the front door and Liz almost spilled her coffee down her dress, stopping herself just before she launched the liquid at herself; instead it just slipped over the rim. That kind of burn would have been more than she needed as a life reminder, and she quickly wiped up the drips from the side of her mug.

Steve answered the door and then poked his head back into the kitchen. "It's for you, Liz." He shrugged a little. Obviously he didn't know their guests.

A little surprised—she hadn't yet made enough friends for house calls—Liz had a moment's dread that maybe her parents had somehow heard about Georgia and had come to drag her home. She hurried out into the hallway.

As it was, two serious-looking young men stood there awkwardly. It took her a minute to place them, and then her brow furrowed. They were part of the young Christian group that went to the church. She stared at them. What were they doing here? And more important, "How did you know where I live?" The question tumbled out of her.

The tallest of the two pushed his glasses a little farther up on his nose and smiled a little.

Liz didn't smile back. "What do you want?" She didn't care if she was being rude. The last thing she needed today was any involvement with St. Joseph's.

"We just wanted to let you know that a special service has been arranged at the church this evening." His voice was low and formal and, Liz decided, very, very pompous. "At eight. A meeting where we can all share our grief at this tragic loss."

Liz watched him bow his head slightly. "Did you know Georgia?"

"Not personally, sadly, but her sister and parents will both be attending, and we on the church council feel it's important to show our support." He paused. "As a united community."

Looking at his slicked-down hairstyle that was about twenty years too old for him, Liz felt mounting disgust in her stomach. Had he said he was on the church council? Why would the town have a student on the church council?

She thought of Mabel's puffed-up pride the previous day. And why was this council being seen as such an important thing anyway? She bit her lip and didn't speak for fear of what may come out.

The other young man coughed slightly. "I take it we can rely on you being there?" Liz stuck her chin out. "No, I'm afraid you can't. I'll be doing my grieving in private."

Steve had stayed in the hallway and she could see him grinning out of the corner of her eyes. The boy in front had pursed his lips.

"Well, we're sorry you feel that way. Very sorry indeed. But if you change your mind, the service starts at eight." He turned toward the door and then turned back. "The church is always there for you, Elizabeth. You know that, don't you?"

She smiled sweetly. "And that shall be a great comfort to me." Rolling her eyes, she slammed the door behind them.

"Well done, girl." Steve slapped her on the back. "You tell 'em."

Angela wandered out of the kitchen. "The paranormal society is meeting tonight as well to pay our respects. That's at eight too. Weird."

Liz looked at Steve and saw her own concern reflected in his face. "Are you sure you still want to go to that club? After what happened?"

Angela looked up, anger flaring in her eyes. "That had nothing to do with Dr. Kenyon's society. Georgia was one of us. And if we want to meet up and talk about her and how we'll miss her, then I know it'll be a damn sight more sincere than any stupid church meeting!"

For once, Liz didn't have an argument.

After they'd halfheartedly attempted to eat some sandwiches, Liz went to call her folks. She didn't have a cell phone, but at least in their divided house there was a phone shared between the two apartments and therefore never a

long wait to use it, unlike she imagined there would be in
the main halls today.

"Hello?"

The tone rang only once in her ear before it was answered, and for a moment Liz had a vision of her mother
sitting in an old rocker all day long, just watching that
phone and waiting for Liz to call and tell them it had all
been a terrible mistake. Or maybe it was more morbid than
that. Maybe they were waiting for the phone call that Georgia Keenan's mother had got. Maybe Mrs. Clapton was terrified that the world had stolen another one of her babies
away from her.

"Hey, Mom. Just calling to say hi and let you know everything's still fine."

"Are you sure? Are you sure you're okay? We pray for
you every day, honey." Her mother's voice cracked slightly.
"We pray for you to come home." She paused. "Where it's
safe."

Listening to her mother's pain, Liz sighed. She sounded
so full of fear; that was the crux of it. Had she ever realized
that her total immersion in religion was perhaps just a
translation of that fear? Probably not. For her mother to
even consider that, her father would have to provide a
voice of reason rather than encourage the obsession. In her
heart Liz hoped that their faith and her own was more true
than that, but hearing so much terror at the edge of her
mother's soft voice left her wondering.

"Oh, Mom. There's nowhere that's one hundred percent
safe. You know that. I could fall down the stairs and die just
as well at home as here. The Lord meant us to be tried,
isn't that what Daddy always says? And that means sometimes being brave and taking the unfamiliar road."

"Are you praying, honey? Are you praying every day?"

"Yes, of course I am." It was true. As she'd lain in bed
each night, she'd found herself saying silent prayers inside
her head. That might not be as vocal as her parents would

want it, but her own religion was the only one she could trust at the moment. Her mother's strain to deal with her daughter rippled silently down the line and set Liz's teeth on edge.

"Look, I can't talk for long; other people want to use the phone." She wondered if Jesus heard her little white lies and whether you were only allowed so many before they accumulated into a full-blown sin. "I just wanted to tell you that I love you all. Try not to worry too much. I'm working hard and concentrating on my studies."

The phone crackled. "I can't hear you, honey. What did you say?" Her mother sounded distant. "Your father wants to . . ."

"Elizabeth?" Having not heard her father's voice for almost two weeks, the warm twang in his accent seemed stronger. Liz's heart leaped a little.

"Daddy?" If her father was starting to speak to her again, then maybe her family was coming around to the idea of college. "Daddy, I love you and—"

"You keep that devil out no matter how he comes to you. You hear, Elizabeth? You keep him out."

Even over the hissing and breaking line the words were clear. "What did you say, Daddy?" Her mouth dried.

"I said you listen to me and you keep that devil out! You get that? You get—" The crackling won and the line went dead. Putting the receiver back in the cradle, Liz didn't move. Flashes of memory hit behind her eyes. Sweating. Fighting. Her dad there. *You keep that devil out, no matter how he comes to you.*

"You okay?"

Liz jumped and bit back a yelp. "Yeah. Yeah, at least I think so. Just having a weird moment." She smiled up at Steve coming down the last few stairs. "I seem to be having a few of those recently." She chewed her lip. "My dad just said something I thought I'd heard him say in a dream. I guess it must just be déjà vu."

"How are they? Getting used to you being here yet?"

"They're still upset. The line's bad though. I didn't get to talk to them much and then it cut out on me." She raised an eyebrow. "They'll probably think it's the devil's work." Laughing, she tried to project a mood she didn't feel. "What are you doing?"

"Angela's taking a shower and then getting ready for her meeting. I figured she could probably use some space. I thought I'd take a walk on the beach. Get some fresh air and try and shake some of today away. You in?"

"Sure, that sounds good."

Steve grinned. "Well, go and grab your jacket, then."

They took the old, mainly unused wooden cliff steps down to the beach from the far side of the college grounds, sneaker-clad feet sliding through cracks as they held on to the rotten handrails for dear life, but thankfully within minutes they were safe on the sand, slipping their shoes and socks off.

Although the sun had shone for most of the day, it hadn't held the intense heat of high summer and the damp beneath their bare soles was cold enough to make them both shiver slightly and their skin tingle. Coupled with the strong breeze coming in from the water, it wasn't long before Liz felt more refreshed than she had all day. Refreshed and glad to be alive.

The tide was on its way out, but the water still fought the drag of the moon, and they didn't have to go too far to let it run between their toes as they walked. In the distance, merely a dark speck against the yellow of the sand, a man threw a stick for his dog, who leaped and chased and ran in and out of the receding water. Other than that, as far as the eye could see, the shoreline was empty. Perhaps the news of a student's death was keeping the residents at home. Maybe they thought it was more respectful that way. Liz couldn't help but disagree. Out here, at the edge of the powerful mass of water, she couldn't think of a better place to remember someone who was lost. There was something about the vastness of the water that reminded her of the vastness of God, and she figured maybe there wasn't so much between them.

Liz and Steve didn't speak as they wandered slowly side by side along the sand below the edge of the town, just occasionally pausing to pick up seaweed or send stones skimming across the surf. At some point, without discussing it, they sat in the sand under the shadow of the church, which was high on the cliffs above them. Seagulls cawed as they chased each other around their playground in the sky. Watching them, Liz wondered how they grieved when they found one of their flock dead on the cliff tops or floating on the waves. Maybe the rest of nature was just more accepting about the inevitability of death than the human species. Her eyes still upturned, her thoughts drifting with the birds, the fingers of one hand gently began tracing circles in the sand.

"Do you think Georgia was taking drugs?"

Neither of them had spoken for a while and the bluntness of the question broke Liz's reverie.

"I wouldn't know, to be honest. My knowledge of drugs is pretty limited." She looked at Steve. "What do you think?"

He shrugged. "I didn't know her well enough to say, but Angela seems pretty sure she wasn't using, and I figure she's street smart enough to know the signs."

"I wouldn't have said she was suicidal, either," Liz added. "I mean, I only met her one time but she seemed stable to me. Although maybe I'm being naive. Who really knows what goes on in someone else's head and heart?" Her fingers moved faster in the sand, cutting circles deeper and deeper.

"Yeah, but if it wasn't drugs and it wasn't suicide, then what the hell happened to her? An accident?"

Liz watched the sunlight glint and wink off the water, calling it back from the sand in its time-old routine. It was hard to believe that where they were sitting would soon be covered with ocean water deep enough to drown them. She sighed, oblivious to the frantic movement of her own hand beside her. "Those joggers said that there was a lot of blood where she was found. What was she doing out on the cliff in the middle of the night?"

"I guess the police will be investigating," Steve said. "If they think there's anything suspicious, then I suppose we'll hear soon enough."

Liz's hand stopped suddenly with the touch of something smooth. Liz glanced down. "Hey, look at this!" She pulled the smooth white stone from the sand and stared at it. "Isn't it beautiful?" The rock was like nothing she'd ever seen in a lifetime of playing on the beaches of North Haven. Unlike the ovals of pebbles, this was almost a rectangular cube with soft curves where its edges had worn.

"Do you think it's some ancient building stone or something?" She grinned. "It looks almost as if it's made from the sand." She held it up for Steve to see. Pink flecks shone in its side, but other than that it glistened like the fine grains that surrounded them. Steve didn't seem too impressed. "I guess if you're into pebbles . . ."

Liz slapped him playfully. "This isn't a pebble." Turning it around, she studied its surfaces. "Look—it looks like there's something carved in it. I can't make out what it is though." She pointed to the strange, almost invisible curved markings on one end.

"Hmm. Looks like a fossil to me."

"You've got no imagination." She paused. "But even if it is just a fossil, then it shows that this stone has been here for maybe thousands and thousands of years." She smiled. "And now I've found it. How great is that?" She got to her feet. "And I'm going to keep it as a lucky charm."

Steve laughed. "If it makes you happy."

She looked at the stone and then at him. "Yes. Strangely enough, it does. Are you hungry?"

"What?"

"Come on. Let's find somewhere to eat. I'll pay."

"All right, then. Sold."

She slipped the stone into the pocket of her jacket, enjoying the weight and the feel of it there. Her other hand slipped into Steve's hand as if of its own accord, shocking her for a second as much as him. But after the initial flinch, neither of them let go. Liz smiled as they walked in easy silence. Maybe it would be her lucky charm, after all.

Al's hands were still trembling as they gripped tight on the painted board. Not as bad as they'd been when he'd first tumbled off the couch and dry-heaved onto the carpet sometime that morning, but shaking all the same. The streets around him were quietly abandoned, too many of the population crammed inside the thick walls of the church for whatever sermon the false prophet was delivering in the name of grief, and it felt like maybe he was the last man standing in the world, who'd somehow missed the passing apocalypse, and was now alone and confused. He trembled a little more. Maybe that was closer to the truth than he liked to think about.

For most of the day, after closing his eyes and tipping two whole bottles of liquor down the drain, Al had wondered if maybe he was just going a little DT crazy. He'd wondered it while he scrubbed and vacuumed and found himself some paint and wood in the cobwebbed garage. He'd wondered it while sitting out on the back porch, looking down at his long-overgrown yard and daubing out words on his makeshift placard. He wondered just how much the hard stuff could own your mind.

Once he'd drunk his fourth pot of coffee he wasn't sure

if the shakes were coming from the lack of spirits or the overdose of caffeine, but whether he was crazy or not, he was starting to feel a little better. Not perfect but better. Surely it was better to be a sober crazy than a drunk one . . . The cuts on his chin stung where he hadn't quite kept the razor steady but it had felt good to be fresh and clean-shaven.

He'd stopped thinking he was crazy when he'd taken his place on the steps of the church early in the afternoon, feeling a little awkward and embarrassed and wondering why he'd listened to a genie who lived in a cheap whiskey bottle. He'd stopped feeling crazy when that priest came out of the house alongside and watched him.

The concept of madness tumbled right away when the priest smiled right at him. That's when Al saw the darkness. It was in the man's face as if his features had been rubbed at with a dirty eraser. Al had looked away, his heart thumping. Until that moment he'd believed that what his mama had said was right, and that the devil lived in the bottom of a liquor bottle. But not anymore. The devil was right here in Tower Hill.

The evening sunshine doing little to warm his thin bones, he looked down at the painted letters on the board that hung around his neck. They were shaky and uneven, but clear enough. GOD'S JUDGMENT STANDS! FALSE PROPHETS WALK AMONG US! WE HAVE LOST OUR WAY! He hadn't been quite sure what he'd meant when he wrote them, but when he had, the genie who'd been sunning herself on top of the porch railings opened one lazy eye and smiled, so he guessed that they would do.

A laugh grabbed him, and turning, he saw a young couple walking hand in hand up from the beach steps. The dying sunlight framed them in halos, and for a second Al held his breath. The trembling in his hands stopped. It was the girl. It was the girl and she was glowing. Watching them cross the road to head farther into town, his legs stumbled down the stairs.

"Hey!" The two paused. He waved at them. "Hey! Guard the light." His shouting bounced from the walls of the surrounding buildings, filling the street and coming back at him, loud, harsh and unsteady. The board banged heavily against his thighs as he ran, the movement itself unfamiliar. He hadn't done much more than sit on the couch or stroll to the liquor store for the best part of three years. It was hard to get the breath to be strong and clear like he wanted.

"Be the light!"

Panting, he made it to the other side of the street. Even out of the glare of the sunlight she radiated warmth. He smiled. "It's fool's gold they're chasing. Fool's gold!" He reached forward to touch her arm but she stepped back a little, the boy with her moving between them.

"Leave us alone."

Al looked into the hard eyes. There was no glow there, but nothing rubbed out either. He tried to smile. "Keep her safe. You keep her safe." The girl tucked herself up behind the boy's shoulder.

Al wished he could tell her not to be afraid but deep down inside he thought that would be a lie and that everyone needed a little fear, everyone needed to shake a little in the presence of the Almighty, and that right now in Tower Hill maybe *a lot* of fear might not do anyone any harm, but he couldn't get the words out. He just stood there and grinned like a loon while she looked at him like he was a madman.

"Come on, Liz. Let's go." The boy took her arm and led her away. Al didn't follow, but stood in the cool shadow on the pavement. Words still spilled from his dry mouth.

"Don't let that devil in, Elizabeth! Don't let them walk among us! You keep them out, you hear?"

When she looked over her shoulder her eyes were wide with sheer terror. The couple's pace quickened. Watching them disappear around the corner, Al sighed. He guessed maybe he'd said something right. Something had hit home anyway; he'd seen that in the frozen fear in her face. Shoulders aching from carrying the board and with rope burns from running, he headed back to the bright side of the road and returned to his position in front of the church.

Back in the pale warmth of the sun, he felt empty. He didn't want to scare her. He didn't want her to be afraid of him. He wished he knew what the words that came out of his mouth meant.

He stood for another hour, carrying his burden that declared angry words to an empty street, and still the church service continued. His legs felt like lead. How long had they been in there? Two hours? More?

Maybe he should have pushed harder to get to the poor bereaved family when they'd arrived, but some of the congregation had cornered him, firmly pushing him back. He didn't like it when they touched him. Their hands had faded bits, not smeared dirty like the priest's face, but kind of rubbed away all the same. Most of the townsfolk that filed in, heads bowed, had looked normal, but not those few. Their eyes were hollow behind the color. What frightened him most was the sheriff was one of them.

He stared at the heavy wooden door and chewed his lip. He should have pushed harder to get to them. He should have shouted. He had been weak. He'd let James Russell, with his big smile and hollow gaze cajole him backward. Tears pricked the corner of his eyes and he felt them raining in his soul.

Something wriggled in his pants, and shifting the board slightly he saw the genie sitting in the seam of his left front pocket. She smiled and he felt better.

"Fool's gold." She said. "I like that. So right." She tilted her head slightly. "Don't be sad. You're doing good. You can't save them all. You're not meant to. Some of them aren't meant to be saved."

Watching her, he wished she made more sense.

"Listen," she whispered. "Look."

She disappeared back into his pocket.

He stared at the door and then leaned inward, pressing his cheek against the tiny gap where two thick oak panels met. He squeezed his eyes shut and listened hard. The tiniest cool breeze tickled his ear and with it came the chant, long and low, muttered by hundreds on the other side.

"Sethenoshkenanmahalaleljaredenochsethenoshkenan-mahalaleljaredenoch."

He gasped slightly, not at the words, which were just more jumbled garbage in his head, but at the hunger in them. It burned like the itch for liquor. The air that escaped with the echoed speech smelled bad and Al stepped away from the door. He thought about opening it slightly and peering in, but the thought of those hollow eyes turning and fixing on him was more than he could bear. He stepped backward. If he looked inside, they'd know he had intent, and then they'd come for him. Better they think him a loon, a crazy. *Poor old Al Shtenko, who never recovered from losing his job at the bank and his wife to another man, and then lost himself in a bottle. He's finally cracked. Nothing to worry about there—it's just Al. He must need another drink.* Yes, it was better they saw him that way.

He stared again at the wood. And as it was, going in would be pointless. This was going to take more than a painted board with some mixed-up words from someplace inside him. He wondered for the trillionth time that day if maybe he was going mad. He thought about what a relief that would be.

Taking the board off and leaving it leaned up against the door, nicely placed to fall on the toe of whoever was first to leave, he stretched for a moment. His shoulders floated like wings with the weight gone. He looked down the coastline. How far away was the next town exactly? He couldn't remember. It had been a long time since he'd had reason to travel, and at least a year or so since he'd sold his car. He sighed. At least the weather was good.

He had a long walk ahead of him.

Steve looked out of the kitchen window and up at the night sky hanging over the small town. A feast of stars shone down bursting with light, and although the air was cool with no cloud cover to keep the daytime warmth in, part of him wanted to go down into the yard and just lie on the grass and stare up at that sky until he fell asleep. Maybe then he'd lose this unsettled feeling in his gut that was tinted with just a touch of fear. The sky looked perfect.

He sighed and sipped his coffee. Liz had gone pretty much straight to bed when they'd got in from the dinner that they'd lost their appetite for after seeing the crazy man at the church. Steve wished he'd hit him hard and shut him up when he'd first run across the street at them. Before he'd said that stuff about keeping the devil out, which had really freaked her.

In the hallway the front door clicked quietly shut. Angela appeared in the doorway.

"It's nearly eleven. Have you been in your meeting the whole time since eight?" Steve asked.

"Yeah. Yeah, we had a lot to talk about."

She sounded drained and for the first time since he'd known her she seemed fragile to Steve.

"You okay? You want a coffee or a sandwich or something?"

She shook her head. "No, I think I'll just have a shower and get to bed. It's been a long day."

"Well, if you want to talk or cry or anything you know where I am."

"I'll be okay." She shrugged. "It's sad about Georgia but if you mess around with drugs, then I guess bad things happen. It was probably her own fault." Turning, she headed out toward the bathroom.

Steve stared and then followed her. "What?" He couldn't believe what she'd said. "How do you mean if you mess around with drugs? I thought you said she wasn't into that stuff?"

Looking at him, her eyes seemed cold in the gloom and dark shadow of the unlit hall. "I was wrong. I can see it know. She had a real drug problem. LSD. It makes you see stuff and act crazy." She flicked the bathroom switch. "Apparently even her parents say so. They hoped Tower Hill would calm her down, but obviously not."

Steve's feet felt numb. Her eyes were unreadable. There was no twinkle or fire in them. It was as if she were somehow detached from what she was saying. He couldn't believe this unemotional calm after the upset of the afternoon.

"I'm going to take a shower now." She looked at him with that cool stare for a moment longer before shutting the door quietly in his face.

The shower was still running an hour later when Steve finally turned in to bed. He thought about knocking on the door and checking if she was okay, but he figured she wouldn't thank him. Or she just wouldn't answer. Lying in bed, restless in spirit, he listened to the quiet patter of water coming from the bathroom; it must have been running cold by then. That sound seemed to sum up everything that was wrong: Georgia, Angela, and the man at the church who was so intent on talking to Liz, on terrifying her with words her dad had spoken only hours before and that she thought she'd heard in a dream.

He didn't know what any of it meant, and maybe it all meant nothing, but the sheer strangeness of everything lived in the patter of that endless shower. He waited to hear it end. For Angela to come out and pad quietly to her own room next to his. But the water ran on and on, and finally, more than an hour later, he dozed off.

CHAPTER TWENTY-TWO

Mabel unlocked the small café just before dawn, and by just after eight the air was thick with the warm smell of baking chocolate and flour and butter. Smiling, she drank it in. My, she could just bathe in that scent, it was so good. She took another long, sweet breath before pulling the door closed and stepping onto the sidewalk, balancing the two boxes carefully.

Her hands tingled a little with the warmth coming through the bottom of the box, and she tossed her curls and picked up her pace. Hot muffins fresh from the oven—that's what would cheer people up. That's what Tower Hill needed, and that's what she'd give them. Some soul food. Across the road, Father O'Brien leaned against the church notice board and tipped her a nod, and for the briefest flicker of a second she almost remembered a dream she'd had of him but then it was gone, lost in the cool ocean breeze that was making her face flush.

She grinned back, her head a little fuzzy, and then pressed on to the library. The priest would approve of what she was doing; she knew that like she knew the tide would come in and out, regular as clockwork, until her dying day, and she knew that it was important in some way that she please him, although she wasn't entirely sure why. Occasionally over the past week, she'd found herself gazing out at the church and wondering where she'd gone. Where Mabel the cynic, the gossip, the earthy lover had been put, and who this godly disciple was that now lived in her shell? Sometimes those moments seemed like a dream.

But today was not one of those moments, and there were no fuzzy confused thoughts in her head. James had smiled and nodded when she'd got up at not long after four and she knew that what she was doing was for the good of the town. And when she saw the bottle of special-recipe chocolate flavoring sitting there on her kitchen shelf, my, had she smiled. Chocolate muffins to spread . . . some good feeling. Her thoughts stumbled a little and she wiped the darkness away. She'd almost thought *to spread the Word* but that would have been all wrong, *ammani paradosis,* and not what she meant. She smiled at her silly head and its wanderings.

First she dropped the smaller box of muffins at the library. The three women who worked there, and old Tom Rogers who cleaned and managed the archives, were all pleased as punch to see her, even if a muffin not long after breakfast was almost sinful. Mabel smiled and said that *not* to eat them when they were warm and sticky would be a sin, and they'd all laughed and obliged. They were still smiling and chatting when she left and that gave her a nice feeling inside. Tower Hill was a community. It was time they remembered that and stood together.

The elementary school was only a short walk from there, a little back from the coastline, and heading out toward the eyesore that was Neville Bright's car lot. Mabel picked up her pace. She had a lot of ground to cover today and the box was cooling in her hands.

There was still a gaggle of mothers at the gates when she rounded the corner, Deputy Eccles' wife, Emma, amongst them.

"Hey, Mabel, good to see you!" Emma beamed the dazzlingly sweet smile that had charmed every boy from

Tower Hill to Castle Rock when she was sixteen and would still melt hearts when she was sixty. "How's James? This business with that poor girl is terrible. I hope he got some sleep last night and isn't working too hard."

Mabel slid the lid from the muffin box. "Why, thank you, Emma. He's fine, but yes, it is so very tragic. And very upsetting for everyone." She held the muffins out. "I thought maybe the town could use a little cheering up today, and how better to start than with some chocolate."

A flurry of gasps fluttered through the group, and she smiled. "Take one, everybody. There's plenty. I'll drop the rest in for the teachers."

Emma grinned and helped herself. "You're an angel, Mabel. That is such a lovely idea." Taking a bite, she planted a chocolatey kiss on the older woman's face. "And these are just too delicious!"

Yes, Mabel thought as she pushed through the low gates. This was shaping up to be a good morning. "I can't stop," she called over her shoulder. "I've got another batch baking back at the café."

After the school she fetched the next load and delivered them to Town Hall just in time for their morning coffee break, and then up to the doctor's lab. She even dropped some in at the car lot, which came as a bit of a surprise to Neville, who'd been out of town for a couple days and hadn't even heard about the poor girl dying on the headland. Mabel figured that Neville Bright wouldn't care much either way, but he still took her muffins. He was reaching for his second by the time she pushed her way out of the steel and glass door. If she remembered correctly, he'd always been a greedy boy.

Striding back to the café, her calves ached a little. This little town was starting to feel bigger and bigger. Everywhere she looked was another business or store or public service building, and she had to reach them all. She *had* to. Maybe she needed to get some help.

By the time Elizabeth came in for her afternoon shift, May was working out front while Mabel baked. May hadn't minded. She'd looked at Mabel and nodded, grabbing her coat and locking up the B and B straightaway. It was church council business, she'd said, and that made it important. Mabel had found herself nodding although for the life of her she didn't know why because surely her baking was nothing to do with the church council. Her head had felt fuzzy for a moment or two after that and then she'd decided that it just wasn't important. What was important was that she had more baking to do, and if May could help, well, then that would be just grand. There were muffins to be made and delivered. Those teachers up at the college could probably use cheering up too.

She had the small window open but still sweat trickled down her hairline as she worked and she could feel it itching between her breasts. Liz stood in the doorway and stared at her.

"What's the matter, honey? You never seen a woman bake before?"

She watched as Liz's face turned, taking in the flour and eggshells that covered the surfaces. Maybe it was a little messy, but so what? She was baking.

"No," Liz said. "It's just that you're making so much. Is there a party or something? Are you doing outside catering?"

"I just thought that people could use some cheering up, and what makes folks smile more than chocolate?" She smiled. "Didn't you see that film with that skinny French girl in?"

"That's a nice thought. Do you want some help?"

"No, honey. You just take care of out front with May. I can manage the baking." Her hands were covered in egg. "But you can just pass me down that bottle. Second shelf, white label."

Liz reached for it and looked it over. "What's this? Secret

recipe? There's no label on it." She unscrewed it and sniffed the opening. Her face crinkled.

"What's the matter? Too sweet?"

"No. No, the opposite. It smells really bitter to me. Is it a dark chocolate recipe?"

Something in the girl's expression irritated her more than the drying sweat under her clothes. Who in hell was she to come in here and criticize? Mabel's hand gripped tighter around the spatula and for a moment her head was filled with images of beating Liz over the head again and again until the girl's brains were spread all over the floor. Then she'd be sorry; then she'd just fit in like everyone else was going to *ammani paradosis* and she'd go to church like a good girl and just do as she was told. And then maybe Mabel would pick up those brains and put them in her next batch of muffins and feed them to all those godless students up at that no-good college.

The oven buzzer rang out and she jumped, the thoughts slipping away, shaken off. Liz turned to put on an apron and then smiled at Mabel.

"Well, if you need a hand, give me a shout."

There was something in that smile that annoyed Mabel and she just couldn't put her finger on why. Maybe she'd misread Elizabeth on that first meeting. Maybe she wasn't the good girl that she'd presented herself as. Slipping on an oven mitt she pulled out two large muffin trays. Maybe after today she wouldn't need any more help in her coffee shop from dirty college girls who don't have any manners.

She took a deep breath of hot, scented air and smiled.

PART TWO

CHAPTER TWENTY-THREE

The wind was cold, all hints of summer gone as Steve and Liz stood in the wide archway of Medway Hall and watched the Keenans standing by their station wagon as solemn students loaded Georgia's possessions into the trunk. Liz glanced upward. The sky was gray and heavy with angry rain. In the ten days since Georgia had been found dead on the headland, the sun had been shy with its favors, taking its warmth primarily elsewhere and preparing the town for the oncoming winter. The day of the cremation had brought with it the first real downpour of the season and it looked as if today they would get the next.

Liz sipped her coffee, liking the heat in her hands. "Georgia's sister's going with them, isn't she?"

Steve nodded. "So I've heard. Seems like she didn't want to though. Her parents and the dean pretty much forced her. They're going to let her pick up her work next semester." He paused. "I don't know why she'd want to stay after this anyway. Her family will need her."

The wind blew a wisp of hair across Liz's face, but she ignored it. "Angela said Georgia's family loved this college. Maybe her sister does too. Maybe staying would be easier than going home and having to grieve properly." Glancing at the paths and stone archways leading into and between the other halls, Liz could see figures like her and Steve dotted around, keeping their distance but wanting to say their final good-byes. She hoped it wasn't just ghoulish curiosity disguised as concern. She hoped that part of her wasn't also feeling that way. There was just so much that was confusing her these days.

Twenty or so feet away from the Keenans' station wagon a police car was parked. The deputy leaned against the closed door, arms folded across his chest, his wide brimmed hat low over his eyes. James Russell stood close to the Keenans.

"Nice of the sheriff to come and say good-bye. Now that the body's burned and nothing more can be done about it."

Steve's sarcasm wasn't lost on Liz. Despite not knowing anything much about these things, the speed of the investigation had surprised Liz a little. Steve on the other hand had found it downright sinister. Within two or three days of her death, Georgia's body had been released to her parents and a cremation swiftly followed. Hardly any of the students had been questioned by the police. Steve figured that at the least they'd be trying to track down her dealer, but there'd been no talk of that in any of the corridors.

Watching the sheriff, Liz sighed silently. Maybe Steve had a point. None of the teachers seemed too bothered by the lack of progress in the case either. They all appeared lost in their own worlds. She figured that maybe Steve was also still angry with Mabel and the sheriff for firing her from the coffee shop. Thinking about it, she felt a sharp sting of hurt inside. If she was honest, she probably hadn't quite gotten over that either, but there was no point in mulling over why Mabel didn't want her there. What was done was done.

Sheriff James Russell muttered some quiet words to the family before tipping his hat to them and walking back to his cruiser. Watching the couple and their daughter climb tiredly into their seats, Liz thought there was an air of confusion around them, as if they'd been caught up in events that they hadn't quite got a handle on yet. They looked as if they were waking up all messed up from a dream, unsure about what was real and what was unreal. Mrs. Keenan glanced down at the urn she held, almost visibly shocked to see it there between her tight knuckles.

The boys who had brought Georgia's stuff down stood and watched as the engine spluttered into life. They didn't smile; their expressions were as black as the first heavy drops of cold rain that fell. Shivering slightly, Liz pushed into Steve's side. "Aren't they the guys from the football team? The ones Angela knows?"

She had whispered the question but she wasn't entirely sure why. There was something about the way they stared that gave her the creeps. Their faces were intensely blank and yet almost empty. "They look weird." Her words disappeared into the watery air and as the car pulled away, the wheels crunching through the gravel, she stared at the other students dotted around. Each of them was focused on the departing vehicle, no smiles of frowns or tilts of the head—just smooth faces and intent, hooded eyes.

She shivered and her fingers found the smooth stone in her jacket pocket and for a second pulled back before encircling it in her palm. She couldn't remember picking it up from the table beside her bed. She must have, but she didn't know when. Still, holding it felt good somehow. Steve nudged her side.

"Hey, look up there."

She followed his eyes, and up on the second floor, hidden in the reflections of the large glass panes, she could make out a row of teachers staring down from the windows.

"That must be the faculty office or something," she said.

"Yeah, but look. They're not talking to one another. They haven't even looked at one another."

Liz watched the silent figures staring down into the quad

and then scanned the outlines and huddles of students that lingered in the doorways and shadows, their features blurred behind the rain.

"No one's talking."

"No," Steve agreed quietly. "No one apart from us."

As the car disappeared and left the campus in silence, Steve and Liz watched as the expressionless students and teachers turned to go their separate ways. There were no waves or calls to meet later or even a single smile or laugh. No one acknowledged anyone else.

"This is too freaky. It feels all wrong." Steve's voice was barely above a whisper.

Liz nodded slightly in agreement. She was watching the sheriff. Standing by the car, he stared at her long and hard before tipping his hat to her. That subtle gesture made her shiver more than the rain. There was nothing friendly in it. She pulled her jacket tight and tucked her head down against the chill drops of water. Steve sniffed.

"Let's get back to the house. Maybe Angela will be up by now. And I need a shower before work."

CHAPTER TWENTY-FOUR

Steve pushed his hands deep into the pockets of his jacket and lengthened his stride as he walked down the long stretch of road from the college to town. The weather hadn't gotten any better since the rain had first fallen that morning, and the cool damp clung to his face. To his left, the ocean waves rolled, the surf battering the shingle and sand with its angry white foam, spraying and spitting at the jagged rocks, the tips of which hinted at their danger a little farther out. The wind that danced on its surface blew inward and up over the cliffs, embracing him and burning his cheeks a little before swirling back out to the vast expanse of water and sky.

Still, despite the chill, there was something good about feeling the elements battering at his skin from the open ocean. It was real. It made him feel alive and he hoped it would dispel some of the churning unease that had settled in his core ever since they'd found Georgia's body out on the headland, not so far from where he was walking now. Shivering slightly, his mind lingered on the weird way the students and teachers had been standing and staring at the Keenans taking poor Georgia's remains home, and he knew it would take more than a brisk walk in the fresh air to clear his mood.

When he and Liz had got back to the house, Angela dragged herself out of bed for long enough to make a cup of coffee, but had soon shambled back into her room with barely any conversation. It wasn't as if she were even grieving for her friend. It certainly didn't look that way. It was more like she was devoid of any emotion at all. She'd seemed confused when they'd tried to talk to her, and although she'd managed to grunt a few words of "yes" and "no" mainly, they'd seemed forced. Where had the bubbly, vivacious girl they'd moved in with gone? Over the past week or so, it seemed she had pretty much left the building.

Liz had been in her room working on a paper when he'd left, her desk light on to fight the gloom, and she'd lifted her head to give him a warm smile good-bye. Although her books had been open and spread around her, he wondered how much actual work she'd get done. The changes in Angela and the weird vibe on campus were taking their toll on her too, especially on top of getting fired from the coffee shop. Like him, Liz had hoped to find some kind of escape at Tower Hill, but things just weren't working out that way. He was even starting to think of the busy hubbub of Detroit with fondness.

The wind returned and lashed at his face, making his eyes water, but he still felt a kernel of warmth in his gut when he thought of Liz. It was funny the way things turned out. If he was honest, when they'd first moved in, it had been Angela he'd been most attracted to. He'd liked Liz, but Angela was the one that dazzled. Things had changed though, slowly but surely, and suddenly it was Liz that was filling his thoughts. There was more depth to her than he'd first realized, and her quiet beauty made Angela's wildness seem a little brittle and damaged.

There was something good about Liz, and that goodness made him feel good about himself. When he was with her, the bitterness of his mom and the hardness of Detroit and the trailer park faded. When Liz was around, he remembered that he had the right to be normal and choose his own way, just like Liz was trying to choose hers. It had nothing to do with not loving their families, strange as they were, and everything to do with just trying to break the cycle.

Maybe this slow attraction would be the start of something, and deep down inside he knew already that, for him at least, it was special. He was determined not to let his insecurities or the ever-present guilt of his overweight mother damage it. This was his chance.

Part of him almost laughed aloud at the naivety of his thoughts and feelings for this pure little church mouse, but he quashed the sound. It wasn't a laugh he liked. He didn't want to be the person who that laugh belonged to. That person lived in a trailer and was disappointed with life, and there was no reason his life had to turn out like that. Liz, and their growing relationship, might be enough to squash that dark part of him once and for all. He didn't want to forget where he'd come from, but he also didn't want where he'd come from to be where he ended up. His mom could keep on telling him that he would never get out, but what the hell did she know? He'd got this far. He smiled to himself. Yeah, who knew where it was going to lead, but he just hoped it would be something positive. They needed something positive.

He stared at the facades of the wood-fronted houses as he made his way into the heart of town. Where only a few weeks ago he'd been charmed by their appearance, now he felt a vague sense of disquiet. The streets were too silent and the gray overcast sky made the pastel colors of the seaside buildings seem all wrong, like a closed-up fair that had no intention of letting the caged rides loose in the night.

It was still early afternoon, but the sidewalks were empty and the trees twisted with the insistent tugs of the frustrated wind, branches screaming out for their lost leaves as he passed underneath them. He sniffed and balled up his fists inside the cotton of his thin jacket, and tried to relax.

Maybe now that the Keenans had gone spirits would lift and people would start acting normal again. At least around the college. The sheriff was never going to win his vote, but Steve could stay out of his way. Neither he nor Liz had any reason to see Mabel or her beau unless they chose to, and he couldn't imagine Liz choosing to pop into the coffee shop anytime soon. Not after how they treated her.

As he turned off Main Street, the rain started again in earnest, falling in large heavy drops, chilled to freezing in their fall, and Steve used it as an excuse to break into a jog, but what he was running from or to, he really wasn't sure.

The electric doors of Hannaford couldn't have slid open more than four or five times in the first three hours of Steve's shift, and even then the purchases made were minimal. One elderly man had come in, his untidy coat dripping from the rain, and stood looking at various brooms and mops for a full ten minutes before going to the chilled meats and instead selecting a packet of bologna and a carton of milk. Happy with his purchases, he scurried out back into the gloomy afternoon. The other three or four customers of the afternoon seemed to be of a similar mind, selecting only one or two items and then leaving. One woman bought only Hamburger Helper and honey. Watching her clutching them at the checkout, Steve was glad she wasn't cooking dinner for him. Who would come out in this weather just for a couple of things they could probably do without? It was strange.

The bright strips of white light that ran the length of the store and in the stockroom lacked any yellow warmth, and having hoped to lighten his mood at work, Steve only found it darkening. He was surprised he hadn't been sent home because it was so quiet, but maybe Mr. Casey was so wrapped up with whatever paperwork he was doing in his manager's office, he hadn't noticed the lack of customers. Steve sighed and wished Mike would come out of the stockroom. It wasn't like him to be so antisocial. Although Steve had ripped his co-workers to Liz and Angela after his first shift, he'd warmed to them since then, and in some ways they reminded him of his friends back home, but without the street-smart hard edge. They were never going to get out of this small town, and they didn't seem to want to.

Amy, the cashier, a pretty blonde just turned eighteen, only really wanted to get married to her boyfriend, Arnold, have lots of babies and live in a nice house near enough to her folks so that they could sit with the kids every once in a while. Mike, who was chubby, dark-haired, and Steve suspected still a virgin at twenty-one, had worked at Hannaford's since dropping out of high school. He dreamed of one day working his way up to store manager. It was a dream he was dead serious about. His plan was to start taking his certificate and training courses when he was twenty-five, and he figured that by thirty he'd be ready to take on the responsibilities of the job.

When Mike had first shared his ambitions with Steve, sitting on a crate out back and eating their sandwiches, Steve had found it hard not to smile at his earnest, chubby face. Joe, the other full-timer, a thin man who rarely spoke, or at least rarely spoke to Steve, had also been there, and he'd just nodded in solemn agreement. Watching them, Steve had suddenly felt shitty about wanting to laugh at their dreams. He'd felt like his mother, and that wasn't a good feeling. Who was he to say what was a good future and what wasn't? And at least Mike and Amy seemed pretty happy, and wasn't that all anyone really wanted out of life?

After that day, Steve kind of settled in to life at Hannaford's and found he quite liked Mike's gentle, shy humor and Amy's effervescence. They were never going to talk politics with him, but at the same time they would never trample on his opinions or try and make him be anything other than himself. After a week or so, he'd gotten the feeling that Mike was maybe a little in awe of him, asking questions about Detroit and what life was like up at the college and saying how he'd never been up there, not even for a dance. Hearing the wonder in his friend's voice made Steve feel humbled for his first snap judgments.

Now that they'd got to know each other, there was an easy friendship between them and their shifts were spent shooting the breeze and laughing while re-forming displays and replacing items on the shelves. The work wasn't particularly taxing and although Mr. Casey would sometimes come out and check on them, they were pretty much left to their own devices unless there was a rush on.

Today though, he was finding it difficult to draw either Mike of Amy into a conversation. Mike had withdrawn to the stockroom with a comic book pretty much as soon as his shift had started, and Amy sat with her back to the register, staring out at the rain, making occasional wet bubble sounds with her gum.

"Hey, Amy," he said to her ponytail. "How about the radio? Let's have some music to pass the time."

Unable to just sit and do nothing, Steve had taken down the big display table of cookie packs and was about to re-arrange it. Amy swiveled her chair around to face him. She looked at him blankly for a second before blowing a large balloon of pink, letting it burst on her face before pulling it back into her mouth with her tongue and chewing.

"I like it quiet. Nice and peaceful." She paused. "Sometimes there's just too much noise in the world. Makes it hard for me to think, you know?" She smiled gently at him and then turned back to looking at the rain.

Leaving the cookies and needing some kind of human interaction to make him feel better, Steve went up through the aisles and into the stockroom. Mike seemed no further into his comic than he had been a half hour earlier, but he stared at the pages with the same intensity as a child gripped in a superhero's adventures.

"Hey. I'm rearranging the cookies. Want to come and help? It's boring on my own."

Mike shook his head and didn't look up.

Steve's foot twitched with the disquiet that nibbled him inside. "You okay, Mike? You seem a bit weird. So does Amy. Is something going on I don't know about?"

Mike dragged his eyes up. "Sorry. Yeah. Yeah, I'm okay." He frowned slightly as if he had to think about it. "It was a late night last night."

Slightly relieved, Steve grinned. "So you were out partying? On a weekday? You animal, man."

"Nah." Mike shook his head. "Nothing like that. It was church. There was a late service. Amy was there too." He looked at Steve, puzzled. "How come you don't come to church, dude?"

Steve's grin fell. Mike had never mentioned religion before. He tried to keep his tone light. "I didn't figure you as a choirboy. And surely church is for Sundays."

"Well, my mom kept going on about the new priest and stuff, so I figured I'd go to keep her happy." Mike looked around, slightly dazed, as if her were just waking up. "And I really like it, I guess." He paused. "Amy started going because she wants Father O'Brien to marry her and Arnie, you know, if he ever gets around to proposing, and I suppose she must like it too, 'cause she keeps turning up there." He blinked hard three times. "I guess all that prayer must drain you. Man, I'm tired." He smiled a little, and looked like the real Mike for the first time since Steve had come in that afternoon.

"That's why I wanted to sit out here. It's nice and peaceful. Quiet. Like being surrounded by nothing."

Steve tried to smile back but the stretch in his face felt unnatural. "How's the comic?"

Mike looked down at it for a second. "It's pretty," he finally said. "Good colors."

"Are you sure you're okay? Maybe you better get an

early night tonight." Steve shifted uneasily from foot to foot.

"Can't, dude. More praying to be done."

Steve stared. "How many times a week are you going to church, Mike?"

Putting the comic down, Mike frowned and shook his head slightly. "Hard to tell. The church is always open for believers. And changes are coming. I think. I think that's what the priest says. Something like that, anyways."

"Maybe you should see a doctor. You don't sound so good. Or at least take a night off from church. I'm sure God will understand." Steve wondered whether he should talk to Mr. Casey about this. Or maybe go and see Mike's mom, or even the goddamned priest. This was all wrong. That much he knew.

A bell rang out loud and long above their heads and Mike sighed and stood up. "Sounds like we're needed out front." He shuffled his chubby frame past Steve and back into the store. With a heavy heart, Steve followed. Amy had probably knocked a display over or something. For a pretty girl, she was very clumsy. There sure couldn't have been a sudden rush of customers. Not in five minutes.

It wasn't an Amy accident or a customer though, but Mabel. Steve grimaced when he saw her, despite Amy's grin and Mike's whoop of hello. She seemed to have got some life out of them and so that was something at least. Her back was to him as she put a box down on the table that should have held the cookie display, and she spoke to Mr. Casey, who'd come out of his office.

"I thought you might be feeling a little peckish, honey." She lifted the lid, and Steve wasn't surprised to see the chocolate muffins, large and inviting, piled on a tray inside. It seemed she'd been delivering them everywhere over the past week or so. He'd seen teachers munching on them in the corridors of the halls, and this was the second time she'd brought some to Hannaford's while he'd been working.

The first time she'd come, she'd told them how she'd been halfway around the town trying to cheer people up with her baking. Steve looked inside the box. Well, he hadn't taken one last time and he didn't intend to this time either. Screw her. She'd screwed Liz over. He didn't want anything from her.

Mr. Casey, on the other hand, beamed. "Why, thank you, Mabel. Such a nice thought on such a miserable day." He took a muffin and Amy followed him, sticking her gum behind her ear before biting such a large chunk of chocolate sponge that she almost couldn't shut her mouth while chewing. Her loose sleeve slid up her arm as she raised it to her mouth, and Steve was sure he could make out a series of small cuts just above her wrist. He squinted. Maybe it was just pen that she'd doodled on there, but it sure looked like cuts. Her arm dropped and the scratches—or whatever they were—were lost.

Mabel turned to Mike and Steve. "Well, come on and help yourselves, boys. There's enough for everyone." Steve followed Mike forward but unlike his friend it wasn't to eat something. It was Mabel he wanted to take a closer look at. What the hell was wrong with her? While Mr. Casey, Amy and Mike wolfed through her offerings, she pulled off the scarf covering her hair and shook the rain from it with a slightly wild laugh. Underneath, her curls were misshapen, one dark twirl of hair falling right down over her left eye. Steve wondered if she'd put the rollers in blindfolded. Her face was made up with equal haphazardness. Red lipstick had slid over the edges of her full mouth and covered some of her right front tooth. Her clothes looked wrong too, and Steve could see why. Mabel had lost weight. A lot of it. Did she even realize she wasn't looking so good?

He watched Mr. Casey smiling at her, and Amy laughing at something she'd said. What was the matter with them all? Couldn't they see that something was going seriously wrong with the coffee shop owner? For the first time since it'd happened Steve felt glad that Liz had been fired. There was no way he'd want her around Mabel now. She looked seriously unhinged.

"Aren't you eating?" Mike spoke through his mouthful of food, and Steve suddenly felt them all staring curiously at him.

"No thanks. Not really my thing." His eyes were drawn to Mike's wrist. There were cuts there too. What the hell was going on?

"But everyone loves Mabel's homemade muffins, silly." Amy giggled. "They're good."

Mr. Casey peered at him. "More than that. They're good *for* you." He paused and shared a smile with Mike and Amy.

"No thanks. I'll pass." His stomach turned slightly. They all had the cuts on their arms, even Mabel. "Um . . ." He couldn't keep the question in. "What's the matter with your wrists? You've all got those cuts?"

Mr. Casey pulled his shirtsleeve up a little. Four long welts were scabbing up, but Steve could still see pink on the white of the man's cuff where blood had oozed onto it. Mr. Casey frowned. "What cuts? I don't have any cuts?"

Mike looked at his own damaged skin and then back at Steve. He laughed slightly, a tired, hollow sound. "You on the weed, dude? What are you talking about?"

Steve's face flushed hot and then cold. "Can't you see them? Right there, on your wrist. It's like someone's cut you. All of you."

Amy tilted her head and retrieved her saved gum. "There's nothing there. You're freaking me out a little, Steve."

Mabel still grinned, but her eyes sparkled dangerously. "You need the church, boy. That's what you need. You need saving. Bringing into the fold."

Mr. Casey and Mike nodded. "Yeah," Mike said. "Come to service tonight. I'll come get you. You'll love it. It's . . . it's . . . it's . . ."

"Indescribable," Mr. Casey finished. "You should be there. It'd be good for a boy like you."

Amy giggled and sighed and wandered back to the checkout. Above him the bright lights were too harsh and Steve felt his legs wobble slightly. He didn't want to stay here. Something was very wrong with these people. His stomach clamped up again, bile rising through his throat.

"You know what, Mr. Casey? I don't feel so good. I think I should go home."

Mabel glared at him, and Mr. Casey's grin froze. "You know what I think, Mr. Wharton?" His voice was low and cool. "I think you should eat one of Mabel's fine muffins. I really think you should."

Steve looked from Mr. Casey to Mabel and then to Mike. None of them were smiling now. Mike's eyes glittered, hard and empty, but more alive than they'd been all day. "Come on, dude. What are you so scared of? They taste great. Real great."

Mabel reached into the box and Mike saw her broken nails and the raw skin that covered her fingers and wondered if she ever stopped baking, even to sleep, and what the hell was she putting in those muffins to turn them all mad, and then he looked up to see Mike and Mr. Casey taking steps toward him.

"Fuck you." He muttered before his feet burst into a sprint, shoving Mabel to one side and sending her box of muffins tumbling to the floor. As he ducked past Mr. Casey and out into the rain, for the first time in his life he was grateful for his past, for the teenage years spent running from gangs and police and his mother. His feet pounded the slick sidewalk but he kept his footing. He didn't look back.

CHAPTER TWENTY-FIVE

Jack's feet echoed a whisper on the soft wood of the Medway Hall floor, his black cassock swinging silently as he moved through the vaulted corridors. It was hard to believe it was still the middle of the afternoon. Where the place was normally a hub of youthful activity, it was now dull and lifeless. Outside, the empty branches scratched on the high windows, the screech filling the hall like the dying cries of a gull.

Jack smiled. His fingers tingled and he raised one to his lips and licked it. He could still taste the lingering sweetness of the fresh apple he'd eaten an hour before. Or maybe the fruity taste was coming from his own sweat. Maybe the apples were becoming part of him. Each day they'd grown larger and pinker and burst with a thousand flavors as he'd sunk his teeth into them, and each day it amazed him how such delicious fruit could appear from a desiccated twig with no moist roots to draw life from the earth.

Occasionally in the night when he couldn't sleep, during those vague moments of wonder at what he and Gray were doing, in which he sometimes felt he couldn't catch his breath, it was the thought of the apples that reminded him that all of it was real. It was all happening. And so much faster than they'd anticipated. The town was half asleep, operating in a numb haze, barely aware of its own actions. Gray's adoring kids were nearly ready. The blood had been mixed and the blood had been shared, just as the ancient instructions had dictated, and as for *them,* those old angry souls on the other side, they were more than ready. They were growing impatient. They had to be; it was the only explanation that either he or Gray could come up with for what had happened to Georgia Keenan. She'd got ahead of the rest; she must have been almost ready, and they'd sensed it, trying to come through too soon and all at once.

They had surprised Jack. He didn't expect that from them. After all this time he thought they'd have learned more patience. But even with the changes bubbling away inside him, he still couldn't imagine all that time and all that anger. He paused at the cafeteria on his left and peered in. A half-empty tray of chocolate muffins sat by the cash register. His smile stretched a little. By the window a boy with unkempt hair stared out of the window, ignoring his coffee. His body was so still he could have been made of marble, but his fingers were frantic with movement, tugging at his fingernails, and Jack wondered if he was even aware that he'd torn them down so far they were starting to bleed. He doubted it. The boy's face was beyond vacant.

Most of the tables in the vast space were empty, only a handful of students filling them, mostly avoiding eye contact with one another or oblivious to anyone else's presence. Against the far wall, two fat girls murmured to each other as they nibbled on sandwiches, peering around awkwardly, unsure about the uneasy quietness that had somehow descended on their lives, catching them unawares. Jack watched them, for a moment fascinated by the meaninglessness of their lives. They were unimportant. They would sit in their rooms and work and pretend that everything was fine and by the time their thick, fat heads figured out that something amazing was happening here in Tower Hill, it would be too late.

Power itched at his fingertips, and for a second his head

felt so full he thought it might explode there and then. Looking at the fat girls, he wondered what would happen if he touched them; if he squeezed their faces with his new and improved hands. Would they just dissolve into the nothing they really were or would his nails gouge into their skin and peel it from their flesh? He gripped the edge of the wall, fighting the urge to act on his impulses. Electricity surged through him as his pulse raced, and under the tips of his fingers the varnished wood bubbled. He watched it and then looked back at the girls. If this was the power he felt now, what would it be like afterward? When he and Gray rose to something more? Excitement tingled through him and he fought to control it from bursting out of his mouth in a scream.

He turned his back on the dining hall and headed for the stairs. It would be easier afterward, he decided, taking the steps with his usual controlled speed. It would be easier because then the transformation would be complete. On the third floor landing he turned onto the corridor and passed the teachers' common room. He didn't go in. Not that it would matter if he had. Most of the faculty were churchgoers, and if they hadn't been to start with, once Mabel had been around with her offerings, they'd all begun turning up. Some were a little confused to start with, but they'd soon been cured of that.

Between the muffins and his special communions, and the blood that had since been drained from their veins, he'd be surprised if even the dean remembered his own name. He grinned and whistled, no longer worried if he and Gray were seen together. They had the dean and the sheriff and most of the town under their spell, most of the residents wandering through their days in a haze. The remaining students could be managed. And that was coming soon enough.

He found MH3 and walked through the empty lecture room and around to the small back office, opening the door without knocking. Gray sat on his office chair, facing away from his desk. He grinned. "Hey, Father. Want to join in on a little original sin?"

"Jesus, Gray. Do you have to?"

Two girls kneeled by the man's chair, both naked from the waist up. One was a pretty honey-colored blonde, and the other was still wearing her no-nonsense, thick-framed glasses as her dark head bobbed up and down in his lap.

"Someone has to." He shivered slightly. "And man, I've been getting some urges." He met Jack's gaze. "It ain't like I'm going to hurt these two. We need them."

"Make sure you don't." Jack looked into his friend's eyes and thought he saw a second set of dark filmy lids flash shut horizontally across the surface of Gray's eyes. He found he wasn't surprised. He was changing and so was Gray. Neither of them could hide it for much longer.

Gray's mouth tightened as he pulled the girl's head away from him by her hair. The blonde's lips took over, sliding automatically over his hard dick.

"Now, tell me, Jack," Gray said, "have you ever seen such a huge pair of tits on such a little girl?" His free hand squeezed each of the student's heavy breasts hard enough to leave red finger marks on her pale skin. She didn't flinch.

Jack looked away. He'd never felt particularly comfortable with Gray's overt sexual nature, and that was something that wasn't changing. "Do you think you could stop for a moment? I've never liked talking to you with your cock out."

His tone was dry and Gray laughed out loud. The sound was the same easy melody that Jack had known since he was sixteen, but there was more resonance to it, as if it hit ranges that were yet to be discovered by man.

"Sure, Jack. For you, anything."

He pushed the blonde away and released the brunette, tucking his erect penis into his pants and zipping up his fly. He leaned forward in the chair, all his attention on Jack.

The two girls' mouths met and they caressed and kissed each other, sliding to the floor. There were silent in their actions as the brunette pushed up her partner's skirt and lowered her head to seek out the delicate area between the other girl's thighs. As her mouth pushed aside the thin panties in her way, she twisted around so that her own legs straddled the blonde's face, pressing herself into it, her dress hiking up above her waist. They writhed together, becoming one as they locked in the sexual act, but there was no passion in their movement, only a sense of slugglishly going through the motions.

Jack watched them with distaste, feeling no arousal at all. He wondered if that too would change afterward. When these bodies were filled with *the others,* and when his own body and spirit were enlightened and empowered. Maybe then he'd start to feel some of the sexual drive that had eluded him all his life. He glanced at Gray. And what would happen to him? What damage would his powers allow him to do if he gave his urges full rein? Not that it mattered. The world would be changed and nothing would be able to stop them. There'd be plenty of young women for Gray to terrify and desecrate if he wanted to. An endless, hopeless supply of female flesh to keep him happy while Jack worked with the returned ones to create a new world. Gray was never the brains in their outfit; never had been, never would be.

Soft, slippery lapping sounds filled the room as the girls' mouths worked. From what Jack could make out, however, there was little enjoyment evident. The brunette's eyes were open, staring vacantly ahead, glazed and empty.

"Do you think they even know what they're doing?" He looked up at Jack, who twisted his swivel chair left and right, and winked.

"Who the hell knows? I'm wondering if I sliced into one of their tits, if maybe then they'd start to make some noise."

"Let's just keep that thought as a wonder."

Gray laughed. "Sure thing, bro." He sniffed and focused his changed eyes on the women. "They're almost empty, aren't they? I think they're on autopilot." He looked back up at Jack. "Weird, huh? We're changing the world."

His voice was thoughtful, and it surprised Jack. Gray normally just went with the flow and rolled with the punches. Maybe this was part of his change.

The electric feeling hummed across the surface of Jack's skin and he could feel it tingling in every inch of his body. "We certainly are."

"We can do whatever we want." The softness in Gray's normal voice was tinged with a sibilant hiss that seemed to slide between the consonants and vowels of the words. "The town belongs to us now. The power's unlocked. I can feel it. It's running inside me. It's fucking wild." He pulled out a cigarette from the pack on his desk and lit it. "Holy shit."

Jack nodded. "Yep, it's something else, isn't it?" He smiled. "But maybe you still shouldn't be smoking in here."

"Why the hell not? It ain't exactly as if anyone's going to come and say anything." He spun the chair around in a full circle, and Jack could see the inner child that had always been in Gray was still very much alive and kicking. "We're the kings, man, and this is our castle."

"Yes, that's true." Jack looked upward. "But the castle still has smoke alarms and sprinklers. And I don't really fancy getting wet."

Gray followed his gaze. "No shit." He snorted back a laugh and choked on his inhale, forcing him to double over spluttering for a few moments. His strange eyes watered as he gulped air, getting his breath back. "Oh, fuck, Jack, sometimes you kill me." He leaned backward and unclipped the window, pushing it open slightly. A cool, wet breeze oozed into the small room.

As it sucked the smoke out, Jack watched goose bumps form on the brunette's white ass as she ground into the face of the blonde beneath her. Muscles twitched erratically at the border of her round cheek and firm thigh and she let out a small sigh. Maybe she was getting something out of it after all.

He looked up to find Gray staring at him. "I hope that doesn't change, Jack. You know, you and me. They way we've been. And I mean it from right in here." He banged at his chest. "You're my family, man. Always have been. I fucking love you, Jack."

Jack shook his head a little. "We've come a long way together, haven't we? Nothing can change that. It's you and me, Gray. In it together."

Gray nodded. "Forever."

The electricity shot through Jack's nerves with the excited power of that word and the truth in it for them.

"Forever."

CHAPTER TWENTY-SIX

Liz had lain staring up at the ceiling for so long that she was starting to see shapes there in the dark of the night. She saw them when she blinked too; gloomy swirls of black that were almost purple dancing behind her lids. She sighed and thought about maybe reading a book for a while. Even with the rain pattering against the small window alongside her, a sound that she normally found comforting, as if it were a natural lullaby, she couldn't relax. The air was completely still and somewhere between sweaty and cool, so when she kicked off the covers she felt too cold, but with them pulled up she was too hot. It was strange weather for the end of a strange day.

She let the shapes dance a little more and thought of the way Sheriff Russell had tipped his hat to her that morning, and despite the sweat on the back of her legs, pulled the covers up a little higher around her chin. Steve had come home early from work, his face flushed as if he'd run most of the way and he'd barely said a word as to why, and she knew better than to push.

They had all been subdued over dinner and as much as she'd tried to get a conversation going, in the end she'd given up. She was just talking to herself. Angela had barely taken a mouthful of her stew, and although Steve had eaten, it had been without enthusiasm, his brow wrinkled and eyes down. Something had happened to him today, she was sure of it, but she figured he'd tell her when he was ready. She just hoped he hadn't had a run-in with the sheriff and told him what he thought of Mabel and the investigation. Steve needed this time at college and arguing with the local law, however strangely its enforcers may have behaved, could make that time very hard for him. She knew what life in small communities was like. People didn't forget.

Rolling onto her side, she stared at the glowing hands of her small clock. One A.M. and still she felt no urge to sleep. It was going to be a long day tomorrow. The small pale stone she'd found on the beach shone in the reflected light and she reached out for it, pulling it back into the safety of her bed. She rubbed it between her fingers, enjoying the smooth, cool sensation and the feel of its strange rectangular shape. It was so close to perfect, she wondered what forces of nature could have battered it into that form. She smiled a little. It was one tiny mystery in the history of the earth, never to be fully understood, but just to be enjoyed. She was glad she'd rescued it from its grave in the sand and shingle. She gripped the rock tightly and felt her body relax a little, letting the sheets and mattress below caress her tired body. For the first time in hours, her eyes began to feel slightly heavy. Maybe she would get some sleep tonight after all.

A bright strip of light flashed on in the hallway, stretching into her dark room from the gap under the door. She blinked, suddenly awake again. It obviously wasn't only her that was restless in the night. She waited for the usual sound of running water and the flush and then the plunge back into darkness, but there was nothing. Silence. Looking at the strength of the light coming from the other side, she leaned up on one elbow. Was the bathroom door even shut? She waited and listened for a few moments, but still no sound of faucets in action or water gushing through the pipes. There was only the quiet and the rushing of her own blood pulsing in her ears. She bit her lip.

Maybe Steve or Angela were getting a drink and thought the bathroom light would be less intrusive than the kitchen one. In fact, maybe it was the kitchen light that was on. One thing she did know was that the movement of sitting up had made her own bladder twinge slightly. There was no way she'd be drifting off to sleep while that tapped away inside her for attention.

Pushing back her covers, stone still in hand, she fumbled for the robe hanging on the back of the door and pulled it on, wrapping it safely around her. Squinting a little, she stepped out into the hallway.

"Angela? Steve?" she whispered. It was the bathroom light that was on, but the door wasn't closed. It wasn't even half closed. Liz moved tentatively forward. "Steve? If that's you, then say so because I'm coming in. Angela? Are you okay in . . ."

Her voice trailed off as she peered into the brightness. There was a scream building in her somewhere, but right there in the moment, she didn't have the breath to carry it. Her lungs felt punched sideways by what she was seeing and she sucked hard to get a breath. The world twisted a little under the glare of the light and she flinched. The blood was too red against the white of the sink and bath.

In only her thin T-shirt and underwear, Angela peered into the mirror to watch what she was doing to herself. One hand pinched her left cheek just below the eye, and with her right, the nail scissors worked awkwardly, trying to cut through the thickest part of the flesh and then up into the lower eye socket, from which her eyes gazed intently, following the progress. Liz's stomach turned and she let out a low moan. Her legs resisting, their energy gone, she forced herself to shuffle in, fighting the dark specks that threatened at the edge of her own vision. The tiles were cold and drops of blood lay in almost perfect circles for a moment before creeping toward each other. She forced herself to take another long, shaky breath. Passing out now wouldn't be good. It might be blissful, but it wouldn't be good. Not good for anyone. Not good for Angela. More blood ran down Angela's slim, toned legs from the cuts there. Liz's hand cupped her mouth. There were stab wounds in her friend's thighs. They were small and jagged, and thick crimson oozed from the flesh there.

"Angela?" She tried to keep her voice calm. "Angela, what are you doing?"

"Oh, Jesus Christ."

Liz's skin almost tore itself free of her as she jumped, before realizing that Steve was filling the doorway behind her. Angela turned to face them, her eyes empty and confused. The hair on the left side of her face was matted and black with blood, her ear a damaged mess.

"What the fuck is she doing?" Steve breathed, and Liz stepped back slightly so she was resting against his chest, needing to feel him whole and healthy behind her.

Angela half smiled. "There's not enough room. In here." She shook her head, a jerky awkward movement. "We need more room. Got to make more room." Her head twitched again, her eyes drifting. "It will be a vengeful God. It will be. It will be." Her free hand lifted to her lips. "Shhh. This is ours. Our time. Our legacy." Suddenly she stabbed herself in the leg, leaving the scissors there. She didn't even flinch as fresh blood erupted from the toned young thigh. "But we need more room," she hissed, spraying the words angrily. "More room."

She tilted her head, her eyes flicking to the shower curtain. "Stay out. Out!" Her eyes emptied again, the edges of her mouth drooping to slack, her upper body rocking a little backward and forward.

Liz's head moved to where Angela had focused. Behind the plastic sheet that covered the shower, a dark shadow was outlined. Without thinking, Liz shot her arm out and dragged back the curtain. Her mind buzzing with fear, she had no thought of who was on the other side, but nothing could prepare her for what she saw. Time stopped for what seemed like forever as the figure became clear and Liz's brain moved in slow motion. She stared, unable to breathe, one hand still gripped on the plastic curtain, and in that moment she thought that her heart had exploded in her chest, and then Steve, who she'd forgotten was there behind her, living and breathing and normal, broke the moment.

"What the fuck?" He stepped forward, coming beside Liz. "How can that be? How the fuck . . . ?"

Liz stared, her mouth open, not able to answer. Angela, another Angela, was standing in the bath hugging herself and shivering. She glanced around, her eyes trembling and flitting between her mutilated doppelgänger at the sink and Liz.

"What am I doing here? What am I doing? What . . ." her voice was hollow and although Liz could hear her clearly, she had to strain to understand the words, as if their meaning had been sucked away.

"It's so cold and I can barely see. Let me back in. I need to get back in . . . please . . . I'm so cold . . . it's so dark." The words broke down as she started to sob, and it was the humanity in those long, heart-wrenching, snotty moans that prompted Liz to act, her fear suddenly overwhelmed by anger. She didn't know who the woman with the scissors was, but she knew that it was Angela in the bathtub, devastated and crying. She knew it right in the core of her soul, regardless of the implications for her sanity or for reason or for logic.

Letting out an irate screech, she grabbed the damaged woman by the arms. Her face flushed with her rage and so did the pebble in her hand as it pressed against Angela's arm. The world shook, and as Liz's gaze met the eyes in

Angela's body she thought she saw too many shades of brown there, and each of them was filled with hate and anger and she knew right then that whoever was in there wasn't poor Angela.

"Oh, dear God, help me." She whispered. Her palms burned but she held on and the Angela filled with strangeness squealed loudly in her grip. The lights above flickered and hummed and one bulb exploded. Glass tinkered to the ground. There was a rush of air and Liz thought the scream that had been locked inside her had finally burst its way out. Maybe it did and maybe it didn't, because then, after the flurry of madness, there was only still, perfect silence.

The arms she held were cool and trembling. The figure in the bath had gone.

"Oh, fuck, it hurts, Liz, it all hurts. What's happened to my face? Oh, fuck, Liz, what's happening to me . . . ?" Liz felt her heart break with relief and sadness. The voice was Angela. All Angela. Slipping the almost forgotten stone into her robe pocket, Liz was glad the light was blown and Angela couldn't see her wrecked face in the mirror. Her own eyes burned with tears. Her stomach lurched as she held Angela close and led her out of the bathroom, hoping neither of them would tread on any broken glass and knowing that Angela probably wouldn't feel it even if she did. She had too many other cuts screaming for her attention.

"I'll call an ambulance." Steve's voice trembled and their eyes met. Liz knew that he'd seen exactly the same thing she had. There had been two Angelas in the bathroom. Crazy as it sounded, even inside the confines of her own head, she knew that something had pushed Angela out of her body. And both she and Steve had seen it. There could be no denying it. She couldn't put it down to shock or a trick of the mind. It was insane and it was terrifying, but it was real. Angela felt fragile in her arms. Thinking about what had happened could wait until later. Leading her friend gently into the lounge, Liz looked in horror at her cut ear, half of it missing, lost into the basin or onto the bathroom floor.

"I'll get some ice." She lowered Angela onto the couch. "You sit there, honey. You'll be fine. You'll be fine."

Angela barely nodded; her face was so pale it was tinged with green.

By the time the doorbell rang twenty minutes later, Steve and Liz had put as many homemade ice packs on Angela's cuts as they could manage, causing small streams of pink water to trickle down her slight body and onto the carpet and couch below her.

Steve stood up. "They took their time."

Liz held a bag of frozen vegetables wrapped in a drying cloth against her sobbing, trembling friend's torn ear, hating the pain it must have caused her. "It's okay, honey," she murmured. "The ambulance is here now. They'll have you better in no time." She was glad Angela was holding a cloth over her cut face. She didn't want to look at it, and she didn't want to think about seeing her gouging at her cheek with the scissors. And she definitely didn't want to have to think about the two Angelas that were in the bathroom.

"Look who it is." Steve's voice was cold as he led the two men into the lounge.

"Sheriff Russell?" Liz felt her breath catch in her throat. "What are you doing here? We called for an ambulance. She needs medical treatment."

"I was wondering the same thing." Steve moved across the room and Liz could see his open dislike of the sheriff clear on his face. Sheriff Russell just smiled as if he couldn't hear the antagonism in the young man's voice.

"It's quite simple, really. The calls come through to the sheriff's office. Sometimes it's quicker for us to drive the patient up to the hospital at Easter Ridge than to wait for the ambulance to get here and then drive all the way back again."

Liz didn't like his smile or the sound of his voice. His words sounded rehearsed. "Don't you worry," he continued, smoothly. "Doc McGeechan can take care of her. We'll get her to the hospital in no time at all."

The other man, Dr. McGeechan, crouched beside Angela and gently pulled her hand away from her face. "She's going to need stitches. Good work with the ice." He gave Liz a half smile and she stared at him. He looked tired and his eyes were slightly bloodshot. She guessed maybe he'd been dragged out of bed to get here and she felt a little sorry for him.

Giving a weary smile back, her eyes were caught by a glint on his chest. There was a badge there. A small silver one with a tiny snake hanging down from a tree on it. Something about it unsettled her, especially as he must have got dressed in a hurry. Why would he pause to put a silly badge on? Forcing herself to look away from it, she stood and helped Angela to her feet. Her fingers slipped into her pocket and rubbed at the stone there. Her eyes scanned the sheriff's shirt and found an identical badge there. Heart thumping, her hand unconsciously gripped the smooth pebble. She watched as the two men led Angela to the door.

"Maybe we should come with you to the hospital."

Sheriff Russell smiled. "Well, that's a nice thought, Elizabeth, but there's no space in the cruiser."

"I've got a car. We could follow."

Russell's grin tightened and behind it Liz could see a flash of anger. His voice stayed smooth though. "Don't you worry. We'll call you when she's settled. I'll make sure to come and tell you how she's getting on myself. You two young people need to be getting back to bed. She'll be fine."

Angela nodded. "I'll be fine." Her words were slurred. "Really. Go back to bed. I'll be fine. I'd rather be on my own."

"You see?"

Liz's feet itched against the carpet. Her heart thumped. She didn't know what to do. She couldn't exactly stop the doctor and the sheriff from taking Angela away without looking crazy herself.

"We'll call the hospital in the morning. Make sure you're okay," Steve said, and Liz could hear the edge in his voice. He was sending a message to the sheriff as well as registering his concern for Angela.

James Russell stared at him. "You do that. I'm sure she'll be very grateful."

The door shut behind them and silence reigned in the small apartment. Liz stared at the blood and water that was staining the carpet and then thought about the mess in the bathroom. Somewhere in there was part of Angela's left ear. Gravity tugged at her limbs and all she wanted to do was crumple into the floor and lay there forever and sleep.

"I guess we'd better clean up." She sighed.

Steve nodded. "And then I think it's time we faced up to all this weird shit and talked about it. That shit in the bathroom really happened." He stared at Liz. "I know I'm not tripping, and I know I saw two Angela's in there. And so did you. We need to figure out what the fuck is going on here."

Liz felt empty fear growl at her insides. If they talked about it then they were going to have to admit that something bad was happening in Tower Hill and that would shatter the dreams they both had of the place. The stone was warm in her pocket; she could feel the heat against her leg through the fabric of her robe. She must have been gripping it tightly to make it feel that warm. Which was strange because she couldn't remember holding it at all once she'd left the bedroom. But then, in all the madness she was amazed she was still standing up straight.

"Yes. Yes, we do need to talk about it," She finally admitted. "But let's clean up first."

It was only when she got into the bathroom that she began to cry.

The streets of Tower Hill were silent as James Russell brought the police car to a halt outside Dr. John McGeechan's pretty two-story, wood-fronted home. It was three A.M. and even the stray neighborhood cats had found quiet spaces to curl up and pass a couple of dark hours before the excitement of the dawn prowl.

"You get on inside. I'll take her from here." The sheriff's teeth glinted white in the gloom.

John McGeechan nodded and peered behind him to the girl in the back. Angela's eyes had rolled back in her head, the painkillers and sedatives taking her on a trip to God only knew where. The stitches he'd given her at his office stood out ragged and clumsy, but they'd do the job. He hadn't put in stitches since training, and that was a lot of years ago. Normally stitching was taken care of over at the hospital, not in the middle of the night in his office with the sheriff watching. He frowned a little. His brain felt gray and fuzzy, as though maybe there was some smoke in there, clogging up his thinking. The hospital. Maybe they should have taken her to the hospital. He bit into his lower lip. He felt confused. He seemed to feel confused a lot of the time when he tried to think too hard these days.

Russell squeezed his shoulder. "Go on. Your wife'll be waiting up. See? There's a light on."

John looked over at his house and the yellow glow coming from the bedroom and smiled. Angela and the hospital faded like the last touch of a dream. He stepped out of the car and into the damp night. "Night, Sheriff."

Standing on the sidewalk he watched the car leave, enjoying the fresh rain on his skin before turning to go inside. He had his bloody shirt undone before he'd even reached the top step of the porch. Inside, he paused at the bottom of the stairs and pulled off his pants. "I'm home!"

Blood was streaked across his chest; it must have soaked through his shirt when he was stitching the girl. He frowned again, the girl already a distant memory. He'd thought about the hospital. Why had he thought he needed to go to the hospital? He vaguely tried to find the answer to the question, but it was only a halfhearted attempt. It didn't seem to matter so much now that he was home. Back home where he belonged and where all was well.

Delicate feminine laughter trickled out across the top landing, and letting it wash him clean of all thought, he pushed open the bedroom door. Shirley, his wife of fifteen years, and Annette, his receptionist, only a few years older than his marriage and who he hadn't been able to resist several months ago, lay entwined on his double bed. They looked up at him, both smiling, their eyes warm and slightly glazed. Chocolate crumbs were scattered across the sheets.

He smiled. "I hope you left some muffin for me."

Annette leaned forward and cupped Shirley's breast, licking and tugging the nipple between her teeth. Shirley sighed happily. Her eyes met John's. "Why don't you come back to bed and find out?"

The doctor glowed, full of love for his wife and his receptionist and slid under the sheets between them, where he belonged. They were warm and giving and tasted of chocolate, and as he felt their hot limbs embrace him all thoughts of Angela and the hospital were lost into the night.

The sheriff closed the door of the cruiser and stared at the road ahead. It seemed to stretch on forever into the darkness. Maybe it was the Midnight Road, a small voice in his head mused. The primrose path to hell. His eyes struggled to focus. He felt tired. It had been a long night and he was ready for it to be over. The wine the priest had given him was warm in his stomach and he glanced back at the house for a second before starting the car. It seemed right that he'd taken the girl to O'Brien. He couldn't remember exactly when the idea had come to him, but then neither could he remember patching all emergency calls dialed in the town through to his cell phone. When did he learn to do that?

He yawned, enjoying the gentle throb of the engine vibrating through his seat. It matched the burn of the wine as it raced through his veins to pump into his heart. He guessed maybe all these thoughts didn't really matter.

Father O'Brien had been pleased that he'd taken the girl there. He'd said as much. He's said it was church business. Sheriff Russell yawned. His eyes felt heavy and his sinuses ached. It seemed like most town business was church business these days. He wondered if maybe that wasn't entirely as it should be, but for the life of him he couldn't think why. He pulled away from the curb, letting the car roll forward. Mabel. Mabel would know. Mabel would be able to help him. She was a clever woman, his Mabel.

But by the time he crawled into his Mabel's arms fifteen minutes later, eyes itching and soul exhausted, his questions didn't seem so important.

Everything was under control.

Just as it should be.

Amen.

CHAPTER TWENTY-SEVEN

Al Shtenko's arms were more tired than if he'd been trying to hold the whole earth up and away from hell, he decided as he daubed paint from the big tub by his feet onto the side of the old church. In fact, just about all of his body was aching with a fiery intensity that he hadn't felt in a long, long time. Still, it wasn't such a bad feeling. It was a feeling with *purpose*. Occasionally he pulled a plastic bottle of holy water from his backpack and tipped a little more into the red goop before stirring it in with the stick. He didn't want to make the paint too runny but at the same time the words had to be powerful. More powerful than if they were just his.

His back screamed a little as he loaded up the big brush and started on the final three letters of the phrase on which he'd decided. It was enough without being too much. There had to be a certain amount of free will; that's what he figured. LEAD US NOT INTO TEMPTAT loomed large above him and he was pleased. He knew that it was good. He stretched a little and sighed.

At least today, even at this time of the morning, the sun was shining and carried a little warmth. It seemed that rain had fallen forever over the past week or so. It had certainly felt that way as he'd walked the miles from one nearby small town to the next, collecting a bottle of holy water here and a bottle of holy water there, until eventually he'd started his long journey back. By then his beard had grown and he had blisters bleeding and getting infected in his worn shoes, but he'd kept smiling. A face could be shaved and he had bandages at home for his toes and heels. And he'd had the genie in his pocket for most of the way, singing songs to keep his feet marching one in front of the other.

He'd been invisible as he'd walked along the edge of the coast road, no cars slowing to stop for him. He didn't expect them to. He looked like a filthy hobo or a tramp and despite his smile and clear expression most folks had forgotten how much appearances could be deceptive in this modern world. Hollywood had reduced us all to children. If it looks good it must be good; if it looks different, then it must be bad.

The genie had talked about that a little on the way out of Angel Ridge. The Good Samaritans had died out. People had forgotten about people. They only cared about *things*. Al had asked the genie at that point if she was a Marxist. She'd laughed out loud at that and then he'd been laughing too, and then he really couldn't blame people for not stopping to offer him a ride; a crazy, dirty hobo, carrying a backpack full of water bottles and laughing out loud to himself right there in the middle of the road.

Still, he was back in Tower Hill now and his cuts were all cleaned up and he'd slept like a log for fifteen hours without so much as a glimmer of a dream. He figured the genie must have been exhausted too, because she hadn't been around since he'd collapsed in his bed in the middle of the afternoon the previous day.

Despite the pain in his shoulders and down the backs of his legs every time he stooped, he whistled quietly as he worked. He thought the genie and the Good Lord would approve. A small line of red dribbled down from the M farther back along the wall. Maybe he'd added too much holy water. Could there be such a thing? He smiled gently.

No such thing as too much whiskey. That's what he used to say over at Joe's Moonshine bar and grill when they'd stop serving him, suggesting that maybe he'd had enough. *No such thing as too much whiskey.* He took a deep breath of the early morning air. He had a new buzz now. Maybe holy water was his new spirit of choice.

He looked down at the bag. He brought plenty. Maybe he'd just rest up for a moment and take a sip for himself. He smiled again and leaned against the wall to enjoy the Lord's blessed sunshine. Just for a moment.

Louis Eccles shut the front door behind him and was pleased it didn't slam. He'd maintained his self-control but goddamn it had been hard. Yawning slightly, he was glad the sun was shining because he sure as hell needed something to brighten his day. It was only half-past six in the morning and he wasn't due at the station for another two hours but he needed some space to cool off. His long legs stretched out under him, putting some distance between him and the house.

What the hell had gotten into Emma? Talking to her these days had become like talking to a stranger. What was it with this God squad obsession she'd developed? It seemed that all her time was spent either at church or at some coffee morning or sleeping. And now she wanted to take Jacob along with her to those long meetings, and the nursery was encouraging it. What kind of craziness was that? Their little boy needed to be playing and learning, not sitting still and praying with a bunch of grown-ups.

He'd tried to tell her but she sure as hell wasn't listening to what he had to say anymore; she either just stared at him vacantly until he shut up, or told him wearily that he didn't understand. Well, she sure wasn't explaining anything to him, so what did she expect? No one else in the family

wanted to talk to him either. It seemed to him that half the
town had gone a little bit mad since that girl died, but he'd
never expected Emma to behave so strangely. She'd always
been so down to earth. That's why he'd fallen in love with
her. All that beauty and charm would normally have made
a girl shallow and selfish, but Emma had recognized it for
what it was. Just a stroke of luck. To him, though, luck had
nothing to do with it. She'd always been an angel.

The fresh air was good for his lungs, and he figured if he
walked far and fast enough, he might be able to fight the
urge to find a pack of cigarettes and smoke them all, one
after the other. He'd quit when they'd found out Emma was
pregnant with Jacob, and he hadn't had a single smoke
since that day. Overall he was pretty pleased about that and
felt better for it, but today he couldn't help thinking that a
cigarette or two would do wonders to ease his mood.

He'd be happier if he could talk to the sheriff about it.
James Russell had been his mentor since he'd first pulled
on his uniform, and in the six years they'd worked together
they'd never had one serious disagreement. In fact, until
this business with the Keenan girl, Louis had never thought
to question anything the sheriff did. James Russell was sharp
and fair and even-tempered. You couldn't ask for more in a
police officer. And more than that, he was by the book,
right down the line. Well, he had been until now.

The wind teased his neck above the collar, tickling his
skin with its cold breath, but Lou barely felt it. What had
Russell been thinking, letting Doc McGeechan examine
the body instead of the county coroner? It was madness,
and he'd implied as much when he'd typed up his report
and left it on the sheriff's desk. Lou had stored a copy of
the report locked in his desk and on his computer at home.
He still felt uncomfortable that he hadn't bitten the bullet
and gone to the county about it, but it was too late to worry
now. The girl was burned and buried, God rest her. Not that
he believed much in any kind of God. There was trying to

be good and kind and that was about as close to a religion as he could believe. That and leaving your genes behind to live on for you.

He thought of Jacob and a shadow passed across his face as he strode deeper into the town. His little boy hadn't seemed as playful recently, and when Lou had got home the previous day the little boy had been sitting in his sand-box, just staring at his red bucket as if he didn't know what he was supposed to be doing with it. Maybe he was picking up on the bad atmosphere between his mom and dad. Lou hoped not. And he hoped the bad atmosphere didn't last. He hated it. He hated how it made his heart feel kind of sick and scared.

The breeze picked up speed, dancing around him, forcing him to notice it, and finally Lou allowed himself to enjoy its fresh touch. It wasn't as good as a smoke but it was a close second. He glanced up and instantly frowned. What the hell? Someone had vandalized the church.

Breaking into a trot, he covered the hundred yards or so in a few easy seconds until he came to a halt at the bottom of the stone stairs. He peered up at the wall on his right that ran to the back of the old church. LEAD US NOT INTO TEMP-TATION was painted haphazardly across it, the final letters tilting upward, just like Jacob's heartwarming attempts at writing his own name did. Lou pulled off his hat and ran a hand through his hair. What in hell? Who would graffiti a church? And with something like that?

A shadow cut across his vision and he turned to see Al Shtenko taking a seat on the gray stone front steps, tilting the bucket of paint at his feet and sighing before taking a long sip from a bottle and tilting his face backward into the sunlight.

"Did you do this, Al?" Louis tried to keep the disgust out of his voice. He pitied Al Shtenko, that much was for sure, but pity wasn't a great way to feel about a man a decade

older than you. He looked at the bottle. It had to be vodka
or rum. "Are you drinking?"

Al Shtenko opened his eyes and smiled. "Certainly am."
He held the bottle out. "God's own water. Try some."

Lou took the bottle and sniffed at its opening. It didn't
smell like liquor but then some clear spirits were pretty
clean. Wiping the rim, he let a small amount run into his
mouth. It was clean and sweet and cool. He stared at the
man on the steps again, but this time with fresh eyes. Al
looked thin, admittedly, but for the first time in a long time,
he looked scrubbed and shaven and his eyes weren't
clouded and angry. Lou looked back up at the wall.

"What in hell did you do that for, Al, if you ain't drinking?"

Shtenko laughed gently and let out a long breath. "I'm
not much of a muffin man. I've never really had a tooth for
sweet things, even back when . . . when I was married." He
looked up at Lou, his eyes crinkling against the sunlight.
"Are you a muffin man, Deputy?"

Lou shook his head. Maybe the poor man had finally
cracked, gone mad from all that cheap poisonous booze
wrecking his insides. He needed to keep him talking. Keep
him calm. That's what they'd said in training, and it wasn't
as if Shtenko seemed dangerous, just a little tragic.

"No, I'm not a muffin man either, Al. I'm diabetic. Have
been since I was a child. That shit will kill me."

Al looked back at the sun. "I thought as much." He nodded a little as if somewhere inside his head it was all making perfect sense. "You want to be careful with people
trying to feed you stuff. Things aren't what they seem." He
stood up and stretched, his knees letting out a loud click as
they straightened. "The genie, she told me to be careful of
the muffins, but I figure they'll try and get you a different
way. So just you stay alert."

Lou stared at him and wondered how a man could say

such crazy things but sound and look saner and calmer than he had in years. The mind was a funny thing.

"Sure, Al. I'll stay alert." He sighed and looked back up at the wall. He had a couple hours before he was due at the station and now it seemed as if he had something to do to fill them. "Why don't I take you home, Al? If I get this cleaned off in the next hour or so, then I don't see the need to charge you." He paused. "But just don't do something like this again, okay?" Maybe he was a little crazy to let the man go without a charge, but there was something gentle about Al Shtenko, and if he'd gone a little nuts, then a charge wasn't going to make any difference. He gritted his teeth. And if it was all right for the sheriff to bend the rules when he felt like it, then there was no reason the deputy couldn't as well.

Al was still smiling serenely, and he pulled two small water bottles from his backpack before picking up his paint bucket and brushes. "Here. Let's drink while we walk. We all need a little pure water running in our veins sometimes. Helps us see clearer, don't you think?"

Lou took the bottle and unscrewed the lid and smiled before taking a long sip, relishing the sweetness. "Let's hope it does, Al." He muttered, thinking of Emma and Georgia Keenan and the changes in the sheriff. "Amen to that."

Al's smile broke into a grin. "Amen to that, Deputy. Exactly right."

"This one's giving out a dead tone too." Looking into Liz's expectant face, Steve put the handset back in the cradle and cursed quietly under his breath.

"Maybe all the rain's taken a phone line down somewhere."

"Yeah, right. That would be convenient. The main phone lines and my cell phone not working?" He stared around at the silent buildings. It may have been only seven thirty in the morning but he'd expected to see some kind of movement in the halls and buildings around him. Early-morning joggers at least. It seemed that Liz and he were the only people awake on campus though.

No one in the apartment below had answered when he'd knocked to see if they had a cell he could try. But then Mona and Dan had both found themselves a partner in one of the halls so were rarely home anymore, and Eric, nice as he was, was a bit of a dopehead metal freak from what Steve could make out, more into staying up late than getting up early, so getting no answer had been no real surprise. He looked up at the sunshine. For once, the clear blue sky wasn't making him feel any better. There was something amiss in Tower Hill and good weather wasn't going to change that.

"Maybe we should go into town." Liz said. "There must be a phone booth on Main Street."

"Good idea." He looked into her blue eyes and smiled, his heart clenching. There was something special about her all right. She was strong and she was good. And she was good for him. Whatever was going on in this town, he wouldn't let it hurt her. The strength of that thought rocked him a little. People often said it, but he knew that in this case it was true. He'd die before he let someone hurt her, and he couldn't help but wonder how that had come to be.

"Come on then." She walked alongside him, her blond hair loose around her shoulders, and her hand slipped easily into his. He squeezed it and she looked up at him and smiled. He smiled back, a little in awe of her bright eyes and clear skin. How the hell did she manage to look so fresh after the night they'd had?

After cleaning up the apartment, both of them silently tackling the mess of the bathroom, Liz sweeping the glass from the floor and Steve grimly cleaning the basin and tiles, the two students had sat together sipping fresh coffee and feeling like their home was suddenly too large without its third resident. Steve had shut Angela's bedroom door, neither he nor Liz needing to see the residue of her normal life scattered around, so at odds with the damaged, mutilated and fragile creature they'd found in the bathroom.

It was only when they'd refilled their mugs that they'd finally started to talk, at first about the impossibility of the two Angelas and then about the changes in Mabel and the people at Steve's work and at the college. They'd gone around in circles wondering if maybe it was them that were going a little cuckoo and the rest of the town was sane. One thing was sure though: by the end of their conversation they both wished they'd gone with Angela to the hospital. Neither of them trusted the sheriff. Liz had remembered him as being different when she'd first met him, just as she still had plenty of good to say about Mabel, but Steve couldn't find any redeeming features in either of them.

By the time Steve's eyes were burning with exhaustion and he was starting to feel a little trippy on caffeine and shock, Liz had whispered quietly that maybe the town had always been odd and it was just that they'd seen it through rose-tinted glasses. Steve had shaken his head, and could see that Liz didn't really believe it either. Something had changed. They could both feel it.

Eventually, as the clock rolled around to four A.M. they resolved to call the hospital first thing and then drive up to check on Angela. They'd stood in their separate doorways for a moment or two, neither relishing the prospect of lying alone in the darkness, and in the end they'd agreed to both sleep in his room, on his double bed.

He kept his jeans on and Liz kept her robe pulled tight, and although nothing happened that would be expected of two hot-blooded students sharing a bed, *something* happened. Maybe something better than that.

He woke up at dawn with her curled up behind him, one arm wrapped over him, her hand across his chest. Despite a cramp settling in his right calf he hadn't wanted to move.

He'd never felt so close to a woman before, and he had been a hell of a lot more intimate with several.

Seagulls whirled across the surface of the ocean as they darted and dipped into the waves, seeking out small fish before snatching them away into the air with a yelp of victory. Steve watched them as they walked. It was better than looking at the quiet town creeping up around them.

"How would someone go about stopping the phones and Internet from working?" Liz asked.

"I don't know. What worries me more is why anyone would want to." He thought of the sheriff leading Angela away and the way Mike and Amy at work had behaved when Mabel had come in with her muffins. There had to be a reason for they way they'd all changed and become so goddamned freaky, but what was it? What was causing all this shit?

As the road curved slightly ahead of them, the church appeared, and it felt to Steve as if Liz pulled in closer to him. He glanced down. Her face had clouded over. She'd told him last night about the strange trances among the church congregation and the almost threatening behavior of the priest. He didn't know what to make of it, but after the two Angelas situation in the bathroom he knew better than to question it. He stared at the gray, forbidding walls that reminded him of the stone of the university, and then frowned.

"Isn't that a police car parked up outside the church?"

Liz looked up, following his gaze. "You think something else has happened?"

"Let's find out."

They picked up the pace and as they approached the front of the building; the wind carried a whistle on it. Following the sound, Steve peered around to the far wall. A slim young man in a police uniform scrubbed at the wall with a broom, every now and then dipping it into a bucket of soapy water beside him. Red smeared down the wall where he'd done his best to wash the writing away. The final two words, INTO TEMPTATION, stared down at them. Steve looked down at Liz and she shrugged a little. Just one more strange occurrence in what had become a very strange little town.

"Hey, Deputy. Sir?" Steve wasn't quite sure what was the best way to speak to a police officer. He'd spent most of his time in Detroit avoiding them.

The man almost jumped out of his skin before turning to face them. "Jesus. You scared the crap out of me." He grinned a little. "I was a little lost in my own thoughts there."

Steve watched him as he put the broom down and stretched a little. He seemed normal enough. Or at least so far he didn't seem to exhibit any of the sheriff's antagonism. He scanned the front of the man's uniform for the little badge Liz had seen on the doctor and James Russell the previous night and couldn't see one. That had to be a good sign. He nodded up at the wall. "Who did that?"

"Oh, just a local with a few problems. He's harmless enough. I don't know what's in that paint though. It's proving hell to get off."

Steve felt Liz's elbow in his ribs. The deputy's sharp eyes didn't miss it either and his friendly smile faltered a little. "You two okay? You're out early for students."

"Well, we've been trying to make a phone call to the hospital to check on a friend of ours, but it seems like the phone lines are down. Do you know anything about it, Deputy . . . ?"

"Eccles. Louis Eccles." The deputy took Steve's hand and shook it. "And sorry, no, I haven't heard a thing about the phones. But then it is still early. Have you got a cell you could use?"

Steve shook his head. "That's down too."

"So's the 'Net." Liz added.

"That's strange." The deputy pulled a small cell out of a holder on his uniform belt and tried it for a moment before flipping it shut. "Mine's down too. Not that it's a surprise. Cell coverage has never been that strong out here."

"Well maybe you know how our friend is getting along—Angela Kelly?" Liz asked. "The sheriff took her to the hospital last night."

Eccles frowned, his hands on his hips. "No, I wasn't working last night. How come the sheriff took her?"

Watching the confusion on the other man's face, Steve's concern for Angela grew. "It was about one A.M. and I called an ambulance."

The deputy poured the bucket of red and dirty water carefully into the drain at the side of the church. Steve's stomach flipped as memories of the previous night's bathroom basin, sticky with Angela's blood, flooded back. He swallowed them down as the deputy faced them. "So how come Sheriff Russell came out to you? Was there a crime involved?"

Steve shook his head. "No, we dialed for an ambulance but the sheriff came with a doctor. He said that often happened."

"Yes, he said that all nine-one-one calls were patched through to him because it was quicker that way." Steve could hear his own uncertainty echoed in Liz's. "That's right, isn't it?"

The deputy took the broom and bucket over to the cruiser and popped the trunk to pack them away. He seemed pretty calm, but his face was clouded. "I guess it must be."

Steve didn't think he looked too convinced. "Are you sure?"

Eccles turned and smiled. "Sure. Look, I'm due on duty in ten minutes or so, so why don't you give me your address and then I'll speak to the sheriff and get back to you? How about that?"

Liz nodded. "I guess we could drive up to the hospital in the meantime."

"Yeah, maybe. But if your friend was taken in late, she'll probably be resting. And the phones should be back on soon enough. Leave it with me for now, okay?" He stared at them. "In fact, you both look like you could use another couple hours of sleep yourselves."

"Yeah, you're probably right." Steve nodded, his eyes still searching the man's face, but it was too hard to read. If they'd raised any concerns in the man about his boss, then he wasn't showing them externally. "Maybe that's what we'll do. Thanks, Deputy Eccles"

"No problem. I hope your friend's okay. I'm sure she will be."

"Thanks."

Liz squeezed Steve's hand and they waved as the deputy got in his car and drove off.

"He seemed like a good man," Steve said, watching the car turn away and disappear.

"Yes, he does," Liz murmured. "Do you think we should wait like he says?"

Steve stayed silent for a moment and then put his arm around her shoulder. "Not a chance. I think we should get up to that hospital."

"I'm so glad you said that." Liz grinned up at him, and then reached up on her tiptoes to plant a soft kiss on his cheek. "Come on. Before the rest of this mad town wakes up."

CHAPTER TWENTY-EIGHT

The town as everyone knew it was gone, at least for a while. Balance of some kind would eventually be restored because that was the way of the gods of nature, but until then Tower Hill was in limbo. Or purgatory. Or perhaps just a period of change, and underneath the buildings and roads, the cliffs and rock would still be there regardless of what the man masquerading as the priest did or did not do.

A few people still moved about normally, bemused by the quiet sleepiness that echoed through the streets. Most put it down to an early outbreak of the flu—because heaven knows there were some nasty bouts of that last year—and they paid the vague-looking blonde in Hannaford's and pointed out to her that some of the fruit in aisle one looked as if it may be getting a little overripe. Her only answer to all comers was to smile and chew a little louder on the pink wad of gum that her teeth slowly moved over as if she'd almost forgotten it was there.

The apples stayed rotten.

Out back in the storeroom Mike stared at his comic book. His brow furrowed but he found the pictures hard to read. He couldn't remember which order to follow them. Was it up or down or left to right? Or right to left? He tried them all. In the end it was easier to just let the colors wash over him. It soothed him. Occasionally he turned a page. But only very occasionally. It was too much effort. Still, the colors were nice.

Outside the streets of the town were empty, as if the bloodless veins of a corpse. No life moved through them, only the wind rushing across their hard surfaces. Most folks stayed home and slept. Some called their offices and left confused messages to say that they wouldn't be in, but only a few were listened to, and then quickly forgotten.

Here or there a worker was found at his desk in a bank or public office because he had a feeling that someone had to make it look as if the town were functioning properly, even though he was not sure that it wasn't. It was just that the sky was too heavy above them all for anyone to think properly. They just did as they'd been told. It was easier that way. That way made sense.

Up at Tower Hill University, most of the lectures were canceled. Sloppily scrawled signs hung on doors and a big blackboard in the main hallways declared there was a problem with the electricity that could be a safety hazard. There was no time line for a return to normalcy. Not a lot of young people turned up to find out, and only a few of them cared enough to try to find a janitor or professor to question. Those who did found none, eventually taking themselves back to their dorms to peer out the windows, a little afraid and unsure before they finally laughed it off. Everything would be back to normal soon enough. Of course it would. This was Tower Hill. Nothing terrible happened here.

In the busy emergency ward at the county hospital in Easter Ridge, a young couple stared in disbelief as the overworked receptionist rechecked her computer records and shook her head. They stood at the counter for a moment longer until she ushered them along to clear a space.

Leaving the building, they stood outside, silently staring at the ambulance that should have come to take their friend away in the night.

They didn't see the senior nurse questioning the young receptionist and then staring after them, chewing her lip. Finally, she went into the nurse's station and quietly dialed one of the few numbers in her hometown of Tower Hill that was working. Her small badge glinted in the beam of the fluorescent lights above.

In his small, wood-fronted house, out in what would be the suburbs if Tower Hill was big enough to have them, Deputy Eccles didn't understand what was happening in his world. His conversation with the students was forgotten. An hour and a lifetime had passed since then. Quiet, sleepy words had been spoken when he'd come home to shower and change after cleaning up the church, and now everything was wrong.

His fingers felt numb as he packed his suitcase and his brain couldn't comprehend why she was making him do this and he didn't know quite how many shirts and pants to take and didn't know why he even cared. Shirts and pants were replaceable. A marriage wasn't. And she'd told him he could "come back later for the rest of his stuff," and that sounded way too final for him to want to deal with.

His legs shook and he felt sick. Taking the framed photo from the side table, he stared at it. It was taken two months ago at most. Emma and him on the beach, with little Jacob sitting high on his shoulders and just squealing with delight. They were all laughing and full of energy. It oozed out of the picture at him as if the paper could't contain it.

His eyes filled a little and he sat on the edge of the bed for a moment, his shoulders slumped. He couldn't believe that she'd kicked him out just like that, and for nothing. She hadn't even stayed while he was packing. Her mother was downstairs, quietly waiting for him to leave. Emma hadn't said where she and Jacob were going. They could be hiding somewhere in the yard for all he knew, listening out for the sound of his cruiser heading away from their home. He wished he could hate her. That would maybe make this easier. And he wished he wasn't so confused.

He put the picture into his small suitcase and shut the lid. He couldn't stay any longer. It was breaking his heart. Anything he didn't have, he could get at the store. Coming down the stairs, his legs were heavy and trembling, like he'd run ten miles at full sprint, and not looking at the woman sitting at his kitchen table he tried to keep his back straight as he walked out the door. The sun was still shining but he wished for rain. He wished the rain would come and wash all this shit away.

He sat in the car for a minute, waiting for his eyes to dry and his heart to stop racing. Eventually it did. The day was too bright, every line and color sharp in his head. He thought about going to James Russell's place. It would have been his natural choice a month ago, but then this wouldn't have happened a month ago. He still considered it for a second and then changed his mind and started driving to May's Bed-and-Breakfast.

When she opened the door and smiled, he got the strangest feeling that she was expecting him.

Liz and Steve drove back to Tower Hill. They didn't know where else to go. The senior nurse had come out after them, all smiles and apologies and flashing bits of paperwork at them. She'd said that the girl they were looking for had discharged herself and gone home, back to her folks. The nurse's smile had stretched. She'd surely be back to college for her things when she was feeling better. Cuts like those looked worse than they were but would still take a while to heal.

The pair had nodded, but Liz had seen her pin and so had Steve, and for a while they had stayed sitting on the bench before they'd seen her watching them from a ground-floor window. They smiled and waved and hoped their expressions looked more convincing than they felt. Eventually they'd got back into her beaten-up old car and sat in silence as the anonymous buildings passed by. They didn't need to say what they were both thinking. If Angela had never got to the hospital, then she'd probably never left the town. It was a black and terrifying thought as they drove the miles back to Tower Hill.

They sat quietly in their apartment on campus, and despite thinking they would probably never sleep again, both fell into a fitful doze for an hour or so. After a while, Steve got up and made them sandwiches, but neither of them ate. The hours ticked by and as dusk began to fall they started to talk, their voices low and earnest as they planned. Liz's hand drifted to her pocket and she rubbed the stone there. It made her feel strong in the face of her fear.

In the old house by the church, a man moved in the dark bowels of the building. The cellar was lit by only a small lamp, the bulb buzzing constantly as if it might fizzle out at any moment. From the doorway Jack looked over at the girl on the mattress and put down the bowl of soup before crossing the room to turn off the soft music and blow out the heavily scented candle. The smoke burned his eyes a little. He turned back.

The girl's hands were tied but it probably wasn't necessary. She was gone. He watched the slight flickering and twitching of her pupils. Maybe the very last bit of her was clinging on, but that was fine. That was pretty perfect. She should be holding on. He thought that they probably had about another twenty-four hours to go until they were all ready. He needed her to hang on until then.

It was funny to think that he had only twenty-four hours or so left of this existence. He wondered if perhaps he should make himself a final supper, and he smiled. If he did it wouldn't be soup, that was for sure. He spoon-fed the girl, careful not to spill any on himself. The liquid was cold but he figured it was probably better that way, given her cuts and the bad stitching. Burns wouldn't help. She barely swallowed; her throat worked but clumsily, as if she'd somehow forgotten how to undergo a natural reflex, but some of the soup must have got down.

He wiped some carefully from the side of her face where it had dribbled from the corner of her slack mouth, and whispered softly to her while he did so, as if she were a child. He was fond of her in a strange way. She was useful to him. In that way he hadn't changed. He still recognized the thing that he needed to progress him. If it wasn't for her and those like her, then he and Gray would have been pissing in the wind out here, however many boxes and candles and bottles of blood they had. This girl was doing him a service and he'd respect her for that.

He stroked a hand down her face, curious to feel the rough stitching. She didn't flinch and he was glad. He'd never been like Gray. Yes, he was a killer, and he didn't mind it; that much was for sure. In fact, he'd proven himself pretty good at it over the years. But he'd never killed for pleasure. Not like Gray, with his thing for the girls. For Jack, killing was just part of what he did and he didn't feel one way or the other about it. It was just something that was sometimes needed to get him where he wanted to be. People were expendable; it was only the human ego that screamed in indignant denial of that. If there was one thing that was true of this earth, it was that there were too many people on it, and if he happened to kill a few, well, it was very rarely noticed for long. But he never got a kick out of it. Sometimes he wished he did. Sometimes he wished he got a kick out of some goddamn thing. Maybe that would all change tomorrow.

Bored, he allowed her a few more slow swallows before standing up and leaving her alone with just the yellow glow of the small lamp. Her eyes didn't move from whatever they were staring at on the ceiling. Maybe it wasn't such a bad thing that she was so far gone. All those cuts would have to hurt.

He locked the cellar door, whistling lightly. He was surprised to find the tune was "O Come All Ye Faithful," and he laughed a little out loud. The faithful were pretty much ready and the others would be joining them soon. He headed back to the office, closed the door behind him and enjoyed the peace. How strange that he now felt so comfortable in a study—a place of quiet. His life had always been so active, so rooted in the physical. But he was changing and changing fast.

The ancient box was open on the old desk and two large apples shone there. He took the closest and bit greedily into it, feeling a shiver run all the way through his insides. Maybe he'd been wrong downstairs. Maybe he did get a kick out of something. He definitely got a thrill out of these apples. They'd become like a drug to him, these fruits of an ancient tree.

Sitting back, he opened the journal he'd been working on for most of the day. The idea had come to him the night before when he'd woken sweaty and shaken in a rare moment of fear at the changes that were coming. *He* was all he'd known and now he would be changed forever. He and Gray would live forever, but not as they were. And he was worried that they may forget who they had been, how they had started and just how remarkable they had been when they had been mere mortals. They needed their story written down and recorded for posterity.

He turned through the pages filled with his tiny, neat hand, the size of each letter never wavering, each equally small in blue ink, filling the lines from edge to edge. Chewing faster, he reached for his pen and continued on the line he'd left off on. There were three hours before the next service and the writing was pretty much all there was left to do. He smiled, barely ripping the last mouthful of flesh from the first apple before reaching for the second.

The pen scratched on the surface and the words flowed. It was his testament.

The New Testament.

CHAPTER TWENTY-NINE

When Gray Kenyon opened his eyes he was knew he was lucid dreaming. It was the only kind of dreaming that he ever did. If and when he slept, it was either out cold like the dead for an hour or so or playtime in the land of the lucid dreamer. This time, however, two things surprised him.

The first was that he was asleep at all. And that was a pretty big one. He was sure as shit that he'd been in MH3, bored out of his mind watching the kids as they meditated. If you could call what they did meditation anymore. You surely had to be conscious to start with in order to drift out of consciousness. He'd started calling the kids his zombie army. His troops from the Land of the Living Dead, like out of that old Romero movie. Even Jack had laughed at that. Serious Jack. Gray wondered if he'd get a sense of humor after the changing. Probably not. But hey, Gray had enough sense of humor for both of them.

He took in the view. He was back in the Afghan desert. That wasn't the second surprise. He'd have preferred to have been cutting up a girl or two if he was going to have a bit of action in his sleep, but given the unfolding events it was no shock that he'd woken up here.

No, the second surprise was the angle of the view. His face was half in the sand, as if he were submerged in the

ocean, peering eyes and nose above the waterline. The
desert and barren mountains stretched out ahead for miles,
seemingly forever under the hot sun. A dry wind beat across
his back and it felt good as he surveyed the terrain. It was
hard to tell if it was familiar from so low to the ground.
What the hell was he doing on his belly anyway? Was there
a sniper somewhere in the vicinity? He listened for shots.
There was nothing apart from the shifting of the sand
whispering around him. So no sniper. Which kind of made
the dream a little less interesting. No girls, no guns. Not a
lot in it for him.

He smiled and laughed. The sound came out as a hiss.
He felt the buzz in his skin. Somewhere behind him a cow-
bell tinkled and he tried to pull himself to his feet to turn
and see the action, but his legs didn't seem to want to oblige.
Instead, he twisted a little, his body shimmying against the
hot earth, the movement and energy coming from his tail
and forcing the rest of his body to slither forward.

His tail.

Well, holy shit, he had a tail. He flicked it and hissed, his
body gliding around with more control until just above the
line of sand he could see the tents set up at the entrance
to the caves. He paused. Now this looked familiar. Inside
he could feel the coolness at his core where the morning
desert sun hadn't yet warmed his cold blood. He wondered
if he'd ever dreamed of being a serpent, or in fact of being
anything other than himself, before. He couldn't think of a
time. It should be freaking weird, he figured as he carved
his way in an S toward the tents, but it wasn't. It felt pretty
damn good. Maybe this dream wasn't going to be as dull as
it first seemed.

The sand parted like water for him and he slithered up
past the cows and thin goats of the wandering tribes and up
to the entrance of the caves, hugging the cool walls and
their uneven edges, reluctant to leave the heat of the sun

behind, but curious to find out which part of his life his mind was exploring.

He tingled with recognition as he pushed forward. He could change the dream if he wanted, he knew he had that in his power, but for now he was content for it to take him where it wanted. It was his dream. He figured his mind wanted him to be here for some reason and who was he to argue with himself?

Ahead he could see himself and Jack, and when he realized the precise point in his history that he was visiting, he would have smiled if he was able. Instead, his tongue darted out and flicked this way and that. They were dressed in the uniforms and dog tags of U.S. soldiers that they'd requisitioned after making sure their original owners had no more use for them. That had been easy enough. There were plenty of soldiers around who were eager to see a Western face and relax around them.

The war on terror had been good to them. Everyone in the world was focused on it, even full two years after 9/11. But not him and Jack. After all, they *were* terror. A different, more personal kind, maybe, but terror all the same. Watching, his cold heart swelled with pride. They'd come into Afghanistan through Iran rather than the Khyber Pass, and traveling had been easier than expected. They began as journalists and then ditched that disguise when they got close enough to the gem mines, instead adopting native dress with a couple of handguns and an M-16 or two disguised in their flowing robes.

Shit, they had been good at robbing those mines while the land around them battled and blew up and made a killing field out of the barren desert. He and Jack had never lost their focus, even though it had almost all ended for good when Jack had stumbled and fallen through a shaft deep into the earth below. It had taken some doing and two nights and a day to get him out of there.

Watching the Jack from the past hunkered down over the small campfire and sipping tea with the Arab, Gray could see the shape of the bandage under his shirt that covered the large gash he'd sustained as his arm had ripped on the way down. He'd had a pretty bruised and swollen ankle if Gray remembered properly. Not that Jack would have showed it. Gray sometimes thought that Jack liked pain. It was something he could *feel*. Jack was the only person Gray knew who was maybe more fucked up than he was. And that was why he loved him.

He hissed in the sand, settling his strange body down and watching his past with a kind of awe. If Jack hadn't fallen through the shaft, then none of this would have happened. None of the changing would be happening. It had only been while Gray had been hauling his ass out of that deep, time-forgotten, foul-smelling pit that Jack had found the chest wedged into the small natural alcove in the wall of the earth, calling up to Gray to hang on, to hold it, while he worked it out of the rock. And Gray had hung on, his arms straining on the rope and threatening to pop out of his sockets, knowing that if he let go, Jack might not be so lucky with a second fall.

But of course Jack had got the box, and Gray had pulled him up, because they weren't like other people and they didn't quit and they didn't die by falling into mine shafts, and as they'd sat there sweating on the floor of the mine they'd so recently raped of low-grade emeralds, they'd laughed and stared and known they'd found something valuable.

They'd never dealt in antiquities before, but hell, Jack had said, there was always a first time.

But then they'd got the box open and discovered the scrolls. And life changed.

"It's a legend, nothing more." The Arab had spoken in low, guttural tones, and watching him from his place in the sand, Gray remembered how he'd smelled of sweet exotic oils, as if he sweated them out from his chubby brown skin. "You should pay no heed to it. Leave it alone."

"If it's just a legend, then how come you sound so freaked out by it?" The Gray of the past lit a cigarette and the dreaming serpent Gray slithered closer to grab some of the secondhand smoke. Seemed like man or snake, he was never going to kick the habit.

The Arab was twitchy. "It suggests here that the impossible may be true. That your Western Bible may not all be—what do you say?—metaphor."

He scanned further through the old parchments. "This garden of Eden was perhaps in the Arab lands somewhere. I don't recognize the place names that it suggests may have surrounded it. But that is not the important part." He turned to a second scroll and sipped his tea before speaking. "The tree of knowledge? The tree of life? Part of it still exists. It cannot die and its last branch is kept safe. Hidden somewhere where man can never again try to take its power for themselves."

Gray watched himself laugh. "I never got that whole tree thing. Why put it there? Stick temptation right in front of people like that? What was God, dumb?"

"I think the temptation was the whole point."

"Yeah, I got that Jack. I'm just saying that he wasn't much of a pragmatist. I still can't believe that Adam, waiting until the chick went first." He laughed again, but Jack's face was serious.

"So, you're saying that whoever finds this tree can share in eternal life? Be like God?"

The man shook his head, his jowls wobbling. "It doesn't seem clear. There is something here about blood. Original blood." He looks up. "The first blood. But alive."

He studied the old scripts, muttering and moving backward and forward between the sheets, unrolled and cracked on the earth below him. "The tree . . . it has some link with the first blood. Those who took the first bite. Only they can truly unlock its power." He sighed a little, his brow furrowed. Gray looked at Jack and shrugged. The serpent Gray slithered forward until the warmth of the small fire touched his scales. That was better. He'd never liked the cold, and this chilled blood was taking some getting used to.

Even from his position on the ground he could see the wonder in the Arab's face as he told the second story in the scrolls. The story of the angry spirits—children and grandchildren of the first man and the first woman, bitter about their inheritance. The tree was in their blood and they could feel its power, but there wasn't enough of it. Their lives were prolonged by hundreds of years; years spent wandering the wastelands, still feeling the wrath of God upon them, and their blood tainted with a power they shouldn't have had.

Gray hissed, enjoying the tale far more during this second telling. The first time around he'd been bored. He could see it now on his tanned face as he blew smoke rings into the fire. Back then he'd just been listening for the angle.

"The grandchildren, Seth, Jared, Enoch—there is a list of names here—sought out a . . . shaman. . . . It's not the right word but the closest I can find. They were old by then. Old and afraid." He looked up at Jack. "There is so much anger in these words."

"What did the shaman say?" Jack had leaned forward, totally concentrated.

"He told them of a way they could have what they wanted. How they could be brought back. And how they could live with the power they'd always wanted. That they thought was their true inheritance." He held up the paper. "It's just madness. Madness and ramblings." The Arab had paled.

"If it's just mad ramblings, then why did you say it was legend?" Gray threw his butt into the fire, watching it flare blue for a moment.

"I have heard talk of this sometimes amongst the tribesmen. Talk of ancient secrets in the origins of the West. I have heard of these wandering spirits. Sometimes when the wind cuts across the desert at night we think we hear in it the wailing of those lost forever between this life and the one after." His voice dropped to a reverential whisper. "We say they are hiding from their creator in the dust around us."

Jack stared at the ground for so long at the dreaming serpent Gray that for a second he thought his friend was really looking at him, had somehow sensed the dream of his friend taking place in the future. Eventually though, he turned and raised an eyebrow at the human Gray.

"Well, that's a great little fairy tale, Abu Mahmood, but if the shaman had told them how to come back, then why the hell didn't they when they died? Seems there's some holes in your story there. What I want to know is if those papers are valuable."

The fat Arab's eyes blazed white as they widened. "Oh, yes. Yes. Valuable for their age and also what they say. Some people would pay a lot of money for these. More than a lot. A fortune. They are priceless." He stared down at them. "But I wish that maybe you had not found them. The reason the lost souls could not bring themselves back is because they need the tree. The tree and the serpent. But the story of their visit to the shaman had reached the ancient holy men and they took the relics and hid them. The children of Adam couldn't find them and they were starting to die. So they did what they could do, which was drain their blood and store it. Some was mixed and sealed in a large bottle. The rest they mixed with wax and made into candles that they chanted the shaman's words over. The 'Dance of the Serpent' the curse was called." He pointed a stubby thick finger at the fragile parchment.

"For anyone that believes in this story then these papers are treasures. They are like finding lost pages of the Bible or the Koran. Priceless."

"And where are the candles and the blood? Do they even exist?" Jack leaned forward.

"I don't know. Maybe on that last sheet there is something." Gray could hear the fear in the man's voice just like he'd heard it the first time around. That was a man who was wishing he could turn into a snake and slither on his belly out of this cave and away from the two Western mercenaries. Because these stories were part of his heritage, and on a deep-seated level he believed them. Despite his wealth and his education, Abu Mahmood was a spiritual man, and whether the deity was called God or Allah, he wanted no part in standing against it. He just wanted to be paid for the work he'd done and then to forget all about it.

They pored over the scrolls until the early hours of the morning, Gray overtly cynical and Jack more subtly so, but both of them with a buzz in their guts that they hadn't felt for a long time.

But the Arab wouldn't translate the location of the candles. It seemed that at the last moment he developed a religious conscience. He was shaking and pale. From behind his snake's eyes Gray watched the man begin to sweat. He wondered if he'd realized by that point that he'd never be getting the rubies he'd been promised and pretty soon he'd be dead in the very patch of sand they were hunkered around. Maybe. Maybe not. People were pretty shitty at accepting the fate that was coming to them. Once Abu Mahmood had screamed into the empty desert night as Gray removed two of his fingers, he'd forgotten his spiritual side and was very much focused on saving his physical one, and then he'd begun to talk. Watching the blood spray, Gray shivered with the memory. The screams faded into the sound of the wailing and were lost as they traveled across the desert on the wind.

The dream shifted to the bustling streets of Jerusalem, and Gray had a moment of vertigo as he found himself upright again. Feeling the sweat sticking to the back of his shirt, he missed the feel of the cold blood of the serpent but shrugged the regret away. He knew where they were, he and Jack. They were six months further on from the caves of Afghanistan. They'd deciphered the riddles and hunted the man down through the lines of his family. He was old, on the brink of dying, but they'd hauled him up out of his stinking bed and drove him out of the house he'd been raised in near the West Bank.

As they ducked through the low, lopsided doorway, Gray thought it was a testament to fate that the home had survived all the shit of the previous decades. Maybe both sides figured a hole like this wasn't worth shelling. An old woman screamed gutturally at them, her dried hands frantically gesturing as Jack dumped the old man in a tatty chair. She shut up when Gray hit her. It felt as good the second time around as it had the first.

They gave the old man a few moments to get his wheezy breath back before he took them down to the cellar and gave them the trunk. He seemed to shrink even farther into his desiccated bones as he relinquished the key and watched it slide around Jack's neck. Alongside the candles and the bottle of blood, there was another parchment—more riddles to be undone. In a breath that stank of damnation, the old man slowly read it out to them. It told of the hidden boxes, of the two that were required and of a third that was the balance, created by the pure of spirit, by the ancient holy men. But it was the first two that must be found for any accession to take place.

They stared for a while at the blood and the candles, and Gray knew Jack well enough to see what he was thinking. He knew Jack's desire to feel, to *be,* more than he was. It was down in that Jerusalem cellar that they'd started to think that there may be something more to all this than their original plan to sell the package to some eccentric billionaire who had a religious streak. Maybe this was something worth trying for themselves. But they needed the boxes. They needed the tree. That's what would make them rich beyond their wildest dreams.

The old woman appeared in the cellar doorway, ranting again and clutching her bleeding cheek, and the dreaming Gray watched as the Gray of the past turned and shot her between the eyes. After that, Jack had killed the old man.

They sat in the house until nightfall, eating the meager stew and stale bread the old woman had prepared. There was a pleasant surprise when the couple's granddaughter turned up. It wasn't such a pleasant surprise for her, but Gray enjoyed reliving the experience in his dream. Reliving it and embellishing it. Hell, he'd been a good boy for what seemed like such a long time. And Jack was so busy analyzing the paper and candles he didn't care what Gray was doing as long as he kept the noise down.

Gray felt her skin tear under his hands, and although the dream wants to pull him forward, he makes it stay there in the warm, fresh young blood. He knew what happened next. The old man sent them west. But first they got the candles dated. The bookish historian turned pale when he handled them and then shook a lot. It was proof enough to them. They killed him too, subtly in the subway. There was no need for a trail. West, the old man sent them. To the land of the crusaders. To England.

He felt the girl's heart in his hand as it slowed to a wet stop. And he sighed. It was a good dream.

CHAPTER THIRTY

Abigail Clapton wrapped the knitted checked shawl around her shoulders and wandered into the small living room. John stood staring out the window, the drapes pulled open in the darkness. She didn't say anything but quietly joined him. Outside the waves roared against the hard rocks but the sky was clear, the moon reflecting blue light from the black water.

She looked up at her husband, loving every line and inch of his skin as she had back when they'd first met and they'd both been so different. Before they'd found their path.

"Were you dreaming again?"

He nodded. When she'd woken she'd reached for him and found only an empty bed under her fingers, the sheet soaked with sweat. The dreams had got worse and worse and even she couldn't ignore them anymore. She watched the shape of the trees change as they bent to and fro in the unforgiving wind, the branches scratching against a pane of glass like fingernails scraping and trying to find entry.

Somewhere, out past the water, lay the mainland. Her stomach knotted with a cramp of fear and for a moment the pale scars on her face twinged with memory, her womb aching with loss. It was a dark place, the mainland. A sinner's place. Not safe like North Haven. Her haven. She loved being here, just her and her family and their time with God, even though it had broken her heart when Liz so quietly stuck to her guns about going away. Oh, she had been terrified for her, even though Elizabeth had insisted that God would watch over her. Abigail sighed, pulling the wool tight across her chest.

"If we got the first ferry of the morning, we could be there by nightfall." She smiled a little, trying to ignore the tremble in her legs. "If the car can still manage that many miles."

John looked down at her and she could see the tiredness and fear so clearly in his eyes. "You don't have to come."

Linking her arm through his, she leaned her head on his shoulder. "Yes, I do." And she knew, despite her fear, that it was true. Her God would not forgive her weakness. And neither would she be able to forgive herself. "She's my baby too."

"Maybe the dreams are nothing. She'll probably be fine."

"Well, if that's the case, then we'll just have given her a nice surprise. She'll be pleased we visited."

"She's a good girl." John sighed. "Maybe I was too hard on her when she left. Maybe I should have understood better."

"We could both say that. But she knows we love her." Abigail smiled. "She's knows she's our blessing."

"I'm afraid for her."

She could feel the tension in her husband's arm and it sent a shiver from her head to her toes. She hadn't seen him afraid for a long, long time.

CHAPTER THIRTY-ONE

"Are you ready?" Steve spoke through the closed bedroom door. It was just after eleven P.M. and Liz had changed into dark sweatpants and a black sweater. Her heart thumped in her chest. Were they really going to do this? They must be crazy. She really didn't know what they expected to find. She glanced over at the Bible and the cross resting on her dresser and felt a tug at her heart.

"Just give me a minute."

She needed some time. There was something she had to do. Something that she hadn't done properly for too long. She felt the void inside her and the sudden realization that her forty days in the wilderness was done. Maybe she didn't need God in the same way her parents did, but she still needed her God. She needed Him walking beside her and she wasn't going to hide it any longer.

Feeling a little ashamed, she rearranged the wooden crucifix so that it was central on her table and then, after putting down the small stone that had become her talisman, she lowered herself to her knees. "Dear God," she started, her voice a low whisper from her bowed head. "I'm so sorry that I doubted, and I'm sorry if I've hurt my family in any way by wanting to choose my own path." She paused, not really sure what she was trying to say.

"Whatever path I choose, I want it to be a good one. A righteous one. And I hope you can see that what we're doing tonight is meant in the spirit of goodness. We're just worried, that's all."

With her eyes shut, Liz didn't see the strange-shaped stone start glowing on her dresser. First the tiniest shard of light escaped from its core like a thin laser beam, and then it became thicker and brighter, a glorious yellow like the sun, dazzling and hot.

Liz continued to mutter her prayers, and then, as the light touched her face she gasped a little, the words lost as she breathed in the light. Her skin glowed as it caressed her, gently easing its way in through her pores and follicles. Her head rolled back and she moaned, bathed in the heat as if she were in the flames of a fire. The minutes ticked out on the clock as the heat and light loved her and she loved them back.

There was a rap on the door and the light shot back into the stone.

"You fallen asleep in there?"

Liz looked up. "No, I'm coming." She smiled at the crucifix. "Sorry, we'll have to finish later. But I love you."

Getting to her to her feet, she reached for her sneakers and pulled them on. She felt good inside, a warm glow burning in the pit of her stomach. Which was weird, because only moments ago all she'd felt was scared and upset and just wanting everything to go back to where it was a few weeks ago. To be normal. Pulling her hair back into a ponytail she wondered at the power of prayer. Maybe that had made her stronger. Or maybe it was the fact that Steve would be with her. Whichever, she wasn't complaining. She was pretty sure the fear would come back soon enough.

They left the apartment and outside the night was cold. The wind driving in from the ocean dropped the temperature even further so that it was almost freezing and their breath hung in the bitter air. The campus lay silent and dark as they followed the path to the gates and slid through them.

"Fancy a jog?" Steve asked, and even though there was no need to whisper, she found herself doing just that.

"Sure. I need to warm up."

Not going so fast as to tire themselves out, they slid into an easy pace, their feet hitting the sidewalk in unison, the soft *whump* of their soles and the panting of their breath the only sounds to fill the night. Houses lay darkly in wait as they passed, glaring at them for disturbing the oppressive peace. They didn't speak as they jogged and Liz enjoyed the feeling of the cold air filling her lungs as her face heated up. It made her feel alive and vital, and she needed that.

Finally the church came into view and they slowed to a walk. Next to it, a light glowed from inside priest's house.

"Shit, maybe he's home," Steve whispered.

Now that they had arrived, Liz's heart still thumped fast and it had little to do with their recent run and everything to do with the return of her fear. But she still felt resolute. They'd come this far, and whatever was wrong in the town, it had something to do with that church. She understood religion and the Lord better than most, and whatever was going on inside those walls had nothing to do with Him. It was not His work. And Steve hadn't argued with her on that one. He'd seen enough strangeness to believe her.

"Let's go take a look."

They creeped across the front lawn and Steve gingerly climbed the steps, Liz right behind him, her breath held in case any noise should give them away. She wondered if her blond hair was glowing in the night, pointing them out like a flashlight beam, and she wished she'd found a hat to wear. But then breaking and entering had never been among her hobbies, so she figured it wasn't so bad to have not thought of everything. Ahead of her Steve peered through the gap of the drapes. "Doesn't look like anyone's here."

She tugged at his T-shirt. "Let's check the church. Looks like there may be something going on in there." She nodded up to the light coming from the stained glass windows. It was thin and pale, but definitely light.

Leaving the house behind, they trotted up the stairs to the church. "What now?" Steve asked. "We can't hardly open the door, peer in and run away." He paused. "We really didn't think this through properly."

Ignoring his frustration, Liz pressed her ear to the thick door. There were sounds coming from inside, but she couldn't make out any part of a service as she knew it. "Well, if there's people in there, then he must be too. Stands to reason."

"Yeah, but for how long?" Steve stood back, his hands pushed into his pockets. "I don't mind running the risk of me getting caught, but not you too."

"They've only been in there fifteen minutes." The low voice came from the shadows behind them, and Liz had to bite down hard on her lip to stop from letting out a yelp of surprise.

Beside her Steve jumped slightly. "Jesus. Jesus Christ." He peered into the gloom. "Who the hell is that?"

The thin man stepped up to the bottom of the steps. His hair was slicked down to one side as if he'd not long been out of the shower, but his nose was red and he looked frozen stiff. "They'll be in there at least an hour. Maybe longer. Seems like the whole town lives in that church at the moment. This afternoon they had a service that went on for two and a half hours and when one group came out another lot went right on in."

Liz stared at the softly spoken man. He looked familiar but she couldn't place him.

"Hey," Steve said, "you're the crazy guy that chased after us that day. You had some placard on." It took a second longer but the memory finally clicked into place for Liz. It was the day Georgia had died. *You keep the devil out,* he'd called after her. She shivered. How could he have known about her dream? At the time she'd tried to convince herself that it was a coincidence, but now she wasn't so sure. Not at all. And then she remembered where else she'd seen him. "I saw you at mass one day. You were looking at me."

He grinned and nodded. "You and me. We didn't drink the Communion wine." He looked at Steve. "And I bet you ain't eaten no muffins either." He raised an eyebrow. "I'm Al Shtenko. Town drunk. Until recently, that is." He held out his hand.

Liz looked up at Steve and then took the man's hand and shook it. "Nice to meet you." The whole ritual seemed surreal, out here in the middle of the night.

Shtenko squeezed her hand tight. "And it sure is a pleasure to meet you. A real pleasure." She felt uncomfortable with the way he looked at her. As if he were in awe.

The stranger looked back at the church. "I'll watch for the door. If you two want to get into that house, I'll whistle long and low if I see anything coming. You hear my whistle, you get the hell out. Go in and out from the back." He shuffled from foot to foot to get warm. "There's a path there that joins up with the sidewalk a little farther on. I don't think the priest will be out but sometimes other people come by the house and check on it. I don't know why. But people do. Like its some special place or something."

"How do you know all this?" Liz asked.

"I been watching, that's all. Didn't know what else to do. I can't seem to get people to listen. I guess that's what comes of being drunk for the past few years. No one wants to hear when you've got something important to say."

"How do we know we can trust you?" Steve sounded defensive and Liz didn't blame him even though she found herself liking this man. There was a gentle goodness about him she couldn't help but warm to. But then she'd liked Mabel and the sheriff at first, and look how they'd changed.

"Well, son," Al Shtenko said with a smile. "I'm out here like you, ain't I? Everyone else is in there."

It seemed like a good enough reason to Liz and she glanced up at Steve. He chewed the side of his mouth.

"I guess so."

"And if I'd been with them," Shtenko continued, "I'd have run straight into that service yelling my head off that someone was looking through the priest's window."

Steve smiled. "Okay, you've made you're point."

"We can't stand out here shooting the breeze all night. We need to get on."

In single file, Liz between the two men, they moved silently to the side of the church. Shtenko crouched a little against wall, lost in a pocket of black there, but still able to peer around and see the doors of the church.

"Listen out for my whistle. It'll be long and low, but loud. I'll give you as much time to get out as I can. Drink may have wrecked my liver a little, but my eyesight's still perfect."

Liz nodded, not sure if Al could still see them. "We need to keep in touch."

"You can find me on Anson Boulevard. Number thirty-four. That's my place." He paused. "You come find me if you need me."

"Thanks." It was all she could think of to say to the stranger, and then she was jogging to keep up with Steve as he padded around to the back of the house. Side by side, they fumbled their way up to the back door in the pitch-black night. There were no streetlight on the ocean side of the building, only the light of the moon to guide their way.

Steve fiddled with the handle and lock, letting out the occasional gasp of frustration, and then the door swung open.

"How did you learn to do that?" Liz whispered.

Steve's teeth flashed white as he grinned. "In some ways I really am the stereotype trailer-trash kid from Detroit."

He stepped across the threshold. "You should see how fast I can get into a car."

Heart thumping in her chest, Liz followed him into the house. A clock softly ticked out the seconds, its old mechanical whir totally at home in the dark wood surroundings. Staying close to Steve, she peered in through a couple of doorways. The kitchen, with its range and small round table sat empty on their left, and to their right, under an archway, was the dining room. Through the dining room was a small lounge, and Liz could make out a long leather sofa with floral cushions that seemed as if it had been battered to softness from too many clerics resting on it.

Her senses wobbled slightly. It all looked so normal. Maybe it was her and Steve and the crazy drunk outside that had the problem. Maybe it was some kind of mass hysteria. It didn't ring true though, even as she thought it. There had been two versions of Angela in the bathroom. Georgia was dead and the town had definitely gone strange. Yes, the house seemed normal, but that was just things and appearance. And appearances could be deceptive.

"Hey. Over here."

She turned to where Steve had pushed open a door on the other side of the hallway. He raised an eyebrow at her.

"It was locked."

They crept in side by side, Liz's heart in her mouth. This was where the light they'd seen outside had come from. It was obviously a study, bookshelves lining one wall, and by the window there was a small drink trolley with two cut-glass crystal decanters and several small glasses on it.

A large desk filled half the room. Several neat piles of paper were stacked on it, partially covering a large notebook in its center. Against the wall behind her was a small, ornate trunk. "What about that? Can you get in it?"

Steve crouched down and studied the lock. "I'm not sure. Seems pretty old. Still, the same principles should apply." Taking what looked like an overcomplicated penknife from his pocket, he tried inserting various attachments into the small opening, his face grimacing with concentration.

Liz picked up the notebook and opened to the first page. The large sheet was filled with tiny, neat writing, the words and lines so closely packed together that it took a moment to focus on it.

"I think I've found something." She looked down at Steve. "It looks like a diary of some kind. We might find some answers in it."

"Good. Because I don't think I'm getting anywhere with this. Which is odd because the locks seem quite normal. The parts just keep sliding away from me. I can't figure it out."

From outside came a long, quiet whistle, and Liz's heart almost stopped, heat flushing her face. "Did you hear that?"

Steve looked up. The whistle came again, shortly followed by the sound of a car pulling up in front of the house.

"Shit." Steve was up on his feet and grabbing Liz's arm. "Let's go."

She clutched the diary. "I'm taking this." It was evidence. There would be proof in it if nothing else. Proof that they weren't the only crazy ones in Tower Hill. Steve didn't look happy about drawing attention to the fact that the house had been broken in to, and she was glad that he didn't have time to talk her out of it.

Their sneakers barely touching the ground beneath them, they sped across the wooden hallway and out into the night, sure that at any second the front door would open and someone would catch them. But it didn't. The back door shut quietly behind them and they ran to the bottom of the yard, clambering swiftly over the fence and hitting the sandy path with a pair of dull thuds.

Liz didn't look back, neither for whomever had arrived at the house, nor for Al Shtenko. She was sure that he'd have kept himself well hidden in the night, and so with one

**hand in Steve's and the book tucked under one arm, they
ran full speed all the way back to the college.**

When Jack came through the front door after one A.M. Gray
was sitting in his office chair, a comforter wrapped around
his shoulders despite overwhelming heat filling the house.
He was sipping whiskey, his brow furrowed as he studied
the Bible.

Jack stared at him, confused. "You okay?"

"Yeah, it's just too damned cold."

"But it's like a furnace in here."

"Is it? I turned the thermostat up. But I can't seem to get
warm." Gray shivered and grinned, and Jack was sure that
the end of his friend's tongue had forked a little. Watching
him pull the comforter a little tighter, Jack wondered what
Gray's body temperature was like these days. Maybe the
changes were making him a little cold-blooded.

Jack perched on the desk and poured himself a drink. He
was tired. There must have been eight hundred people
crammed into the church tonight, and that had been the
second service of the evening. It was too much concentration. Looking down at his hands, he looked at the red stains
on them. The stone slabs around the altar were still slick
with the red substance. He hadn't bothered cleaning it up
tonight. Every day it seemed less and less important to
cover their tracks and maintain a sense of normalcy. Nothing was normal anymore. They'd all drained and drank.
The blood of this town was as one now. And also as one
with those on the other side who'd died so long ago and refused to move on.

The people of Tower Hill were ready to be drawn on
whether they knew it or not. There life energy was now ac-
cessible to the first blooded. The primary life. Sighing, he
sure as hell felt as though he could use some extra life energy. How ironic that he was this close to ascending into
something altogether more powerful, leaving mortality and

humanity behind and becoming a new level of man—man as he was supposed to be, created truly in God's own image, and yet he'd never felt so frail and human.

"Did you sort out that car?" The sheriff had told him about the Clapton girl and her friend going up to the hospital, and it had left him feeling some unease. He didn't want them leaving town again so easily.

"Yeah," Gray nodded. "They won't be going anywhere in a hurry. I did the whole college parking lot just to be safe. It took me the best part of two hours. Probably why I'm now freezing my ass off."

Jack smiled. That's what he'd always liked so much about Gray. Under all that charm there was a real eye for detail. "I can't believe you're reading the Bible."

Gray looked up and grinned. "I was hoping it had pictures."

"Ha! And there's probably not enough sex and violence in there for you either." He raised an eyebrow. "How are the kids?"

"Totally zoned out. Fucking zombies, mostly. You thinking tomorrow night for completion?"

Jack nodded.

"I'll bring them down tomorrow evening then," Gray continued. "We can lock them in the church. They won't know how long they're in there for. They don't even know what day it is. I think they're out more than they're in most of the time."

"Good." Jack paused. "One more day, Gray. Can you believe it? After two years, we're finally doing it."

Gray put down the book. "Yeah, I can believe it. Because we always succeed, don't we, Jack? That's what makes us so much better than the rest." He paused. "You know, I was thinking today about all the adventures we've had, you and me. We've had some of the best, haven't we?"

Jack looked at Gray's open, handsome face, and thought

for a moment that he looked sixteen again. "Yes, my friend, we have."

"Well, don't ever repeat this shit, because you'll embarrass me, but part of me is kind of sad that they're over."

Jack smiled, thinking of Gray's new eyes and tongue and the electricity running through his own veins that hinted at so much.

"Hell no, Gray," he said finally. "They're not over. They're just beginning."

Picking up the decanter, Jack refilled their glasses. "To us. To our past adventures and an eternity of future ones. To us, Gray."

"You and me forever, dude. Best friends."

They drank and laughed and reminisced until dawn slowly began to break, and then quietly tumbled off to separate rooms.

It was only when Jack woke two or three hours later and wandered into the study to do some more writing that he realized with a stab of cold anger that his journal was missing.

CHAPTER THIRTY-TWO

Deputy Louis Eccles stumbled down the stairs of May's Bed-and-Breakfast, his eyes burning from lack of sleep. He was the only guest staying at the big house, and it felt full of ghosts of life and energy who silently watched from every fold in the drapes, aching to be remembered.

There had been a time not so very long ago when anyone driving past in the late summer afternoons would see May and Ted sitting out on the porch and laughing like they'd only been married a week and were still in the flush of the early days and busy nights of marriage. But those days were gone now. Ted was cold in his grave and May kept on going and smiling but there was a sense that she was just biding time until she saw him again on the other side of the dark veil of night.

Lying in the starched, itchy sheets, Lou hadn't been able to sleep, suffocated by the thoughts that whirled in a confused tangle in his head. Despite May's best efforts, he hadn't eaten the dinner she'd sent up to his room, leaving it untouched under a silver cover like the good hotels use. He'd taken the tray down before turning in for the night, after May had knocked on the door to say she was going to church and asking him if he wanted to join her. She hadn't been happy when he'd politely declined, her voice shrilly declaring that Emma would most likely be there. He'd gritted his teeth and shut the door on her. The church he could do without.

After that, listening to the wind cutting through the trees outside, he'd locked the bedroom door and put a chair up against it. He'd felt a touch foolish but it hadn't stopped him from making sure his gun was loaded and handy. He wasn't entirely sure why he'd done either thing, but perhaps it was that policeman's gut instinct that was always talked about so much in the movies. Sometimes it didn't hurt to be safe. He'd heard May come in sometime after one A.M. and listened to her turning the lights off and sending the house to sleep. She didn't try his door handle but he'd still left the chair where it was. He wasn't sure, but in those few hours before dawn, he thought he may have dipped into a swampy dark sleep where invisible hands tried to drag him into suffocation, but he kept resurfacing, struggling to break the surface of consciousness and waking, gasping for air, confused and not entirely sure whether he'd slept.

Having reached the lobby, the dull dawn light staining all the furniture gray, Lou sat on the bottom step to pull on his running shoes. He was tired but wired with energy and needed to do something to stop his heart and head from exploding. A couple of miles workout on the beach was probably just what would save him from driving straight over to Emma's and begging her to take him back

"Morning, Deputy."

Looking up, surprised, he saw May coming toward him with a mug of coffee.

"I heard you stirring," she continued. "I thought you may want some coffee." She smiled but it wasn't the expression Lou remembered from her days of laughing out on the porch.

He gave her a soft smile back. "I wasn't expecting you to be up after getting in so late last night. I didn't wake you, I hope."

She shook her head. "No. I only sleep for a couple of hours these days. Don't need any more than that at my age." She held the mug out toward him. "This'll help wake you up."

Lou took it and placed it on the wooden stair beside him as he tied the laces on his second shoe. "That's real nice of you, May." He stood up and she watched him intently as he held the drink.

"There's plenty of cream and sugar in there to keep your strength up. And I'll have a hearty breakfast waiting for you when you get back. You could use fattening up a little." She paused. "Now you drink that all up. It'll be good for you. Trust me."

The surface of the liquid frothed at the edges and it seemed to Lou that there was a tiny film in its centre. Something Al Shtenko had said to him yesterday morning niggled at the back of his mind. Some shit to do with watching what people gave him to eat.

Feeling May's intense gaze unwavering on him, he raised the china to lips and mimed drinking it. A cloying smell, almost disguised by the coffee aroma, hit his nose and he couldn't bring himself to let the warm liquid touch his lips. There was something wrong with it, he was pretty damned convinced about that. It seemed his policeman's gut instinct was growing stronger. And who cared if Shtenko had also talked about a genie, he figured. Maybe that genie had been talking some sense.

Apparently satisfied, May smiled and turned to go back into the dining room and kitchen. Lou stared after her, the drink forgotten. May's skirt was tucked up into her pantyhose, which appeared to have been put on backward, the gusset covering her oversized underwear. It looked like half her long skirt was caught in that elastic waistband. He frowned. Surely she must feel that? This wasn't like on that ad on the tube where the sexy girl has her tiny mini skirt hitched into her underwear. May was carrying half her outfit there. *Wrong,* he thought again. *This is all very, very wrong.*

Walking to the front door, he paused by a potted plant and, carefully watching the dining room for any shadowy hint of May's return, he poured the coffee in the soil. There was no way he was going to be eating or drinking anything without having watched it being prepared for a while. He was beginning to like his gut instinct. He could get used to having it around.

He left the empty mug on a table and stepped out into the early morning air and over to the cruiser. He'd drive down to the clear stretch of beach where there was more sand than shingle and then run his heart out. And when he was cleaned up and ready for work, then maybe he'd call in on Emma and see if she'd had any second thoughts. He couldn't believe that she'd end things like this. So suddenly. So *absurdly.* It was the only word he could come up with that covered it. Emma, little Jacob and him—they were a unit. A unit of solid love. Surely nothing could have broken that without him knowing it? Not something as abstract as the church? Surely? His heart battered at his ribs with frustration as he turned the key in the car. Why the hell didn't anything make any sense?

Ten minutes later and Lou was heading down the wooden steps to the beach. It was still not even seven in the morning, and the wind coming off the water stung his cheeks. It felt good. Not bothering to stretch, he let his frustration loose and started to jog. Within a few seconds his strides were long and despite his tiredness, he'd fallen into his natural running rhythm, enjoying feeling the resistance of the sand beneath his feet. Air burned in his lungs and for a while he almost zoned out, letting his muscles do the feeling instead of his emotions, his tired brain allowing itself to be carried by the up-and-down pounding of his body.

After a mile or so, however, he squinted. A dark shape stood out against the tan of the shore. He picked up his pace, his curiosity engaged. What was that? Why would someone be sitting out on the beach at this time in the morning? Who would do that? Summer was well and truly gone. Whoever it was must be freezing.

He hoped to hell it wasn't Al Shtenko again. He hoped that Al was tucked in bed, getting his mind back with a good night's sleep. He was a gentle man, Al Shtenko, and Lou didn't want to have to lock him up in the holding tank for any crazy misdemeanors. Hell, the way he felt at the moment, he'd be happy to deface the church himself.

He came to a halt a few feet away from the figure sitting with his knees bent up, arms wrapped around them, fiddling with something in his hands. Leaning over and panting, perhaps more heavily than he needed too in an effort to look like he'd stopped casually, Lou could see straight away that it wasn't Al Shtenko on the low dune. It was a kid. A boy from up at the college; a football player, judging by his red jacket. He didn't look at Lou but stared out over the water. His eyes were bloodshot and barely open and he looked about as tired as Lou felt.

"You okay, son?" Maybe there wasn't so many years between them to make the term appropriate, but Lou figured there was a lot of growing up done between your teenage years and your twenties, especially when you'd had the experience of bringing a new person into the world. It changed your perspective.

The boy didn't look up. His face was pale, almost drained. Lou took a step or two closer. What *was* that he was playing with so absently? For a moment he stared, confused, before he realized that what he was seeing was not an early Halloween prop painted green and ready to scare the college girls, but was a nauseating, swollen extra hand being passed between the boy's pale fingers.

"What's that you got there?" Keeping his tone light, he stepped forward and crouched in front of the teenager. The boy continued to stare forward.

"Found it on the beach. Must have washed up."

Pulling his sweatshirt off, leaving his thin body only the protection of a T-shirt against the strong ocean wind, Lou leaned forward and used it as makeshift gloves to take the severed hand from the boy. He relinquished it without looking down, and as it dropped into Lou's possession, the deputy noticed the cuts running up the boy's arms and disappearing into the sleeves of his jacket.

"What's your name, son? You from the college?"

"Yeah. Yeah, I am." The kid paused and frowned, his eyes finally drifting away from the hypnotic movement of the waves. He looked at Lou and then down at the hand with mild surprise.

"Dennis. My name's Dennis." He sighed. "I saw the ring in the sand. Right here. That's how I found it."

"What were you doing down on the beach so early? That tide can be dangerous, you know."

The kid shrugged. "Dunno. Just dunno."

Watching him struggling to get the words out, Lou wondered what sort of shit they were smoking up at the campus this year and made a mental note to maybe get James Russell to organize a surprise visit to the dorms one night.

"Well, you sit right here for a minute or two, Dennis. I've got to go and call this in. Okay?"

The boy nodded slightly but his eyes had been called back to the water. Lou figured he wasn't going anywhere in a hurry, but still gathered some shingle into a pile to mark the spot before starting the run back to his car and his CB radio, the only kind of damned communication that seemed to be working in town.

Tired and sweating, Lou wished he hadn't run so damned fast to call the sheriff. Not judging by the man's complete lack of interest.

"But look, James. The hand's been chopped off with something. This is a pretty clean cut."

"Sharks can bite clean."

Lou fought the urge to shake the man he'd known and respected for so long as the sheriff was busy getting the kid in the back of the cruiser.

"Sharks? In this water? Since when?"

"You heard of global warming?"

"Jesus, James. That's bullshit and you know it." He leaned across the car's hood so the sheriff couldn't avoid looking at him, and pointed down at the grotesque appendage still wrapped in his sweatshirt. "This girl wasn't out for a winter swim. Her nails are painted. He looked again at the piece of jewelry that now looked ready to cut through the swollen finger. In the center of its silver frame sat a large emerald-colored stone, ironically probably worn to draw attention to those pretty painted nails, but now pretty much blended in with the skin around it.

"And that ring may not be worth much, but you wouldn't wear it out in the water. No young girl would. The rest of her is going to come up on our beach in pieces—I fucking know it. Surely you're going to call the county or state in for this one? Or shall I just drop the hand off at John McGeechan's office and he can sign it off and incinerate it before a proper investigation gets in the way?"

Despite the heat of his anger, Lou felt the chill settle between them as Sheriff Russell turned to look at him. For a moment the older man said nothing, but just stared out from a face that was thinner than Lou had seen it in a long time.

"No, Lou. You're not dropping it anywhere. The only thing you're going to be leaving with me is your gun and your badge. I'm suspending you from duty"

"What?" Lou Eccles felt the world shift unnaturally beneath his feet for the second time in two days. "What the hell for? Because of this? Because I'm disagreeing with you?"

"No, not because of this." The sheriff let out a long sigh.

"It hurts me to say this, Lou, because we've always been close and I would never have believed it of you."

"Believed what of me? I don't know what the hell you're talking about."

"Oh, come on. I'm talking about Emma. Did you think she'd just stay quiet? She called me over yesterday evening just before church. Told me about how you beat on her and how she's worried you're going to start in on little Jacob soon."

"I what? She say's I've been doing *what?*" The sheer incongruity of what Russell was trying to say knocked the air from his chest. "She's saying I hit her? Why would she say that? No . . . shit. She wouldn't say that. She just wouldn't." He stared at his friend and boss, and at his empty eyes. "Surely you don't believe her? How can you believe her?"

The sheriff pulled a handkerchief from his pocket and blew his nose. "Damn this sea air." He held his hands up. "Look, Lou, I'm not sure what I believe. She has a nasty black eye and someone must have given it to her."

"And you think it was me?" Maybe he was in a dream. Maybe the whole past twenty-four hours was just some surreal nightmare. "And what do you mean Emma's been punched?" The thought of Emma with bruises ripped at his heart. But why the hell would she say he'd done it? Maybe she was afraid of someone. Maybe it was the only choice she'd had. But it didn't make sense. Who the hell would Emma be afraid of? He remembered her dead expression when she'd told him to leave. It had been like talking to a stranger.

"You can keep the car to drive back into town with once you've showered and got your shit together. But I want it back at the office with your badge and gun by ten." James Russell paused. "And don't go home, Lou. Emma wants one of those restraining orders on you. I've told her that's not necessary. Don't force my hand."

Lou stared at him, his guts turning to water. "Jesus,

James. What the hell is going on in our town? Seems to me you've all gone a little crazy."

The sheriff didn't answer, but picked up the hand from the car's hood and climbed into his car. "You can get your sweater later. I've got a burglary to investigate at Father O'Brien's place, and then I'll get to this precious hand of yours." He paused, his face clouding for a moment before clearing. "Town business comes first." Without looking at Lou again, he turned on the engine and drove away.

Louis Eccles stared after him until the police cruiser had disappeared, and then tilted his head back and joined the gulls in a cry of rage, screaming out his anger and frustration into the dust and the sand and the sky, until eventually he fell silent, his throat sore and his heart empty. He stood there in the cold, letting the wind beat him until his skin was numb and his teeth chattered, biting at the inside of his mouth.

CHAPTER THIRTY-THREE

Liz and Steve had banged on the door of the downstairs apartment for several minutes before Steve eventually tried the handle. It was open and they'd let themselves in, calling to see if anyone was home. There was no answer. Eric's room was emptied of his possessions and the heavy metal posters were gone from the walls. Maybe he'd just dropped out, or maybe they weren't the only ones getting a little freaked out by the way people seemed to be changing in Tower Hill. Whatever the reason, Eric was gone and there was something slightly disturbing about his room, now devoid of any hint at his existence. It was almost as if he'd never been there.

Back up in their own apartment, Steve made them coffee and Liz began scanning through the diary, lost in the tiny words and craziness that oozed from the pages. Steve had bolted the front door and was perched on the back of the couch, where he could keep an eye out the window for anyone approaching. If it came to it, they could get out by the fire escape down the back of the building before anyone even knew they'd been there. That was the plan, anyway.

Still holding the book, Liz stood up and began pacing. She couldn't believe what she had just read. It was madness. Insanity poured out onto the page. Still, her heart hammered in her chest. Steve looked over at her briefly, his face bemused.

"So, what you're saying is that the tree of life, the one out of the Garden of Eden, was real? And still exists?" He shook his head. "That's crazy. It's just a story."

"I know, but that's what it says. And there's more." She flicked back and forth through the thin sheets. "With the rise of Christianity, the relic of the tree branch was kept first at the Vatican. This caused too many problems with statesmen from the other great European nations, who felt that the Vatican should share this responsibility with the other monarchs since they were God's appointed on earth also, and by spending time guarding the relic, this would help show their strength and faith to God. And so, every ten years, the relic would be safely transported from one state to another and into the safekeeping of the monarch there. And that state of affairs went on for centuries, despite all wars and conflict. Regardless of the diplomatic state between nations, if it was time for one leader to pass the tree to another, they did so, in the greatest of secrecy."

Steve stared out the window. "So how the hell does this tie in to what's going on over here?"

"I'm getting to that." For a moment she'd forgotten the fear and danger that surrounded them and was lost in the history. "During Henry the Eighth's reign, the relic came to be in England for its turn there. But Henry had a secret. During the Crusades a few hundred years previously, another relic had been brought back from the East, a cryptically sealed box purporting to contain the shed skin of the serpent. Henry had taken it from the monastery that guarded it and kept it in his own strongroom as he did with the relic of the tree. For ten years he'd had them both close by and accounted his health, success and vigor to their proximity. He couldn't bear to give them up." She looked up and smiled. "This is just amazing. Maybe I should write my thesis on it."

Steve shook his head. "This is not the time to be thinking about assignments." She could see that he was as fascinated as she was by it though. "So what happened next?"
he said.

"Well, Henry had become bored with his wife and was
lusting after Anne Boleyn, and he used the situation to
force a break from Rome. He knew that the Pope would
never give him a divorce, so he allowed himself to be ex-
communicated, and then set up the Church of England.
And kept the relics."

"No wonder the Brits were always at war back then.
Sounds like those relics sent him a little power mad."

"Yeah, it does. Especially when you think how blood-
thirsty and self-centered he became. He married Anne Boleyn, and three years later accused her of witchcraft and
adultery and had her executed."

"Nice man," Steve observed wryly.

"And that's just the start for him." Liz smiled. "He
wasn't much nicer to the next four wives either. But we're
veering." She flicked over to the next page, poring over the
words.

"When Elizabeth was on the throne she had both relics
placed in the care of priests, and an order of special monks
was created to guard them. They were kept in a secure
monastery at Tower Hill in London"—she paused long
enough to see Steve take notice of the familiar name—
"with the most devout believers watching over them constantly. Right at the end of her reign, when she knew she
was dying and would have to hand her crown over to James
the Sixth of Scotland, she had the relics and the monks sent
over to the New World, where they traveled up the coastline to an isolated area, and the monks set up an outpost to
hide the relics. A stone church was built, and a large
monastery with high towers for seeing out over the vast
lands where the boxes were buried.

"But as the years passed and the New World grew, the

guardians forgot their place and the priests drifted away
from their calling and became townsmen, taking wives and
learning trades, and they started forgetting to teach their
children their true heritage. They stopped passing on the
word of the Lord. The story of the town's origin was forgotten. The church was maintained, but none of the priests that
worshipped there realized the burden that should have come
with the job."

Steve snorted. "Well, this one seems to have some fucking idea."

Liz nodded, and closed the book. Father O'Brien was
key to whatever had changed in the town; she was sure of
it. Puzzled, she looked back at the first page. "But he isn't a
priest," she muttered. "At least he's not Father O'Brien."
She looked up, pointing at a small name written into the
hard inside of the front cover. "Jack Devaine. That's who
he is."

Steve took the book from her and stared. "So who the
fuck is he?"

"I don't know. He hasn't said much about himself yet.
So far it's all been the history of these relics." She took it
back. "I'll skim ahead. He'll tell us soon enough."

"Yeah, well I'm not too happy about us staying here. I
think we should get out of town and read the rest of it
someplace normal."

"Sounds good to me."

Grabbing sweaters, they headed back down the stairs,
and Liz was glad Steve went in front. She trusted him to
look after her and it was as a simple as that, feminism be
damned. She wasn't sure whether she believed what she'd
read in the book so far, but she did know that there was a
lot of weird stuff going on and she was very glad to have
Steve with her. She thought about what she'd read about
Henry VIII and her head swam. There was just too much to
take in. And then she remembered how Angela had looked
when she'd brought her out of the bathroom, all bloody and

confused. That was what was important, not events from hundreds of years ago. She owed it to Angela to find out what had happened to both her and Tower Hill. The thought of her missing friend made her feel sick.

Outside, her heart sank when the car wouldn't start. It wouldn't even turn over. "It's never done this before," she said. It wasn't until Steve had mentioned getting out of town for a while that she realized how appealing the idea was. Just to sit somewhere normal surrounded by the bustle and noise of human life rather than this sluggish ghost town seemed like heaven to her.

"Pop the hood." Steve was already getting out, his face grim. Pulse racing, Liz tapped the steering wheel. Maybe it was just a loose connection. Eventually, just as Liz's fingers started to feel the first touch of numbness from the chill air, Steve slammed the hood down, shaking his head. Liz stepped out, clutching the notebook to her chest.

"What is it?"

"Someone's ripped some of your wires out. This isn't your car breaking down. This has been done on purpose."

"What?" Liz couldn't believe it and immediately looked around. Who would have done this? With a heavy heart she realized that there were probably quite a few people in town who could fill that slot.

"Wait here. I want to check something." Steve trotted over to another car, parked across the way in the small lot. He dropped to the ground and shuffled his torso under the vehicle. After a couple of seconds he reappeared. "Shit. This one too."

Liz stared around them as he walked back to her. "I guess someone doesn't want us to leave town."

"Maybe they don't want anyone to get out. We could walk, I suppose."

Liz shook her head. "No. We'll stay. There must be someone we can talk too. Maybe we can track down that man from last night. Or the deputy. He seemed okay." Her insides felt warm. "I'm tired of being afraid. Whatever's happening in town, it's bad, but I'm not going to run away from it."

His focus somewhere over her shoulder, Steve grabbed Liz's arm and tugged her sharply down, so they were hidden beside the driver's-side door.

"What? What is it?" Her voice automatically dropped to a whisper, the hairs on the back of here neck prickling.

Steve put a finger to his lips and nodded over the hood of her car. Before anything came into view Liz made out the sound of an engine and tires on concrete, and a few seconds later a police cruiser pulled up outside their house. She ducked a little farther down and slid along so she could peer through the windows of her own car.

Sheriff Russell got out of one side and the dean of the college the other. They spoke quietly, their voices just a low rumble to Liz, and then they stared up at the apartment. There was no disguise as to which of the two interested them. Liz held her breath as the two men knocked loudly and pressed the buzzer a few times before the dean pulled a large ring of keys from his pocket and opened the door. They disappeared inside.

"Come on." Steve tugged at her sleeve, and keeping low they ran to the cover of the bushes and trees, needing to get hidden again before the two men got into their flat and were able to see out the windows. Liz didn't spend any time wondering what they might be looking for. She was carrying the answer to that tightly in her arms.

Crouching behind the hedges, they peered out through the leaves until the men emerged a full twenty minutes later. Liz was glad they weren't so close that she could see their expressions. They waited until the car was gone before creeping out and running up the stairs to check on the apartment. Following Steve in, Liz gasped. The place was a wreck. Automatically, they reached for each other's hands as a comfort against the desolation and moved from room to room in awe of how much mess had been made in the short space of time.

In the kitchen the drawers were ripped out, their contents tipped all over the linoleum, and the cupboards hung open. Liz was amazed that given how much damage the two men had caused that they hadn't smashed the plates. Maybe they just didn't want to make too much noise if they could help it. In each of the bedrooms clothes littered the floors, personal belongings of each of the three students chucked carelessly in all directions. Staring at her things, treated so badly by people who should be looking out for her, Liz felt her stomach contract with fear and more than a little anger.

"Well," said Steve, picking up a broken CD case from the floor of his room, "I guess they don't really care that we know that they've been here." He looked up at Liz. "Maybe it's a test. To see if we'll call the cops or not." He tossed the plastic case back on the floor.

Liz looked out at the gray sky and then down at her dresser. It was almost empty, her Bible and cross thrown to the floor. Alone and forgotten on the wooden surface sat the small, strange-shaped stone. With an overwhelming sense of relief that she didn't fully understand, she snatched it up and squeezed it tight, almost unaware of the way it buzzed in the palm of her hand.

"I think it's too late in the day for games. This isn't a test." She rubbed the stone gently across her cheek. "The sheriff doesn't care whether we know he's been here. We're just an irritation to him." She turned to face Steve. "The town can't go on like this. Something's happening. And it's happening soon. Can't you feel the tension in the air?"

Steve shrugged. "If you feel it, that's enough for me. Do you want to go into town and see if we can find someone else like us? Someone who doesn't seem to have gone completely insane? I don't think we should go into any of the halls. If the dean sees us it might not be good."

Liz straightened her shoulders, the rock in one hand and the journal in the other, and looked into Angela's room. The ache she felt for her friend, wherever she was, was enough to give her strength. Sometimes you have to stand firm in the face of evil. "Town sounds good to me. Let's go. Thirty-four Anson Boulevard is the place we need to get to. That's where the man from last night said he lived."

Liz grabbed their jackets and found Steve gathering up some of the larger kitchen knives from the floor and wrapping them in a towel before putting them in his small backpack.

Liz stared. "Do you think we'll need those?"

He raised an eyebrow. "I'd rather find out later that we don't need them than find out that we do."

Liz couldn't argue with his logic.

CHAPTER THIRTY-FOUR

"It was a hand. A hand just sitting in the sand, and he didn't give a shit. What kind of sheriff is that?"

Deputy Eccles sat on one of the small park benches on Main Street, not far from the turn-in for Hannaford, his bottle of vodka not even hidden in a brown paper bag. Listening to him, Al Shtenko just nodded. He'd give the young deputy a few more minutes before dragging him back to the problems of the present. Beside them on the bench, the genie filed her nails and whistled to herself. Al didn't recognize the tune. He wondered if she was cold in her tiny, sheer dress. He figured not. After all, she seemed cheerful enough sitting there all cross-legged and dainty, and it wasn't as if she was ever shy about speaking out.

She'd woken him this morning by pulling at the hairs in his nose. His eyes had been watering when he'd opened them, but she'd just smiled and wished him good morning. Then she'd told him to shift his butt and get a coffee in him. It was time to gather the faithful. The crusaders of the light, she'd called them, and it seemed to Al that after their encounter yesterday at the church, that Deputy Eccles might be a good place to start. The genie hadn't disagreed.

He'd waited in a recessed doorway across the street from the sheriff's department starting at eight A.M., and although he'd seen some strange people coming and going from there in the first hour, the deputy wasn't among them. Most of those who had drifted in and out of the doors were prominent men of the town, and a few years ago Al himself would have been counted among them. There was Neville Bright from the big car lot where just about everyone in town felt obliged to get their rides; Tom Jackson from the Chamber of Commerce, who Al had never liked for his smug talk of raised business taxes and big expense accounts; that smarmy Dr. McGeechans and the smug downtown lawyer whose offices and fees were way too big for what he really needed.

Yep, he'd thought from the doorway, *that's them all right.* But if it hadn't been for their builds and hair he wouldn't have recognized them at all. They all seemed a little confused and untidy, but it was hard to tell with their faces rubbed out like that. It was much worse than when he'd first noticed it outside the church. This time it made his eyes ache just to look at them. It seemed as if a great big dirty thumb had smeared their features into a mess, dark and blotchy and shifting across their skin. It wasn't pleasant. It wasn't good. But it was surprising that they didn't see it in one another. Given they way they shambled in and then out to go about whatever business it was that had summoned them there, he had wondered if they were seeing anything much at all.

The mayor came by at just after nine, lost in a world of his own, his smart pants on but without a jacket, his shirt hanging loose at his waist, the sleeves rolled up messily. He paused outside the department office but didn't go in. Instead he turned in circles and scratched his head a little. "Is there enough blood?" he muttered to the pavement and then the sky. "There must be more blood."

Fascinated, Al watched from the doorway as the older man stared down at the insides of his arms, examining them and tugging at the skin. "I can see it in there. I can feel it. Too much blood. Not enough blood."

Eventually he wandered off again, still mumbling, and the genie, leaning out of Al's top pocket and resting her elbows over the edge, snorted a little. "And people think *you're* crazy."

"Well, to be fair," Al said, "I have had my moments."

She shook her tiny head emphatically. "Not like that. And you're no fool, Alvin Shtenko. That's what's seen you through. You've had your time in the wilderness and now you're back."

Al guessed that he was, but a part of him felt ashamed at how much of that wilderness he'd created for himself.

"And when the time comes," the genie said with a mouthful of tiny hairpins as she rearranged her sixties hairdo, "you'll be strong."

Al figured he'd take her word for that.

The deputy had turned up at about five after ten, not in his uniform, but rather jeans and a sweater. Al had stood up alertly and watched as Lou Eccles disappeared inside the building, abandoning the cruiser right outside on the street rather than parking it in the small lot in the back. He came out less than ten minutes later, his clear face like thunder—no rubbing out to block the expression there. He strode determinedly through the town, and Al fell into place behind him even though he doubted the young man would have noticed if he'd walked along beside him dressed as Colonel Sanders singing "Yankee Doodle" and waving fried chicken under his nose. He watched the man in front as they walked. Deputy Eccles looked so very young without his tan uniform and hat adding weight to him, but Al wondered whether that was just that he himself was getting old. It seemed that once you'd hit forty, anyone under thirty was a baby.

He and the genie watched from Main Street as Lou went

into the small liquor store next to Hannaford. From the determined way he was moving, Al figured that if the store had been closed the deputy would have just knocked the door down.

"Shall I go after him?" he'd asked the genie, but she'd shook her head.

"Let him get what he wants. He's a good boy. You can stop him from drinking too much, but a shot or two is probably just what he needs."

Al waited for him to come back out; Eccles emerged with a bottle of spirits in one hand, and Al watched as he strode back to Main Street and the nearest bench. It was only when he sat down that Al saw the strength seep out of him. As he unscrewed the cap and took the first long gulp, Lou Eccles kind of crumpled a little inside.

"Now go after him. We've got some shit to clean up today and we're going to need him sober."

Al nodded. He sometimes wondered where the genie got her language. At times she had a tendency to sound like something from a cheesy straight-to-DVD movie.

"A hand, you say?" They'd been sitting on the bench for ten minutes now and it seemed to Al that young Lou Eccles was not having a great couple days. He watched him take another hit from the bottle and almost felt the burn down the back of his own throat. He didn't feel tempted though. Not anymore.

Al gently eased the bottle out of the deputy's grasp. Eccles wasn't a drinking man, any fool could see that, and this wasn't the day for him to start becoming one. There was maybe an inch or two of the liquid missing from the bottle, but he'd sober up soon enough from that. Lou stared across the street.

"Emma says I beat on her. Why would she say something like that? I've been trying to figure it, but I just can't." His voice was soft, the fight going out of it and a maudlin tone creeping in. Al ticked another box on his mental checklist.

Yep, it was definitely time to stop the young deputy from having any more.

He slipped the small bottle into the right-hand pocket of his jacket and pulled another out of his left. He unscrewed the cap and handed it to the policeman.

"Here, drink that. It'll make you feel better." Watching the deputy take a sip and flinch at the purity of the water after the sting of liquor, Al Shtenko smiled softly. "Don't be so hard on yourself, Deputy. It ain't your fault. No more than anyone else's. It's all in the blood." He took the bottle back and allowed a sip of the sweet water for himself.

Sometimes he heard the words coming out of his mouth and didn't know who was really speaking them, him or the genie. He figured it didn't really matter. Louis Eccles wasn't really listening. Al stood up.

"Come on. I'm taking you back to my place. I've got bacon and eggs and good strong coffee waiting there, and I'm pretty damned starving. We've got a lot to talk about." He glanced around at the closed-up businesses. "And I think it would be best if we stayed forgot for today." He hauled his reluctant companion to his feet. "Now let's get moving." As they started to walk, he felt the genie settle down in the warmth of his top pocket for the ride.

CHAPTER THIRTY-FIVE

The hoods of their sweatshirts drawn up over their heads, Liz and Steve cautiously walked through the town, avoiding people wherever possible. Not that too many of the residents seemed to be taking to the streets, and those that were shambled like zombies through the gray morning chill, an air of confusion about them as if they'd forgotten where they were supposed to be going and the reason they'd come out.

Liz frowned a little as they moved swiftly past a slow-moving, scruffy, middle-aged man. The sheriff and the dean hadn't walked like that when they'd seen them up at the house. And what they'd done to the apartment had taken a lot more energy than the few people littering Tower Hill's streets seemed to have. Whatever was going on, it was having different effects on different people.

Outside the town hall they studied the huge map proudly displayed on the wall and found Anson Boulevard out toward the edge of town, at the opposite end to the college. The map had trees and plants and laughing children carefully painted on it. Looking around, Liz didn't see anything on the wall that she recognized. That town was gone for now. She made a mental note of the directions they needed to follow and then they headed off again, picking up the pace a little. The deserted streets were making her feel uneasy.

As they veered toward the more residential part of town, Steve paused and pointed down the wide road on their left. "Who's that? What are they doing down there?" His voice was low even though the figures were a few hundred yards away. Liz stared at them, her heart thumping.

"I don't know. I can't make it out." Her voice was almost a whisper, as if subconsciously she were afraid her words would carry all that way in the quiet. Steve squinted, and for a few seconds they watched the two men as they crouched on either side of the street, laying something out between them before getting up and pacing the line, checking it.

"Stingers," Steve muttered. "They're laying down stingers to blow any tires." He paused. "This road leads out to the main coast road. Guess they don't want to encourage anyone in or out of the town."

They, they, they. Liz's head spun with confusion over how a *them* and *us* situation had arisen in the town. She pulled Steve to their left, into the shadow of a building. "Do you think they're doing that on all the roads?"

"I guess so. It would make sense if they're doing it on this one." He looked at her. "I guess we're stuck here. Who knows if people are watching for anyone trying to leave." He stared back at the road. "This is some weird shit, Liz. Really weird."

Having no answer for that, Liz started walking. They'd seen what they needed to and there was no point in watching the men working any longer. It only risked drawing attention to themselves. After what the sheriff had done to their apartment, she could bet that whoever those men were, they'd been told to keep an eye out for two students that couldn't just sit quietly and believe what they were told. She hoped that whoever they were, the deputy wasn't among them. She'd liked him. He'd seemed like a good man.

CHAPTER THIRTY-SIX

The crossing had been choppy from the moment the small ferry had pulled away from its island home, as if even the tides and winds thought their leaving was a bad idea. John Clapton had thought his stomach would give up its small breakfast contents on more than one occasion. His legs trembled weakly beneath him, bouts of nausea attacking him with every throb of the feisty water; but whereas he just wanted to die quietly in the small uncomfortable cabin, Abigail stood firm at the rails.

He watched her from the small open doorway, her slim hands gripping tight onto the metal as she stared out across the angry ocean to the land they approached. Her face was flushed from the constant wind, and with her hair flying out behind her coat, he thought he hadn't seen her looking so alive since they'd first met, before life had scarred and changed them.

So far there was no sign of the fear that had eaten her up and driven them from the city to the safety and isolation of the island. Her eyes were focused and clear, no twitchy edginess or darting from side to side, seeking out danger in every corner. His seasickness momentarily forgotten, he thought—and not for the first time—that she was as much a mystery to him as the wide depths of water surrounding them. He'd thought her inner strength had died all those years ago, and sometimes over recent weeks he'd begun to wonder if Elizabeth was right in her judgments of them. Perhaps they had hidden in God. Maybe there was a kernel of truth in that, but he wouldn't change it. One day Elizabeth would come to see that. It may not be everyone's way but God and his family was all John needed.

Trying to ignore the burning feeling rising from his gut, he stepped up along his wife. "You all right, Abby? Did you manage to get any sleep?"

She smiled, a sweet expression that filled her face. "I dreamed," she said. "I think an angel came to me. My dream was full of light. It was beautiful and terrible." Her voice was wistful. "He's given us so much, our God. So many blessings. But life is like the world, isn't it? No matter where we live. I see that now. Life is beauty and terror all rolled up, so sometimes you can't tell one from the other."

He nodded. "That's why we went to New Haven. To escape the terror."

"Yes, yes we did." She sighed. "And the Lord's respected that and been good to us. He's given us our peace and our beautiful daughters." She squeezed her husband's arm. "Maybe now it's time to give something back. I think there will be sacrifices made before the day is out, John. Some beautiful and some terrible." She flicked hair out of her eyes with a quick, elegant tilt of her slim neck. "I just hope we get there in time to do our part."

Pulling her in close, John shivered. There was something about the calm acceptance in her voice that chilled him to the bone.

CHAPTER THIRTY-SEVEN

Al Shtenko poured the deputy a fresh coffee from the warm pot and took a packet of Aleve from the cupboard above the stove. Lou could see him trying not to smile. Not that he blamed the other man. He was probably an amusing sight in a vaguely pathetic way. If he was going to try a career as a drunk now that the police department didn't want him any longer, then he was going to have to toughen up his liver. No more than three inches gone from the vodka bottle and he had a hangover.

Shtenko carefully put the mug down on the table, and Lou added sugar and cream before swallowing a couple of the tablets with it. He flinched at the hot liquid. Al pulled up a plastic chair opposite him.

"I don't see you as a spirits man, Deputy."

"No. No, I'm not. A couple of slow beers out in the yard with Emma is more my style." He raised an eyebrow. "And I'm not a deputy anymore, Al. I'm just plain old Lou Eccles."

Shtenko shrugged. "You're still the deputy to me. And being a beer man sounds pretty fine. I don't think you've got a drunk in you." He shook his head a little and looked away. "A man can waste a lot of time in that self-pitying wasteland of blurred vision and confused thoughts. It's not a good thing to wake up with your mouth burning and poisonous stomach pains that you think'll kill you if you don't get another drink quick." He looked back at Lou. "You're better than that, though. You're tougher than I ever was; that much is for sure."

Lou frowned, feeling the hollow space at the core of him. "I don't feel too strong."

"You don't have to. It doesn't change that you are."

They sat in silence for a few moments, Lou enjoying the quiet as his head buzzed slowly back to normality. When he finally spoke, it was softly.

"What the hell is going on in our town?" The question was rhetorical but he figured if anyone had an idea, then it was likely to be Al. And why the hell not? The town drunk seemed more sane and together than anyone else had over recent days.

"Fool's gold, that's what it is."

Lou stared. "How do you mean?"

Al rested his arms on the table. "There has only ever been one battle on this ground, and it has probably raged even from before man walked on the earth. And that's the struggle between ultimate good and ultimate evil. Sometimes we're just pawns in the hands of those two eternal powers." He smiled. "We're paradoxical in our worth. We are each special and with a purpose, but for some that purpose in to merely be toyed with or to serve."

He nodded a little, his eyes sharp as he met Lou's gaze. "And some of us . . . some of us just aren't happy with what we have allotted to us. Our three score years and ten, and the miraculous power we have to love and to hate and above all else, to *choose*. To exercise our free will."

Lou's hangover pressed against the inside of his skull. "I'm not really following you, Al. What has this got to do with fool's gold?"

"Sometimes things can be made to look like they're important, and promise wealth and happiness and your heart's desire, but it's all a veneer." He leaned in. "It's all about temptation. It's *always* been about temptation. Any fool knows that. And in this good and evil battle, there's only ever been one real prize. Immortal power on earth." His forefinger tapped the vinyl surface of the cheap kitchen table. "And that's not for any man's hands, no matter what they are led to believe. The idea that man can have that power is like fool's gold."

Lou frowned. "Where do you get all this stuff from, Al? I never took you for a philosopher." He bit his tongue to stop from adding *and I don't have the first idea as to what you are talking about, you crazy drunken loon. And what the hell has it all got to do with my town?*

"The genie." Al let out a gentle laugh. "Oh, I can see what you're thinking, Lou, and maybe you're right. Maybe the genie is just in my mind. But you know what? I've given that idea a lot of thought recently because even I know that there's something definitely unusual about having a tiny genie in my pocket, but I figure it don't matter so much. I believe in her whether she's real or not. She got me sober and she kept me safe. She told me about the temptation. The fool's gold."

Despite the throbbing head, Lou had lost the woozy vodka feeling, and he was glad. "Who's being tempted?"

"Hell, we all are. All the time at some level. Sometimes we're just tempted to take the easy path. Maybe not such a great sin but if too many of us turn our back on the true way then what happens to our world?"

Lou thought maybe he was supposed to say something, but he just shrugged helplessly.

"Just look around," Al continued. "War, poverty, crime and terrorism surround us. We call it a result of the flaws in our society. But we *are* our society. We make our choices.

The people of our town have made their choices as their forefathers did before them. We've taken the easy route and now the wolves are through the door and we didn't even see it coming."

"Shit, Shtenko. Maybe I'm still drunk, but I need you to stop talking in metaphor."

"Have you read Shakespeare, Deputy?"

Lou shook his head. "Not since high school, and I didn't pay much attention back then."

"Well, he wrote a play called *Macbeth*. It's a great play. When this is all done you should try and see it. It's about a man brought down by his ambition and there's a line in it that goes something like, 'Oftentimes, to win us to our harm, the instruments of darkness tell us truths.'" He laughed again. "I love that line. That Shakespeare knew some stuff, I'm telling you." He paused. "Here in Tower Hill? We're caught in a loop of darkness."

Eccles ran his fingers over the lumps and bumps of his aching head. "You got any more coffee? I'm going to need it if I'm going to have a chance of understanding any of this."

Shtenko slapped him lightly on the back. "Don't you worry. The girl will be here soon. She'll make it clearer. Those students are better with words. In banking it was all numbers."

"What girl?"

Al smiled and Lou almost caught his breath. He'd never seen anyone transformed by an expression before. Al's face was almost beautiful. "She's the light."

"How do you know she's coming?"

"The genie told me, of course."

"The genie. Of course."

Lou wondered for a second whether there had been something in the water Al Shtenko had given him to drink and used to make the coffee. Still, he thought, as he sipped the last dregs from his mug, if you can't beat them, as the old saying went, you may as well join them. And he couldn't deny that the coffee tasted good.

Still, crazy or not, Al and his genie had been right. Twenty minutes after he'd finished his coffee, and luckily just as the Aleve had fully kicked in, the two students from the college had turned up just as predicted, eyes wide and shaky, the blond girl clinging to her friend's arm. Lou recognized them from their meeting outside the church the previous day and he nodded at the boy, Steve. As the two shook hands, a look of mutual understanding passed between them. Lou wondered why the girl smiled at Al so openly, both pairs of eyes twinkling with recognition, and how the hell the two kids had known to come to this house.

"Did you get what you were looking for last night?" Al asked. The girl nodded and pulled out a large hard-covered notebook from inside her jacket.

"I think so. We found this. It's incredible. We started reading it but then the sheriff turned up and wrecked our apartment. The only place we could think to come was here."

"This is where you're supposed to be."

Lou stared. "The sheriff did what?"

Liz continued talking to Al, as if the deputy weren't even there. "I guess he knew it was us that broke in. Maybe he knew we'd tried to find Angela at the hospital. Who knows?"

"He had the dean with him. They really wrecked our apartment. That priest must really have a hold on this town." Steve pulled off his jacket, and there was a clink of metal as he put his backpack down.

"Yes, the priest and that Dr. Kenyon and his stupid supernatural club," Liz added.

Lou could feel his impatience rising and a flicker of memory from the early morning flashed in his head. What had James said? Something about a burglary at the priest's place. Was it these kids who had done it? And how the hell was Al involved? For a moment their words were just a syrupy blur in his ears, and then he snapped.

"Will someone just tell me what the hell is going on?"

Two hours later, Lou had stopped worrying about whether he was crazy. He figured that when the majority was insane, then that must surely become the status quo and therefore any sane thinking would be pretty damned insane. The paradox of the thought made him smile. Al's weird logic must be rubbing off on him. His head was a whirl. From the frying pan came the smell of eggs and hot maple bacon sizzling in oil, and his mouth watered. If it was going to be a last supper, then he could think of worse.

"So, let me get this straight." He paused, not really sure what to say. He'd skimmed the book and Liz had talked him through most of it at least twice, but it was still hard for a simple small-town boy to grasp. "These two mercenaries have murdered the real Father O'Brien and now have the whole town under some sort of hypnotic spell? What about the college teacher? How did he get in there?"

Steve raised an eyebrow. "It seems that as well as being a complete psychopath, if this journal is to be believed, he's also a bona fide doctor of archaeology. I bet a small college like ours would have snapped him up if he'd written to them and said he wanted to teach here."

"And it's not hypnosis," added Liz. "It's worse than that. When we found Angela in the bathroom, it was like she'd been pushed out of her body or something. Our Angela, the real one, was in the shower. Someone else was using her body."

Al Shtenko put down in front of Lou a plate laden with two eggs, bacon, a couple of franks and some beans. "And not just anyone else either." He said. "The children and grandchildren of Adam and Eve, cast out into the wilderness all those millennia ago, where they lived out their extended lives." He grabbed a bottle from the refrigerator. "Ketchup?"

Amazed that he still felt so hungry in the midst of this surreal conversation, Lou nodded and added sauce to his plate before passing it to Steve. Al placed a pot of fresh coffee in the middle of the table alongside a basket of bread. "Go on, then." He smiled. "Don't let it go cold."

Lou picked up his fork but Liz stopped him before he could take a first mouthful. "Wait." Her pale skin flushed a little. "I think maybe we should say grace."

Feeling slightly embarrassed, Lou put his cutlery back down.

Al nodded. "Given the events around us, I think that's a fine idea." He closed his eyes and lowered his face, and Lou found himself doing the same thing as Liz spoke softly.

"For what we are about to receive, may the Lord make us truly thankful." Her breath hitched a little. "And for whatever may be coming our way tonight, please make us strong."

Opening their eyes, they all ate quietly for a while, as if the meal was indeed blessed, and it was only while he was mopping up the last of the egg and bean juice with a thick slice of bread that Lou spoke again, breaking the silence. "So, if none, or at least some of Genesis isn't metaphor and all this actually happened, how come some of the descendants of Adam and Eve lived for such a long time? What did you say? Hundreds of years? How is that possible?"

"The apple," Liz said, sipping her coffee. "It gives eternal life. It makes man equal with God, at least in some ways. It holds knowledge and life in its fruit. And because Adam and Eve had eaten the apple it was in their blood so the small portion of power they'd absorbed was passed down in their line in the form of extended life."

"That's what they're so bitter about." Al swallowed his last forkful of bacon and leaned back in his chair. "Imagine having a taste of all that power and feeling it itching at your veins but not being able to really use it." He sighed. "It would drive the wrong person mad. Some of the children would have lived their long lives out and realized that maybe in a way they'd been blessed, but a few just couldn't get past it. And it's those few that we've got the problem with. They're the ones that left their blood behind in the candles and the bottle, and set everything up for someone to find the tree of life and then bring them back. They want to take what they see as their inheritance and eat their fill of the tree. Are you following?"

Lou Eccles nodded, his head a whirl. "As much as I can." He rubbed his eyes. Damn his head was tired. "So, that's what the supernatural society was about? Getting bodies lined up for these people to come back into?"

"I know it sounds crazy"—from across the table Steve could obviously see the confusion on Lou's face—"but I'm telling you, if you'd seen Angela, you'd know it was true. As soon as she went to that society and started doing that weird meditation shit with those candles, she changed. She went into a haze, like she was disconnected from us."

"That was the point of the meditation, I guess." Liz began gathering up the plates. "To start maybe separating the soul from the body a little. To make it easier for the others to get in."

Lou thought of Emma and little Jacob and their taste for Mabel's muffins and Emma's sudden religious conversion. "And what about the rest of the town? Why have they messed with them?"

"Surplus energy if required. All that life force to take if they need it to get back. The whole town's connected now, through the muffins and the Communion. They've all shared that blood." Al frowned. "And all gods need their faithful followers."

Lou's heart ached. There must be something they could do to get the people back to normal. There had to be. "So when are they supposed to be coming back, these spirits?"

Liz looked at Steve, who shrugged. "We don't know for sure, but the last page or so hints at tonight. I'd bet on that too. The town is falling asleep and there must be other people like us who are looking around and thinking they've been transported to the Twilight Zone and wondering what the hell is going on. There's only so long people will go on with their heads in the sand pretending nothing's wrong before they get out of town and raise an alarm. Those men have been putting the stingers down to keep people in as much as keep people out." He paused. "So I think it'll be tonight."

Liz nodded. "And strange as it sounds, I can feel it. I don't know how, but I can feel the energy buzzing in me. I can't describe it."

Outside, the afternoon light was fading to blue-gray, draining color from everything it touched.

"It's the final scroll," Liz said. "He has to read the final scroll to summon them back. It's sealed. He hasn't even opened it to see, but it's supposed to contain the word of the Lord. The paradosis." She shrugged. "And now that all the necessary parts are in place . . ."

"By parts you mean people," Steve interjected.

"Now that they're all in place," Liz continued, "when he opens the scroll and reads the words they'll be brought back. That's what the journal says."

Al peered out the window, apparently as drawn by the changing light as Lou. "But it's all fool's gold. Fake. At it's simplest it's a con and our adventurers have been too dumb to see it."

Liz and Steve both turned to face Al, and at last Lou felt that he wasn't the only one running to catch up.

"Explain," Steve said.

"Take away all the gimmicks and blood and death and you're left with what's always there. Temptation. It's all about temptation. Those spirits ain't lost like they think they are. They're damned. Damned for their bitterness." He shook his head. "So stupid and such a waste. They think they have the power, but just like those two mercenaries they've fooled, they've been fooled themselves. Ego will blind you. Every time." He turned to face the room.

"If they come back, it'll be the devil that comes with them. Satan himself or whatever name people choose to give him. He'll ride in on the backs of their foolishness, and then he'll have the tree and the knowledge and will be equal with the Lord." He took a deep breath. "It'll be Armageddon. The end of the world as we know it."

"How in shit do you know that?" Steve asked, his eyes narrowing.

Al started to open his mouth, but Lou interrupted. "I'll bet the genie told him." He raised an eyebrow. "But don't knock it. That genie knows stuff." He pushed back his chair and stood up, his legs cramping with tension. Shit, they hurt. It had been a long day since that run on the beach and he was pretty sure it was going to get longer.

"If God is all powerful," he started "then can't He just do something about all this?"

"Sure. He can send the faithful to stand for Him. That's how it works. Faith and temptation."

"So, where in the hell are they?" Lou had a feeling he knew the answer that was coming before the question was out.

"Right here, of course," Al said, as if it were the most obvious thing in the world. "We're the faithful." He smiled.

Lou tried to return the gesture, but felt his countenance turn to a grimace. "But I don't believe in God." He paused and wondered if that were true given the way events were unfolding. "Or maybe I should say, I never have believed in God. And after this shit, I'd still leave the whole damned religious thing alone if I was given the choice again."

Al's lips stretched into a grin. "But that's fine. I reckon young Steve's just the same. You don't have to believe in God to be faithful. You have to believe in *good*. And you two are good people. It shines out of you like the light shines in Liz." He laughed, and the sound tinkled around the room like ice against glass. "Yep, we're the faithful, all right."

Lou looked at Steve, who raised an eyebrow. "Well, regardless of whether we're the faithful or the faithless, I guess it's time we figured out where we go from here. If they're going to do something, they'll be doing it soon."

The gloom gathered into dusk outside, and Lou thought of May. "Their service was at eleven last night. May got back to the B and B at about one. I figure it'll be the same tonight."

"Of course," Al muttered. "They'll be aiming to bring them back at midnight. To start a new seven days. Not Genesis; no creation this time. This time it will be destruction." He gazed back out at the trees twisting in the wind.

And for a while after that nobody spoke.

CHAPTER THIRTY-EIGHT

The tension had been slowly climbing as the clock journeyed painfully, relentlessly around from day to night, and it felt to Steve as if the unease clung to his feet like thick sea mist as he twitched to get moving. The waiting was worse than the fear, and he wished he had some of Liz's faith to help him through. She and Al had gone through to the small living room to pray for a while, leaving him and the deputy to gather whatever they could that may help in either their defense or attack.

Despite the lack of faith in both of them, neither had argued that taking a few bottles of the holy water would do any harm. He'd gone through Al's meager wardrobe and dug out a couple of thick belts they could use to hold knives at their waists, and although they'd found an old revolver, there were no bullets that he could see. Still, he brought it through to the kitchen and added it to the small collection of weapons on the kitchen table.

"Hey, look at this," Lou muttered quietly. "Something's happening."

Steve joined the other man at the window and pushed two of the blinds slightly apart to peer out into the dark. Shapes moved slowly on the sidewalk as figures silently stumbled by the house, no energy or conversation apparent, just a steady flow heading into the center of the small town. They moved like the exhausted refugees shown on TV sometimes, worn down by war and lost in their own worlds as they trudged toward the flicker of hope for a better existence, heads down and closed off from humanity.

Steve's heart caught somewhere in his throat for a second before he swallowed it back down. "Your timing was pretty exact. It's coming upon ten forty-five." On the other side of the street an elderly couple came out of their house and joined the passing human traffic, leaving their front door wide open and seeming as unaware of each other as of any of the people around them. "We need to join that crowd if we want to get into the church unnoticed."

Lou nodded, his jaw tight. Steve wondered what he was thinking and then instantly answered his own question by wondering if the deputy's wife was out there in the passing crowd somewhere. He watched the grim expression on the older man's face. Lou Eccles was a good man. If he'd been working the trailer park beat back in Detroit, then maybe Steve would have stayed out of trouble a little more in his early teens.

Behind them the kitchen door opened and Al came in with Liz a couple steps behind him. Looking at her, Steve smiled. There were so many things he wanted to say but knew he couldn't. Not tonight. Not this night. Her face was open and clear and strong despite everything that was going on around them, and telling her how he felt about her would just be selfish. It wouldn't change anything and they didn't need any more confusion or anything more to distract them when they were in the church.

"Is it time?" Al said. He tugged a dark, well-worn overcoat from the back of the door.

"Yep." Lou nodded. "I do believe it is. There's a crowd out there heading toward the church. We need to lose ourselves in it. It's how we'll get in."

Steve picked up the gun. "Have you got any bullets for this thing?"

"Just one. In the drawer by the stove." Al frowned a little. "But guns and knives aren't going to win this battle, Steve."

Rummaging through the wooden drawer stuffed with take-out pizza menus and old unpaid utility bills, and not wanting or needing to ask why Al Shtenko kept only one bullet for his gun, Steve felt the cold metal cylinder under his fingers and tossed it over to the deputy. "That may be, Al, but it's always better to be on the safe side." He turned to Liz. "If you put one of those belts on over your jeans but under your jacket, you can tuck a knife into it and not cut yourself." *I hope,* he nearly added. He was sounding a lot more confident than he felt. But then he couldn't really feel any less confident. The world had gone mad and the trailer-park boy from Detroit was about to go into a battle between God and the devil. Now that was some kind of fucked-up shit. He almost smiled at the street language creeping back in. Maybe he needed it in order to be brave.

Liz stared at the table but didn't touch anything.

"Go on." He frowned. "Liz, take one of the knives. We've got to get going."

Looking up at him, she shook her head. "No. You guys take them. Not me."

"What?" He squeezed her arm. "Look, that's crazy. I know you might not like the idea of stabbing someone and neither do I, but we have no idea what all these people will do. We don't know what the hell is going to happen when we get in there and you need to be protected." He paused. "It's not as if the odds are on our side." He looked over at Eccles for support, and the deputy nodded.

"Steve's right. I'd be a whole lot happier knowing you were protected."

Liz smiled. "I will be protected. I have you three and I have God. What more do I need?"

Beside her, Al Shtenko nodded serenely, and in that moment Steve wanted to punch him in the face. "Well, God helps those that help themselves, remember?"

She shook her head again. "I can't explain it, Steve. It wouldn't be right. For the first time in a long time I feel at home with my faith and I'm going to trust in it." She smiled at him, and Steve didn't see an ounce of fear in her face. He didn't know if that made him more or less afraid.

"And I'm going to trust in you," she added softly. "So let's stop arguing and get going."

"Amen to that." Al Shtenko buttoned up his battered jacket. Steve stared at them both, frustrated and confused, but was pleased to see that Shtenko at least took a knife and tucked it into the pocket of his oversized coat, along with two bottles of the blessed water. Something was better than nothing, he guessed.

Lou Eccles tugged on his own coat and looked over at Steve. "I don't know about you, but I intend to hedge my bets both ways." He picked up three knives, wedging them around his waist, and then took a small Evian bottle filled with the water, opening it and taking a sip before tucking one away.

Steve smiled. "I like your thinking, Deputy. When this is all over, you'll be getting my vote for the sheriff's job."

Lou nodded. "Well, let's get rid of the current one first, shall we?" That grim expression was back.

CHAPTER THIRTY-NINE

Out on the street, Al fell into step behind a fat man he recognized from his respectable days. From the days before
the booze haze had taken hold of his life. The man was an
avid quarter collector and he'd bring in his huge jars of
coins to be changed every six months or so with a pleased
but slightly embarrassed anecdote about what he'd spend
his money on. Funny, the things you remember sometimes.

Keeping his head low and mimicking the man's shuffling gait, Al wondered if he even realized he'd come out in
his pajamas and slippers. He must be awful cold in the
crisp night air. His heart ached. The man's name was lost
in his head somewhere and he wished he could remember
it. That would be respectful at a time like this. But the name
was gone in a bottle of vodka drunk too long ago and it
wouldn't be found.

Two or three people ahead he could see the young
deputy walking between two old women, his head lolling
slightly, mimicking the movement of the travelers around
him. Fighting the urge to sniff in case it drew attention to
him, he let his nose run a little in the chill before the irritation got to be too much and he slowly raised his hand and
wiped the mucus away. No one turned to look at him or

scream or identify a stranger in their midst, but just kept on walking slowly forward.

The silence, broken only by the soft slap of shoes on pavement was eerie, and he was glad when the road veered around and carried them into the heart of the town, its sidewalks lit with bright lights that helped him pretend that all was well. But all was not well. Looking up, it took all his control not to gasp.

Hundreds of townspeople, just like those around him, wandered in silence toward where the church sat on the cliff's edge, maneuvering around so that no one touched another, as if they were islands of numb flesh and bone, no hint of personality as they moved like zombies, steadily onward.

You keep calm, the genie said. *You keep calm and you keep strong, Al Shtenko.* He looked down to where she peered out of one of his pockets, toned thighs wrapped around the cap of the water bottle she was perched on.

"Shhh," he muttered, aware of the movement of every limb around him.

Her laugh tinkled loudly. *I'm not stupid, Al. I'm talking inside your head. See? No lips moving.*

He looked down. She wasn't lying. It was a strange sensation. *Can I answer you in my head?* He thought the question.

Of course. Would be pretty silly if you couldn't, wouldn't it?

So you can read my thoughts? Al knew she was sitting in his pocket, but it felt as if she were also making herself comfortable somewhere in the gray mass of his brain, padding down a soft corner and lazily lying on it.

Only the ones you talk to me with. Anything else might be a touch impolite.

Al fought the urge to laugh out loud. He liked the genie. He liked her a lot. For a moment they walked along in both mental and physical silence and Al weighed up how he felt about having her in his head. He watched the silently moving individuals around him. *Maybe I'm the only person in Tower Hill tonight that isn't alone.*

No. The genie spoke softly. *You're not the only one. Very few people are ever truly alone, Al. They just forget about the footprints in the sand.*

The church loomed into view ahead of them, and Al glanced over at Liz and Steve dragging their feet along a few feet to his left. They seemed miles away, as if he'd never touch them or speak to them again. It was crazy, he knew. They had a long way to go yet and he hoped they'd be all right. In fact, he hoped they'd all be about okay when the new day came.

Seeing the gray building lit up against the dark of the ocean behind it, Al felt the first real moment of terror gripping him since all this had started. He'd been afraid plenty before over the years, and right at the beginning of all this when the genie had first showed up he'd been sure that maybe he was going plain crazy. But terror? Terror had been saved for the end.

Will you stay with me tonight?

He felt the genie smile inside his head. *Sure, buddy. It's you and me all the way, Al. Right till the end.*

Her voice seemed a little sad, and he hoped that she had some faith in him. *I'll try and do my best, you know,* he thought. *I really will.*

And that's all anyone will ever ask, Al. Just try your best.

Despite his shaking legs, Al trudged on toward the church steps.

Chapter Forty

Steve had followed the shuffling line to the base of the steps, his legs feeling awkward with the slow movement. Looking up at the light pouring so confidently outwards from the open church doors, his heart pumped so hard that he could feel the veins in his head throbbing. The tips of his fingers tingled with cold, adrenaline, and more than a little fear.

Dark figures stood on each side of the heavy arch, supervising those shambling forward; from outside, surrounded by night, it was hard to make out who the ushers were, but he was pretty sure neither was big enough in build to be either the sheriff or Dr. Kenyon. Keeping his head low, he glanced up for a second to see Lou Eccles crossing the threshold into the building and disappearing into the crowd and yellow glow within, his lurching body movements identical to those lost people around him. He wasn't stopped, sliding invisibly in. Steve's pulse raced some more as he tried to keep his breathing even, and he focused on his feet taking one step at a time forward.

He was on the second stair up to the church when he realized what was happening. A dark shadow cut across his vision and he looked up to see what was blocking the light, and then it all became clear. Shit. Oh shit. His mouth dried.

There was a small tug on his sleeve and he found Liz beside him, her eyes wide as she too realized that things weren't going to go according to plan and that maybe they'd be thwarted before they'd even begun.

They stared for a long terrible moment at the closing doors ahead. "Oh, shit." He finally said out loud, and after a hesitation that seemed like forever, he threw himself forward, pushing past the walkers around him and launching at the last gap, the final strip of light. But it was too little, too late. His body slammed into the cold, heavy oak as it closed on him, a vibration running up through his shoulder and rattling out through his teeth. He stepped backward. The light was gone and they were left out in the cold night.

"Shit!" he said, in the direction of the barrier that had shut them out. He turned to face the darkness. "Shit," he whispered, the word the only one he seemed able to form. Apart from the shadows of Liz and Al coming toward him, everywhere was still. The sea of bodies stood frozen, as if with the doors closing all their energy had been drained from them. They were lifeless, unmoving statues staring emptily at the church that had been the holy grail of their silent journey. The other two joined him on the top step, Liz panting slightly, her breath catching with panic.

"Why have they shut the church? Liz said quietly, her voice little more than a tremble. "Why would they do that? What are we going to do now?"

Al sighed. "We should have thought. There are way too many people. They were never going to fit all these people in and I figure they don't need them, either. I guess it must be pretty crammed with life in there."

"We should have moved faster. We should have run here. Oh, God, we can't have failed already."

She was either swearing or making a plea to her God; Steve wasn't sure. Al wrapped a thin arm gently around her shoulder. "Lou's in there. And either we'll find another way in or he'll find a way of getting that door open as soon as he can. He's a good man, and a clever one. He won't let us down."

Steve nodded but his heart had sunk. He didn't rate Lou's chances very highly, being in there on his own. There must be five hundred people packed into the ancient building. How was Lou going to get the door open? "Shit," he muttered again. "Shit. We should have thought. We should have been here earlier. We should have been hiding out nearby."

Liz took his hand. "It's okay. We've got some time." She looked out toward the twinkling ocean. "It won't end like this. It can't."

Al nodded, and in the gloom his eyes looked like twin moons in the dark space of his face. "She's right, you know. It won't end like this." He turned away as if speaking to the shadowy figures that silently surrounded them, but listening to what came next, Steve wondered with a shiver if he just couldn't face them.

"It won't end like this because we haven't made our stand. We haven't made our sacrifices." He shook his head slightly, his words dancing out over the still bodies whose occupants slumbered somewhere deep inside, if they were there at all. "So, let's see if anyone's left the back gate open for us."

"No." Liz shook her head. "You stay here. If Lou manages to get the door open, we're going to need someone here so that we know. You can whistle for us." She paused. "Or just yell."

CHAPTER FORTY-ONE

Head down, Lou Eccles slid into the throng of people who were overflowing from the pews, losing himself in the crowd, his face flushing in the damp heat before he realized that the heavy doors had closed only a few people behind him.

Without the cold night air wafting in, the church became stifling within moments and his skin prickled beneath his coat, his own sweat adding to the sickly scented blend of hundreds of varieties of human perspiration. Judging by the strength of the odor, he figured that some of that sweat was less fresh than others and his nose wrinkled slightly in disgust. Ever so slowly, he slightly turned, allowing himself a glimpse behind. His eyes hooded, he scanned the view. There were no eyes there seeking him out. His heart sank. None of the others had made it inside. He was on his own.

Using the man beside him as a shield to stay partly hidden, he studied the back of the church. Both sides were completely crammed with people in all manner of dress, from underwear to full coats and hats, some sitting up on the backs of the pews to make room for more to squeeze in front, but between them all the aisle was clear, apart from the odd leg or shoulder that drifted into the gap.

The two men who had been guarding the open doors now shuffled up to the front and took their places nearer the altar, and a familiar figure stepped up to stand in front of the door with the old-fashioned wooden bar pulled down to keep it firmly shut. James Russell folded his arms and stared forward. Lou watched him. His old friend and boss wasn't looking so good. He hadn't shaved, judging by the stubble that covered his chin and neck, more flecked with gray than the hair that sat messily atop his head. There were bags under his eyes that Lou could see quite clearly from where he was standing, and there was no denying that the sheriff had lost a lot of weight. And fast. If it weren't for the belt cinched tightly around his waist, Lou was pretty sure that his uniform pants would slip right off. Under Lou's fear, his heart ached a little. What had they done to his friend? And how the hell had he let it happen? James was always so god-damn together, and now he'd been turned into someone else's puppet in what seemed like the blink of an eye.

Lou bit the inside of his mouth, the sharp pain making him refocus, and he let his eyes slowly drift around. He knew he had to think about finding a way to get the others in as soon as whatever crazy service was planned finally started, but first he needed to satisfy the aching question inside him. Despite the small part of him that didn't want to look at all, that preferred not knowing whether Emma was amongst these living dead, the policeman that some-where over the years had become *the man* instead of just *the job* knew he had no choice but to try to find out.

A child coughed somewhere up ahead at the same time as strange, hypnotic music piped into the silence, pushing it back against the walls. Lou's heart jolted. Could that be Jacob? He willed the sound to come again but there was nothing. Above the lights dimmed to nothing, leaving only the candles spread out along the walls to light the space. He gave his eyes a moment to refocus and then let them drift along his line. He found a few familiar faces gazing blankly

forward, but none of them was Emma's. His heart thumped
out its slight relief.

A door creaked open up at the front of the church, and
using the noise to cover his own, he eased himself along
the row until he reached the far end. The bodies around
him gave way to his movement as if they were made of soft
clay, bending themselves to let him through and then right-
ing themselves again, as if he'd never been there. Stepping
out of the pew and into the gloom behind a pillar, Lou felt
a shudder of revulsion at the people around him. James
Russell may not have been looking too great, but compared
to the rest of the town that was out tonight, he was in peak
condition. Lou stepped up to the next row, scanning the
lines of each slack face for the features of his wife, his
stomach flipping with relief each time he didn't find her.

The volume of the music rose, and something in the
crowd changed. Moving slightly forward, he studied the
face of the old woman at the end of the closest row. Her
eyes had shut, her head lolling back slightly, and her mouth
began to move. Just tiny twitches at first, and then slowly,
bit by bit, the sounds came, breathy and harsh and in perfect timing with everyone around her. "*Sethenoshkenanma-
halaleljaredenochsethenoshkenanmahalaleljaredenoch.*"

The strange words came out in a chorus of rapid, jerky
breaths, harsh whispers filling the room, awkward mouths
spraying saliva with the consonants. His shoes shuffled
backward. What the hell was this? Pressing into the wall
behind him, he edged himself forward, toward the front of
the church, trying to get a better view. His heart caught in
his throat. Emma's mother sat five rows from the front, her
mouth chanting incoherently like all the others, her head
listing slightly to her left. He strained in the gloomy candlelight to see either side of her. Emma and Jacob weren't
there. Surely if they were inside, they'd have been sitting
there with her mother. . . . Surely they would have been.
His insides screamed with frustration.

He knew he was just trying to convince himself because right now in Tower Hill there was no "surely" to be found in anything.

From up ahead a laugh rang out, deep and rich and warm and completely out of place amongst this collection of chanting zombies.

"Holy shit, Jack. We've fucking done it." The man laughed again. "Look at this shit. Just look."

Lou's whole body tense and alert, concerns for Emma and Jacob boxed away in his heart, he crumpled his tall frame down a little and trotted up to the pillar closest to the altar and peered around it.

"It seems we have, Gray. We're very nearly there." Father O'Brien, or whoever he damned was, grinned at a tall blond man dressed in jeans and a white shirt. Lou's eyes narrowed. He must be the college professor Liz and Steve had talked about. Beneath his thick blond hair he was a handsome man, but there was something wrong with his skin. Lou frowned. It looked rough and scaly in places, running up his neck from under his collar and spreading up across his cheek, as if he were suffering a nasty bout of eczema. Kenyon trotted down the stairs and stood in the middle of a circle of chairs.

"Where do you want me?"

"You can stay right there if you want. You did all the ground work with the kids. You'll get the best view of them changing from the center of the circle."

Why the hell was the O'Brien impostor still bothering with the priest's outfit now that the deception was no longer necessary? Maybe there was something about its inherent power that he liked. Still, it seemed a little insane to dress like God's servant when you were trying to become equal to God yourself. But then, he reconsidered as he tried to get a better view of the chairs, this whole thing was insane, and the fact that he was even here showed that he'd been touched by it himself.

Kenyon stood in the center of the circle and O'Brien moved around each of the twelve chairs, unwrapping what looked like ancient daggers from individual cloths and placing one on the lap of each of the seats' occupants. Looking at the kids there, Lou felt his anger rise. One girl had rough stitches covering her face and he figured she must be Liz's friend Angela, who James was supposed to have taken to the hospital. Next to her sat the boy he'd found staring out at the sea that morning, holding the severed hand in his own. Just a college football jock. Jesus.

Despite their thinness and vacant expressions, their clothes belied them all as the kids they were. They'd come to his town full of life and expectations and thinking they'd be safe, and this had happened to them. His fingers itched to do something and he curled them into a frustrated ball. There was nothing he could do on his own. He needed to find a way to get the others in.

"Why do they need the daggers?" Kenyon played with the long blond hair of one of the students as he spoke, tugging it roughly this way and that, bemused by her lack of reaction.

"It's just part of the ceremony. They're from the ancient days of human sacrifice." O'Brien stood up straight and surveyed the circle. He seemed happy.

"This shit is blood-blood-blood all the way. You gotta love it."

"You certainly do." The priest looked over to the blond man and smiled. "You ready for immortality and the life of a God, Gray? Our biggest adventure?"

Kenyon laughed again. "What do you think, Jack? I think I've always been ready."

Their conversation, so normal against the backdrop of the whispered chanting, set Lou's teeth on edge. It was wrong. Everything about this was wrong. He peered into the gloom along the left side of the church wall, hoping to see some kind of door there, but there was nothing but solid stone. Shit. The church must have a second doorway, but it was obviously somewhere on the right, beyond the altar, and maybe in a vestry. There was no way he could get there without passing James Russell or cutting straight across the aisle, and there was no way he'd manage that without being seen. Shit. He was pretty much screwed.

On the altar sat an old trunk, and O'Brien opened it. Taking some kind of ornamental bottle from it, he used one of the cloths that had held the daggers and went over to the pews, smearing thick red liquid that could only be blood onto the foreheads of the people sitting in the front row. Lou saw plenty of faces he recognized there: Mabel, Doc McGeechan, the dean of the college and the mayor were among them, all pillars of Tower Hill's small community. A line of blood trickled down Mabel's face and into the untidy folds of her bosom. She didn't wipe it away, lost in whatever reverie she had been lulled into. The priest put the bottle back and carefully lifted out a scroll.

"Are you sure we're ready?" Kenyon asked.

"There were no apples in the box this morning," O'Brien answered. "It's time."

The two men looked at each other and smiled.

"Let's do it, then. The paradosis. The secret word of the Lord." Kenyon grinned. "Break it open, dude."

The priest held the seal over a candle. "So let us begin."

Lou looked from the awful scene at the front of the church to the door at the back, which was guarded by the sheriff. Above the wet mutterings of the crown he heard the parchment unravel, its bloody wax melted. The sea of people in front of him let out a collective sigh before restarting their chant.

Lou stared at the door at the back and the man blocking it and thought of Jacob and Emma and all these people that he'd sworn to protect. He knew what he'd have to do if Liz, Steve and Al couldn't find a way in. There was no other choice. He'd just have to take the sheriff on. Looking at the size of the man and knowing the strength that James Russell had in those arms, and knowing that his holster would be full, Lou felt his stomach flip with more than a little fear. He sighed and hoped that there really was a God. He really hoped there was.

And the man at the front of the church began to speak.

CHAPTER FORTY-TWO

Liz and Steve trotted around the building, peering in the gloom for any sign of an entrance. "There'll be a back door somewhere by the vestry," she whispered. "But it'll be solid. I'm not sure of your chances of picking it." She didn't know why she wasn't speaking loudly. It wasn't as if any of the residents of Tower Hill were even aware of them. Shivering, she glanced back at the dark shapes scattered and unmoving, far into the distance. They were like pillars of salt.

The Genesis story shifted in her head and she wondered whether that was what she and Steve should have done. Just turned and left and not looked back. She squeezed the pebble in her pocket. That would have been safer maybe. But it wasn't the path for them. Their purpose was here.

Her feet invisible in the darkness, she felt her way around the far end of the church as they jogged. "We have to get in, Steve. We have to find a way. We can't stop them from out here."

"I know," Steve answered. She couldn't see his face in the night, but his voice was grim. Their breathing was raw against the gentle lap of the ocean behind them as they came to a halt by the small wooden door at the back of the church. The earth had been cut away and a few uneven

steps led down to it. Steve went first and Liz sat on the top
step, not wanting to block any moonlight he might need to
work by.

The stone was cold, eating through her jeans and numb-
ing her skin, and she chewed her mouth impatiently while
he fiddled with the lock, trying varying combinations of
equipment and movement.

After five minutes, Liz couldn't keep silent anymore.
"What do you think? Can you unlock it?"

Steve stood up and sighed. "Yeah, I can unlock it. But it
won't do any good." He paused. "It's bolted on the inside.
We can't get in this way."

Nausea ate into her heart. She'd been sure, positive, that
they'd get in. They had to—inside was where the battle
was going to be. God couldn't be this cruel. Were they just
supposed to sit on the sidelines and watch? The wind coming straight in off the water beat at her face but she barely
felt its sting. Maybe it wasn't God. Maybe it was them.
They'd let him down already. They'd left too late. They'd
been complacent.

So many images of failure filled her head: the priest,
Mabel, the sheriff leading Angela out of the apartment.
They'd let God down on each of those counts. Surely she
could have done something by now. She remembered
her doubt and wanted to cry. How could she have doubted
her faith? Why couldn't she have separated her doubt of
her family and her belief in God? And now it seemed that
maybe God had lost his faith in her.

The clouds drifted overhead, clearing the way for the
moon to shine down in all its glory. She stared at it for a
moment, its full white circle perfect against the black of
the night sky, before biting back a sob and shaking herself.
This was no time for self-pity or tears. She was giving up
before they'd begun. And the faithful didn't do that.

Steve took her hand and pulled her up. "Let's get back
around to the front and see if Al's got any ideas. He seems

to be pretty overloaded with karma and wisdom, for the town drunk. And I could use some of his good karma right now."

Halfway around to the front of the church, Liz felt her center of gravity shift slightly and she almost tumbled over onto the damp grass. Steve grabbed her to keep her from falling. "You okay?"

"Yeah." She nodded. Something fizzed deep in her core and for a second her legs almost buckled. She was okay and not okay. "Didn't you feel that? Like a kind of pulse of energy? It came right up through my feet."

Steve shook his head. "No. No, I'm fine."

A dark terror gripped her gut and she dragged him back around to the front of the church, her jog turning to a sprint despite the disorientation that kept hitting her in waves. They joined Al at the top of the steps.

"There's no way in from the back," Steve panted. "It's bolted."

"And whatever's going on in there, it's started," Liz added, her voice low. "I can feel it, like an awful, dark power coming up through the earth. It's making me feel like I've been breathing gas fumes. All sick and headachy." She looked at Al. "Can you feel it?"

Al shook his head. "No, honey, I can't. That's why you're so special." He sighed. "But you'd better get ready, because I think that door will be opening soon and then we're going to go into battle."

"How can you be so sure?" Steve asked.

Al shrugged. "Just call it gut instinct."

CHAPTER FORTY-THREE

Al stood to the right of the girl and peered into his pocket. He figured that gut instinct wasn't that much of a lie.

Sitting in that safe well of warm cloth, the genie wiped away a small tear and then stood up. She sighed. *Are you ready, Al?* she asked in his head.

He thought about it for a few seconds before deciding that the answer was almost irrelevant. The moment was upon them. He *had* to be ready.

Sure, I guess if you are, I am, he answered. *How come you're crying? Are you frightened?*

He wasn't sure he liked the idea of the genie being afraid. In fact, it scared the living shit out of him.

No, no I'm not afraid, Al. She sighed. *It's the deputy. He's a good man. Sometimes the true beauty of human nature just gets me all welled up, you know? Sometimes the precious gift you'll give away for the sake of others just takes my breath away.* She smiled up at him. *And that's why we'll stand today, Al Shtenko. For the beauty of mankind.*

Al smiled back. He liked the genie's sentiment but wondered if she'd forgotten the kind of pain that often accompanied that beauty. His heart thumping, he felt more alive than he had in years. It was funny what a little terror could do for you. He stared at the door. And waited.

CHAPTER FORTY-FOUR

As soon as the priest began to speak, things changed in the church. A sharp pain shot down one side of Lou's head and, gritting his teeth, he had to lean on the pillar to get back his balance.

The ground beneath his feet throbbed and the people that filled the pews swayed from side to side, as if even in their lost state they could feel something building in the air. Something coming that was remarkable and terrible and unnatural.

Their voices rose as one, a mockery of a choir, the discordant slurring chant threatening to drown out the one clear voice reading from the scroll at the front. A foul-smelling breeze rushed past him, and he turned to see if by some miracle the others had made it in from outside, but there was no sign of them. The rotten air, a veil of sickness and disease, swept back, blowing in all directions at once.

God, it was foul. His heart pounding, Lou's stomach fought to keep down the eggs and bacon he'd eaten earlier. This wasn't a natural wind. This was coming from within the church. It was being created here or somewhere that was trying to *be* here, conjured along with the souls that the two mercenaries were trying to bring back.

Knowing that if he didn't move now, then fear would

probably keep him rooted to the spot until it was far too late, he pushed away from the pillar and jogged toward the back of the church. Stopping at the third to last pew, he pushed his way in amongst the people there and slowly edged along their line. He fought the urge to go faster, knowing that despite his fear that he'd left this until too late, he needed to be cautious.

The priest was occupied with his words but Lou couldn't see what Kenyon was doing, and he couldn't afford to risk being noticed by either the professor or the sheriff.

His ears aching with the chanting that roared around him, he moved on, ignoring the unpleasant film of liquid forming on his face from the hot tangy breath that damply spat onto him as he passed each individual.

He didn't look for Emma anymore. Either she was in here or she wasn't. There was nothing he could do about that now and all he could do for her was this. His business now was to get the door open. And that meant getting past James Russell.

Reaching inside his jacket, he carefully pulled out the old pistol and released the safety. He had one shot at this, literally one chance. He couldn't blow it. His head and heart ached and he tried to stop his hand from shaking. Taking a deep breath, he stepped out into the aisle.

Behind him the cacophony of noise continued, and for one blissful moment as he took a few steps forward, bringing himself only a few feet from the man he'd considered his very best friend despite the gap in their years, he thought that James Russell was as lost in all this as the rest of the poor town, and then Lou saw the glazed eyes focus on him, widening a little in surprise.

Lou held up the gun, pointing it at his boss. "Step away from the door, James. I don't want to have to—"

Someone punched him hard in the stomach, knocking the rest of the sentence away into nowhere. He doubled over, staggering sideways into the crowd. *Jesus, that hurt.*

Stars flickered at the edge of his vision and, trying to stand straight, he looked down, confused. Who had hit him? How? He pulled his hand away and stared. Blood. His hand was covered in blood. In the doorway, James Russell raised his gun again, and Lou almost smiled through the burning pain that was now filling his guts.

The sheriff always had been a fast draw. Not that either of them had ever had much call to use their guns in the streets of Tower Hill. In fact, Lou realized, this was the first time he'd so much as raised a weapon in his whole time as a deputy. How was that for irony? But he'd still practiced. James had insisted they keep themselves sharp, just in case. In all those afternoons down on the range, laughing and talking and shooting the breeze as they took out the targets, he figured neither of them would have ever guessed that one day they'd be shooting each other. How about that for things turning out funny? He wished he could laugh about it. Or maybe cry.

His legs felt heavy, and for a moment he thought the white light that suddenly glared in the building was inside him, but then he realized it was coming from behind him, from where the altar and the circle of chairs were. The voice at the front grew louder and despite his cloudy thinking, Lou knew the priest was building up to a crescendo.

He stayed a little hunched over for a second, wobbling more than he needed to, although Jesus himself knew that he could happily sink to the floor and stay there. He shut his eyes for a brief moment.

"I forgive you, James," he whispered under his breath. "And I know you'll forgive me. Amen."

Using all the energy he had, he whipped himself up tall and in the same moment raised the pistol, and with a clear eye focused on his target, pulled the trigger. A small red hole appeared in the middle of the sheriff's forehead, right between his surprised eyes.

For a moment he just stood there, and it seemed to Lou

as if for an instant his friend was back and looking at him, wondering what the hell they were both doing in the church with bullets in them, and then the light faded and he crumpled to the floor. His friend was dead.

The door seemed like an age away rather than a few feet. Dropping the pistol, Lou kept one hand over the warm, wet hole at his middle and used his free one to prop himself up from one pew to the next. Finally, just before the blackness at the edge of his vision threatened to take over, he reached the door. Stepping over the dead body of the sheriff, he lifted the bolt with arms he could barely feel, and just as the priest finished speaking, yanked open the door. He was dimly aware of the others staring back at him from the cool crisp night and he tried to smile, but he wasn't sure he managed it. His legs gave way but a pair of strong arms caught him before he collapsed.

"I got you deputy." Al's voice seemed distant, too far away to be coming from the man holding him, and in the background Lou saw Steve dragging Liz into the church and her turning and staring at him in horror. That look probably didn't bode well for him, he decided. Not good at all. Cold began settling in his limbs. The fire in his belly had gone out and had been replaced with shards of ice. His teeth chattered.

Outside, Al sat him down against the wall at the top of the steps. Lou looked up at the kind face that blurred a little in front of him.

I can't feel my fingers, he tried to say, but just wheezy breath came out.

"You done good, Deputy Eccles," Al whispered, softly. "You done real good. You sit here and rest now."

Al's fingers felt hot on his skin as they pushed the hair out of his face, and Lou wondered how Al could be so hot and yet he was so cold, and he knew there was a reason but it was all getting vague and messy in his head, so he just thought of Emma and Jacob and held their faces in the gloom behind his eyes. There was nothing confused about them.

"I hate to leave you here, son." Al's voice was growing more distant and Lou wished he wouldn't sound so sad. "But I've got to go inside. I've got business to take care of in there. I hope you forgive me."

Lou tried to nod. It seemed there was a whole lot of forgiving being done tonight. Hadn't he just forgiven someone? He couldn't think who. He was vaguely aware of Al Shtenko getting to his feet and walking away. He didn't mind so much. His eyes were tired. In fact, all of him was tired. Maybe he should just sleep. Maybe he should just—

And then he was gone.

CHAPTER FORTY-FIVE

Steve tugged Liz away from the pale and bleeding deputy and in through the open doors. Somewhere over the mad cacophony of noise pouring out at them he could hear her screaming at him to stop, but he pulled her forward, his heart aching.

He'd seen the thick dark blood seeping out between the young man's fingers as the deputy clutched at his leaking guts, and he knew deep down—in that place where his survival instinct was raging at him to turn an run—that Lou Eccles was dying. And as much as he wanted to stop and sit with him and say a thousand things, he knew there wasn't any time.

"Come on!" He yelled. He was damned if he was going to let Lou Eccles die in vain. He was damned if he was going to let any of them die in vain.

Stumbling over the body of the dead sheriff, they entered the madness. A foul wind beat around them, blasting up through the aisle, and Liz raised her arm to protect her eyes from it as it whipped her hair around her neck and face.

At the far end of the aisle, the kids from the college sat in a circle of seats, white light erupting from their ears, eyes and mouths, bright and painful like a nuclear blast. In the middle stood Kenyon, his arms out wide, laughing as he turned and turned, his hair standing on end, crackling with electric light. Steve paused and stared, terror gripping his soul. This was some far-out shit. What the fuck was he doing here? How could they stop this?

"Oh, God, we're too late. *We're too late,*" Liz shouted above the moaning and screeching of the crowd, whose chanting blurred into animalistic wails. Some of them tugged at their hair, others turned in circles, and some just swayed from side to side, their heads unsteady on their necks.

Although the wind was blasting around him and Liz, it didn't seem to affect the congregation, who remained lost somewhere in a world of their own. He figured maybe that wasn't such a bad thing. If all these people turned on them they'd be dead in seconds.

Light bled from the bodies at the front, joining the unnatural wind and spinning fast at the edge of the circle, creating a small tornado blocking their path. Despite the fetid air blasting toward him and burning his eyes, Steve looked up beyond the altar to where Father O'Brien stood staring down at them, his face glowing in the light. He smiled mockingly, the open scroll in one hand.

Their eyes met, and Steve was sure that the other man's burned red for a moment. What the hell was happening to him? Did he even know? Liz was still fighting to make her way forward, her hand in his, pressing against the wind to get closer to the action when the priest waved the scroll in their direction, smiling at his victory.

As if the scroll were some kind of fan directing it, the tornado exploded toward them. Liz's hand was ripped out of his as the fierce shock wave of light and air hit them, lifting them right off the ground.

"Liz!" He barely had time to get her name out before seeing her slam into the opposite wall and collapse in a heap on the stone floor, and then his own skull cracked against the pillar and all the lights went out.

CHAPTER FORTY-SIX

Jack had heard of paradise and had never believed in it. How wrong he had been. He *was* paradise. *This* was paradise. He had created it and it tingled in every cell of his being.

Behind the circle of bright light everything was still and silent, and standing in the midst of that small island of calm he watched the changing unfold as though a composer in awe of the orchestra playing his finest piece of music.

He had no interest in the townspeople that filled the pews of the church. They were sheep and cattle, available for slaughter as required, and what would be done with them after would be decided after. They were slaves.

A shiver of pleasure ran through him, so strong that he sighed. He felt as if he were in the first delicious waves of orgasm but with all of his faculties intact. Yes, maybe slaves were what he would need. Slaves and worshippers. It made him smile. Even his face felt different, as if he could feel every nerve and fiber that moved there.

Beyond the first row the light was so bright that the crowd was just a sea of bodies, but he had no more concerns. The teenagers were out cold somewhere at the back and the scroll had been read. His face stretched farther, his teeth gritting as he grinned.

In the circle, Gray turned, laughing, and Jack could see him calling something out, but the words didn't penetrate the wall of silence. Still he had a good idea what they were. *This is fucking great* was what it had looked liked and he laughed, a tinkling melody of sound. Nothing could change Gray all that much. Gray had always been different.

The light that had poured so aggressively out of the students lost its strength and gathered like a mist in the high vaulted ceiling. Jack looked up. What next? Was this it? Were they coming? His heart thumped in excitement.

The white mist changed color, going through a spectrum of pinks and then darkening to crimson, swirling faster and faster before dividing into twelve jets and shooting like lasers into the bodies below.

As the final strip of light vanished, Jack caught his breath. The church descended into silence and he could see it all now, lit only by the burning candles. In the rows of wooden seats people slumped across each other, not unconscious but not conscious. Their legs no longer able to support them, they'd collapsed where they stood, landing on a bench, the concrete or one another, not seeming to mind which. The church doors were open and outside the night was black.

"Hey, Jack. Look." Gray's voice pulled his attention back to the circle. One of the students was moving. He looked at her more closely. Not one of the students. Not anymore. She'd changed.

Where earlier her face had been a web of infected red and angry stitching, now the skin was fresh and pale and completely smooth. Jack smiled at Gray. He wondered if his friend could feel the changes to his own face, now half covered in pearlescent scales that glinted with every change of expression. Gray had always been so proud of his looks. Was he still proud?

The girl moaned slightly and struggled to clutch the dagger on her lap but couldn't muster the energy. Her eyes opened and flashed angrily sideways to the front pew, her gaze locking on one of its occupants. Mabel rose to her feet, and Jack watched as consciousness refocused in those dull eyes. The red blood on her forehead glowed and for the first time since he'd known her, Jack saw fear in the fat bitch's face. She was her old self, the daze induced by the blood gone, if only for a while.

Her feet shuffled forward despite her feeble attempts to hold on to the back of the pew. "What's happening?" she said. Her body was drawn by glare of the girl and she had no hope of resistance. "What's happened to me? Help me, Father!" Ignoring her plea, Jack smiled. He wasn't her father. No faked priesthood for him any longer. He was her God.

The others in the circle were twitching now, resurfacing after centuries of slumber and, needing more energy than the healthy young bodies could provide, they sought out those marked in the front row. One by one the church council was hauled to its feet, confused and anxious and dragged helplessly forward to their fate.

Mabel fell heavily to her knees in front of the dark-haired girl. She was whimpering a little now, and Jack found he liked that sound. He could feel his own power in it. He watched as her chubby hands reached into the girl's lap and unsheathed the dagger, tears running down her badly made-up face.

"No . . . no . . . no . . . no . . ." she called out against the actions of her own body, but there was nothing she could do. She couldn't stop herself.

Her eyes pleading with Jack's to do something to stop this madness, she plunged the knife into her own neck and yanked it out again before using whatever was left of her energy to raise the gash to the girl's mouth. Jack watched in wonder.

Drinking greedily, the girl gripped Mabel's hair, nearly ripping her head from her shoulders as she devoured the blood. The room filled with the screams of the council, the good doctor sobbing as his legs dragged him relentlessly toward a boy in a red football jacket. One of the odiously sanctimonious young Christians peed himself as his bony knees hit the concrete, and somewhere underneath, the old Jack nearly laughed. None of it mattered though. In moments, the screaming was done and for a few long seconds all that could be heard was the soft sound of sucking before the bodies were discarded, creating a second, lifeless circle at the heart of the church.

When they were done, they looked different. Jack couldn't put his finger on it, but each of the twelve students had a glorious glow and he fought the urge to go and hug each of them as if here were their father. Which he probably was in a strange way. He had brought them back. He'd given them life. And all the riches of the universe were his in return.

His head was filled with knowledge, an expanse of it that ran and bubbled and fizzed beyond limits, and although he was afraid that if he turned inward he'd never find his way back again, at the same time he relished every aspect of his physical being. He could feel it all both inside and out. He was God made man, and it was beautiful. He was beautiful.

He wondered if it was the same for Gray, still standing in the midst of the circle. Maybe it was. Or maybe Gray's power was different. Time would tell.

The twelve stood as one and looked at one another, recognizing each soul from the eyes and laughing. For a few moments, as they studied themselves and one another, they looked around Gray as if he weren't even there, until a blond girl, who had been pretty before but now had a shining beauty, ran her slim fingers over the bloody dagger in her hand and giggled.

She looked up at the others, meeting each one's gaze with a sly nod.

"Kill the serpent. Eat of the tree." Her voice was low and

guttural, the first few words stilted as she readjusted to her mouth and tongue. "Kill the serpent. Eat of the tree."

Nodding, the others joined in the chant, and as all twelve pairs of eyes focused on Gray the hissing words filled the church with a clarity that the earlier congregational mumblings had never had.

"Kill the serpent. Eat of the tree. Kill the serpent. Eat of the tree." They raised their daggers and stepped inward.

Jack stared, a little confused despite the infinite wisdom that itched his fingertips. What were they doing? This hadn't been in any of the scrolls. This wasn't familiar at all.

He was vaguely aware of a man coming in through the open doors at the back of the church and crouching to shake awake the girl on the floor, but none of that mattered. None of that could harm him. He stared wide-eyed as the first hint of fear showed on Gray's face.

His friend laughed nervously in the center of the circle as the returned ones stepped closer.

"Hey, hold up. I'm your God. I brought you back. Take it easy."

The blond girl raised her knife and brought it down in a fast arc. Gray ducked but it slashed into his forearm. "Jesus! Shit!" He twisted around as another ripped through the back of his shirt, bright red blossoming in a line there. "Jesus, stop it." the knives came down fast, cutting into every part of him. "Jack!" he called. "Jack, man, do something!"

From behind the altar Jack watched as Gray tried in vain to escape the circle, screaming and collapsing as a dagger took out one hamstring and then the other.

He thought about helping him. Somewhere in the information that danced like lights inside him he could see twenty years of his and Gray's adventures playing on a loop. There was lots of laughter and lots of blood. A lot of good times.

He sighed, watching the power in his breath ripple out, distorting what it touched for a moment. Yes, he loved

Gray. But was there a place for Gray in this new world? Probably not. Gray appeared not to have evolved fully in the changing process. Maybe it was better this way. Flashes of brilliant color sparkled in the corner of Jack's eyes, each sending a shiver of pleasure through him.

His friend's screams had gone beyond fear and into agony now, and he tried to zone them out. They were unpleasant. A world should have only one God, he decided. Not two. Gray's time was done.

He looked down at the bloody, writhing mass and decided it was all academic. There was nothing of Gray left worth saving. The screaming stopped but the twelve brought down their daggers over and over into the dead corpse with angry vehemence until finally they were done. Her hair now pink with blood, the blonde raised her hand.

"Kill the serpent. Eat of the tree." She smiled and the others nodded. Jack wondered if maybe they'd missed a parchment with part of the ritual on it. Maybe.

As the returned ones turned toward him, all smiling, he felt a slight unease. He'd expected more gratitude. More humble adoration. He'd brought them back after thousands of years of purgatory. He had become a God; he could feel it.

Watching them coming toward him, he looked in the trunk for the box with the tree branch in it. It wasn't there. The house. He'd left it at the house. The unease gnawed a little toward fear in his gut.

The blonde and the football jock were at the top of the few stairs, their movements fluid and lithe and fast. The others followed, forming a crowd around him. Glancing over his shoulder, Jack looked for the vestry door. It was open. If he could get there and unlock the back door then he'd be out. It seemed a long way away.

He turned to the strangers who circled him. "I've left the tree in the house. We'll have to go and get it." He smiled. "And then our reign can begin!" He pushed his fear away.

It was crazy. He was powerful. He was changed. He could feel it in everything he knew that he hadn't known before.

The girl who had been Angela laughed and shook her head. "So stupid. So very, very stupid." She flicked her head backward and the vestry door slammed shut.

"What?" Something in his new intelligence screamed at his human vanity that he'd missed something. That he should have seen something coming but that it was too late.

The football jock tilted his head. "You *are* the tree. You have become the tree."

They began to laugh as the realization seeped into him, his jaw dropping slightly and trying to find something to say, something that could get him out of this, but all he could see were the apples. All those apples. All those apples he'd eaten.

"Kill the serpent. Eat of the tree. Kill the serpent. Eat of the tree."

And then, mouths open, they fell on him.

CHAPTER FORTY-SEVEN

When her eyes opened, Liz thought maybe she was just coming out of a dream. Her head was bleary. She was in bed. She was safe and none of it had ever happened. But her bed was cold and hard and slowly the blackness lifted as a hand shook her shoulder. Who was that? Couldn't they just leave her alone?

Lying there, she at first thought the screaming was coming from the pain in the back of her head where a lump throbbed, but as the nausea washed over and away from her, replaced by a shivering clarity, she knew the two things were separate. The image of the bleeding deputy filled her head and she gasped, everything falling back into place.

"Are you okay, Liz? Can you stand?" Al gingerly pulled her to her feet, not waiting for her answer. Her legs wobbled a little but kept their ground.

"Steve?" Twisting around, she searched for him. He had to be all right. He had to be. Her heart thumped with relief, setting a new round of pain off inside her skull, as he pulled himself to his feet on the other side of the aisle. He stared at the altar. "Oh, sweet Jesus."

Following his gaze, Liz clung to Al's arm. They were too late. It was carnage. Dead bodies slumped around the empty chairs, bloody and destroyed, and in the center of the circle the twelve students stabbed at a screaming body, who finally fell silent. As one, it seemed, they turned to face the priest at the altar.

Staring at the mess of a corpse in the middle of the ring, Liz saw a glimpse of thick blond hair. It was Kenyon. They'd killed him. Gazing around her as if she weren't really there at all, tears stung her eyes. "We're too late," she whispered. "It's all over."

Al shook her. "No. No, Elizabeth. It's only just beginning."

She stared at him, her mind confused. What was he talking about? How could it be? They were back. The scroll had been opened.

"They were fooled too, remember?" Al said. "This isn't about *them*. It's about *him*."

And as the priest began to wail, the foundations of the church rumbled beneath them. "He's coming," Al continued. "And we can't let him! The word of the Lord as been spoken by his people. It's called him, and if he gets here and possesses it and the tree, it will be Armageddon."

Liz grabbed a pew as the solid concrete beneath them rippled in waves. She looked up to where the priest was shrieking, her eyes widening as she realized with horror that those who had taken possession of the student bodies were eating him, ripping his flesh from his bones with their bare teeth.

"We haven't got much time. We have to send them back." He paused. "*You* have to send them back. Them being here is wrong. It's helping him return. You have to send them back, Elizabeth."

Steve stood to the other side of her, rubbing the back of his skull. "How the hell is she supposed to do that?"

Al smiled, but Liz could see the terror quaking in his eyes. "She's the faith, Steve. The faith and the light."

"That doesn't make any sense! That doesn't—"

"It was fool's gold. It was always fool's gold! She needs to send them back, and we need to destroy the scroll."

Liz could hear them arguing. Somewhere in the back of her mind she could hear it but her fingers had found the stone in her pocket. Her talisman.

She thought of her mother and father and their prayers and how they'd done their best to protect her from the world, and how they'd never stopped loving their God no matter what life had thrown at them, and in fact had loved him in spite of it. She knew that they would never have let themselves be tempted or led like the people of Tower Hill. They hadn't gotten complacent and self-serving.

The stone was warm in her hand and her own human heat mixed with it until the rising temperature ran up her arm. She felt full of love for her God, and she knew that maybe she would die here. The heat burned at her organs, and for the first time, she became aware of it.

She thought of Lou Eccles letting them in and stumbling out dying into the night. There was no *maybe*. *Probably* she would die here. But she would fear no evil. She stared at the abominations ahead of her and, as the water in her eyes tingled and bubbled, she pitied them. She pitied them their bitterness and the greed that damned them, and she wept for them.

Suddenly she was filled with a purifying heat that overwhelmed her, scorching her insides, and she knew what her God wanted her to do. He wanted her to send them back. And she knew how. Smiling, unaware of her hair rising and fanning out around her head, she began to walk forward.

"Jesus. Shit, Al. What the hell is happening to her? What the fuck is going on?"

Liz's body blazed in golden light, both men flinching as they looked at her as if they were staring directly into the sun. The glorious brightness shone from her eyes and her hair and her mouth and her pores. She and the light were indistinguishable. She had *become* light. Her feet took tiny steps, their touch burning the stone slabs beneath them and making the surface sizzle. She didn't look back. Maybe she

didn't even know they were there anymore. Steve's mouth
had dropped, his eyes wide with fear, but Al could see only
the beauty in the light of the Lord.

With each step she took, the church walls growled. Al
felt a shuffling of tiny feet in his pocket. The genie was impatient. They were running out of time. It was a long, long
way up, she said, and he was so very nearly here.

Al grabbed the young man. "There's no time for expla-
nations. Get the sheriff's gun and get up there with her." He
pointed back at the vestry. "And get that door shut in case
they run."

"You want me to shoot them?" Steve tugged the gun
from the dead sheriff's hand.

"No, leave them to her. The gun won't work on them."
He waved at the crowds. "The gun's in case they draw on
any of these to help them. I'll get the scroll. It must be destroyed before he gets here."

"Fuck." Steve shook his head slightly. "Oh, fuck the
devil. Let's do it."

The genie told Al the words and he spoke them loud and
clear as he followed Elizabeth up the groaning aisle of the
ancient church.

" 'Thou are the anointed cherub that covereth; and I have
set thee so; thou was upon the holy mountain of God; thou
hath walked up and down in the midst of the stones of fire.
Thou wast perfect in thy ways from the day that thou wast
created, till iniquity was found in thee. . . . ' "

Above him, dust crumbled from the ceiling, small pebbles of old cement landing sharply on his head, but he
didn't pause, the words sounding out above the agonizing
yelps and moans coming from the altar.

" 'By the multitude of thy merchandise they have filled
the midst of thee with violence, and thou hast sinned:
therefore I will cast thee as profane out of the mountain of
God: and I will destroy thee, O covering cherub, from the
midst of the stones of fire.' "

As he spoke, Liz grew brighter, her aura of golden heat and energy spreading until everything around her seemed in shadow. Over in the corner Al made out Steve's shape emerging from the vestry area, the door secure.

" 'Thine heart was lifted up because of thy beauty, thou hast corrupted thy wisdom by reason of thy brightness: I will cast thee to the ground, I will lay thee before kings, that they may behold thee.' "

As she passed the front row her hand caught the edge of a woman's jacket, and the jacket burst into hot white flames. As the woman began to scream, the fire taking hold of her, a shot rang out and she was silent, her body sliding to the ground and quietly burning.

Beneath Al's feet, steam rose in a hiss from the gaps between the stones, and the stench of sulfur burned his nose and throat. Watching the girl in front, Al willed her forward. He needed her to get the twelve beings away from the priest so he could get to the scroll. It wouldn't burn near him. Nothing would burn near him. The tree of life was indestructible.

" 'Thou hast defiled thy sanctuaries by the multitude of thine iniquities, by the iniquity of thy traffick; therefore will I bring forth a fire from the midst of thee, it shall devour thee, and I will bring thee to ashes upon the earth in the sight of all them that behold thee.' "

Steve stood watching the sea of people. Somewhere in the back row he could see Mike and Amy from the store, dazed and vacant. He barely recognized them. He tried not to stare at Liz and the amazing light that burned from her. He also tried to ignore the foul stench that rose up from beneath his feet and the way the building roared and shook as if it were going to collapse at any moment. If he didn't believe in God, then he sure as hell didn't believe in the devil.

He smiled for a moment, finding bravery in his poor joke, and then scanned the crowd for signs of movement.

Dark spots danced in front of his eyes from when Liz had first started to glow, and she had only gotten brighter since then.

Behind him, something snarled, and turning, he saw what used to be Angela stepping away from the devoured body of Father O'Brien and wiping her mouth. A blonde, the football star's girlfriend, if he remembered correctly, stood with her. Their eyes were golden and full of ancient hate. He thought for a moment he could get lost in that millennia-old gaze, or maybe fall to his knees and pray in awe of them, and then Liz was up the stairs. Her whole body a beacon of light, she reached out and grabbed the girls' wrists. Smoke rose from where she held them and they whipped this way and that in a frenzy of shrieking and panting. But Liz held strong and it seemed as if it was no effort to her at all.

"Go back." Her voice was thick and syrupy, and Steve thought it may make his ears burst if he had to listen to it for too long. "Go back. You're not welcome here."

Red light oozed out of them and suddenly two of the congregation were up on their feet, wailing and charging angrily toward him. He raised the gun at the old man in pajamas first and shot him in the chest before turning it on the second, younger man, coming up from farther back. Both slid to the ground and despite everything, Steve hoped they weren't dead. He hoped he wasn't that good a shot.

Peering backward for a moment, he watched Angela and the blonde change, turning into dessicated corpses in front of his eyes, the rot starting at their wrists and spreading up through their torsos and down to their limbs. Liz shook them and they crumpled into dust at her feet. His stomach turned. Angela. Any hope for Angela was gone. With renewed anger he gritted his teeth and waited for more movement in the congregation, all thoughts of mercy gone.

Stepping forward, her heat and light grown stronger with the deaths she'd caused, Liz reached out again, catching a

large-breasted girl by her thick black hair and a boy in a
red football jacket in her hand. Steve turned his gun back
to the crowd and waited for the next two to charge at him.

Coming out from behind Liz, Al flinched as the pulpit to
his left shook and then brick by brick imploded into a tumble of dust and rubble. He took the stairs in one bound, his
knees creaking a little as he did so. For a terrifying moment he thought that in that pile of destroyed bricks on his
left, he could see a molten core burning, a fiery angry pit of
hate, and then there was just the dust again. There was still
time. Precious little of it, but time all the same. And where
there was time, there was hope.

   Having heard the screams of their dying number, six of
the remaining eight lost souls had turned to see who had
come among them to spoil their plans, but two still fed on
the body of the priest, greedily stripping his bones of meat,
lost in their own gratification. The scroll was held in the
priest's hand, and for a moment Al thought he'd have to
fight them to reach it and then as Liz spoke, he flinched and
turned automatically to face the sound.

   Go back. Even with his eyes shielded, Al could see Liz's
skin burning red beneath the light and his heart ached for
her, for all of them and for those that hadn't yet arrived,
and he wished, not for the first time, that the genie hadn't
given him so much knowledge.

   Liz stretched out her palms, spreading her fingers. "You
are not welcome here." Light shot from her fingertips,
seeking each stolen body and sucking the red light back inside her. "You are not welcome here."

   Al watched as the two still feasting on O'Brien rocked
back on their heels, drawn against their will to the light,
their faces frozen in a moment of pain and disbelieving an-
guish, before the rot took them. They turned to ash, remaining intact for a moment before finally losing integrity

and becoming nothing against the gray, bloodstained slabs beneath them.

Al stared at the dust. All those centuries of waiting. All that planning and still they came to dust. He touched the pile. *We all come to dust,* the genie said in his head.

Even you? he asked.

She smiled. *Even me, eventually, Al. As and when I choose. When I feel it is the right time.*

Two gunshots rang out behind him, closely followed by a third. And then there was a lull of silence and Al reached across to grab the scroll from the priest's fingers. Somewhere in the bloody mass that had once been his face, O'Brien let out a slick, damp sob, his eyes following Al's.

"Jesus Christ." Steve was beside him, staring down. "He's still alive." He panted. "But that's not possible. Look at him."

Al did. The man's rib cage was visible, the skin and flesh torn from it, and although some of his guts hung loose, his organs had been ripped out and eaten.

Shaking his head, Al spoke softly. "He's the tree of life. It can't be destroyed." He paused. "He's in agony."

A loud crack reverberated about them and the two men turned in unison as the back row of wooden benches crashed into a chasm below, semiconscious people tumbling in with it.

"Oh, shit." Al repeated the genie's words without hesitation. "Lucifer's coming."

Clutching the scroll he ran toward Liz, who'd turned to face the oncoming destruction, her arms still held wide. Facing her, crouching against the immense heat, he tossed the old paper in her direction.

It fluttered uselessly back, carried on the hot wind.

"Try again!" Steve called, and Al did so, failing once more. Behind them a second row took its occupants into the pit, their wails tumbling with them for an eternity.

Clutching the scroll, Al knew what the genie had held back. *This isn't going to work, is it? Not like this.*

She shook her head. *No, Al. But you can do it. You need to take the word back to the Lord. It needs to be burned in the Lord's fire.*

Al looked up at Liz, the heat coming from her making his eyebrows curl, even from several feet away. He drew himself up tall.

Well, I guess this is good-bye. I figure it's time for you to get off this ride. He smiled down at the genie in his pocket. *It's been a pleasure knowing you.*

She shook her head, her eyes merry. *I'm coming with you. It's the time of my choosing. It's you and me all the way, Al. Right to the end.*

Inside, Al felt love fill him in a way he never had before, not since the first days of his marriage, and with tears of joy in his eyes, he put the scroll in his pocket beside the genie and stepped up toward Liz.

He took a last hot breath and let his words ring out loud and true.

" 'All they that know thee among the people shall be astonished at thee: thou shalt be a terror, and never shalt thou be any more.' "

Somewhere behind him, he heard Steve call out for him to stop, but he moved forward. He held out his arms and wrapped them around Liz's waist. As his skin burst into flame, there was just one moment of terrible white pain. He had time to decide it wasn't such a terrible price to pay, and then he and the genie and the scroll were gone.

The church was silent. Just for a moment. The ground was steady and firm beneath his feet, and even though the back few rows of pews were missing, there was no gaping hole or open void, just the worn old flagstones. The people who were left slowly came to in their seats, looked about them in confusion and then horror and ran for the door. None stopped to ask what had happened. None stopped to ask if they were okay.

Watching them flee, Steve found a weird comfort in that thought. Everything was back to normal. Most people were like that—just interested in saving their own skins. He shook as he sank down and sat in the dust. Maybe in time they'd learn from this. From the grace and bravery of Al and Lou Eccles. And Liz. Or maybe they wouldn't.

"It hurts, Steve." Liz's voice was her own again, but full of pain. Looking up, Steve expected to find her back to normal, but although the glow had lessened, it was still there. He moved toward her, but she stepped back.

"Don't touch me. I'll burn you." She sobbed and the tears hissed in steam on her blistering cheek. "It's burning me. I can feel it in my insides. I can't get rid of the fire, Steve. It's too strong inside me." She paused. "I think it's killing me."

CHAPTER FORTY-EIGHT

John and Abigail Clapton abandoned the car after the tires blew on the outskirts of town, and although neither of them had done much exercise in years, Abigail found that her legs could still carry her pretty fast when they needed to. For a while, she and John matched each other's pace, and then as he slowed down, she pulled away, remembering for a moment her days of track running and the freedom she'd loved about it when she was younger than Elizabeth was now.

She heard him some way back calling for her to slow down and wait for him, but she couldn't. She wondered if maybe she should call something back to him, something meaningful, but she couldn't find any words that could sum up their years together, and then she realized that she didn't need too. Their love didn't need a sound bite. It was whole in itself, spoken or unspoken.

Feet slapping against the concrete, she weaved between the frozen people randomly paused on the sidewalks and streets, her gut instinct, mother's intuition and love of God all leading her in the right direction.

The wind coming in from the ocean was cool against her hot skin, and she sucked it in, enjoying the raw feeling in her lungs. It was funny how unafraid she was. So many years spent being afraid. She wondered if the Lord thought she'd wasted her time, tucked away with only her family and her prayers, but she figured it was too late to worry about that now. Only this moment and her Elizabeth mattered now.

As she drew into the center of the town, the statues around her woke up, dazed and disoriented, and started quietly wandering home. She ignored them, as she did the fleeing groups of people who were crying and running from the church as it came into view, ancient and glorious and terrifying beneath the full moon. Her legs tired beneath her, she slowed to a walk and climbed the stone steps. The doors were wide open and for a moment, as she took it all in, her breath was lost. So much destruction. So much loss. She tasted the lingering sulfur in the air and knew who had been here. Who her daughter had fought.

"Mom?" Her baby looked up at her in wonder from where she sat on a step by the altar next to a boy with his head in his hands. "What are you doing here?"

Abigail looked at the blisters covering her daughter's skin and the light that shone out from her dried, red eyes, and she fought back her tears. "Me and your daddy, we had dreams. We had dreams that you were in terrible trouble."

Liz nodded. "We were. But we stopped it. We won."

"Does it hurt, Elizabeth?" She stared at her daughter, who was so special, given to her by God, and she knew in that instant what she was here to do. The devil had been faced and was gone. She was here to take care of her baby, as simple as that.

She watched the steam rising from Liz's cheeks. "It burns, Mom. It really burns. I can't make it stop."

Abigail smiled. "I'll make it stop for you, honey." She sat down on the cool step and took in the sight of her eldest daughter, treasuring her. It was a long last look. "Don't you worry baby, I'm going to make it all better."

Swiftly putting her arms out, she pulled Liz into her chest and hugged her tight. "I love you, Elizabeth," she whispered before the heat engulfed her and she sucked it in, burning in its brightness and feeling the power at its core.

"It's beautiful." She sighed as she took it all back from her child. Her skin popped and blistered, but she welcomed more, savoring the light of the Lord. "Truly beautiful."

Moments later the light was gone, and so was she.

CHAPTER FORTY-NINE

Three days later Steve, Liz and her father stood on the headland looking over the ocean. The water was a crisp, clear
blue, and it washed to the shore gently, the waves lapping
against the shingle for a moment or two before retiring back
to the safety of the deep.

The town had begun to return to some semblance of normalcy, albeit shocked and dazed and grief-stricken at the
loss of so many of their number in the fire that had destroyed the church. Those who had vague memories of coming to, squashed into the pews in the middle of the night
and fleeing for their lives kept it quiet and convinced themselves it had all been a dream. It was never spoken of beyond the occasional long, questioning look of strangers
who found something familiar about each other as they
passed in the bank or at the checkout in the store.

No one had seen the three silent and weeping survivors
of the battle take the serpent pendant that had reappeared
on the dead Kenyon's chest, and then shovel the still-living
and silently screaming corpse of O'Brien or Devaine or
whoever he might really have been into a plastic garbage
bag.

They piled the corpses at the center of the circle of
chairs, and Liz had placed the journal and the scrolls and

artifacts that they found in the priest's house on top. It was these they doused in gas and lit first, watching them burn before the fire took hold and forced them out. Still, they stared silently from a distance until the morning light came and the town emerged from its long slumber and went about the business of getting back to normal. They buried the pendant the next morning, down deep in the ground under the pier.

Liz still had the stone in her pocket, but it was cold and ordinary. She'd hide it somewhere, maybe up at the college, but she figured if it ever needed to be found, it would find the person it wanted. Just like it had found her.

"Are you sure you want to stay here, Dad?"

He nodded, the expression strong, despite the grief that lined his face. "This place needs a guardian." He smiled. "I thought I might start my own church here. Nothing extreme. Maybe I'll go back to being a Baptist."

She smiled. "A minister. You'll be good at that."

"And I figure your sister will like the change from island life."

"What are you going to do about . . . the thing?" Steve stared out at the ocean.

"I'll bury him." John Clapton's voice was soft. "He committed some terrible deeds. But he's in living agony and he's paying for his sins, don't you doubt that. If I could kill him I would. It would be merciful."

"You're going to bury him alive?" Liz had thought that little else could horrify her, but the idea of what was left of Father O'Brien being placed conscious in the earth forever shook her to the core.

Her father nodded. "Yes, I am. And I'm going to have to live with that."

They stood in silence. "Will he live forever?" Steve asked.

"Maybe. Although I think at some point maybe in a hundred years, maybe a thousand, maybe ten, he'll shrivel until he looks just like a twig from a desiccated tree, ready for the next fool to dig up." John Clapton paused. "It's all about temptation, after all."

Liz nodded. After a few moments, she linked her arm in his. "I love you, Daddy."

"I love you too, princess."

Two hours later and the battered station wagon with the MAINE BORN AND BRED sign in the rear window was loaded up and ready to cruise out of town. The boy and girl smiled as they got in, the girl holding the road map, the route to Detroit highlighted in red, and then the trip to New York completed in dots.

Life was for living and that was what they intended to do. They drove in silence through the streets of the town, and although none of the residents lined the streets to say farewell to their saviors, a few curtains twitched and hearts felt heavy for a moment.

Emma Eccles, clinging to Jacob's hand and lost in her grief, paused and watched as the car drove by and wished in a way that the two young people inside would stop and maybe talk to her for a while.

She didn't know why she felt this way. She'd never seen them before, but in her grief, some part of her knew that they had answers that she would never have. But the car didn't stop, and it was another four years before Emma Eccles could sleep without nightmares that she didn't quite understand of her husband dying alone.

"Hey, look at that," Liz said, about thirty minutes out of town. "A new Burger King is opening." She looked at the banner. "They've got a special offer. You want to stop?"

Steve looked over and then shook his head. "Not unless you do."

She looked again at the roadside restaurant. "No. Let's not. I want to keep on driving." She smiled at Steve and he smiled back, and they felt complete in their love.

"Then that's what we'll do."

Turning the music up a little on the radio, Liz leaned back in her seat. On the other side of the road a sign flashed by and she caught it in the side mirror.

TOWER HILL—40 MILES.

And counting, she thought.

What would you be willing to do for
TWO MILLION DOLLARS?

Michael Fox answered that question for himself. He was
just about to commit suicide when a stranger approached
him and offered him two million in cold, hard cash. All he
wanted in return was Fox's right arm....

But the mysterious surgeon's plans go far, far beyond one
simple limb. And Fox is not his only "donor." Once Fox
is trapped behind the operating room doors, he discovers
there is no escape from the madness, as bit by bloody bit
his body is taken from him...and gradually replaced....

THE JIGSAW MAN

GORD ROLLO

ISBN 13: 978-0-8439-6012-9

Bram Stoker Award–winning Author

BRIAN KEENE

Everything from ghosts to a goat man are said to haunt the woods of LeHorn's Hollow. So it's the perfect place for Ken Ripple to set up his haunted attraction. Halloween is near and Ripple knows folks will come from miles around to walk down the spooky trail and get scared witless.

But those ghost stories aren't just talk. Evil really does wait in the woods....

GHOST WALK

ISBN 13: 978-0-8439-5645-0

Gary A. Braunbeck

Coffin County

The small town of Cedar Hill is no stranger to tragedy and terror. Nearly two centuries ago, when the area was first settled, a gruesome mass murder baptized the town with blood. More recently there was the Great Fire, the notorious night the casket factory burned down, taking an entire neighborhood with it. But no one in Cedar Hill can be prepared for what is to come—shocking murders that grow more horrendous with each victim, and a trail of taunting clues that point to the past…and to an old, abandoned graveyard.

ISBN 13: 978-0-8439-6050-1

JACK
KETCHUM

Burned again. Men never treated Dora well. This latest cheated on her and dumped her. The last decent guy she knew was her old high school boyfriend, Jim. He'd said that he loved her. Maybe he did. So with the help of Flame Finders, Dora's tracked him down. Turns out he's married with two kids. But Dora isn't about to let that stand in her way…

OLD FLAMES

Includes the novella,
RIGHT TO LIFE

ISBN 13: 978-0-8439-5999-4

NATE KENYON

"A voice reminiscent of Stephen King in the days of 'Salem's Lot. One of the strongest debut novels to come along in years."

—*Cemetery Dance*

A man on the run from his past. A woman taken against her will. A young man consumed by rage…and a small town tainted by darkness. In White Falls, a horrifying secret is about to be uncovered. The town seems pleasant enough on the surface. But something evil has taken root in White Falls—something that has waited centuries for the right time to awaken. Soon no one is safe from the madness that spreads from neighbor to neighbor. The darkness is growing. Blood is calling to blood. And through it all…the dead are watching.

BLOODSTONE

ISBN 13: 978-0-8439-6020-4